Also by Gay G. Gunn

One Day. Someday. Soon: Book I, Culhane Saga
Nowhere to Run
Pride and Joi
Everlastin' Love
Dotted Swiss and Gingham

By GiGi Gunn

Never Been to Me
Cajun Moon
Rainbow's End
Living Inside Your Love

MIGHT COULD BE

By Gay G. Gunn

Might Could Be is a work of fiction. Names, characters, business organizations, places, events and incidents are the product of the author's imagination or are used fictitiously. Any resemblance to actual persons, living or dead, events, or locales is entirely coincidental.

2016 Different Drummer, LLC Trade Paperback Edition

Published in the United States
By Different Drummer, LLC

ISBN: 978-0-692-61732-8
eBook ISBN: 978-0-692-61733-5

To the Veterans of the American Wars and their families:

Great-great grandfather, Doc Davis, U.S. Colored Infantry, Pioneer Co. Calvary Division 16 Army Corps... U.S. Civil War   (DOB: 1842-1929)

Two Fathers:
Richard N. Gunn, WWII
Sewell D. Horad, WWII
Father-in-law:
Marvin E. Gunn, WWII

And to all veterans who fought "over there" to preserve our freedom "here"... Thank You.

To all jazz greats and not so greats who sacrificed, persevered and endured for their art yesterday so we could have the pleasure of their music today. We thank and salute you.

Gone but not forgotten.

Book II

Culhane Family Saga

Part I

Chicago, South Side
November, 1941

"Excuse me," Selena accosted the woman who'd rolled her eyes one too many times at her in the hallway of her new apartment. "Mazeda is it?" Selena pretended to hazard a guess at her name, knowing it was true.

The woman posed in her own apartment doorway, answering with a steely stare.

"I don't know what your problem is, but our husbands seem to be friends. You think we could try to at least be cordial?"

Mazeda let out a weary sigh of annoyance but didn't slam the door in Selena's face.

"Either you had a thing for my husband or you had a friend who did."

A silent Mazeda leaned against the doorjamb and eyed Selena with stony interest.

Got her attention, Selena thought and continued, "None of that matters now. I won. Game over. He is *my* husband and he's gonna stay *my* man." Selena didn't let on that she'd overheard Mazeda's disparaging comments, most of which summed up Selena as being "country." Mazeda wondering how this "hick Selena" landed Hoyt Colson; how his new wife didn't know how to dress, dance, talk or act; how she knew nothing but how to get a ticket straight-up from "Hicksville."

"The choice is yours," Selena offered. "Whether you do or not makes me no never-mind. I got enough friends. But I got one question for you." Selena walked toward Mazeda, who straighten in her doorway, looked the woman dead in the eye and asked, "Who does your hair?"

Selena smiled into the mirror as she put her fingers directly on the permanent-waves set by Mazeda's best friend and hair dresser, Sugar Dee. That'd been over a year ago. As newlyweds, that first year had flown by and she and Hoyt enjoyed each other's company almost exclusively. He'd taken her everywhere with him as he photographed up and down the east coast.

Being with her husband, watching him work and exposing her to, not only white folk, but her own people as well, proved exciting in and of itself. Having been raised in the all-black town of Colt, Texas, white people had never been an issue—there were none. First time she'd encountered them to recall was when she traveled to her Aunt Summer's in St. Louis to attend teacher's college. She found them rude, arrogant and ignorant but not "racists," a term she'd heard but wasn't sure what that meant. Any conversations with them always ended with one question, "You not from 'round here are you, girl?" Whites had no place in her rearing and seemingly weren't going to have any in her successful adulthood, so Selena largely ignored or dismissed them as inconsequential. Her own folk were another matter altogether. Her own people puzzled her to distraction. They seemed to put stock in the oddest things; traits that no one could do much about. Skin color, hair texture and facial features, all fixed at birth. In Colt, Texas none of that mattered as much as what a person brought to their community; brains, skills, attitude, willingness and ability to work toward shared goals. Folk in Chicago were hard on one another; whereas in Colt, Texas, no one bothered with complexion or rating one's worth on the lack of melanin. No "paper bag" test, which Selena and her sisters would surely have failed. They'd deemed themselves "brown-skinned beauties" in Colt. Here in Chicago, they called you "dark," hurling their best compliment, but "cute for a dark-skinned girl."

Far more perplexing, the subject of hair: what you had and how you could or couldn't make it straight. As Selena walked toward the vanity, she thought of hair texture in her family for the very first time to remember. Her mother sat on a thick, salt and pepper-colored braid. Her father's hair looked wiry but felt soft to the touch and straight at the root like her brother, Hep's. Her older sister, Orelia, had hair more like their mother's, but Selena and Star, her second oldest sister, had hair short and courser than their mother's, but cottony. In Colt, Texas hair was hair, it grew, when a child you braided it, as an adult, you cut it. She'd never known a straightening comb until Chicago. She just combed and brushed her hair into a bun without applying heat. But now Sugar

Dee would croquignole, or wave or Marcel it for special occasions.

"Don't go changing too much on me, Lena," Hoyt had teased. "If I'd wanted a fancy-girl, I'da married one." Selena studied the whole skin-color/hair thing like she was taking a class in it. Selena dealt in logic and none of this made much sense as no one should be judged by these superficial characteristics.

"C'mon, Lena. You can't improve on perfection." Hoyt stuck his head into the mirror's frame. "We're gonna be late."

Selena blushed as much as her dark brown complexion allowed, left her image and slipped into the fur jacket her husband held out for her by the door as he donned his signature porkpie hat. *So handsome*, she thought as she strutted through the door he held open for her.

"Have mercy," he remarked in appreciation. "Your body's making eyes at me."

As the couple strolled arm in arm toward Itch's, the local club, to meet friends, Selena reflected on her past as she squeezed the hand of her future. Hoyt Colson'd exposed her to so many things over the past year plus. Having grown up on acres of land in a big house, she'd taken to apartment living, sharing walls and floors with folks not your family... strangers who preferred staying that way. Hearing other folks' noise, smelling their food and listening to their comings and goings proved exciting as long as she had Hoyt beside her. His apartment,

5

clearly set up for a bachelor photographer, accommodated them both. A two bedroom with the largest converted into his dark room and the smaller one their bedroom. He'd ditched the single bed and maneuvered a double bed in after he brought his bride home. His dream of buying a building and opening his own photograph studio down on State Street on the first floor and living upstairs on the second, zoomed to the top of his list. Before he took a wife, the progress had been slow because he made a comfortable living traveling wherever summoned and had little need for a space to snap photos of families and clubs against stationary backgrounds. Musicians and stars called on him to do their photo album covers and publicity shots and, as he'd showed Selena in the Colt, Texas library, the government hired him on referral and recommendation, oftentimes not knowing he was black.

The thump of the drums throbbed through the quiet night sky and beckoned the couple from the wide boulevard to the club's entrance. They disappeared under "The ITCH" sign into the vestibule, where the horns joined in the musical cacophony and silhouettes of black folk morphed into sweaty flesh and blood bodies standing and seated, jumping to the rhythms spilling from the tiny stage. Selena's and Hoyt's eyes adjusted and through the smoke-filled room, Mil and Mazeda Yarborough waved them over. The smell of old, worn-out deodorant, new liquor and cheap perfume wafted through the air and "Hey Hoyt," was the greeting from several tables as the couple made their way to the table for six near the band. Hoyt helped Selena out of her coat and draped it over the back of her chair and slapped five with Mil and Shanghai.

"You all always late," Sugar Dee said with a wink at Selena.

"Newlyweds," Mil decreed with a wide grin, his harmonica visible from his inside breast pocket like an old friend.

"You know we wouldn't miss your farewell party," Hoyt chimed in and ordered drinks for him and his wife.

"You got some catching up to do, man," Shanghai said.

"I see," Hoyt said looking at the empty glasses on the table.

Zack Fluellen jammed on the sax, as the piano, horn and drums strained to follow his riffs. At the end of the set, he came to the mic and announced, "Wanna say fare-thee-well to Shanghai and Sugar Dee, going all the way to Los Angeles to set up a place for us to stay when we get there."

Everyone clapped and cheered. "We here at Itches and Chicago gonna miss you, man," he growled, "but save me a room." The audience laughed. "Square business. Best of luck to you all, man."

"I cannot believe you are really going," Selena said to Sugar Dee as the men carried on their own conversations.

"I don't know what is to become of her hair," Mazeda teased Selena.

"Look who's talking," Selena shot back.

"Hey, got to go where my man wants to," Sugar Dee said. "I ain't never been to California so I'm really excited. No more winter."

"Besides, you'll make a mint," Hoyt chimed in.

"That's the plan, Stan," Shanghai quipped. "Not many places for brothers to hole up as it is. Bought a real big house so they'll have a decent place to stay when they do gigs in L.A."

"Right now there's the Dunbar Hotel over on Central Avenue or you have to crash on friends' couches or stay in tourist-traps and bad motels on the wrong side of town. Musicians can't even stay in hotels where they play."

"It's a damned shame. Get instruments stolen. Bad food," Sugar Dee added.

"I wouldn't play where I couldn't stay," Selena offered naively.

"Then you'd starve."

"Mine is gonna be a class place. Clean. Reasonable rates. Close to the action," Shanghai offered.

"You sold me, man," Hoyt said. "When my bride and I do California... we'll be there."

"You ever been to California?" Shanghai asked Selena.

"Nope. But I'm ready." All laughed, Sugar Dee went to talk to a soon-to-be-ex customer, and Selena noticed Mazeda's preoccupation. "What's up? You're not your usual jovial self."

"I don't know what 'jovial' means but I'm not happy."

"About your hair? 'Cause Sugar Dee's leaving?" Selena teased. "We'll do our own."

"Oh, God. No. Mil is going to see his mother."

"So? You don't like her?"

"I never met her and how could I not like the woman who birthed the love of my life?"

"Amen. So what's the problem?"

"She lives in Florida."

"Oh." Selena understood. Most folks were coming this way. Leaving the south for the north in a migration for jobs, a better way of life and to escape Jim Crow laws. Few ever went back, not even to visit.

"Mama doesn't want to travel?"

"Can't. Mil got a letter that she's dying and wants to see him."

"Well, you can't fault that, Mazeda."

"I know. But he'll lose that good job at the slaughterhouse."

"Mazeda!"

"We have plans to buy a house and start a family."

Selena rolled her eyes.

"I just have a real bad feeling about him going down there."

"Then go with him."

"Are you kiddin'? I don't want him to go and he even says it'll be better if he goes alone and comes back fast. Apparently, Ocala is not a place to linger."

"Sounds delightful," Selena offered sarcastically.

"Besides, suppose my job at the phone company comes through while I'm gone. I don't want to stay at the pencil factory forever."

"I know that's right."

"We're saving real good now. But I just got a gut feeling about him going down there."

"Don't even put that in the wind. You kiss him good, love him hard, wish him well and welcome him when he comes back."

The morose Mazeda just looked at her friend and supposed this was how black folks acted when everything always went their way.

"Hey, Lena, they're playing our song," Hoyt interrupted, standing with his hand extended.

Even over the din, Selena recognized this song she'd never heard before and listened to the lyrics, the haunting complicated melody. She melted and rejoiced in how it made her feel in the arms of her husband who held her so tenderly. Hoyt had introduced this classic to her as he'd introduced so many other things to her. Lovemaking being the most exquisite, until this song. Like a kid with a new Christmas toy, Selena sang "Stardust" all around Chicago as they walked past The Loop at sunset when the purple haze graced the sky. She sang it around the house before and after making love and now, Selena sang "Stardust" in the shower as she readied to join Hoyt's photograph session with Cab Calloway and his band at the Regal before their show. Hoyt lay in bed listening to

10

her voice and thought it was more than just "love." His wife had a quality like no other.

"Ah! You're still in bed? Don't blame me for being late," she said, going to the small chest of drawers rummaging through for a pair of stockings without runs.

"It only takes me a few ticks." He watched her pull on one nylon over her shapely brown leg, and attach it to the garter. "Have mercy. C'mon back over here." He patted the side of the bed.

"No. We got to get going."

"Si. C'mon. Right quick." He winked at her.

"So, I'm 'Si' now and not Lena, huh? I know what that means." She slowly gave him a show as she pulled the stocking up on the other leg, snapped the garter in place, checked if the seams were straight and shimmied her slip down to cover the view. "You don't want a reputation for being late, do you?"

"Once they see my wife they'll understand." He reluctantly hopped out of bed, slapped her on her derriere and headed for the shower. "Rain check?"

"Always," she grinned, taking the dress from the closet. She'd been excited to return to the famed Regal Theatre where Duke Ellington had anointed her as a "good luck piece," and all other musicians had followed suit. When first married, she went to all of Hoyt's photo sessions with him. Hoyt'd chat with the fellas as he set up, getting them to relax, do whatever he deemed necessary to get the shots he wanted. Composing pictures that would capture not only their images but their personalities. That's why they loved Hoyt Colson, "the man who sees beyond the lens."

Early on, Selena had spotted a piano over in the corner and asked, "Mind if I sit?"

"Naw," was the usual answer. Missing her piano at her family home, she initially played spirituals that affected the stars in various ways. "I remember that. My mama..." they'd begin. Hoyt snapped sober, reflective shots of otherwise wild, outrageous musicians.

Then, depending on who, she might launch into one of their hits, adding her own spin, playfully tinkering or launching into full, rich orchestral chords. Some artists recognized the difference. Others just responded to the music itself, dancing around, letting the music carry their bodies. That's how her husband got those uncharacteristically spiffy shots of Billie Holiday, using the smoke from her cigarette as another layer. For Count Basie, she'd mimicked his trademark tinkering, and the same with the sophisticated rhythms for Duke. Miles Syphax, of the Syphax Trio, had recognized that Selena'd had formal training. "Now add singing to that piano playing and you got yourself a career. Happened to me," he shared.

"My wife is happy being my wife for the time being, Miles," Hoyt teased.

"Well, if you're ever in the market to make some money," Miles gave back, just as his wife, Maxine, came to claim him.

On the rare occasion when Hoyt appeared at a session without Selena, they always asked, "Where is the little lady?" "Your better half?" "I need my background music." Hoyt'd come home with a list of folks who'd asked after her. It made Selena smile then and now. *Always nice to know that your talent is appreciated*, she thought, as Hoyt bounded out of the bathroom almost fully dressed.

"You shaved!"

"That's for later tonight," he teased and yo-yoed his eyebrows playfully. "Our little tete a tete."

The couple made their way to the famous Regal. Cab Calloway had made his mark, but Selena remained most impressed by his older sister who'd had her own band, "Blanche Calloway and Her Joy Boys," back in the 30s; first woman, black or white, band leader of an all-male band. She wondered if Star knew about this pioneering woman. Selena realized that she'd met or been proximal to most of Star's idols. Selena wondered how many Star had run into since leaving home to pursue her own career at eighteen years old in 1933. In companionable moments, Selena never failed to ask the stars or musicians if they knew of her sister, Star Culhane or "Cherokee" as she once went by. Hoyt hadn't heard of her but perhaps others had and Selena always held out hope that one day someone would say, "Star Culhane? Yeah. I knew her. That girl could blow." Besides "I love you," spilling from Hoyt's sensuous lips, that was the second thing Selena wanted to hear a human being say.

~*~

Hoyt answered the door with Mil and Mazeda on the other side.

"Hey!" Selena yelled from the kitchen making her way to the trio who stood awkwardly around a bouquet of flowers.

"These are for you," Mil said, thrusting them toward Selena.

"Thank you," Selena replied, "But don't go changing on us now, Mil. Why the manners?"

"I'm told when folk invite you to dinner you should bring something," he repeated rotely.

"How about booze next time," Hoyt said, breaking the ice.

"Damn, man," Mil said on a breath of relief as Mazeda sucked in her teeth. "I could use one right now. What you got?"

"C'mon. Get your own. You ain't company," Hoyt said, guiding him to the small portable bar caddy in the corner.

"Mazeda, what you want?" Mil called out.

"You can take the Negro out of the country but not the country out of the Negro," she said to Selena following her to the kitchen.

"What gives?" Hoyt asked his friend.

"Trying to make these last few days for her bearable. Doing almost everything she wants before I leave."

14

"Monday?"

"Bright and early. That's why Sunday got to lay it on her long enough to last till I get back."

"Doesn't sound like a bad gig," Hoyt teased. "No sweat."

"I'm praying for a lot of sweat, man." He chuckled and continued out of earshot, "Lookit. Want you all to look in on her while I'm gone, man."

"Didn't even have to ask, man," Hoyt said.

"She can be a real piece of work, man, but I love her."

"Any man with eyes can see that."

"Dinner's ready," Selena sang out. "Take your usual seats, please."

"Great Gawd Almighty, is that your mac and cheese?" Mil shouted.

"It's my mama's, but I did the best I could."

Mil eyed the table and identified the dishes—all his favorites. "Act like this is my last supper."

"Have you met this woman?" she referred to Mazeda. "Oh yes I did if I wanted an ounce of peace."

"My Mazeda can't cook a lick, but she got other skills, don't you, sweetie?" Mil kissed the cheek of a mock-mad Mazeda who melted at his touch.

"But she knows how to get you what you want," Hoyt shot.

"She do," Mil agreed.

"I can't sew like her either. We all have our talents," Selena said, sitting in her chair, as Hoyt scooted it under her. "So speaking of which, did you bring Myrtle?"

Mil tapped his breast pocket.

"After dinner, we'll turn off the phonograph and have some live music up in here."

With bread pudding and pineapple upside down cake consumed, the foursome gathered around the piano Hoyt had surprised Selena with last Christmas and jammed. Mil poised the harmonica between his lips, barely visible, and played it like it had a mind of its own. Selena's fingers danced up and down the black and white keys and the two-tone deaf individuals, Hoyt and Mazeda, sang their hearts out.

"The old lip harp going with you?" Hoyt asked.

"Tried to let Mazeda hold it for me, but she said that'd be bad luck."

"Myrtle has to go where he goes. For protection," Mazeda said.

"For recreation too," Selena offered. "I hear not too much goes on in Ocala."

"Most of the time 'we' are the recreation," Mil said, immediately regretting his reference to lynching.

As Mazeda frowned not getting the reference, Selena piped up, "It'll be good to see your family. Always is."

"Yep," Mil quickly agreed. "I only plan to be there a week or two tops. If Mama goes to glory, we have to bury her."

16

Selena wondered how this conversation turned so sullen.

"And on that note," Mil slapped his thighs and rose from the piano bench. "I think we best be goin'."

"Yep," Mazeda agreed and they walked to the door.

"Wanna take something? Chicken at least. I know you all won't want to stop and cook tomorrow."

"No," Mil and Mazeda's gaze fastened only on one another.

Hoyt and Selena smiled.

"Hoyt ol' buddy, I'd appreciate it if I could say my goodbyes now 'cause we don't want no interruptions of any kind all day tomorrow."

"You got it, man," Hoyt said, shaking one hand and clapping his shoulder with the other.

"When I get back, we'll take you two to dinner. Our treat."

"Sounds good," Hoyt said.

Selena kissed Mil on the cheek, stepped back and said, "I know you got the hall phone number, but you have ours too. Call day or night."

"Got two phones here in Chicago. Problem is finding one in Ocala to use." They all chuckled uncomfortably. "Probably be easier to post a letter. I'll be back before it comes to that."

"We'll all be glad and relieved when you get home," Selena said.

"Me too. Look out for my sweetie," Mil asked.

"As much as she'll allow," Selena quipped. "Don't worry about her."

And they were gone.

Hoyt reached for Selena's hand which she gladly gave him. He brought it to his lips and kissed it. "Can you imagine? Being separated like that."

"Let's not. Help me clear the table?"

"My pleasure."

Baby It's Cold Outside

The hawk swung high into the clear night sky, gathering up icicle-cold air to swoop down to nip and peck at the necks of Hep and Range as they made their way to the barbershop. The frigidity of Chicago temperatures debuted new and lethal when compared to Colt, Texas, as any exposed skin was deemed fair game for the beak of the hawk. They tucked in their chins and further shrouded scarfs around their mouths, jamming hands and fingers deep into the pockets, attempting to hide them from the winged assailant. The rotating barbershop pole summoned them closer until they barreled into the tiny shop and slammed the door behind them.

"College boys!" Roscoe greeted in an announcement. "Cold enough for ya?"

"Colder than a witch's tit," a shivering Range said.

"Had some of them since you left home, huh?"

A shrieking scream came from the back room and a man, head covered in slick whiteness, ran out and into the bathroom, sticking his head in the toilet for relief from the burning lye applied to his tender scalp to make his hair straight.

"He ain't got hair like you," Roscoe pointed to Range, "so he conks it to try and get it."

"Ain't gonna happen," a customer chimed in.

"Got mine from my mama and daddy," Range said, blowing warmth into his hands.

"Sit over there in the window so folks think they can get your hair in my shop."

"Trying for smooth, straight hair that the good Lawd spared 'em. Like Duke, Cab—"

"Pain? Too high a price," Range dismissed.

"What's your pleasure?" Roscoe asked Hep.

"Trim."

"Homecoming, huh?"

"No. That was a few weeks ago. Just regular maintenance," Hep said, getting into the chair.

"Any Negro girls for you to date up at the college?"

"No," Range piped up. "None that'd give it up. That's why we come down here."

"I know you get plenty of play down here. College boys with good hair?"

"They think they'd died and gone to heaven." Everyone chuckled.

"You must have 'em lined up."

"We don't do bad," Range smiled, his even-toothed grin blossomed in a handsome face.

"You mighty quiet," Roscoe said to Hep.

"Got a lot on my mind."

"You didn't get no girl in the family way did you?"

"No," an offended Hep answered. *Wish it was that simple*, he thought.

"I know your folks gave you the 'birds and bees' talk and probably some rubbers too," another barber said with a laugh. "You got a future to protect."

The comment made Hep recall the talk with his father before he left for college. It was a little late, but he listened out of respect for his dad. Hep had only kissed and fooled around "over clothes" with Feather Criqui, Range's younger sister and his future wife, but he'd go as far as any girl'd let him… and Hep Culhane got pretty far. Last summer at home with Feather, things had changed. He didn't know exactly what to make of the fact that she'd been willing to go farther than he had anticipated. There were things he was sure of and her being a virgin on their wedding night had been one of them. That had changed along with his academic status at Northwestern University where he had an academic scholarship. Again his father's words rang in his ears about how he represented the Negro race and how he was to continue to excel to make it easier on the next black student who applied for a scholarship. Hep was "but a link in the chain of excellence… don't break it. I can afford to send you to school, but the next black man who doesn't have that option depends on you to make it easier for him."

Hep received the official report today that his scholarship was rescinded due to his falling GPA. Speculation and prayers were over. He'd thought of telling his folks that college was too hard. But it wasn't. He may be a lot of things but liar wasn't one of them. He thought he could just make it up in time but he'd made questionable choices just before midterms. He could blame it on the two Billies: Holiday playing at the Strand and Eckstine at the Regal. Hoyt and Selena invited him to not only see his two favorites but meet them afterwards. They'd gone to clubs on the south side and Selena thought that Eckstine made his living replicating her brother's rich baritone voice. Hep held no such illusions, and only heard his dad, Papa Colt, saying, "When you point the finger of blame at somebody or something, three other fingers point back at you. Take responsibility for your actions." That piggybacked his father also saying, "Even if you do something wrong, it better be your idea. I raise leaders who think for theyselves not followers. Unless you lead dog, the view never changes." It seemed Hepburn Heath Culhane's world was spinning out of control and it was time to pay the piper.

Two other things happened before this report that gave him pause. After dinner one Sunday as Hep and Range finished up before returning to campus, Hoyt called him over.

"Hep cat," he summoned, "a word please."

Hep left Range and Selena to clear the table as he walked toward his brother-in-law.

Out of ear shot Hoyt said, "Citizen of the world. My man. Found a rubber package in my bedroom when Selena and I came back from D.C."

Hep could have crawled under the floor and slithered his way back to the dorm.

"My bedroom," Hoyt repeated in a lethally low tone. "Mighty glad you're using them, but not here. Not in my home. Your sister's home. In our marital bed."

Hep felt lower than a snake's belly. He couldn't meet Hoyt's gaze.

"We gave you a key to use when you can't make it back to campus in time," Hoyt continued. "When you get too plastered to make it back. When the weather is bad. But not to use our home as a cheap motel. Not to bring strange women into my house."

"You want the key back?" Hep said, reaching into his pocket.

"No. I want you to respect our home and use it as it was intended. You and Range. Period. Capische?"

Hep nodded his embarrassment.

"You're young. Thinking with the wrong head. Just wanted to set the record straight. Next time. I'll want the key."

"Not going to be a next time," Hep promised and for the first time looked earnestly into Hoyt's waiting eyes. "Did you tell Selena?"

"Man-to-man. You'd know if I told your sister—" Hoyt said with a chuckle.

"Yeah," Hep agreed, knowing she'd pitchabitch.

"Just want to set you back on the path to being that 'citizen of the world.'"

"OK."

"Like I said I'm damn glad you're using rubbers…but not here."

"OK."

"Everywhere else is just fine," Hoyt tried levity.

"You all finish your little pow-wow over there," Selena asked from the kitchen counter.

"We're fine," Hoyt said and Hep offered a nervous smile.

"Dessert," Selena announced.

"Thanks," Hep said to Hoyt who slung his arm around the boy's neck and ushered him over to the goodies.

"I was young once."

Hep felt like crap days after that and while he remained tense, Hoyt was his old self.

The second event occurred when he and Range were at Black Cat's and two girls that he'd been dating laid claim to him. Range thought it exciting and Hep felt good about the attention, trying to diffuse the situation with his deep voice and suave use of words that always impressed the women. But when one girl drew a knife, then blood on the other, Hep froze. "Aw shit!!" Overestimating his prowess, he'd lost total control of the situation. His daddy, mama and all of Colt, Texas would be ashamed and embarrassed.

Now, a number three punch suckered him earlier this morning, the grades, and loss of scholarship. As Range would say when they were kids, "You in deep doo-doo." Hep grew consumed with his options. A way out of this hole he'd dug for himself. He could have his father pay tuition but not without admitting he'd messed up in the first place. Hep couldn't see any way out of this humiliation for him, his family and his hometown. Disgraced. His father had never had one moment of disgrace that Hep knew or ever heard about. Colt Culhane survived slavery, being beat by an old massa at nine years old, emancipation and hard times in Washington, D.C. before being orphaned and totally alone at 12, hopping a train west, where he scouted for wagon trains, fought Indians, ramrodded trail rides, bought a piece of land, settled down with the woman he loved, founded a town and ran a successful horse and cattle ranch in west Texas. And he, Hepburn Culhane, couldn't survive four years of college. Hep, his legacy, his only son, who'd had all the advantages, was a colossal disappointment.

"There you go, college boy!" Roscoe declared proudly, swinging his chair around and presenting him with a mirror so he could inspect the back.

All Hep saw reflected: A failure.

Do You Know What It Means to be in New Orleans?

In passenger seats, Selena and Hoyt jostled as the train clickety-clacked across the Huey Long Bridge over the mighty Mississippi River heading for New Orleans. In all the places they'd traveled, absent from their Chicago apartment almost as much as they were there, Selena had her favorite haunts: Washington, D.C., Harlem, New York and New Orleans.

Only her second time to the Crescent City, she'd fallen in love with it the first time she visited the French Quarter and walked its skinny, exotic streets hand-in-hand with her husband. Hoyt, a terrific guide on these sojourns, pointed out various places of repute and ill-repute left of the infamous Storyville section closed by the military in 1917. While the couple had resided in the lively Dew Drop Inn in uptown on LaSalle, this time Hoyt selected Jardin Lautrec for him and his wife, two blocks from Bourbon Street on Chartres, an ideal locale both peaceful and close to the action. Her husband loved being in the thick of things but when he slept he wanted it quiet.

"There it is," Hoyt pointed out the small club to Selena.

"The Onyx," Selena read the tiny sign of Star's first gig or, at least, the first place from which her big sister'd sent a flyer while Selena was still a teen in Colt, Texas waiting for any word from her.

The management of The Onyx had changed since 1933, and no one recalled "Star." But Selena dissected and absorbed the last place she'd known her sister to be. She looked around at the tiny tables, the stage from which she'd sung, and when Selena used the bathroom she imagined Star had used the same stall and washed her hands in the same grubby basin with the broken mirror above. Selena only hoped that when Star was here, it was a better-kept club. Despite the disappointment about her sister, Selena liked the current owner and his wife, and Hoyt got along with everyone. While in Nawlins, they frequented the club with some regularity and Selena's impression of the appearance changed as the Chicago couple got to know the regular patrons who'd been coming there for years.

"Sure. I remember her," the deep chocolate-skinned woman with the wide smile answered Selena's millionth-and-one question about Star.

A flabbergasted Selena lit up like Christmas, smiling from the woman to Hoyt. "Really?"

"Yeah. Star. Star? Ummm. Cull…" the woman snapped her fingers asking for assistance with her memory.

"Hane!" Selena shouted. "Star Culhane!'

"That's it." The woman agreed like she'd just won a contest. "She was a sweet girl. And, boy, she could wail."

"She was my sister!" Selena offered proudly.

"Really? How is she?"

Selena's heart and face dropped. "I was hoping you could tell me."

"Oh." The woman sipped her drink. "My name is Zenobia. Zenobia Stubberfield. Zen for short."

"Pleased to meet you," Selena replied rotely.

"When was this you knew Star?" Hoyt piped up. "How long ago? Where did she live back then?"

"Wow," Zen replied as Selena perked up with her husband's questions.

"I didn't *know* her, know her, you know? I mean, I'd come here like everyone else to hear her sing. Like I said, she was a sweet girl. Probably too sweet for Nawlins, if you know what I mean."

Hoyt nodded knowingly while Selena's eyes meet theirs with skepticism.

Zen noted the different reactions and treaded lightly. "She had a voice, no doubt, but she didn't have the street smarts. Like people took advantage of her."

"What?" Selena asked.

"I mean. I heard they didn't always pay her on time and she lived with the Sisters of the Sacred Heart which didn't help her rep as a jazz singer."

"What?" Selena asked incredulously. "Catholics? We weren't Catholic."

"They ran a charity—"

"Charity!"

"Well, not a—" Zen looked to Hoyt for help.

"Like a place for where you could let reasonable rooms," he added.

"Yeah. Like the 'Y' for white girls. She had a room and helped out with the meals and all. Helped talk to other girls and what have you," Zen stumbled to the end.

"When was the last time you saw her?"

"Years ago. Last I heard she was heading for New York City. She'd saved up for a cabaret card. That's a lot of money but she knew you needed one to play in the clubs up in New York where they served liquor. She was smart... and very trusting."

At that point Zen had verified Star's story as Selena knew it. Hep had received a birthday card with a New York City postmark but no return address. Zen confirmed that Star went to NYC. For a moment, Selena had a connection with her big sister. Upon his wife's request, Hoyt took her to the Sisters of the Sacred Heart where Star had lived for a while. No one remembered her. Selena and Hoyt strolled the streets that Star had walked as Selena tried to envision her sister there. What drew her to Zen in the first place was her resemblance to Star. Same coloring, same stature, the way she sat and stood, but clearly it was not her.

As the southbound train slowed into the New Orleans station, Selena and Hoyt gathered their things. Selena anticipated seeing Zen again as they'd kept in touch. She'd decided not to share the info with Hep since there was nothing new to report about their sister's whereabouts. At this point, just confirmation. She hoped that one day she'd be able, not only to give info, but bring Star to his front door. "Guess who this is?" she longed to say. He'd look at her and guess right away. Such happy tears the trio, back together again, would share.

It'd always been the three of them. Orelia, their oldest sister, always seemed like she was waiting for them to be returned from whence they came. Her parents had a stillborn child before her, so Orelia was the indulged child; the first born and, in her mind, remained an only child with four younger siblings. Henley died when he was ten, leaving Star, Selena and Hep. The Trio. Star would smuggle 78 LPs in to play on Dad's Victrola. He didn't seem to mind as much as their mother, Keely, who named it "devil music." Choir leader and organist for the Mt. Moriah Gethsemane Baptist Church, she wasn't partial to secular music. At eighteen, Star decided to leave the nurturing bosom of Colt, Texas to pursue a singing career. Her father said "no." She defied him by going and he told her if she left, she was "dead to me and have no home to ever come back to." A rift that still loomed large and permeated every nook and cranny of their house but, of which, they never spoke.

Selena recalled her first Christmas home after she was married and, while the annual Culhane Christmas party bloomed in full swing, her father carved out time for a private conversation with her. The kind of talk enjoyed by parents with their grown children, touching base adult-to-adult. She'd never seen her father so interested in her and what she was doing and saying.

They spoke of New York City where Colt had never gone and Selena wowed him with the Empire State Building, its one hundred and two stories, the elevator that took them there stopping on the observation decks on the eighty-sixth and one hundred and second floors. She spoke of the underground subway and the escalator at Macy's, the mammoth department store at Herald Square with ten and one half stories that took up an entire city block. Colt countered his daughter with his knowledge of Seneca Village where in the 1820s free black families built homes and lived on property they owned and attended one of three churches and a school until city government claimed the land through "eminent domain," evicted the residents which included Irishmen, and razed their homes to create Central Park. The father and daughter shared the discussion of Washington, D.C. where he and Aunt Pearl went in 1868. Papa Colt never mentioned slavery and leaving the plantation but her mother'd supplied the details. Selena told him how D.C.'d filled in a canal and named it Constitution Avenue, and that Gideon's Tavern was now in the middle of the block but clearly had a plaque "established in 1859." She and Hoyt couldn't find the alley street that her father and Aunt Pearl lived on, but Maryland Ave was still there as was Union Station where he'd hopped a train west at twelve years old. Without mentioning Star, Selena told her daddy that she loved New Orleans.

Her father got a faraway look and a faint smile graced his lips as he whispered, "Never made it to New Orleans. Was invited."

"What you thinking on Daddy?" Selena asked, mischievously.

"Just thinkin'." He couldn't wipe the grin from his face. Memories of him and Ruby de Mouton overwintering at Fancy's flooded back. She'd taught him all he needed to know about pleasing a woman.

"Sounds like rememberin'," Hoyt interjected.

"That too."

"We're going out to California," Selena shared.

"Been there too. Seen that wide Pacific Ocean."

"How'd you get there?" Hoyt wondered.

"Horse." They laughed at the prospect of riding a horse all the way to the west coast. "How you all going?"

"Either train or drive," Hoyt interjected.

"That'd take us weeks just to get there," Selena said. "Can't leave my students 'high and dry.'"

"You teachin'?" Colt asked.

"Piano. I give after school lessons to children three times a week."

"When she's there," Hoyt teased.

"Precisely. Can't take a month off."

"Suppose it was Paris," Hoyt chided.

"Well… I'd have to think hard on that," Selena said with a chuckle.

She'd come to teaching by accident. After hearing her play, one musician's wife asked if she gave lessons.

32

Selena agreed and began teaching three students for fifty cents a lesson in her house. After some middle class parents found out she had a degree, they wanted Selena to come to their houses to teach their little ones, preferring their precious babies not go to the South Side to take up the instrument. Selena knew immediately which students were taking piano lessons for themselves and which took them to please their parents. Additionally, she had three students she taught for free because they didn't have the money, but had a real love and aptitude for tickling the ivories; one little boy sat there for hours until she fed and shooed him home. A real virtuoso in the making.

"You play?" Colt asked Hoyt.

"'Chopsticks,' 'Heart and Soul,'" Selena joked.

"I can pick out the opening for Beethoven's 'Fur Elise'."

"Yes, you can," Selena conceded in patronizing baby-talk.

"Hummm. Is there any place you haven't been?" Hoyt asked Colt.

"Nawlins…" he said and laughed, wondering how Ruby had fared. Her fiery red hair surely gray by now.

"It's never too late."

"Oh, yes it is," Colt declared.

As was the tradition, Colt sat at the piano where he and his daughter regaled the guests with carols and a few "secular" songs he'd learned at Fancy's that winter and Selena'd learned in Chicago and New Orleans. During their lively repertoire, Hep'd gone over and kissed his mother who'd joined in, happy for the health and homecoming of her family. In that first Christmas, Selena hoped they'd always be this happy family. After their father/daughter set, Colt gathered his flip and sauntered out to the cemetery gravesites of his boys; Micah, Criqui, Pincus, Banyon and Durango. A tradition he'd begun after their deaths; during the Annual Culhane Christmas party, Colt'd visit and pour each of them their favorite drink while bringing them up to speed on his family and theirs. They'd followed him here, helped him build his house before settling here and building their own. They'd founded Colt, Texas, Rudd County.

~*~

The couple'd been home from New Orleans only a week before leaving again for Washington, D.C. Upon arrival, a cold rain fell on the city which disappeared the next day leaving a slight nippy-bite to the southern town. After noting how the leaves of the trees were touched with crimson and gold, Selena let the sheers drop back on the tranquil sight.

"OK," Selena said into the telephone while staring down on the traffic crawling up 15th Street. "You know I had to call and check on you."

"I know, thanks," Mazeda replied. "Have a good time in D.C."

"Without you?" Selena teased. "I'll try."

Selena hung up and Hoyt asked, "Better?"

"Who? Her or me?" She went over and hugged her husband. "I cannot image a life without you."

"That's something you don't have to worry about."

"Promise?"

"Promise." He kissed the tip of her nose. "Unless you mess up big time."

"Aw!" she swatted his butt.

"I thought she was feeling better since she received Mil's letter?"

"That lasted all of three days. Then the worry crept in again."

"It's gonna take some time for him to bury his mother and get out."

"You make it sound like he is escaping?"

"He is. From Florida. They lynch us there too."

"Just know that I can take, maybe a week of not hearing from you. No more than that."

"Good to know. I don't think you can do a week."

"Oh really?" She sassed, then quickly added, "but don't put me to the test."

One of her standby favorite things to do in the Nation's Capital was leave the hotel and walk up the steep 15th Street mountain and be rewarded by Meridian Hill Park, twelve acres of pure delight which sat high on its perch due north of the White House. The unobstructed view of the city below always gave Selena pause. Having already snapped photos of the Henderson Castle across the street, Hoyt liked the four statues in the park; Serenity, Joan of Arc, Dante and James Buchanan, and the concrete benches, urns and patterned walkways that reminded him of Europe. "We gonna get there together one day," he always declared to Selena as they held hands and strolled to her treasured spot, the terraced fountain with thirteen basins of the cascading waterfall on the 16th Street side. The park had been dedicated in 1936 but completed and open only a year. For Selena it remained a cherished find as she sat atop the Italian renaissance styled structure surrounded by the French baroque gardens. Like many others mesmerized by its beauty in the middle of the city, the couple sat wrapped in each other's arms watching the sun set. Streaks of brilliant red-orange giving way to regal purple as the fiery yellow orb bid a final farewell for the night. The light spray from the water misted her skin, and the muted glow illuminated her husband's handsome face, and Selena began singing "Stardust" to him quietly in honor of the tiny points of brightness rising in the sky to accompany the moon. Without fail, at the end of the song, a smattering of applause thanked her for her vocal gift. They'd descended the hill towards U Street to have a bite before returning to their hotel room and made love under the stars she'd just serenaded.

But on this chilly night, the Colson's had plans. Selena donned her mink coat as she laced her arm through her husband's and walked through the Dunbar Hotel's lobby making a left on U Street. They passed the Lincoln Theater where they'd seen yet another Oscar Micheaux film heading for 11th Street and the Crystal

Palace with its stalactite and stalagmite décor and the Louis Jordan band. This club's historical pedigree reached back to 1926, where, during prohibition, they served brined pork chops and liquor in tea cups while the jazz age raged on. On top of the famous club now sat Davis Drugstore on the first floor.

During this promenade, they passed black-owned and operated barbershops, cleaners, clubs, hair salons, clothing stores, grocery stores, fine restaurants, diners, pool halls, shoe repair shops, furniture stores, watch and radio repairs, everything required to be a self-sustaining black community that functioned quite well without white people. Selena thought that D.C. and its Black Broadway, reminded her most of Colt, Texas in its ability to meet all the needs of life independent of outsiders. Besides a selection of clubs like Club Bali, The Casbah and Murray's Casino, there were several movie houses they could attend freely; The Lincoln, which had the Colonnade in the basement for big events and dances, The Republic and The Booker T. This area had its own Post Office on T Street, a great Chinese laundry, Jonnie Lew's, on 11th, Thompson's Dairy and Industrial Bank since 1919, across from their destination. Although no Sugar Dee, Selena'd had her hair done at the Lula B. Cooper French Beauty Salon where the stylists wore all white uniforms like nurses. True Reformers Hall, a benevolent society that offered insurance and banking for Negros without any white involvement, housed in the substantial four-story building, not only offered meeting places for the community but elegant ballrooms for D.C.'s tuxedoed men and their gowned society-type wives as they were entertained by native Washingtonian, Duke Ellington. This building also housed the Metropolitan Police Boy's Club which used their gym for physical fitness and their other activities. The YMCA on 12th was the first in the United States erected for blacks and, besides reasonable room rates and a gym, it served as a gathering and meeting place for various civic and civil rights endeavors.

Around the corner, the Howard Theater, which predates The Apollo by three years, provided a larger venue and the surrounding houses supplied rooms for the stars who played there. Hoyt'd often asked where she would like to live and eventually start a family and Selena thought of the places she'd visited; thus far, D.C. was number one. She didn't know what lay beyond the Florida Avenue boundary and thought of that old warning on ancient maps, "beyond here lie dragons," or more recently "Negroes need not apply," but she did like the LeDroit Park area with its three and four story homes on the edge of Howard University. She liked that this progressive area invested in one another and that the school system had black teachers and administrators. Like Dunbar High School, famed for producing leaders of the local and national Black community, was proximal to this rich and vibrant neighborhood. Selena thought despite the fact that her father couldn't wait to leave,

D.C. proved sophisticated and hit most of her marks for family living.

Hoyt admired D.C. because it was the capitol of the free world and showcased all the landmarks and monuments everyone flocked to see. Thanks to Hoyt, Selena'd visited them all multiple times, Hoyt always finding something new to shoot. When he stopped and stared at a scene or people, she knew he'd seen a shot and was about to go through his paces. When he took off his porkpie hat and replaced it, she knew he'd found something worthy. He'd push his hat back on his head, out of the way, raise his camera and she'd hear "Click. Click. Click" turning in time to see a big grin beaming on his handsome face when he knew he'd nailed it. While Selena was enthralled with the Lincoln Memorial, the gargantuan figure of the emancipator, the stately, marble edifice itself, her husband would shoot a charwoman there to clean up... her mop and bucket prominently displayed in the picture. Or walking downtown, he'd shoot a well-dressed Negro woman in pearls and heels with her equally coiffed daughter in ribbons and anklet socks with black patent Mary Jane's outside the Greyhound bus station, making sure "Colored Waiting" was in the frame. Her husband had an eye for social commentary or injustice. While she was trying to figure out where her father's place was in Northeast Washington, Hoyt took pictures of happy, dark-skinned children in rags playing stickball in the street, the domed capitol looming large in the backdrop of the shot. "America's Children," he called them.

She was proud of him because the one picture he'd snapped in New Orleans won the prestigious Oglethorpe Award. A nattily-dressed little white boy with matching coat and cap, sitting in the very last seat of the "white only" section of a city transit bus so he could hold the hand of his black nanny who sat in the first seat of the "Colored" section. The intertwined, interlocking clasping of black and white hands evident. Entitled "Separate but Equal," this picture had been widely circulated and reproduced in both the black and white press; *Life* and *Look* magazines. Selena, positive that this picture made it into the Colt, Texas Library, would have to check when they got back. The prize money would afford them a trip to California to visit Shanghai and Sugar Dee while he shot public works projects, military installations, impoverished slums and migrant camps for the government.

Now, if Mil would just return safely to Mazeda, all would be right with the world.

You Were Meant for Me

In Chicago, the hawk threatened to appear, full-throttle, ahead of schedule as Hep and Range devoured the sumptuous Sunday meal Selena'd prepared for them as she loved to do whenever she and her husband were in town. Selena noticed that her brother had eaten but failed to fully engage in the discussion like Hoyt and Range.

"What's going on with you, boy?" she asked playfully.

"Nothing." Hep shrugged his massive shoulders.

"UmmHumm," she said. His not immediately objecting to being called "boy," foretold of some inner crisis that he apparently wasn't ready to share. "You see how he's acting?" she whispered to Hoyt. "When is he going to tell me what's on his wee little mind?"

"Maybe never," Hoyt mused as he helped her clear the table while their guests were out of ear range.

Selena looked hurt and left out.

"Growing pains, Lena," Hoyt continued. "All young men have them. Don't take it personally that you are not his 'go to' person now. Maybe never again."

"What?"

"That's normal. You got to let him make his own mistakes. Nudge him in the right direction is all you can do. You can't force him to do anything. Just be there if things don't work out. With open arms, though, not criticisms and critiques."

"Did you go through this?"

"All men of any ilk do. A man who doesn't have pain, isn't growing." He went and sidled up behind her as she washed the dishes. "He'll be fine." He grabbed the dish towel. "All 'citizens of the world' have their challenges. Part of their passage to greatness."

"Well, I'll see how he acts at Christmas."

"Woman, did you hear anything I said?"

"I'll take it under advisement."

"You a hard-headed, tender-hearted woman."

"And you love me for it." She turned into him.

"Humm." He dropped his dishtowel and filled his hands with her flesh. "Preach on."

"What are you gonna do?"

Hoyt bend down and covered her lips with his.

"We're leaving now," Hep announced near the door.

"As always. Copacetic and thanks," Range said with a grin and a shake to Hoyt's hand.

"You all be careful," Selena said, eyeing her brother thoughtfully and saying, "Any time. I'm here."

"I know. Night."

Selena let the door whine closed. "Range doesn't seem any the worse for wear."

"Range is Range. Doesn't have the same sensibilities as Hep-cat." He grabbed his wife. "I thought they'd never leave."

"What did you have in mind, Mr. Colson?"

42

"Some quality time with my woman."

"We'd better hurry. Your wife will be home soon," Selena teased and ran to the bedroom with Hoyt in hot pursuit.

~*~

"This house is huge!" Hoyt exclaimed as they lit from the cab and stepped into the California sunshine. "Almost as big as your Colt, Texas home."

"Bigger," Selena agreed. "They have an extra floor on the top," she said, smoothing down her traveling suit.

"They're here!" Sugar Dee's loud voice blasted from inside before she pushed open the screen door and screamed her delight. She ran from the porch, down the steps and grabbed Selena in a bear hug. "My girl. You are a sight for sore eyes."

She kissed her friend's cheek, then Hoyt's and put her arms around both just as Shanghai swaggered out on the porch with his apron.

"Hey, man," he greeted Hoyt. "And your better half." He kissed Selena on the cheek.

"Man," Hoyt continued, "this is some big-ass house."

"You like?" they climbed the steps. "C'mon in and let me show you around."

They entered into a large reception room and to the right, the living room had been converted into a lounge-room with places for sitting and eating which included a bar. A jukebox sat in the corner with Ella Fitzgerald singing "A Tisket A Tasket," from its colorful façade.

Interesting, Selena thought.

Behind this room, in the hallway, Sugar Dee had a couple of chairs and a beauty parlor set up; hot combs, pressing irons, hair pomades, hot curlers, clips. She pushed a door open into the kitchen, a screened-in back porch with a freezer and washing machine with rollers on top for wringing out clothes before putting them on the line, could be seen over the stove. Back in the hallway by her beauty chairs, pocket-doors tucked on an angle opened into their big bedroom with a bathroom and closet.

"This is immense," Selena noted.

"Used to be the dining room. And you can't hear nothing from the rest of the house," Sugar Dee said, elbowing her friend.

As Shanghai grabbed the phone, the trio climbed the big staircase in the reception room to five bedrooms. The stairs narrowed and continued up another flight.

"Whew, we do get our exercise," Sugar Dee said. "Two more bedrooms up there," she added in answer to Selena's questioning eyes. "Bathroom at the end of the hall," she concluded as she swung open a door. "This is your room. You got a sink and a closet and these two windows."

"You have done so much in such a little bit of time," Selena complimented.

"All it takes is money, honey. We still got a lot to do. I want a piano in the downstairs parlor. More furniture in these rooms. More sheets and such. You always need them and a maid to clean 'em. I'm tired."

"But you look good," Selena said.

"California's good for what ails you!"

"Hey Hoyt!" Shanghai called up the stairs. "C'mon make a run with me."

"Bye," Selena said to him, popped open the metal clasps of the suitcase and began unpacking.

"So how's our girl, Mazeda?"

"She's got two letters from Mil in all this time. Carries them with her everywhere and will not go anyplace but to work, scared she'll miss a call or letter or him coming through the door."

"She got my prayers."

"She needs every one of them," Selena said, changing the subject. "So how's business?"

"Ebbs and flows. Sometimes we turn away business 'cause we're all full up. Other times we can't give a room away. It all depends on what's shaking on Central Avenue, the main drag for entertainment here in the black community."

Through the window, Selena looked at the house down the street. "I believe you and that big gray house down there are the largest I've seen."

"Yeah, mostly open lots and small bungalows around here."

"That house give you much competition?"

"Not hardly. We got different clientele, shall we say. I had to get that straight the first few months out here. We don't do no hourly rates. Know-what-I-mean? We have a two-day minimum stay. They got the message."

Selena looked quizzically.

"That gray house is a bawdy-house. They call it 'House of the Rising Sun' or 'Setting Sun'…whatever. It gets lit up like Christmas about eight, settles down about dawn-ish, real quiet through the afternoon then starts all over again. They not short on clients but we ain't after the same folk." Sugar Dee chuckled. "Although a lot of guys who stay here make their way down there from time to time. I make sure they know they can't bring them gals up here. Do their business and come back here—alone. It's a hard rule to maintain when the bands get to jammin' but we got Big Boudine at the door and the base of the steps to refresh their memories. "

"Sounds like he's got the stuff to keep them in tow."

"No doubt. Pretty boy musicians and their little chippies ain't gonna challenge him." Sugar Dee lifted the empty suitcase onto the stand. "Running your own business is a real hoot. Gotta be clear on what you want to be and stick with it. Regardless of the money. We run a clean and respectable place. Period."

Selena let the curtain drop, concealing the sight of the gray house from view.

"It's a selling point. Convenience for my clients," Sugar Dee continued. "Got that house down the street and

Central Avenue only a few blocks away. Most of the guys walk to their gigs."

Selena laughed, "One thing about you, you do see the positive in everything."

"Got to, or you'll go crazy. Learned that in Oklahoma City where they knew and appreciated music. All the greats. Every city worth their weight in gold has an entertainment center like D.C and U Street. Central Avenue here and mine was the Deep Deuce. That's why I got a good ear."

"You left?"

"Oh yeah. When you from someplace the only thing left for you to do is go. Leave it. Once away, either you appreciate it or you find something better."

Selena thought of Star. Her leaving Colt, Texas for something better. She sure hoped her sister found it. Even if she never let them know.

"But I do go visit. Although it's been awhile," Sugar Dee confessed. "Everybody I loved is gone."

"Hey Sugar Dee!" Shanghai yelled up the steps.

"Speaking of loving somebody, that man only knows how to yell." She smiled and shouted back, "What!?"

"Hoyt and me going down to the wharf to buy some fish. What you all feel like eating tonight?"

"Wanna take a ride?" Sugar Dee asked Selena.

"Sure."

The four piled into their Packard and rode down the palm-lined streets, wide and broad and clean. Selena let the warm and comforting sunshine hit her face not believing that it was the end of December. Eyes closed, she shared with Hoyt, "This is nice."

"Another contender for a place to live?"

"Don't know yet. It's far away." Selena watched wide grassy lots with wild poppies poking through the dry dirt shoot past her window soon to be replaced by low-rise commercial buildings, train tracks and then modest bungalow after bungalow with yards, driveways and fences so unlike the South Side of Chicago.

"It snowed six inches yesterday," Hoyt informed.

"Brrr...the cold, white stuff?" Children played ball in the street, moving to let them by. Girls jumped rope as parents sat on the porch steps. "Black people live here?" Selena asked Shanghai and Sugar Dee.

"A few. This section is called Watts. Working-class folks. Came in the 20s. Was a labor camp for workers on the Pacific Electric Railway."

"Before you leave, we'll go over to where the uppity Negroes live."

"Really?"

"Every city got a place for them too."

"Not in the south. We all live together. Rich, po' and otherwise."

Down by the wharf, they walked along the beach and Selena marveled at the expanse of the Pacific Ocean just as her father had seen years ago; another experience she'd share with him at Christmas. Removing her shoes, she watched her dark toes disappear under the white sand. When the warm water reached her feet, she giggled.

Returning home they cooked, ate and sat on the porch watching the antics at the House of the Rising Sun, before deciding to go to bed. They couldn't wait to honor their reservations at the famed Club Alabam, Shanghai and Sugar Dee hoping it'd be a dry run to convincing the Colson's to come back for their New Year's Eve party.

The couple sauntered up the steps as Shanghai locked the front door and Sugar Dee bid, "Goodnight you two," and winked.

Hoyt entered their room and clicked on the too-bright overhead light, cutting it off in favor of the lamplight on the nightstand. Selena walked to the window and raised it higher letting in the cool refreshing California night air on a stream of moonlight ushering in the smell of night jasmine. She eyed the House of the Rising Sun, all lit up and the tinkle of errant music waves reached her ear. "Not as loud as the South Side of Chicago."

"Not as cold either." Hoyt came up behind her and squeezed her tight. She lay her head on his shoulder and relaxed in his safe and welcoming embrace. No matter where they roamed and where they stayed, Hoyt Colson remained her safe place. Her home. She began swaying her body in response to his even though they couldn't make out the tune from down the street. It didn't matter, they had their own music that played for them and only them. Heartbeat to heartbeat. Their own rhythm wrapped in love and tenderness and need one of the other. She turned into him and noticed how the streetlight cut across his chiseled face. She never lost sight of how happy he made her feel. She watched him close his eyes and tilt his face so his lips could devour hers full-force. His tongue flicked and licked as his hands moved down sending shock waves up her spine. Slowly he peeled her dress from her body. Their frames fused and she felt his projectile, like a heat seeking missile, aim for her soft parts and tender spaces.

No longer hearing any music but their own, their breathing grew heavier and more urgent, as her hands traveled beneath his shirt and up his back, skin-to-skin. They rocked and filled in any spaces between them as he gathered her and carried her to the double bed. He removed her panties leaving only her garter belt and stockings, his body laid upon her and while kissing, he expertly removed her bra, freeing "the girls" and then treating them one by one to the rough-smooth texture of his tongue. She moaned, caressing a handful of his hair as he traveled toward her hairy triangle.

Once he'd arrived at the moist abyss, he stood and shed the remainder of his clothes so that his maleness showed etched against the California darkness. She reached for him and he allowed her to touch his daunting hardness, holding him in her hand, massaging, filling him to overflowing. He took himself from her and lowered his pulsating maleness into her dewy center and they moved as one. She then flipped over so she ended up on top, and held the bedframe as she moved against him, with him, thrusting until he rolled her over in a final climax of mutual ecstasy. Flesh-to-flesh, they panted in unison waiting for the restoration of their breaths. The rumble of laughter began in their sweat-soaked stomachs which made salacious sucking sounds; they giggled nose-to-nose. He gave her butterfly kisses. She giggled, covering his delightfully-athletic haunches with the sheet.

"You think they heard us?"

"Does it matter?"

"No. I think we gave the House of the Rising Sun a run for their money."

"They got nothing on us, Selena. I love you."

"I love you more."

"Impossible." He rolled from her and she snuggled in his arms.

"California love ain't bad."

"Loving you anywhere ain't bad. You're a tigress and I love it."

"Got to keep you interested."

"Don't ever worry about that."

They fell asleep and in a few hours Selena rose to remove her garter belt and stockings, relieve herself and run and jump back into Hoyt's welcoming arms. He nuzzled her and she relaxed, joyous and satisfied. He made her happy. She wondered if all women felt as she did. She hoped so. So loved and cherished by her man in and out of bed. Knowing when he looked at her, she was his and he hers...completely, unequivocally. She vacillated between thinking that all women felt this way to she was the only one who could feel that way because she had Hoyt for a husband. They shared an unwritten and natural intimacy that no other person could compromise. No one could put asunder. No one else had that power. She fell deeper and deeper in love with him with every waking day.

She thought, *To answer your question, Hoyt Colson, I could live anywhere with you on the face of this earth and beyond.* With the faint laughter and tinkle of music wafting down from the House of the Rising Sun, Selena fell back asleep.

The next day Hoyt kissed his sleeping wife goodbye and headed to the military base to pick up his assignment, returning for dinner before they dressed and headed out to the Club Alabam on 42nd and Central; one of the happeninest clubs on the L.A. scene, known for booking the best bands and entertainment. Selena delighted in seeing Miles and Maxine Syphax, whose road-show, *Shuffle Along,* had folded in L.A. and they decided to stay. "Not bad. Hard but not as cold as Chicago," Miles'd summed it up. "In more ways than one."

All too soon the Colsons trained back to Chicago so Hoyt could develop his work and send it back before their Christmas in Colt, Texas and possibly a return to California for New Years. A cataclysmic thing happened to prevent his best laid plans from coming to fruition. A change for him and the world.

America the Beautiful

Saturday, December 6, 1941

"Man, you are bringing me down," Range told Hep as his friend covered his glass so the bartender couldn't add more brown liquid.

"I'll meet you back at the dorm," Hep said, paying his tab and leaving Range with the two girls.

"Must be his time of the month," Range joked. The women did not. "Maybe some other time." Range settled up his tab and ran outside to catch up with Hep. He'd vanished into the dark night without a trace.

"Man, where did you go?" Range blew warmth into his hands as he entered their dorm room. "You got them extra-long legs."

"I *have those* extra-long legs," Hep corrected.

"Man, it is Saturday night. How many more of these we got before we have to go home and face the music?"

Hep stretched out on his bed face up, hands behind his head. "We don't have to act like jackasses right up to the day do we?"

Range hated went Hep got serious… too serious. "We're young. We're supposed to make mistakes. That's what the 20s are for."

"You know what our fathers were doing when they were twenty?"

"Aw. Not this again, man. We're not our fathers."

"Pity." Hep swung his legs to the floor. "My father was on his own at twelve. Had to make a way out of no way so that his children wouldn't have to struggle or suffer. Look at us. Look at me. How are we going to find a dignified way out of this?"

"I vote for just telling them we lost our scholarships and then they'll pay for tuition and we can finish. C's in this ofay school ain't nuthin' to spit at."

Hep hated Range's nonchalant attitude, his ability to settle for the easy way out. He took nothing seriously. Too good-looking and spoiled for his own good. Girls, women, married and otherwise, vied for his attention, which he freely gave to whomever he fancied at the time.

"You graduate, go home and take over Cherokee Ranch, marry my sister and have pretty brown babies. Ten years from now none of this will matter."

"We need a miracle," Hep said quietly.

"You worry too much about what other people think."

"Only one person."

"Papa Colt," Range answered for him.

"OK, two. Myself. I do not like myself right now."

"You'll get over it, man."

"I'm going for a walk." Hep grabbed his hat and coat.

"I'll go with—"

"No. I need to clear my head."

Range sank back on his bed. He wished for some way to get his best friend out of this slump. He wanted his friend back. Fun-loving, crazy Hep Culhane. If he knew how, he would. All these years he'd been more brother than friend and he missed them both.

An hour later, Hep slipped back into the dorm room to find Range spread out over his bed, fully clothed, ready to go if Hep called. If Hep needed him.

"You back," Range managed through a haze of sleep.

"Yeah."

"Good," Range muttered, using one foot against the other to remove his shoes before turning over and going back to sleep.

Hep chuckled and lay on his bed. Range loved and annoyed him like his own mother bore him; the second generation of Culhane and Criqui men to share this bond. Hep dozed then settled into a fitful night's sleep.

The college boys woke to chaos on campus. Not sure whether a bomb threat or a fire, looking out the window showed the green lawn covered with frantic, agitated bodies. Students running and rallying but Hep couldn't make sense of the melee.

Hep opened the door and snagged the arm of one of the guys as he ran down the hall.

"What's going on?"

"Didn't you hear?" he asked breathlessly. "Japs bombed Pearl Harbor this morning. We're going to war."

He shoved a newspaper into Hep's chest like it was a ticket for the black guy to set him free.

The two-cent Final Edition of the *Chicago Daily Tribune* headline read:

U.S. and JAPS AT WAR.
Bomb Hawaii, Philippines, Guam and Singapore.

Hep stared at the words, threw back his head and laughed. Laughed and laughed like a crazy man as he put the paper into Range's hands. A great lightness and relief washed his face.

"What the hell is so funny?" Range raged at his demented friend.

"This is it. This is our way out."

"What is?" Range didn't follow Hep's train of thought.

"Don't you see?" He grabbed his friend by the shoulders. "We go to war."

"Say what!"

"We do the honorable thing. You know everybody's gonna be signing up to fight. Especially the white boys."

"I say let 'em. I ain't gonna fight and die. I got too much living to do."

"How you think the women are going to feel with you here and all the men out there fighting?"

"Good. Oh, I'm gonna make them feel real good."

"Range, this is perfect. We couldn't get a better out. This is heaven sent. We fight and become heroes. Colt,

Texas' finest. We may not even get overseas. Papers say it'll be over before we know it."

"They said the same thing about the Civil War. People used to go see the fighting with picnic baskets and blankets. They were wrong, then and now."

"C'mon. Imagine the women you could pull in uniform?" Hep appealed to his friend's vanity and horniness.

"I do not want to be shot at."

"Like it's the first time. Lookit, this way our folks will never have to know about our pitiful academic mess. That we let them down and the whole damned race. This way we'll look like men stepping up for the cause. They not gonna let Negroes fight. With some college, we'll probably do clerical work somewhere. It's the best way. Don't you see?"

"Naw. I'm not feeling it."

"I'm going, with or without you."

Hep challenged Range's competitive spirit.

"You'd do that wouldn't you? Leave me here then come back and get all the women and praise 'cause you volunteered."

"Got that right." Hep saw the wheels in his friend's head turning. "We ain't gonna die. Bad things don't happen to us. We're 'citizens of the world.'"

"Damn, man. That ain't me. That's you."

"Regardless, what do you say? It's the most exciting thing that's happened to us in a long while." Hep's eyes glistened with hope and resolution. "What do you say?

Hep-cat and Hipster for a year or so. Come home and it's all gravy."

~*~

Keeping up appearances that everything remained normal, Hep and Range trudged through new-fallen snow to Selena and Hoyt's for Sunday dinner.

"Now, you all seem like the cat that swallowed the canary," Selena noted. "What's up?"

"Nothing," Hep replied.

"That's the second time you told me that lie."

"In due time. Want to tell everyone at Christmas."

"Oh? Good news or bad," Selena pressed.

"Depends."

"On what?"

"Wait like everyone else."

"Have you lost your mind talking to me like that?"

"Maybe I've found it." He got up and went to the bathroom.

"Hoyt, talk to him and find out. He got some girl pregnant."

"I don't think so, Lena."

"What?" She could count the times her husband had told her "no."

"His news. Have to wait like he said." He gathered her into his arms. "Gotta respect a man's privacy."

"He's twenty."

"He's a man."

"Is not. You all—men—are a strange breed." She wrestled herself from her husband's arms. "Gotta finish up dinner," she dismissed.

Smoke Gets In Your Eyes

"The hell you say!" Colt jumped up almost knocking over the dining room chair. The grandfather clock in the grand hall chimed predictably.

Hep expected this reaction, and met his father's outburst with quiet dignity.

"What the white man *ever* done for you, done for us, but keep his boot on our necks?" Colt began pacing in front of his fireplace and back, never removing his eyes from his son. "Now you say you want to join up in this fight? His fight?"

"Yes sir."

"No sir!!" Colt shouted. "It don't make no sense!" Colt tried to harness his rage. "This ain't our fight, son. Them Japs not marching down in Colt, Texas. Not bombing Cherokee Ranch. White folks tried. White folks failed. 'Cause they the devil incarnate."

Hep remained silent but remained continually impressed with his father's knowledge of the world around him.

"Range talk you into this mess?" Colt knew better, but had to ask. "This the kind of fool-brained impulsive shit his father would have pulled. Thinking it'll all work out."

"No sir," Hep said evenly.

"You all cook this shit up together? Blind leading the blind. What you think you gonna gain from this? Huh? If you wanna die, there's other, quicker ways to do it."

In his entire life, Hep could count on two hands the number of times he'd heard his father curse. He knew his father was mad-dog mad.

Colt sat back in the chair with a huff. "Most ignorant-ass thing I ever heard; a black man volunteering to fight the white mans' fight. You got to fight the white man over here. Why you going over there to fight *for* him and *with* him. You sure ain't gon' be *beside* him. *Equal* to him."

"Enemy of my enemy is my friend."

"Don't sass me, boy. Don't throw my teaching up in my face." He tried to calm the wild look in his eyes. "The white boy is always gonna be your enemy. Can't help hisself. He may make promises and sweet talk you into fighting with him, but don't trust him 'cause he'll turn on you in a heartbeat," Colt snipped then asked, "Is that it? How-some-ever you think you go over there and fight with them, it will make the white boys respect you and all will be right with the world when you get back? Might could be you think you gonna 'prove' to them white boys that you are worthy of their respect?" Colt eyed his son. "Damn their respect. That's a fool's errand boy. They ain't never gon' think on us as anything but their lackeys. We always gonna be blacks that overstayed our welcome and outlived our usefulness."

It was Colt's turn to sit quietly and internally try to make sense out of nonsense.

Hep'd never thought of what it'd be like when he returned victorious. Hep wondered if, subconsciously, that was part of it. Not as sage and quick as his father, but maybe Hep was doing this for now *and* later. Initially, enlisting proved to be the dignified way to cover up his C average and educational failure of losing his scholarship and having his father foot the tuition to graduation. But he liked what his father said about furthering race relations; proving to them and the Army and the Japs what superlative men of action and honor the Negroes were.

Hep looked at his dad, again and almost resigned. He knew how well and hard he'd fought for Cherokee Ranch. A place where his children and their children could soar and flourish. Be free to "be who they are." But his dad's world was not his world... and his world was changing. He'd seen that in just the two years he'd been at Northwestern. Living in Chicago and traveling to and fro; changing train cars when they reached the south to Jim Crow cars behind the sooty engine. Hep hated that. He'd witnessed the way they were looked upon, talked to like they were an ignorant nuisance to be tolerated.

"Dad?" Hep tested.

Colt held up his hand as if he just couldn't discuss it any longer. Hurt stood in his eyes. *You my only son. You gon' go off. For what? I busted my ass to give you everything my family could ever want,* he thought. And none of you all wanted it. Henley died. Star left and now you are leaving too. "Is Cherokee Ranch so bad, son? Is this life so bad you want to leave?"

"Just the opposite, Dad. It's you who taught me to be the best. That I am just as good… no, better than any man out there. It's you who had me grow up with a strong sense of who I am. What I am and I am proud of it! You gave me the confidence to go out there and be a 'citizen of the world,' 'cause I have the heritage and background to tackle anything."

Hep'd learned that a little late after the South Side clubs and women got the best of him, but it was a lesson well-learned and one he would never forget. Ever in his life. He remembered Star's leaving and her saying to him, "Promise me if you have to leave, you will." A ten-year-old Hep didn't understand then, but did now. This one conversation with his big sister clarified pain for him; their father's mixed with fear and Star's need to go. With this one conversation, he confronted his parents with a decision they didn't want or understand, but they saw his determination to go, as something he had to do for himself. Not for them, not even his country but he as a man needed this definition. He intended to come back alive and well, but if he died, he'd do so pursuing his destiny. It was his choice. The appropriate epitaph to the son of Colt Culhane.

Colt sighed deeply and looked earnestly into the ebony eyes of his only living son. Not wanting to make the same mistake as he had with Star, he said, "I cannot give you my blessing, son. But I can tell you to be careful. Your mother and I will be waiting for you when you get back. This will always be your home."

"Thank you, Dad."

"Umm," he rose then capitulated, "Don't be no hero. When you find yourself in hell, keep on going. You might get out before the devil knows you're there."

Later that night Keely and Colt lay in bed, neither able to sleep.

"Did we fail them, Keely? Our children."

"No, we gave them roots, deep, strong and lasting. But we also gave them wings to fly away if they had a mind to."

"Ummm." Colt thought on it.

"We gave them the confidence to go out into the world and make their own way."

"That's pretty much what Hep said."

"Fail or succeed it's their life, Colt." Keely said quietly, snuggling closer to him. "Can't live it for them."

"Helluva Christmas present. Our son going off to a war I thought would never touch us." Colt couldn't recall anyone from Colt, Texas fighting in WWI. That Prohibition or Depression didn't bother us either nor the massacre of Rosewood, Florida or race riots in Tulsa, Oklahoma or wherever else."

"Our little hamlet is too small and safe for our children. They got big plans."

~*~

"That was it? You joined the U.S. Army," Selena confirmed, breaking off a piece of her mother's famous chocolate cake, licking the white icing from her finger.

"Yep. I wanted to tell Mom and Dad first."

"I can understand that. What I don't understand is why go at all? Doesn't seem your style."

"I'm still learning what my 'style' is."

"You got to get shot at to figure that out?"

"It might make things clearer. Certainly make me appreciate my life more."

"I just don't need that kind of clarity," Selena teased. "What about Feather?" she asked of his Texas sweetheart. "Her brother *and* her man signing up for a war."

"Not taking it well. Let's just say things are in turmoil at the Criqui home."

"Hey," Hoyt said, joining the siblings who were on the front porch swing. "Any more of that cake left?" he asked, sitting on the porch bannister. "Chilly out here."

"Not as bad as Chicago. Yep. Want a glass of milk with it?" Selena asked her husband.

"That'd be great. Thanks." He watched his wife disappear behind the screen door which concealed her fine brown frame as much as that wool coat, but he knew what lay beneath.

"Heard what you did. Honorable man," Hoyt told Hep.

"We'll see." Hep pushed the swing into motion with one foot. Always admiring Hoyt like a big brother he asked, "Would you?"

"Doesn't matter, man. Your life. Your decision. Your success or your failure. Whichever. Own it."

Hep nodded.

"I'm proud of you, man."

"Thanks." Hep's face broke into a wide grin; Hoyt being the first to acknowledge his decision as a man in a positive, supportive way.

~*~

The Culhanes and the Criquis stood on the rail platform at River Bend Station like they had years before seeing Hep and Range off to college. This time, a smaller farewell party bid them goodbye and safe journey; Feather Criqui visibly absent. Then the final destination had been Evanston, IL. Today the train would drop the pair off at Ft. Benning, Georgia for basic training.

Life had taken a turn.

~*~

Hoyt spirited his wife back to the warmth of Los Angeles to celebrate New Year's Eve in the presence of friends and take her mind off the fact that her baby brother would be spending his Christmas in basic training. Despite the nation's preoccupation with the war, his scheme seemed to work.

The day after their arrival, they lounged until time to dress for their reservations at the Club Alabam with Duke

Ellington and his Band. Sugar Dee did up Selena's hair and she slinked into a beautiful beaded cobalt blue off-the-shoulder dress. The foursome strolled in the balmy weather to the club and occupied a prime table up front, so close that Duke's sweat almost hit them.

Hoyt was so proud of the way his radiant wife looked, he thought he'd burst. When the band took a break, Miles stepped up to the microphone and crooned "*Stardust.*"

"They're playing our song," Hoyt said, extending his hand.

Selena took it and melted into his tall lean stature. "This is so perfect," Selena oozed into her husband's ear. Eyes closed, he glided and guided her with his own body.

"Out of all the girls in this world, you're my one and only girl," Hoyt whispered to Selena as they danced to Miles' smooth, soulful voice. "Now, forever and always."

They rejoined Sugar Dee and Shanghai, who had the goofiest look on his face, but did not speak.

"Hey, man? You having a stroke?" Hoyt asked.

"I saw you over there talking to Lena Horne, man. The *Horne*," Shanghai marveled. "You *know her*? More importantly she knows you! Damn!" Shanghai enthused.

"I know a lot of famous people," Hoyt demurred, nonchalantly. "Had to introduce her to my beautiful wife." He kissed Selena's hand.

"She invited us to see her at the Café Society in Harlem," Selena interjected.

"She's no Dorothy Dandridge," Sugar Dee chided.

"How you know her?" Shanghai continued.

"I did some publicity pictures for her way back when she was just a teenage chorus girl at the Cotton Club. Her daddy kept tight reins on his baby girl."

"We gon' have to talk later," Shanghai reached out his open palm, waiting for Hoyt to give him some skin. "You gon' leave me hangin', man?"

Hoyt reciprocated and gave him the evil-eye that asked, *What the hell are you doin' disrespecting our wives like this?*

"Nothin' more to tell, man. Let's just enjoy our lovely wives on this new year's eve," Hoyt dismissed and gazed into Selena's inquiring eyes. "More champagne, Lena?"

He inwardly cringed at using his wife's intimate sobriquet in public. Selena cut her eyes agreeing with his bad timing.

For the second set, comedian Redd Foxx warmed them up, after which the Miles Syphax Trio played background music while they dined on filet mignon, baked potato and asparagus tips with Hollandaise sauce. Dancing resumed and, as it neared midnight, everyone plucked their noisemakers from the table centerpiece.

The countdown began and then… Happy New Year! Balloons fell from their nets in the ceiling, streamers whizzed by the banner that read "1942." As confetti rained around them, Selena and Hoyt kissed and wished each other a Happy New Year and the band launched into

"Auld Lang Syne." Like a phoenix, the party rose and morphed into an old-fashioned jam session as band leaders from other clubs came to Club Alabam. At four in the morning the foursome headed back home proclaiming that as *the* best New Year's any had ever had.

Back at their room, Selena began to peel the sweat and smoke-filled cobalt-blue dress from her body. "So. You've slept with Lena Horne?"

"No, I did not."

"But you wanted to?"

"No offense, but every man wants to, Si."

"What happened to 'Lena?'"

"We haven't kept in touch—"

"Not her. You calling me 'Lena?'"

Hoyt looked at his wife... speechless.

"I've never known you to be so discombobulated," she teased. "You know. I don't care who you slept with then. Before me. But it better not happen now," she warned. "Or I will chop it off and send it to her."

"I have steak at home. Why would I want hamburger?"

"Good answer." She sauntered off to the bathroom.

Hoyt raised his eyes to the ceiling in a mute "Thank You, Jesus." Then he looked into his pants. "I don't want to lose you, buddy."

That next week Hoyt snapped new photographs as the assignments changed with the attack on Pearl Harbor. He took a lot of impressive pictures of military outposts and troops and factories changing from one thing to munitions plants, airplane production and uniforms, gearing up for the fight with the Japanese. Selena preferred not accompanying him on those shoots and stayed with Sugar Dee. The big sister tried not thinking about her little brother, still in basic, but he shared nothing with her. Hopefully, he did with Hoyt and her father, but she believed, with men's strange code of silence, there was little information flowing between them either; just an unstated sense of support. Since the universe had taken Hep from their immediate reach, she hoped it would return Mil to Mazeda. It had been months now. The Colsons left California's warmth and trained back to Chicago. Hoyt developed his photographs to send back and packaged them up in the living room as Selena looked out on the blanket of fresh snow filling Chicago's streets below.

"I think I'm pregnant," Selena confided quietly.

"What?" Hoyt asked, looking up from his task.

She turned to have her eyes meet his. "I think we're going to have a baby."

"My Blue Heaven" played lightly on the radio. "How? When? Why?" he began grinning.

"I think you know how—"

"Yeah, that's always fun." Hoyt came over and enveloped her from behind.

"I guess in California and because the rhythm method doesn't always work."

70

"There are plenty of Catholics who agree with you."
He rubbed her stomach. "How do you feel about it,
Lena?"

"I don't know. How about you?"

Hoyt let out a whoop she was sure the entire
apartment building could hear.

"Hoyt! Shush!"

"Why?"

"It's such a strange time. The war—"

"Besides Hep and Range… it's got nothing to do
with us, Selena."

She turned and looked into her husband's gleaming,
hopeful eyes.

"It's my first. How about you?" He teased her.

She laughed and melted into him. "You crazy man."

"Crazy about you. And our kid."

"He or she is not a goat."

"Oh, Lawd. OK, Miss Schoolteacher." He held her
tightly, nuzzling into her ear. Even her correction
couldn't destroy his mood. "A baby."

"We didn't plan—"

"I wasn't planned either. Neither was my sister. You
probably were. Regardless, this baby. Our baby may be a
surprise but you know what I call that?"

"What?"

"God's idea."

She blushed and kissed his neck.

"Know what else?"

She looked up at him.

"This baby is going to be loved and cared for." He massaged her flat stomach tenderly.

She shook her head in agreement. "I'm taking care of him—

"Or her. Or them. Twins run in your family," He reminded.

"Whoa. Orelia has twin girls but that's a fluke. Probably from the Rudd side."

"You get two for one."

"Spoken like a man whose life will change little."

"Untrue. My children will know me. Know that I love them."

His comments met Selena's silence as she realized she knew very little about Hoyt's background.

"Have I told you all this?" he asked, reading her mind through her eyes.

"Tell me again," she prompted.

"Born in east St. Louis moved to Kansas City at ten after my mother died. Lived with my sister and her husband for a couple of years until he decided he wanted to try farming. Moved to a remote area and it was hard for him... and my sister. One day I took the biggest piece of chicken and the last of the buttermilk. He took exception and threw me out on the coldest, dreariest day ever. I stayed in the barn for two days. My sister brought me food until he found out...he beat both of us and I left on my own for good. I was fourteen... alone, made it back to town. Did odd jobs and a lady gave me a camera." He smiled. "Mrs. Petway. She saved my life.

The camera saved my life. I could focus or control the images any way I saw fit. When she died, she left me five hundred dollars. That was a fortune back then."

"It's a fortune now," Selena added.

"She reminded me of your Ms. Felicity Rudd." Hoyt looked up questioning. "I don't think she had any children of her own."

"She had you."

"And a few others. We'd hang around her house. She fed us. Encouraged us. One cat played the piano. Another one painted." He looked at his wife. "I haven't thought about that in a lot of years."

"Well, now you have a reason."

"Yeah. My child will have all he or she needs before, during and after I'm gone."

Selena never realized how much Hoyt's life paralleled her father's. On their own at a young age, vowing to take care of their yet-to-come family at all costs. Without knowing the details of his background, she'd been drawn to him... drawn to a principled man like her dad.

That night they didn't make love, but she'd never felt more treasured and cared for as she slept in his arms. She'd been momentarily mortified when she first suspected. None of her friends had children; Mazeda, Sugar Dee or Zen. She'd have to make all new friends with children. She also realized that many of the female singers had no children yet: not Billie, Ella, Sarah or Dinah. Selena supposed that their lifestyles were not conducive to family. Male musicians, if they had children, left their wives back home to care for them while the musician-husbands lived like single men on the road until they got home. Selena wasn't ready to give up traveling with her husband on photo-shoots. She certainly could not take a baby "on the road," not as an infant or a school-age child. She didn't want to be left behind caring for a child, trying hard to keep a connection with her traveling husband. Trying to make his time at home special while giving all her mother had given to them growing up. It sounded exhausting.

Selena was tired already.

You're in the Army Now

"Next time I'm gonna punch him in his mouth," Range spat as they made their way from the mess hall to the barracks.

"No, you won't," Hep advised as he flicked ashes from his unfiltered cigarette. "You can't let them get to you. You fall into their trap. Then who gets sent to the brig?"

"You can't disrespect a man like that and not expect to get punched out," Range fumed.

"You ain't a man to him. You're a boy. Don't you know that?" Hep halfway teased his friend.

"Ain't funny, man."

"No, it is not," Hep agreed, entering the building and sitting on his bunk.

"This ain't what I expected, man. Cut off all my hair. Have me wearing these ugly-ass vines. These roach-killer shoes and got to get up early in the morning. How long we got to do this?"

"Coupla years."

"No way, man. Gotta find a way out of this. Blow a toe off or flatten my feet or something."

"Go crazy," Hep offered.

"I might just do that. That's how I'll be if I don't get poontang on a more regular basis." He stretched out on his bed. "Going to town with us tomorrow?"

"Yeah. There's a Micheaux flick Hoyt told me about."

"Man, I ain't talking no flick. If I'm flicking it won't be no movie."

Hep chuckled.

After a night on leave, they walked back to their barracks. Reveille came early in Ft. Benning, Georgia. Despite that, the pair sat outside for a last smoke.

"You think we'll kick these when we muster out?" Hep asked.

"I ain't kicking in. These things are disgusting. I prefer gum," Range declared and looked up at the full moon. "Wonder what the folks in Colt, Texas are doing?"

"Sleepin'," Hep said on a stream of smoke.

"How long we in for?" Range kept asking, hoping the length of time would change.

"The duration, I guess. The only way out now is in a box with a flag on it."

"Or wounded so badly you're no good to them."

"Neither is an option for us."

"Ever wish we'd have found another way? Just sucked it up and gone back to school?"

"At first, yeah. But now that I'm here with all these other guys who are so gung-ho and patriotic. Well, it's rubbing off on me. Like it's an honor to serve your country."

"Oh, man. Don't let your daddy know you've fallen for the okey-doke propaganda," Range said.

"So what's your plan?"

"Well, live. Go back whole. Maybe take one of those French gals with me."

"To Colt, Texas?" Hep asked. "You're better off getting shot."

"Possibly. Maybe I'll get all the French poontang I can handle. Then go back to Colt. Marry a nice local girl ten years younger. Have a lot of babies and live long and prosper."

"Sounds like the Criqui tradition lives on."

"What about you?"

"Finish up college."

"Oh yeah. I say we go to Howard University this time. Some fine women up there."

Hep chuckled.

"I plan to settle down by thirty. I can't keep this up for long; plus, by then I'll be bored by a stream of lovely ladies. There is more to life, you know."

"Really?" Hep took another drag on his Lucky Strike.

"After graduating, then what? Marry my sister, run Cherokee Ranch, have babies?"

"Feather has taken exception to my military detour."

"She'll get over it," Range predicted.

"Dunno. We didn't seem to click like usual at Christmas."

"You had this crazy scheme on your mind," Range offered. "Once you strut into Colt, Texas a war hero—she'll forget all about this little stint."

"Humm," Hep murmured, thinking about Feather, who wanted to get married now and said she wasn't going to wait for his finishing up college before they married.

"You're right. Let's survive first and worry about the rest later."

~*~

The next morning a dispatched soldier interrupted the platoon. The drill instructor inspected the orders given to him by messenger.

"Culhane!"

"Yes sir."

"Fall out. Report to Colonel Stryker."

Hep took the orders and eyed Range as he made his way toward the colonel's office.

Once there, Hep took a seat as instructed and waited for almost an hour, wondering what the colonel wanted with him. He scoured his mind for offenses but could recall none. They'd made a humungous deal over his sharpshooting, but Range had come in second and he was still back drilling. Hep realized he was missing the ten-mile speed march and relaxed.

"Culhane," the white soldier called and showed him through the open door of the colonel's office.

"Sorry to keep you waiting but—" the colonel looked up for the first time. His jaw dropped. He shuffled the papers on his desk and found the correct one. "You are Hepburn Heath Culhane of Colt, Texas?"

"Yes sir." Hep still stood at attention as the colonel had not instructed him otherwise.

The Colonel scanned the recommendation: Student-scholar at Northwestern University, Chicago, IL. He'd not only scored nearly perfect scores on all Army testing but a perfect score in math. According to his drill instructor this soldier had excelled in all basic infantry training: machine gun and barbed wire infiltration courses, map reading, hand-to-hand bayonet fighting drills, close order drills, night patrol and night maneuvers and endurances. It showed two runs over full combat style obstacles every day, thirty-two mile forced marches and two mile double-time. The Colonel looked up again and then continued his quiet perusal of this man's record. The most impressive to this officer was Culhane's proficiency with a gun. 16 "bullseyes" out of 16 shots at 500 yards. A shoe-in for the Special Forces sharpshooter program. All manner of details were in his folder, even how they felt his scores were suspect and that the target-pit officer was contacted to make sure there was no "fixing" of his scores. But nowhere in the pages of these reports stated that the soldier was a Negro.

"At ease," the colonel finally said. Culhane's validated obvious intelligence, physical shape, endurance, map-reading skills and shooting were unparalleled by any other soldier at Ft. Benning. *A nigger,* he thought, but asked, "How tall are you?"

"Six three, sir."

"Shoe size?"

"Twelve, sir.

"Dismissed."

Hep saluted and left. Walking back to his barracks he thought, *What the hell? All of that for stats.*

When Range returned he couldn't wait to ask his buddy what'd happened.

"Well, you're still here," Range said.

"For the time being."

The following day, Range Criqui endured the same questioning from Colonel Stryker…with the same results. Neither Hep nor Range could figure the inquiry out. But they were in the Army and belonged to them for at least two years.

"As much as I hate to admit it, Culhane is the best for the assignment," The colonel acquiesced. "A nigger." He'd continued a vigilant two-week search for another soldier, but none came close to Culhane's credentials and stats. Critical time wasted when the inevitable stared him in the face.

"You want to win the war or keep a prized buck down on the farm, sir?"

"I'm not that prejudiced. As long as he gets the job done and doesn't want to marry my daughter. We'd be fools not to use him."

"Maybe he'll die."

"That's not funny."

"Sorry sir," he cleared his voice nervously.

80

"We got to requisition special uniforms… and boots for that big buck."

"Yessir," the soldier said simply, not knowing how to reply.

The colonel stamped the order "Special Forces," and with that gesture, the life of Hepburn Heath Culhane changed forever.

What A Difference A Day Makes

The door of apartment 3G whined open and Hoyt stepped into uncharacteristic pitch.

"Selena?" he called out, setting his suitcase and equipment down before turning on the light.

"Oh, hi," Selena said weakly.

"Lena, what you doing sitting here in the dark?" He went to her and sat beside her on the couch.

"Just enjoying the quiet. Listening to the sounds of life around me."

"Did something happen to Hep?"

"No. Not that I know of. Do you know something?" she tumbled to an end.

"No, Si."

"I bet you're hungry. How was your trip?" she said, rising.

He grabbed her hand. "Sit," said he. She obeyed. "Now. Tell me what's wrong." He stroked her hand. "Is it Mil?"

She shook her head and took his hand in hers.

"Mazeda?"

"She's been with me all day. She got that job at the shipyard. A riveter. Can you imagine?" Selena chuckled. "It's good money. She hated that pencil factory."

"Selena." Hoyt took her face in his hands, forcing her to look directly into his eyes. "Talk to me."

Selena listened to the phone ring in the hall as a door opened, and an occupant ran to answer.

"That's been happening a lot. That phone rings day and night."

"I bet. Selena." He quieted her trembling lips with his.

His kiss calmed her and when he stopped she blurted out, "I lost the baby."

Hoyt embraced his wife and held her.

"I'm so sorry. I lost our baby, Hoyt."

"It's OK, Selena," he said, holding her tightly so as to keep her grounded and with him.

Tears sprang from his eyes. "I should have been here with you." He sprinkled her forehead, her nose, her cheek with tiny kisses. "I am so sorry."

"It's not your fault," Selena managed before her crying resumed. She thought herself all cried out.

"It's not your fault either." They embraced each other as tears flowed freely between them.

"We got to get you to a doctor."

"No need. Mazeda and I took care of all that. Called a doctor. Just heavy clotting for a few days. Then spotting. I wasn't even showing yet."

"I am just thankful that you're alright, Selena."

He squeezed her so hard she had to laugh. "Hoyt, you're choking me."

"If anything ever happened to you. I couldn't—"

"Not to worry love of my life." It felt good for her to give care and comforting after receiving so much from her friend. She'd had days to get used to the idea. Hoyt remained devastated.

"Doctor says there's no reason we can't try again after a while."

"I don't even want to do that. As long as I have you—"

"Hoyt." She looked up at him. "We'll be fine."

He stopped sniveling becoming embarrassed that at a time like this, his wife gave him the comfort. He wiped his hands over his tear-drenched cheeks, clearing the wet away.

As if reading his mind, she said, "That's what marriage is. You build me up and I build you up. We're a team. You and I."

"Yes. We are," his emotion-choked voice trembled.

He thought himself away too long. Selena didn't want to go because of the length of time she'd be away from her students and she didn't want to travel south. His rigorous assignment was to photograph the Color Guard at Ft. Bragg, North Carolina, Camp Lejeune's Montford Point basic training for black marines then over to Parris Island in South Carolina before the training of black pilots at the Tuskegee Air Field in Alabama. Pride had swollen his chest with every picture he snapped of the black servicemen, making an historic stand for America, but there was something enviable about the black pilots at Tuskegee that gave him pause and a longing to be one of them. Hoyt had much to share with Selena in the retelling of his southern adventures but her news took precedence.

Hoyt remained cheek to cheek with his wife. Serene. Speechless. Comfortable. He then placed his cheek at the edge of hers and fluttered his eyelashes against hers. It tickled. She laughed.

"What are you doing?" she asked, happy for the diversion and half return to their playful normalcy.

"Butterfly kisses," he answered reverently. "My mama used to give them to me to cheer me up."

Selena fluttered her eyelashes back in response and grinned. "It works."

Soldier Boy

"Hey, man," Range said during Hep's farewell beers. "This ain't the way we planned it."

"Sure isn't. We were supposed to be together until the end of our duty. Hop a train back to Colt, Texas and take up where we left off."

"Hey, man. Don't forget the Howard University detour."

"Cool. Where do we meet up?"

"Depends on where we muster out."

"Yeah. Let's get out alive first. The rest is just details."

Beside them, the other guys laughed at some raunchy joke.

"You don't know where they're going to send you?'

"Top secret."

"Can't even go home for a visit to say goodbye to your folks?"

"Neither will you."

"Yeah, only the boys who are within hours of their family get to do that. Army ain't payin' for nothin'."

"Three hots and a cot."

"Like prison, man."

"Maybe this 'top secret' stuff will get me out early."

"That could be sweet, man. You wait for me. Don't start Howard without me. 'Hep-cat and Hipster' got to show up together."

"Yeah," Hep said, as an unexpected melancholia settled in between them.

In all their years from toddlers to now, except for sleeping at home, they had never been separated. A day hadn't gone by when they didn't see each other from riding and racing their horses to chasing girls. From crayons, recess, aftershave, high school football to college scholarships, they'd been joined at the hip. No one in Colt, Texas ever expected to see one without the other. And now Hep was shipping out and Range was staying put. Like losing half of yourself to some unknown. Losing a leg or an arm and expected to function.

"I was thinkin' since they're splitting us up, I'd try for that black pilot school down there in Tuskegee. Fighter plane escorts."

"I think you need a college degree for that," Hep offered.

"Or those paratroopers. Jumpin' from planes."

"Man, you get me up in a plane the last thing I'm going to do is jump out of it," Hep chuckled. "You're more like your dad than you think."

"He was hot-headed, thrill-seeking, stubborn and impatient," Criqui recalled what he could about his father. "But he was my Dad. And I loved him."

"Yeah. Can you imagine our fathers tearing up the west?" Hep gleaned. "They were supposed to end up growing gray together sitting on that side porch."

"That'll be us. Surrounded by all our children and grandchildren. We'll carry on where they didn't."

"Not if you're flying and jumping out of planes," Hep teased.

"Or fixing roofs," Criqui added the reality of how his father actually died.

Their laughter faded.

"It's gonna be rough."

"But we're rougher. We can handle it," Hep said. "Colt, Texas Proud," he repeated their football chant.

"We make it through this shit? We'll be golden," Criqui said.

"We were golden before and messed it up."

"Yeah, well, what does Papa Colt always say, 'there are no mistakes, only lessons.'"

"Lesson learned."

"Be safe, man. We got things to do." Range slapped skin with his brother, blinking back tears at the reality.

"You too." Hep grabbed him awkwardly in a bear hug, clapped him twice on the back and released him.

"Hang tough, bay rum and buttermilk."

"I'll do my damnedest."

Unable to bear more sentimentality, Hep'd risen early, looked over at a sleeping Range, left him two packs of Juicy Fruit gum and reported to his post. He'd eaten with his new unit and walked to the waiting truck for transfer. Hep looked over at his old guys and spotted Range going through his calisthenics, the rising sun glinting off his coal-black hair. When all were down on the ground for push-ups, a recalcitrant Range remained standing and saluted his buddy from a distance. Hep returned the salute, got on the truck, took a window seat and watched Range be reprimanded by the Drill Instructor until he was out of sight. Hep chuckled. Range Criqui; his brother, his buddy, his partner in crime, his best friend, remained one-of-a-kind.

~*~

Snow fell on top of snow in Chicago with the delicious smell of a pineapple upside down cake perfuming apartment 3G as Hoyt tried to explain the military system to Selena who found it hard to believe that the Army did not allow Hep a visit home to say goodbye to his mother and father.

"Not a garden party, Lena. He'll come home when his duty is over. Or before," he stopped. "But not likely unless he's wounded or of no further use."

"So we're to hope that he stays alive and keeps fighting?" She cut her eyes. "Ain't that a blip?"

Across town, Mazeda loved her new job as 'Rosie the Riveter' and volunteered for extra shifts, anything to take her mind off of Mil's loud absence. Selena and Hoyt managed to drag her to an Oscar Micheaux film and dinner one Saturday night.

The nation remained immersed in all things World War II. Everyone did their part in the effort. Shanghai and Sugar Dee spoke of how buses came around day and night in Little Tokyo, loading up Japanese Americans on trains and taking them to internment camps. Zen was elated because the Blue Plate Mayonnaise Plant moved from across the Mississippi River to mid-city New Orleans making it not only more convenient but a raise to keep workers from leaving for the better paying wartime jobs in the shipyards around the Port of New Orleans. "Soldiers need mayo too," she'd quipped.

World War II cast a huge shadow over the U.S. perhaps uniting the country in a way it never had. Everyone was affected by the war effort through their work, or had someone fighting, tended Victory gardens or bought War Bonds. Selena's desire to participate was satisfied when she accompanied Hoyt to the USOs that popped up all over the country, and took peacetime pictures of soldiers at leisure en route to battlefields. Selena greeted, served sandwiches and filled punch bowls, danced with the guys and played the piano and sang when a star was either late or more rarely cancelled. Famous and not so famous celebrities always stopped by the South Side USO Canteen, reputed to be the liveliest and Selena loved volunteering and boosting the morale of soldiers passing through and it showed. Initially, Selena was identified as Hoyt's wife, but slowly they looked forward to her at the piano as she established a following in her own right. Initially she declined to record a V-DISC, which they sent overseas for the troops, until Hoyt encouraged her. A nervous wreck when she appeared at the studio for her first record, "*Stardust*." Only with her husband there in the background was she able to muddle through and do it justice after three false tries. "Singing with all those people around, into a mic, with a big band is something I'll never get into," she told Hoyt. "You'd be surprised what you can get used to with the right motivation," he'd countered with a smile. "You were good, Lena."

"Really?"

"Really."

Volare

"Get down!" Hep yelled, yanking the man down beside him into the foxhole. Biblical rain had fallen for seemingly forty days and forty nights and every time they stepped into the mud, their feet sank past the ankles like quicksand. The sucking sound loud every time they took a step and pulled their foot out of the muck; trench foot in the making. Cold, wet and miserable... but alive.

"Grazie," the soldier thanked Hep for pulling him out of the line of fire.

"Prego," Hep replied.

"Ah. Parlay Italiano?" his face broke into a wide infectious smile.

"No," Hep replied, taking out a Lucky Strike and offering him one.

"No. Grazie," he said haltingly.

"You're a real Italian?" Hep asked. "From here?"

"No. American born in New York. Brooklyn. My parents from here. At my house in America, we speak only Italian."

"Come ti chiami?"

"Ah, parlay italiano?"

"Un po. I'm learning."

Over the last few months Hep had shared space with many foxhole mates, the most exotic an Arab mercenary fighting for a price, not a cause. But an Italian not from Italy… an Italian-American who spoke horrible English… curious, but no worse than the Italian Hep was trying to master.

Hep'd made few allies since leaving America on his new detail. They'd departed from Hampton Roads, Virginia for a nine-day crossing on the ship, *Billy Mitchell,* weaving through the ocean with enemy submarines beneath them. The officers had their own private quarters but the rest of them slept six to a cabin in bunks. When darkness fell, to avoid detection, they were prohibited from even smoking on deck, and given all types of small musical instruments and games to play to occupy their time and keep them from going stir-crazy. Mostly, Hep played cards as he noted his comrades; some anxious to see action, others petrified they would, many resigned and others already praying for their safe return. Many regretted leaving home and the things not said. Not done. Hep savored and dreaded the last hot meal they'd have on the boat when they landed as there'd only be C rations for sustenance from that point on. His company landed in Casablanca and had taken a slow "40 or 8" train, either 40 soldiers or eight horses, to Oran, North Africa before boating through the Strait of Messina to Naples, Italy. The ravages of the war not yet fully fought showed up in the trash, and rubble strewn all over the ancient city accompanied by the smell of hopelessness and a desperate, visceral need to survive. Besides begging the soldiers for food, glassy-eyed women picking lice from their children's heads seemed the only activity. Men, conspicuously absent from the scene.

"Tavio Orsini," he introduced, with appreciation.

"Hepburn Culhane."

"Piacere."

"How'd you get picked for this?"

"I shoot good."

"Me too. But it hardly seems to be all we need to do over here."

Hep felt the unspoken prejudice of his unit and he began to understand what his father'd said about righting wrongs and being treated fairly. He'd made few "friends," but they regularly called on him to take out an enemy, especially those who held bunkers. With one shot, Hep's intended target slumped forward or spun around with the impact of his perfect aim.

"Hot damn! That nigger can shoot," was all the applause he received.

Just as his daddy predicted, Hep felt "tolerated not celebrated." He ate his rations alone until Tavio began to join him. As an Italian-American with "not good English," he too was a persona non-grata. A guinea. The two necessary outcasts formed their own bond, aiding one another with their languages. Hep would teach Tavio better English so when he returned stateside he could get a better job. And Tavio taught Hep Italian and other colloquialisms for his survival over there. Phrases and inflections that would make Hep seem like a native

94

Italian. Besides being an expert marksman, with the Nazis already occupying France, he learned that his company was the advance team to plot the eventual southern invasion of Italy.

In time, Hep's company subdivided into a smaller group of four: Orsini and two Alabama crackers. Due to the secret nature of their mission, unless called upon to shoot, little about the actual operation was shared. It seemed to Hep that there was a race to see who could accurately detail the terrain and get back to the powers-that-be with the correct information. Both quick learners with the right motivation, Culhane and Orsini learned their respective native tongues making them functionally bilingual, complete with conversational expressions and regional dialects.

"A wop and a nigger speaking the same foreign language jus' don't seem right," one Alabama, red-neck soldier commented to another before Hep stood and stretched his healthy 6'3" frame, intimidating the soldier without speaking a word.

Buoyed by their mutual affinity for languages, Culhane and Orsini spoke exclusively in Italian and, to make things interesting, tackled and mastered Morse code and sign language. In so doing, they learned about one another's families, hopes and dreams, filling their non-fighting hours with discussions, unaware of the connection they were creating. Tavio was not Range, but he became a close second in a short time. The Orsini family grew the finest olives in the Tuscany region, nudging them from the rich volcanic loam on the terraced hills of their small village. His great-grandfather and his grandfather before him produced the finest, sweetest yet earthy-tasting olives only their soil could provide. His grandfather began an olive oil company with his father and uncles, grooming them to take over. His grandfather dreamed of exporting oil to America but instead, when a three-year drought with no signs of stopping continued, it was them, the family, that was exported. "My grandfather and father, never got over losing their groves. My father went back and forth to Italy many times before convincing his father to come to America. He finally came... only to die from the loss of his homeland and a broken heart. He hated America. "My father tolerates it because now with the war... there is nowhere for us to go. Our ancestral home was ravaged."

"I make this vow to you, my friend. If I'm ever in the position to revive your family's' olive oil business, I will."

"Grazie. And if I ever get lots of money, I will make sure your family is taken care of."

"Deal," Hep agreed although he couldn't imagine his Papa Colt ever needing such a handout, but wouldn't insult Tavio with this observation.

"What does this 'deal' mean?"

Hep explained that and countless other terms as they sloughed on through hilly, slippery terrain and in late spring, the rains ceased and the sun slanted, dabbing the hills with its rays. Culhane and Orsini had rejoined their company as their mission-rhythm had become to join, get further orders, and separate and rejoin and separate. Still, Hep paused as he viewed the bright spring day and remarked, "This is beautiful country, Tavio."

"Si. But you should see Tuscany. Bellissimo!"

"If I were your grandfather, I wouldn't want to leave either."

Early the next morning his company came upon a burnt out villa. The Nazis announced themselves by taking out three of their men simultaneously. The enemy held the stone edifice stronghold with ease, their ammunition capacity seemed endless. Night fell and there appeared to be no way to kill the well-entrenched Nazis. Hep volunteered for advanced recon with his company staying behind. He applied mud to his face and when the Alabama red-neck started to comment, Hep silenced him with a lethal stare.

Hep moved stealthy along the perimeter when a waiting Nazi stood and threw a grenade toward him and his men. Within a split-second, reminiscent of his football days, Hep pitched, rolled, gathered up the grenade and chucked it back into the tower with innate, mechanical precision. A split-second later the grenade exploded taking out the tower and the building below. The men followed up with a volley assault lighting the skies above like a 4th of July celebration. Through the thick smokescreen, American tanks lumbered in crushing the doors, the ensuing fire fight, deafening.

When the smoke settled, it was clear they'd decimated the Nazis. Whoops and cheers erupted from all... black, white and otherwise, expressing their awe and amazement at Culhane's quick action and presence of mind and body to execute the initial assault.

"A white man would get a commendation for that act of heroism," the major mumbled.

"He's a long way from white," his lieutenant answered.

~*~

Spring 1942

Hey Hep cat,

Where are you? I'm somewhere in France.

Still working that Top Secret mojo, huh? I've written you about two letters none answered so I thought I'd just send them to Cherokee Ranch. We can drink beer and re-read them on the porch when we get back.

I send the obligatory 'everything's fine' letters home to Mom, but I can tell you the real deal. Got to thank you for this... I'm with the 3916 Quartermasters Truck Company. You know they don't let us do nothing serious, but man, I'm driving trucks all over the French countryside carrying supplies to the troops. It's thrills without front line danger. They had us trying to drive trucks to qualify and I stripped all kinds of gears, but two hours later, I got the hang of it and I've decided what I'm going to do when I get out. Never thought a born horseman would defect, but I'm going to run a truck company in Colt, TX. These machines are the future, man. They're talking about GI's going to college for free, so I'll still go to Howard U. like we planned, get that sheepskin so I know how to manage a successful business, get a co-ed wife and return to Colt, have a passel of cute-kids and run trucks and cars. I figure by that time, I'll be ready to settle down but right now? Ah, man, this is a blast. I can hot-shot a car in two seconds. We're supposed to wait on the entire convoy to roll out, but by the time we all get together we've wasted valuable time, so I just take off and we roll, man with supplies, ammunition, jerry cans of gasoline, food, even bombs, whatever they need on the front line. They were going to reprimand me, but General Patton himself commended me for my 'initiative.' I'm calling my shop the Red Ball Express 'cause that's what they call us. Nuthin' can stop us... and the women... French women are Ooooh La La.

These cats are wild. Red is the blackest nigger I ever seen. Miss Felicity Rudd would call that a "play on words." When he closes his eyes and his mouth, he disappears into the dark without a trace. Invisible. Red "SkeeKee" Benton and I exchanged seats mid-drive, man. Going 50 miles per hour over hilly dirt roads and didn't even stop. He's from Chicago and knows all the places we went. We probably saw him and didn't know it. I told him all about you. Did I mention the French women? ... Lawd have mercy! I know I can't bring one home to Colt...so I'm having all the fun over here now.

Enough to last a lifetime. Hope you are sowing oats so you can settle down when we get back. Feather says she's not going to Spelman because she likes the job she has at the Town Hall. Go figure. That ain't got nothing to do with me. But you probably already know all this.

Anyway, man. Just catching up. Hope everything is copacetic with you.

Will write later.

Miss you, man.

Range

~*~

Oblivious that there was a war on, nature eased the spring rain and volleyed into summer on schedule. Sun shone and warmed the grass, coaxing wild flowers into budding. While other men wrote letters home, ate rations, cleaned guns and savored their down time, Hep and Tavio often wandered around the nearby environs, familiarizing themselves with the local roads, rivers, hills and the area's general topography. The oddly matched soldiers often took natives by surprise and Tavio, with his easy manner and toothy smile, would quip in flawless Italian, "My cousin fell in love with a Moor. What can I say?" Hep would follow up with an impeccable Italian phrase and all would laugh before the salt and pepper pair would move on down the road.

Hep never thought that racism would save his life. Germans, Italians and other Americans knew that the United States services were segregated, and blacks could only clean up latrines and dig graves, certainly were not

100

working intelligence or anything of value... and speak Italian? Negroes couldn't speak English. To avoid over exposure the curious pair traveled on side roads along the waking countryside, sleeping in old barns or shelled out farmhouses once filled with loving families.

"I'm definitely coming back here when the war is over," Hep promised one night as he lay in a bed of old hay, gazing up through a hole in the roof at the stars. The same stars under which his parents and Feather slept. "Bella notte."

If their unit hadn't caught up with them, the pair wound their way back to the company and awaited their next assignment. After Hep's heroic feat at the villa, Major Taggert often called "Culhane" in to aid in his map-reading to the obvious objection of other soldiers and, on occasion, visiting top brass.

"Culhane. Your thoughts?" The major asked as the visiting officers bristled at the audacity of asking not only this infantry man's opinion but a Negro to boot.

"Sir. The river is on the left not the right as indicated by the map."

"Are you saying this map is wrong?" the colonel boomed indignantly.

"Yes, sir. I am."

"Dismissed," his major ordered before the profanity flew.

Destroying the peace of the night, a verbal ruckus between the colonel and major ensued in the tent before the unit was issued new orders based on Culhane's recommendation.   Subsequently, the unit flanked the Germans, surrounding them on two sides, the river on the left, while the soldiers hit them hard and Hep and Tavio picked off the runners.

"What's that boy's name?" The colonel asked begrudgingly. "He left no POWs."

"No sir. He did not," the major replied.

I'll Never Smile Again

Selena glanced out the window at the fight between Chicago winter's refusal to demure to the anxious stubborn buds on the trees trying to fling themselves into the spring season.

"It's a dream come true, Lena." Hoyt beamed.

Selena's face crumbled as she handed him a dish to be dried.

"Aren't you happy for me?"

"Do they know you're black?"

"I dunno or care. I get to go overseas and shoot the real action there. Maybe I can get into newsreels and come back and do films like Micheaux."

Selena struggled to grasp this threat to her idyllic life. "I can't go with you? Over there."

Hoyt stilled. "Well, no. It'd be too dangerous for you—"

"But not for you?"

"Lena, I'm a man. They'll protect me. I'm not fighting. I'm taking pictures—"

"Oh? So now who is naive?"

"War correspondents and photographers go over there all the time. They come back."

"And enemy bullets know the difference," she sniped.

"When I get back—"

"*If.*"

"I can write my own ticket," he ignored her negativity. "We can have that house you want and have babies." He went to her. Embraced her tenderly. "Lena, please don't ask me not to go."

That's what she always liked about her husband. Straight. No chaser. Truth was she didn't want him to choose between her and this assignment. Truth was she wasn't sure he would choose her. This was something he'd always wanted. To break barriers and show, given the chance, how good blacks were in everything. She was new to his life. He could start over again. She could not. He was her everything. Why did things have to change? Why did she have to fall in love with a visionary; 'A citizen of the world.' This was the price she had to pay. If he stayed, he would loathe her with every breath he took. She couldn't stand to see disappointment in his eyes and know she was the one who put it there. In time, he would resent her and leave her and she'd be alone anyway. "Okay," she whispered.

"Really?" His face reclaimed its ebullient smile. He squeezed her hard, lifted her feet from the floor and swung her around. "You won't be sorry."

I hope not, she thought and suddenly, she understood and felt as hopeless as Mazeda.

In the days before his departure, the inseparable couple rifled through old pictures Hoyt kept in his office. Attempting to sort them into a manageable order,

104

categorizing them for easy access and making space for those he'd bring back from overseas, Selena came across a sepia picture of a woman who could have been Star. Selena had no idea how Star would look now... in her late twenties. This woman stood in a waitress uniform in front of a plate glass window, splattered across her face in all cap letters: COLORED ONLY. Selena held the image in her hands as Hoyt noticed and looked over her shoulder and said, "This is why I'm doing this. So pictures like this will be obsolete. Old. Archived and left for history books."

Selena looked into her husband's hopeful eyes.

"I want to help usher in the 'New Order,' Lena. I fight injustice with a camera. I expose and prove wordlessly."

"A picture is worth a thousand words," Selena murmured.

He smiled that Hoyt Colson grin that warmed her heart like nothing else. "Listen to my edumacated, wife." He kissed her forehead and caressed her tightly. "Once we prove ourselves over there, they have to take note and treat us the way we deserve over here."

"You are a romantic, my husband."

"It's the right thing to do."

"When have you known ofays to 'do the right thing' with any black or brown people?"

"You're in a mood," Hoyt observed.

"I can go and sing for troops," Selena ignored him and offered a solution to their predicament.

"Yep. You could. You'd be protected too. But there's no guarantee they'd send us to the same place. You can stay here safe and sound and they already love you at the South Side Canteen."

"They do, don't they?" Selena smiled and then added, "Just promise me that you'll come home safe, sound and be the Hoyt Colson you are now."

"Promise." He turned her in to him and she straddled his legs and felt his nature rise immediately in her soft spot.

"You'd promise me anything now," she teased.

"Sure would," he answered, planting tiny kisses all over her face as his hands drifted down to her soft, moist center. "Humm," he moaned. He lowered his head to kiss her breast through her thin slip.

"And promise me, after that, you'll never leave me again."

He began moving against her and she stopped him cold. "Promise."

"I do, Lena," he managed huskily, inhaling a whiff of her scent released before they made love.

That verbal assurance carried Selena through his last days, her tearful departure and back home alone.

Their apartment door creaked open and she clicked on the light... then clicked it off again. She didn't want any company... not Hoyt. She walked to the open window and shut it against the impending storm. The smell of rain swirled around apartment 3G. Without realizing it, Selena had spent three days alone, weighing her prospects. Still in love with her new high-paying job, Mazeda spent much of her time working. Selena's parents invited her home for a visit to Colt, Texas but, being with a couple who'd never been separated all the years of their lives, didn't sit well with the grieving newlywed... and that's how she saw herself. A perpetual newlywed. Hoyt made her feel that they'd only just begun. He always made her feel beautiful even though she knew she wasn't. She cleaned up well, but a beauty she was not... but her man made her feel so. And now he was gone. So was all the touching, the feeling, the looks and anticipation of making great love. So Selena visited the South Side Canteen, greeted like a returning hero. She continued to serve punch, dance, socialize with fellow soldiers, take requests for the piano and her voice, all making her feel connected to her husband and her brother... out of reach and so far away.

"That's good," Hoyt had enthused when told over the phone before shipping out.

"I feel lost," she admitted.

"I'll be back before that happens."

Silence. Selena didn't want to beg him not to go. He'd given her that chance and she'd blown it.

"I'll be around you so much you'll be tired of me," he continued.

Selena covered the mouthpiece of the phone so he couldn't hear the muffled sobs.

"I love you," he stated simply. Boldly. Honestly. Straight, no chaser.

"Love you too."

Hey Hep-cat,

I guess these letters are piling up in Colt, TX. I'll fill in the blanks while you're smoking Lucky Strikes and I'm eating your Mom's pound cake. I'm on track, are you? Howard University, here we come. C ration stew tastes good when you warm it up on my truck engine. Well, maybe not too good but better. Need some hot sauce. Got into a situation last week and thought of you. Reminded me of me and Yvette. What was her last name? Same as her husband's. Then, I didn't know she was married until he interrupted us and I jack-knifed out that window butt-naked. You asked me where my clothes were and I told you I had to leave 'em. Your daddy always said there are no mistakes only lessons. I learned to ask a woman if she's married. I did that last week... but apparently she lied or I don't talk as good of French as I thought. These women make it hard on a man to honor their vows. I can't respect a woman who lies or takes me to her marital bed. That's as low-life as you can get. A lot of things Papa Colt told us didn't hit home until now. I guess I'm one of those who has to learn by doing. After my daddy died, yours took over without even knowing it. Or maybe he did. Got to ask him when I get back. He made me burst with pride when he'd tell me, "You jus' like your daddy." Maybe I'm, as they say, growing up. I've seen some things, Hep-cat. Things I want to forget but don't think I ever can. But I guess you have too.

Let's just meet in Colt, TX and take the D.C train to HU from there. In the high times I'm OK. But in those quiet times. Well... I've learned to appreciate where I came from and a lot of times wish I was back there. Doing normal natural stuff, riding horses. Helping my mother out. God, eating her food or your mom's. A long drink of clean Texas water. From the pump. The smell of my mama's lilacs out near our front fence gate. My own bed. Trying to sneak a peek of pubic hair or a hard nipple from the girls at the swimming hole. Inez Foster making a hot night hotter. Mt. Moriah Gethsemane Church. Your mama on the organ, your daddy on the porch and any of your sisters in the choir. Founders Day races. I let you win a couple of times. Enough for now.

Miss you, man. See you soon...

Range

P.S.

I learned how to open a beer bottle without a church key. Beer is my liquor of choice now. You can catch ofays spitting into a bottle of beer. Looking forward to sharing a few COLD ones with you soon. Double V.

Ave Maria

The thirsty Italian countryside absorbed the two men as they traversed the overgrowth on the hill. Hearing a jeep, they plastered themselves against the mountain until it passed on the road overhead and continued on in its direction. The smell of gunpowder assaulted their senses as they closed in on their target, even though they could not yet hear the engagement. Culhane and Orsini'd been on their own more often than not, doing better alone than when with a unit. Stealthily, they moved with the undulating fields, undetected, taking their targets by surprise. By the time their unit caught up, no one was left to kill. The pair, leaving bodies in their wake, moved on to the next destination. Once the major saw the bodies of the enemy, he knew his guys had been there. "Killing machines," he observed of the two.

Hep and Tavio snaked their way back toward their next assignment, checking out Nazi strongholds fastened to Italian terrain. Lighting his last cigarette, Hep nudged the snoring Tavio who snorted and turned over. Hep took a long satisfying drag of the filterless, thin white reed wondering exactly when he'd begun smoking. He'd picked up other bad habits he hoped to shed once home. Home, in the tranquil evening he allowed himself to think of it this one time. Had Feather started Spelman as planned? How were his folks? Not including basic and all the other fundamental training, he'd been in Italy for almost a year. He hadn't written to anyone in just as long and, without news otherwise, surely they all thought him dead. He relished returning to Colt, Texas and surprising everyone with his health and regaling them with the tamer stories of his travels. Highlighting the Italian countryside, the olive groves, contorted, ancient grape vines, rich volcanic soil, eliminating the fact that he'd become a sniper for the U.S. Army. Neither embarrassed nor proud of this accomplishments, he never kept count. He did his job, kill or be killed. His objective was to get home. Having grown up all his life with firearms, he thought nothing of his skill. Didn't know when he learned to shoot. Guns in Texas were a way of life; he passed a Winchester and a pair of pearl-handled Colt revolvers hanging on the hall fireplace every day of his life. Guns his father used to tame his section of west Texas. Used to defend his Cherokee Ranch for his family. Guns, a necessary implement to keep what he'd worked so hard for.

Hep took another drag, realizing that the Army'd kept stats on him, but Hep knew whatever they attributed to him would have to be doubled with all his kills of Nazis in the field. He looked forward to putting this all behind him. 'Throw away the bad and keep the good, as his mother used to advise.

With the crackle of brush underfoot, Hep jerked back to the alertness required. In one smooth gesture he flicked his cigarette far from him and reached for his pistol.

"Halt!" a lone silhouette shouted, blazing a light in Hep's dark face. The soldier's uniform, unmistakable, and the look registered on his face, a mix of confusion and superiority.

Hep froze as ordered, his mind ablaze with options. Tavio remained quiet and Hep didn't want him to awaken and draw fire. Realizing that he couldn't bullshit this German in Italian, he only needed a spilt-second to take this Aryan out.

The blue-eyed soldier cocked his gun.

I can't die like this, Hep's only thought.

Suddenly, Tavio lunged towards the German allowing Hep enough time to pivot, gather his pistol and shoot him between his surprised, transparent-blue eyes. A wild shot discharged from the soldier's gun.

"Prego pisano," Tavio complimented of the executed, unspoken plan of men whose lives depended on one another.

"I'll take my kudos once we're back in the states," Hep said, picking up his gear, rolling over the dead Nazi taking his P08 9mm luger and looking out over the dark terrain. "Make a nice souvenir. Let's get outta here. I'm sure that shot was a calling card for his buddies."

Hep moved a few steps with Tavio behind him, then, heard him fall.

Hep rushed to his side. "You hit man?"

"He missed my arm," Tavio managed before passing out.

Hep hoisted his comrade over his shoulder and whispered, "You'll do anything to get a free ride." He felt the wet, warmth of blood trickle from his friend's gut.

Once in the clear, Hep inspected Tavio's wound and packed it as best he could. The mission had changed. He had to find his friend help. Hep walked east away from eminent danger of the Liri mountains. Daylight came and went twice before Hep happened onto a remote farmhouse. Hep cared little for the political affiliation of the residents and more about their ability to take care of Tavio, ready to have them help him at gunpoint if necessary. Luckily, the Vittadinis belonged to the resistance and sprang into action. The middle-aged man plucked the lone bullet from Tavio's mid-section. Hep heard the "pling" into the tin cup, announcing its successful removal.

As his wife, Rosalie, served Hep the first hot meal he'd had in weeks, Carmine said in his native dialect, "The bullet is gone but he's lost much blood." He slapped the black soldier on his shoulder and said, "Only rest and God can save him now."

Hep remained in this precariously dangerous situation for two more long agonizing days, risking discovery, missing connections, but it mattered not as long as his buddy was in jeopardy. Hep patrolled his environs during the day but when he returned, there was little change in Tavio's healing. Watching the daily demise of one so full of life, for life and his country wore on Hep. Once lively eyes roamed indiscriminately around the beams of the house not resting on anyone or anything. The once full lips covering the toothy smile, murmured indecipherable nonsense. The olive of his complexioned turned pale and sallow. Death ran rampant through his body, infecting and setting it fever-hot to the touch. Hep felt powerless, helpless and useless for there was nothing he could do to restore this vibrant man to his former self. Nothing he could do to save the life of the man who had saved his.

Old hurts, buried pain and forgotten losses reawakened in him; the death of his brother, Henley, when he was ten. The loss of his big sister, Star, going off to pursue her singing career not to be heard from since, mingled with the inevitable loss of this friend. Only now Hep, in a foreign land without family and friends around for support, made this loss more acute.

Hep returned to the farmhouse two days later to find Tavio covered in a sheet. He walked to his side and Carmine shared, "He passed this afternoon."

Tears sprang to Hep's eyes. "I should have been here."

"There was nothing you could do," Rosalie comforted.

Hep folded back the sheet revealing Tavio's face; peaceful with the hint of a smile.

"He must have seen somebody he knows," Carmine explained.

Despite the streaming tears, Hep chuckled.

As Rosalie prepared the body, Hep picked the spot, nestled into a sloping hill under an ancient tree. Carmine and his sons dug the grave—deep—so no sadistic Nazis or any other predatory animals could disturb Tavio for all eternity.

Hep removed Tavio's dog tags and the intertwining crucifix he'd received from his family at his First Holy Communion. For safekeeping, Hep slipped them into his sock.

Hep and the family carried the wooden casket to the open grave, setting it down gently as if Tavio could feel their intent. Hep breathed in the clean air filled with the fresh smell of earth devoid of any wartime pathos. Hep fought for composure and, reaching his goal, in the impeccable Italian his comrade had taught him, shared how much his friendship meant. Carmine Vittadini read a passage from the Bible before Rosalie and her daughters sang an unfamiliar old folk song.

Hep stood there, stoic, erect, as the male Vittadinis hoisted dirt upon his friend's makeshift casket. His heart filled and without explanation, Hep's rich baritone voice rose and bathed the verdant valley in an impassioned rendition of "Ave Maria," wetting the eyes of the cantor and the Vittadinis. Carmine, anxious to move this soldier out before he was discovered, ushered him forward. Hep looked back, returned and knelt by his grave. "Goodbye, my friend. Thank you for everything. I promise that I will never feel this helpless and powerless again. In your honor, I will name my first born son after you; the man who will allow me to have a son where you will not. Until we meet again." Hep gathered a handful of dirt and slipped it into his pocket.

"You come back and see this land, your friend and us when this war is over," Rosalie invited. "If there is anything left," she added. "God be with you."

Carmine folded Hep's tall frame into the false bottom of his hay wagon; twice, unsuccessfully bayoneted by Nazis patrols. Carmine connected him to the resistance and he was transported to Foggia to be reunited with his company. While waiting, he had his first hot shower, compliments of First Lt. Sewell Horad of the 366th who'd rigged the contraption for his men as well as setting up an "Officer's Club" for his soldiers so they could drink and successfully make it back to their bunks, bypassing the MPs, an arrest and a stint in the brig. Hep learned that First Lt. Horad'd graduated from Howard University, an omen and sign, which solidified Hep's and Range's intentions to go there.

Once his company returned, Hep informed the major of Orsini's passing and subsequent burial.

"Great loss," was all the major said which angered Hep beyond his ability to express it. Their lives meant nothing to these officers and never would.

"His dog tags?"

"No." Hep would give them personally to the Orsini family.

After a day back, Hep received another assignment.

116

"I ain't gon' go with no nigger!" the other soldier spat.

Hep eyed the major.

"Soldier, you will go where you are assigned!" Major Taggert bellowed. "You are to take orders from Culhane. He might just keep you alive."

The white soldier seethed. "Unless I kill him first."

"What did you say?" Major Taggert shouted.

"Nuthin', " Murphy glared at him. "Sir," he added spitefully.

Hep eyed the Major knowingly without uttering a word.

As the pair disappeared into the night, the major experienced an uneasy feeling.

Two days later, Culhane was found slumped in the road by a member of his company who called in the major and medics. Culhane's shoulder had been shattered by a bullet and blood flowed freely.

The major ordered Culhane shipped to a medic unit which airlifted him to an Army hospital. Hepburn Culhane survived the surgery and endured three weeks of physical therapy to get his shoulder and arm back into working condition for a return to active duty.

While there on other matters, Major Taggert paid Culhane one visit attempting to find out how Culhane'd received his injury. "It's all in the report, major."

"Yes. Well, there wasn't much in that report."

"Don't recall much," Culhane stated. "I was hit. Blacked out and then you all picked me up."

117

"Where was your backup? Murphy was it?"

"Don't know." Hep eyed the major.

"Did he do that to you, Culhane?"

Hep squared the major in the eyes. "Not that I can prove."

In five weeks' time, Culhane braced for orders to return to combat. The orders received stated that he was "to return home. Father ill."

Hep stood on the ship's deck worried about his father. Squinting against the sun's strong reflection bouncing off the water, he'd just received ship-to-shore confirmation that his father was in good health. For two more days, Hep tried to figure out the conflicting reports and paperwork regarding his father's health. He realized he was returning a different man than when he'd left. Isolation, life and death experiences had fashioned him into a more confident man with a broader world view, clearer priorities, a respect for life and a healthy acceptance of things beyond his control; beyond his ability to influence or change the situation. As he smoked his Lucky Strike, he deduced that going home early was more than a clerical fluke. He surmised that the major had changed his orders. Hep didn't know or care why. Hep'd done his duty, served his country and he was going home.

Many hadn't. Many wouldn't but Hepburn Culhane was... he'd make the best of it.

Do Nothing Till You Hear From Me

The long gone hawk'd been replaced by the devil's heat settling in on Chicago as Selena tried dressing and getting out before sweating up all over again. In her husband's absence, the South Side Canteen proved Selena's saving grace. Although initially she'd met Ella, Billie, the vivacious Bricktop, Duke, Count, Cab and Dizzy and many others through Hoyt, she was learning them professionally and they her as she gained their respect for her talent and work ethic. Lonely and feeling beyond useless, Selena increased her time at the Canteen becoming a regular occurrence as everyone was consumed with the war effort and what they could do to make it easier for "our boys." Celebrities hawked War Bonds. Short films on growing Victory Gardens and discussions on gas rationing became part of every movie showing. Often Selena opened the acts before the tardy stars breezed in, some staying longer than others. They all glimpsed, first hand, what Selena Colson could do musically and vocally as she seemed delighted to be among the soldiers. And the uniformed men in turn loved her. Becoming their "regular," her way of being close to her husband and her brother while they were overseas. Unlike the movie stars, Selena wasn't on contract neither did she have busy gigs to fulfil, her payment remained a soldier's rapt attention, his shouting out a request or giving a simple "Thanks. You make it feel like home here."

Selena reveled in her role as a volunteer mainstay at the local USO Canteen... whether serving snacks, taking coats, fast-dancing with the guys, playing the piano accompaniment or singing on stage. She was committed. This was the only activity that guaranteed her a good night's sleep when she got home and slept alone. When she remained too jazzed by activity at the Canteen, only thoughts of Hoyt could calm her down, when there, only her husband could give her the release she needed so she could sleep. Still, some nights she tossed and turned trying to warm the cold sheets where Hoyt used to lay. Should be laying now. Sometimes, she could feel his hands on her skin. Hot to the touch. Smell his lime-soap cleanliness. Sometimes, she jerked awake, feeling his presence in the doorway. Sometimes, she got out of bed, lit a cigarette and went to the window to watch humanity below move on with their lives without him... without her. "I'm looking at the moon but I'll be seeing you."

On a few occasions, she managed to drag Mazeda along and, once there, her friend ended up having a good time. She used to think waiting on Mil's return was just habit for Mazeda, but now with her man also gone, Selena fully understood. Humans all have their own coping patterns; Mazeda's release was working and saving for when Mil came home, sewing and learning to do hair like Sugar Dee. Selena's drug of choice, going to the Canteen. At least it wasn't cocaine, alcohol or other men as Selena'd witnessed in other women. When Sugar Dee invited Selena and Mazeda out to L.A. to join all the other Negroes going there for the abundance of jobs available to support the war effort, they both declined. Waiting for their men, where their men left them, their sole purpose until their returns came to fruition.

Hoyt and Selena's shared few letters, some attached to negatives he'd managed to send home for safekeeping. She preferred the immediate gratification of talking to him on a crackling phone line that made him sound millions of miles away, but the essence of him, the connection seemed more real. Trying to forget the reason he was away, they made plans for when he came home which began with the money he sent to her for bank deposits for their house.

"…Attending Negro League Homestead Grays game at Griffith Stadium tops my list of things to do when we return to D.C."

Selena laughed. Then challenged, "That's the first thing you want to do?"

"Well, no. Not the first thing," Hoyt countered in a husky-sexy voice. "Certainly won't be staying with Dr. Seth. We gonna be so loud!"

After a few more randy comments, he was gone. Again.

That call left Selena feeling especially hopeful, upbeat and horny. In trying to redirect her sexual needs, she recalled how Papa Colt had rescued the orphaned boy, now Dr. Seth Trask from River Bend, and taken him in as his own son. Before she was born, her father'd raised him the rest of the way and sent him to Howard University undergrad, then medical school where he met and married his wife. They lived in a beautiful four-story row house in LeDroit Park, steps from Freedman's Hospital where he was now Chief Administrator, and only a few blocks from the Wonder Bread Factory around on Seventh Street. The squishy white bread in no way resembled the thick, textured bread of her mother but the aroma was reminiscent and intoxicating. While staying with the Trasks, Selena'd missed lying in bed as the smell of fresh bread wafted over her and perfumed the air. Once married, she missed that aroma by staying at the Dunbar Hotel which was more considerate to both couples. She and Hoyt were going out as the Trasks were turning in for the night, often coming home when they were rising to go to work. Both Selena and Hoyt loved the Trask home, but hated their compromised privacy. Sometimes they didn't tell the Trasks when they were coming to D.C. as, despite their conflicting, topsy turvy schedules, they always wanted the young couple to stay with them. "I have to give up the Wonder Bread smell for privacy because you are too loud," Hoyt'd say.

"Me?" she'd counter as she rubbed up against him and added, "You shouldn't be so good."

"Can't help myself." He'd cupped her derriere and moaned. "Look who I'm lovin'."

Selena shook her head free of the sensuous thoughts and said aloud, "The tradeoff is well worth it."

Selena shook her head free of thoughts of Hoyt and recalled how she and Mazeda sometimes spotted Hoyt's name in the credits for the newsreels at the movies. Indescribable pride and joy would consume Selena and she'd whisper sotto voce, "Hurry home, my love."

I'll Be Seeing You

In mid-August, the days blazed hot but shorter, when Hep's size twelve's sent up a cloud of dust into the evening sky in River Bend. He'd come full circle, leaving on his own odyssey first to college and now returning from the Army; honorably discharged with commendations he'd yet to receive. The attendance for his initial send-off included his parents, Feather and half the town. For the return... he stood alone, his memories trudging through Europe his only company. The River Bend train depot hadn't changed, but he had. He tapped his jacket pocket and heard the quiet jangle of Tavio's dog tags and crucifix as he decided on a shave before venturing home. *A few more hours won't matter. Can't go home to mama without a proper shave,* he thought. A few hours later, the barber slapped Bay Rum on his clean-shaven cheeks and Hep smiled thinking of Range's calling him "Buttermilk and bay rum."

He hired a cab to take him the few miles home. As he paid the man and set his trunk off road, Hep hoisted up his duffel bag over his shoulder and eyed the ranch. Probably the same place his father spoke of when he'd brought his mother there for the first time. Hep's silhouette etched out against the twilight of converging night and he inhaled the fresh air. Free from acrid smells and the spoils of war. Flush with clean. In the distance, he made out the outline of his childhood home. The lights predictably off, save one in the hallway near the steps upstairs. He couldn't see it from this distance, but Hep knew it to be burning. He lit a Lucky Strike and started walking on the dirt road. His footsteps began to make noise and he automatically stepped on the grass to muffle the sound for a quiet advance. He smiled, realizing he didn't have to do that anymore. Home now, safe and sound, he didn't need such precautions. He wondered how many other practices he'd unknowingly brought home. As smoke filled his lungs, he relaxed and eyed the land that would someday be his; to have, hold, love, protect and pass on. At least now, he felt he'd earned it. Deserved it.

With only his footfalls for company and without warning, tears sprang to his eyes. Overcome with indescribable relief and sheer happiness that he'd made it home in one piece. That he could finally see his life in color again with hopes, dreams and depth. Emotions swirled around him. In that house he approached, lay parents who loved him unconditionally; a mother and father who'd welcome him with open arms. Overseas he seldom allowed himself to think of "back home" much, of normalcy, the mundane and routine. He now looked forward to boredom. He'd settle into Colt, Texas slowly and try to mend fences with Feather, if no Morehouse man had turned her head by now, while waiting on Range to come home. If his buddy hadn't returned by fall semester, Hep'd enroll at Howard U and by the time Range came out, Hep'd have an off-campus apartment for both of them. He'd come up with a way to decline Dr. Seth's offer of a room in their LeDroit Park home. What he and Range had in mind wouldn't do for a respectable doctor's house. Hep chuckled and took another drag of the cigarette and imagined seeing Range for the first time since they'd volunteered. Since Range'd defied the drill instructor to give Hep that final salute as he boarded the truck. *First on the agenda,* Hep thought, *beers and the swimming hole where he'd listen to the detailed exploits of Range and all the French women.*

Easing his key into the front door's lock, Hep knew it hadn't been changed since Star's leaving—just in case she came home. He set his duffel bag on the front hall hearth under his Daddy's guns, smiled and tipped into the kitchen heading straight for the refrigerator and a healthy swallow of buttermilk.

Standing in front of the refrigeration, he heard the click of a gun at his back and the words, "Raised by wolves, were you? Come up in here like you belong?"

Mid-gulp, Hep held up his hands and turned slowly, "I thought I did. It's me, Daddy."

"Well, I'll be got-damn!" Colt uncocked the gun in time to accept a hard embrace from his son. "Look at you! Keely," he screamed into his son's ear and up the stairs. They hugged again, father squeezing son's flesh to make sure it wasn't a vision. Tears soaked both their eyes.

126

Keely bounded down the steps and when she reached the bottom, she stared in disbelief. "To God be the glory!"

"Yes, ma'am." Hep beamed and caught his mother in a bear hug.

"My boy. My baby. My only son. Home!" Keely sobbed uncontrollably with delight.

"Catch your breath, Mama."

"Why didn't you call? Why didn't you write? Where have you been?" all tumbled out in one sentence as she slapped him playfully on the arm.

"Well, I didn't want to disturb you. I couldn't write and Italy," he answered in order.

"Italy?" Colt questioned. "You been to Italy?"

"Yep, and North Africa. I'll tell you *all* about it. You'll be sick of my stories, but I've got until I leave for Howard University."

"Say what?"

"Range and I are going to finish up there. Is he home yet?"

Hep didn't notice how the smiles froze on his parents' faces.

"Yeah. He's here!" Colt piped up.

"Hot damn! Oh, excuse me, Mama."

"I expect I'll have a lot to get used to." She walked toward her son and touched his cheek. "I'm looking forward to it, son. Praise be to God."

They bantered on for another hour when Hep finally asked, "How long has Range been home?"

"Been a few weeks," Colt answered.

Hep rose and went toward the phone.

"Who you calling this late?" Keely asked.

"Range. I know he's still up and if not—I'll get him up!"

"Young man. You may have been out there on your own, but you will not disturb the Criqui home this late with such foolishness. You were raised better than that," Keely mandated and the trio chuckled.

"OK. I'll see Range and Feather tomorrow."

"That's time enough."

"Finish off that buttermilk. There's more where that came from," Colt said. "Your room is just as you left it. Your mama still changes the sheets weekly like you were coming home."

"I knew he would," Keely whispered, holding her heart.

"Thanks for the faith and prayers, Ma."

"'Night, son," Colt said, guiding Keely up the stairs.

"Big breakfast tomorrow so sleep tight!"

The jubilant parents climbed into their bed as Keely asked sotto voce, "Should we have told him?"

"No. It'll keep until tomorrow." Colt gathered his wife in his arms. "Let him get one last, good night's sleep."

Hep poured a glass of buttermilk to accompany his revisit of his home, taking inventory and basking in the comfort of just being there... safe and sound, after all the noise, chaos and uncertainty of war. He walked into his daddy's study which remained unchanged since he, Star and Selena listened to jazz records on the sly. He sauntered across the hall into the dining room past the breakfront that housed the flash-ruby set his parents brought back from the Chicago or was it the St. Louis World's Fair? He moseyed beneath Orelia's, Star's, Selena's and his high school diplomas on the wall and Orelia's and Selena's college degrees, thinking he'd be adding his in short measure. He meandered back into the hall and stood with a glass of buttermilk, eyed and then toasted the Henry and Winchester rifles, the cowrie shell and eagle feather that hung over the mammoth hall fireplace. "Thanks for bringing me home."

The next morning Hep slept late, awakened only by the smell of bacon poking at him. Not just any bacon but his mama's. Washing up quickly, he bounded down the steps where the familiar sight of his parents sitting at the dining room table almost brought tears of joy to his eyes.

I got to stop this wimpy shit, he thought.

"Hungry?" Colt asked from behind the newspaper.

"You can't imagine."

He sat in his old chair and his mother gleefully served him until full. Colt couldn't tell who was happier—mother or son.

"Wow! Thanks. Umph, umph, umph." He leaned his seat back on two legs.

Keely shot him a reprimanding glance.

"Oh, sorry." He grinned, righted the chair and she laughed. "Well, let me catch up with Range."

Hep jumped up. "Love you, Ma. Thanks for breakfast. Can't wait for dinner. I'm sure Range'll join us."

"He's waiting for you out back," Colt stated plainly.

"Yeah?" Hep grinned his way to the kitchen door, but didn't see him. "Where?"

Hep looked right and left waiting for his father to answer him or for Range to pop out and surprise him. Hep looked right again over to the church cemetery where his dad's boys were buried.

A sharp knowing bit Hep's heart, grabbed hold of it and wouldn't let go. Suddenly, Hep couldn't breathe. Standing stoically in the screened doorway, he waited for the feeling to pass. His mind somersaulted with conflicting musings until finally it congealed into one gnawing vexation... The impossibility that he came home and Range did not.

Colt and Keely sat at the dining room table staring into one another's eyes, waiting for their son to rejoin them with his questions. Instead, they heard the screen door slam closed and Hep's footsteps fall on each riser. Keely began to weep. Colt stretched his hand to her. She seized and squeezed it.

Hep walked slowly over to the graves. He didn't run, he didn't jog, giving his friend ample time to come up behind him, snatch him around the neck and say, "I was just jivin', man" after which Hep would curse his ass out. But Hep walked haltingly to the graves, past the headstones he'd known since childhood, coming upon

130

one with more freshly turned dirt and faded flowers. Buried behind his father, the tombstone read: Range Criqui...

The mere sight of his name forced Hep to his knees. He reached out and, despite the heat of the day, felt the cold stone beneath his fingers... like reading braille, Hep let each letter form under his fingertips. He stared at and stayed with his friend for two days before his father came out.

"I know what it is to lose one of your boys, son. All of mine are buried up here."

"They weren't this young."

"No. They lived long lives but that didn't help the hurt none. We are never ready for those we love to leave us. Whether it's sudden or they been sick for a long time."

His father's words did nothing to soothe him.

"I don't care what people say," Colt continued. "I'm here to tell you, you never get over it. You don't." Colt turned to face his son whose features were swollen with tears. "They always with you. If you real quiet, you can hear them talking to you. But unless you gonna crawl in there with him...you got to move on. Ready or not."

"How? What happened?"

"He came home. Early discharge 'cause he lost his leg below the knee."

Hep held his head, and rocked, his eyes shut tight against the pain and suffering Range must have endured.

"Seemed to be in good spirits. You know Range. Hopping around on one leg, making jokes. He loved cars so he was working down at the fillin' station. He still planned to go off with you to school but he said he was going to run a car shop. 'Mechanics' he called it. It's what he learned in the army. He'd had a accident over there in France. Came home and the same thing happened. He and Canaan Redbird were racing and Range got his pant leg caught in the gear. Couldn't get away. The car flung Redbird away but rolled over and onto Range. Crushed him."

Hep plastered his body against the headstone and held himself at the elbows.

"He sent these letters here while you all were away." Colt held them out to Hep who didn't touch them. Colt put them on top of the headstone. "Read 'em when you're ready."

Colt walked back into the house. "It's done," he told Keely as he walked straight through from the back door onto the front porch and sat in his porch-swing, his back to the cemetery.

The parents watched their son from the house. One day he was missing and so were the letters. Hep'd taken them and a six pack of beer to the swimming hole. He unsealed and read the letters from his friend; laughing mostly and crying when he finished knowing this was all he had physically left of his brother from another mother. With his back against the mulberry tree, he recalled the hours he and Range spent at that swimming hole. If they weren't riding horses or chasing girls, they were there diving from its banks or jumping from the tire Papa Colt had hung for their amusement. He chuckled and took another swig of beer as he remembered how later on the game was to sneak a peek of some girl's hard nipple or pubic hair, armpits or mustaches didn't count. For the days to follow, Hep realized that Range's spirit lived at the swimming hole not at his grave and Hep stopped going every day. He could see it from his bedroom which proved close enough. The last time there a visitor sauntered up.

"Hi, Hep."

"Hey, Inez," Hep said, annoyed by the intrusion.

"How are you?"

"How do you think?" he snapped and immediately regretted it. "Sorry."

"I loved him too." When there was no response from Hep she continued, "I came to say goodbye."

"Where are you going?"

"To California. I hear that's the 'land of milk and honey' with all the wartime jobs. Richmond Shipyard in Oakland is hiring Negroes, men and women, and Henry Kaiser is offering medical care."

"Good luck to you," he dismissed.

She stood there with Hep, both just staring at Range's name stamped on the tombstone.

"I thought we'd always end up together. You know, after all his running. He'd realize that I was the one who really loved him."

Hep looked at her.

"I know. I had the 'reputation' but that was the only way I could get his attention." She looked at his name etched in the cold granite. "He was my first. You never forget your first." She returned Hep's gaze. "I would have taken him with a half of leg. No leg. Anyway, he came back to me. But—" She snapped herself out of the self-made doldrums. "I can't stay here. In Colt, Texas without him. Without hope of his ever coming back to me. Well," she sighed. "Bye. Good luck to you too."

As Hep made his way to express his condolences to Mrs. Criqui, he thought about Inez Foster. Was she in fact Range's true love and he didn't know it? Would they have ended up together in a few years? His dying freed her to pursue another life, because as long as he lived, she would have held out hope.

Hep rang the doorbell, feeling odd that Range wasn't there to answer. Feather opened the door; in a heartbeat, he felt like they were simpatico again. Like no time was lost. Despite his neglect of her, he wanted to fall into her arms and be comforted like only she could. He smiled at her. She smiled at him and then, instinctively, she rubbed her stomach.

"It's good to see you, Hep. I'm glad you made it back all right."

He grinned, then noticed that Feather Criqui, love of his life—was pregnant.

"Thanks," he managed to say. "I guess I've been gone longer than I thought."

134

"Who is it?" Wilma Criqui called out from the kitchen.

"Hep Culhane, Ma."

"Tell him to come on in."

Although he and the mother of his best friend had an amicable, tearless visit, Hep couldn't take his eyes from Feather each time she entered or walked by the room.

"You know, she waited for you," Wilma began. "Any word from you at all. But nothing. She began working at the Town Hall and liked it. Decided not to go to Spelman. Joaquin Banyon started courtin' her. She agonized about it but when someone was paying attention and you weren't... She stopped making you the priority when apparently she wasn't yours."

Hep shook his head knowingly.

"Buck up. He's good to her and for her. But he's not you." She winked. "And you're no Range."

"There was only one Range Criqui."

"Amen! We'll all miss him. Life goes on, Hep. You keep on too."

Hep shook his head again.

"What are your plans? I know it's not Colt, Texas. Neither you nor my boy were gonna stay here for long."

"Going to finish up college and see what the world has to offer. I liked the political science and government classes, so I might try law," Hep reasoned to Ms. Criqui, realizing he was really probing the subject for himself. "Maybe law school. I dunno. I'd like to be the first black mayor of a major city." He didn't know where that came from.

She chortled, before recognizing he was serious and said," Well, that'd be good. Whatever you do, you'll do well and don't be a stranger, Hep. I lost one son, I don't want to lose his best friend too."

"Yes, ma'am."

Feather showed Hep to the door. "Congratulations, Feather."

"Thank you. If you were here, I'd've invited you to the wedding."

"If I were here, there would have been no wedding."

"You've never been short on ego."

"Something Range and I have in common." He smiled.

"Wherever you're going, you'll need it. World doesn't take kindly to the timid black man."

Hep shook his head in agreement. "See you around."

"Not if I see you first," she answered in the banter they'd enjoyed as kids.

I was told about Range, but not Feather, he thought, as he jogged down the steps. Well, this life just gets more complex with surprise after surprise. He didn't feel as bad about losing Feather as he'd thought. Happy, she was happy, he moved on to his options. He wasn't going to Howard University without Range so he'd apply to Fisk University in Nashville, Tennessee, closer to his folks, and to Hampton Institute in Virginia. He'd study political science and government and, having been out in the world and in the army, he'd seen some things he'd like to change. Knowing feelings cannot be legislated, he knew laws can be changed and feelings may follow. One thing Hep knew for sure—he'd be gone by the time Feather Criqui Banyon's baby was born.

Accepted to both colleges, Hep selected Fisk and had five days before Labor Day and his reporting for the first day of class.

But first... He had one promise to keep and one stop to make.

O Sole Mio

The tall black man left the 18th Street subway station and wound his way through narrow streets in the Bensonhurst section of Brooklyn, New York known as Little Italy. Hep heard the many dialects of the inhabitants who commented and eyed him suspiciously, never suspecting that he understood every word, good or bad, uttered about him as he sought the address on Cristoforo Colombo Boulevard and 18th street. Looking up, Hep glimpsed snatches of cerulean blue sky knifed by the roof tops of the tenement buildings; many family-owned shops housed on the bottom floors, crowned by living areas above. The visual squalor of too many bodies compacted together in tight spaces, a complete antithesis to the rolling hills of the Lazio region of Italy and certainly not the Tuscany Tavio had described with its wide open spaces studded with wild red poppies. *They've voluntarily left their homelands for this,* Hep thought. *Hot water, electricity and flushing toilets, but they were together.*

The aroma of sumptuous food simmering for hours on the back burner of stoves overrode and permeated the skinny streets and ushered more heat into the already steaming hot flats, forcing folk outside until called for dinner. Those lucky enough to have a small parcel of yard nurtured gardens of garlic, basil, artichokes and vertically-staked tomatoes, that, thanks to Tavio, Hep knew were San Marzanos. The owners of these hot houses set tables outside where they dined *al fresco* under a canopy of grapes the tenants grew and made into their own homemade wine, which stood in unmarked green bottles. *Next to black people,* Hep thought, *Italians would be next best.* To Hep, Italians were black people with "good hair"; large, close-knit families, loud, expressive, wary of strangers, and food central to all their gatherings. They too fussed among themselves, but "no one better not say a bad thing about kin."

Hep approached women and children sitting on the stoop of the Orsini address and politely asked about the family. "Me scusi, dove' la familia Orsini?"

The women held their tongues, but the children spoke and pointed, "Grazie," Hep said and began the climb to the third floor. The delicious fragrance of what loving hands can turn into luscious meals made his stomach growl. He knocked on the door and the little boy who'd told him where the Orsini's lived, had followed Hep up the stairs, opened the door and shouted, "Nonna!"

Hep stood at the front door waiting to be acknowledged.

A woman came to the door, closing it into a slit so Hep could not see inside and inquired, "Que?"

From the heart-shaped mole beside her lip, Hep knew this was Tavio's mother. In the perfect Italian her son had taught him, Hep explained that he was Tavio's friend from the Army and her son'd taught him Italian in exchange for Hep teaching Tavio English. Instead of Mama wrestling with whether to trust this big black man at the door speaking flawless Italian, Mama melted at the sound of her son's name being spoken in such a loving way.

"Come in!" she insisted and shouted "Papa! Venga."

In moments, the entire apartment filled with Italians with Tavio's toothy grin. Aunts and uncles from downstairs and up flooded the small living room to see the man who'd last seen their "Tavi," marveling at Hep's command of their language and giving full credit to their relative.

After numerous introductions and stories of their exploits all in Italian, Hep finally shared, "I've brought you something, Mama Orsini."

From his breast pocket, Hep pulled out Tavio's tangled dog tags. At the sight of his intertwined communion crucifix, his mother and grandmother burst into tears. Retrieving a used handkerchief from her apron, his mother dabbed at the river of tears flowing from her eyes.

"You must eat with us," the father declared and Hep did. Folks disappeared, returning with plates piping hot with food they'd been preparing, all brought to this apartment to share with this soldier. Instantaneously, a party sprung up with manicotti, spaghetti and meatballs, lasagna and sautéed spinach, eggplant and zucchini. Hep was served the best food he'd ever feasted upon. They shared photos and stories of their beloved Tavi. Hep lingered with them over delectable homemade wine and Papa had Tavio's nephew run and get spumoni for dessert. As Hep vacuumed the meal, all he could wonder was "what must their food taste like when there was no war on and there were no rations?"

Finally, he left the Orsinis with an open invite to return any time, "You come back to celebrate San Genaro, patron saint of Naples in September. It starts next week and lasts eleven days!" Papa Orsini enthused.

Hep descended the stairs to get back to Uptown early enough to catch the sights. On the subway, he thought how welcomed they made him feel. How good he felt that he'd kept his promise to himself—to personally return his buddy's possessions and not surrender them to the major. He shared his vow with the family that if he was ever financially able, he'd revive their olive oil plant. The Orsinis offered him polite, patronizing smiles of gratitude, never imagining that would happen but appreciated the thought. No one could think beyond this war ending. Since Feather would not keep the money he'd had the army send from Europe for them to start their family, Hep had withdrawn it. Giving it directly to the Orsinis had failed, so Hep left it for them with a note: "Grazie por cena!" under the flour canister in the kitchen. Hep'd kept that promise and he'd keep the vow that he'd never be out of control again.

On Selena and Hoyt's recommendation, Hep went uptown and took a room at The Theresa Hotel. He washed up and took off for the sights: Savoy Ballroom, Cotton Club, Small's Paradise, Minton's Playhouse and caught Redd Foxx at the Apollo. He'd spent two days there traipsing around Harlem and its hot spots and, like an old man at the club, it all seemed lackluster. Like his time being thrilled by these carnal pleasures had passed. He felt lucky and blessed to have returned, but also abjectly alone and lonely. He missed his side-kick and buddy Range, knowing this hole created by his death would never be filled. Hep checked out early and headed toward Tennessee, changing trains in D.C. to board the segregated Jim Crow train further south. He braced himself for his next adventure. His only goal, to complete college and use the degree he'd earn for good.

Part II
1942

Iron Butterfly

Lorette Javier sat in her chair next to the window and doodled absently on her notepad. Circles, hearts, squares and nonsymmetrical figures while she contemplated her life. She glanced out at the Fisk campus, homecoming over, leaves abandoning branches and soon it'd be cold. The fifth and final "Javier girl" born to Alexander and Fern Javier wondered what life held for her. Her being crowned Sophomore Homecoming Queen, riding on the float, waving her hand regally had been sabotaged by her sister Corrine's news. All of her sisters had graduated college and married well... doctors, lawyers, Indian chiefs, but Corrine with her sandy-colored hair, light eyes, freckles and big brains had *become* a doctor, which ruined Lorette's debutante season, prom and graduation, but then ...she, Dr. Coke, married one to boot. In addition to their private practices, they both taught at Meharry Medical School. Her best friend, Gay Iris, was there at Fisk with her, but her other best friend, Effie, was at Oberlin studying to be a concert pianist; both content with their directions in life. Why wasn't Lorette?

The young co-ed had more fun at Pearl High, but this college life wasn't what she'd expected. The boys there weren't much more interesting than the boys in high school. All seemed so easily impressed with her looks and she tired of hearing how much she resembled actress Lena Horne. Lorette supposed the real men were fighting in the war leaving these pukey-lame male residues. Because her prominent father ran three Javier Mills and the new aggregate quarry, everyone thought her natural beau would be Theopolius Parker, heir apparent of the sausage family. Those two families ruled the social, economic and cultural encampment known as Evelyn, Tennessee. She and Theo had dated throughout high school and after he graduated from Howard University everyone expected they'd marry... everyone except Lorette. She found Theo nice but tiresome and still very much under the thumb of his family, pleasing and doing all expected of him to fulfill his central goal in life; the idea as boring as he was. Somehow marrying the entrepreneurial, wealthy son of the "Sausage King" failed to offer the generational security of the college-educated, professional pedigree of her sisters' husbands.

"How do I love thee?"—a rich baritone voice pierced her musings—"Let me count the ways."

Lorette's head swiveled her attention to the front of the class where a strapping six foot something man stood reciting the sonnet. A man... not a boy, faced her with gigantic shoulders which crowned an athletic body. His dark complexion brightened by red undertones and the texture of his mustache over full lips, perfectly matched the hair on his head. His high cheekbones caught and held the sun, ferreting her gaze to his distinctive nose and back up to his deep-set eyes. He was unlike any male

Lorette had ever seen. Exotic. He exuded confidence, boldness and control. Upon completing his recitation, Lorette's eyes followed his swagger back to his seat.

Mrs. Thurma Davenport clapped her delight and gushed, "Magnificently rendered, Mr. Culhane," just as the bell rang.

Lorette quickly gathered up her books and threaded herself to his seat by the door. He was gone. She scurried into the hallway, but despite his mammoth size, he'd disappeared. She ran down the steps, pompadour falling, threw open the door just in time to glimpse his pant leg vanish around the corner of the building.

"Damn!" she cursed her short legs, no match for his long ones.

"Hey Rette," Gay Iris sauntered up. "Your hair is a mess."

"Did you see him?" Lorette accosted her. "That tall drink of water."

"A guy?"

"Just because you have a boyfriend you need not be oblivious to all others." Lorette pushed her hair back up out of her face, extracting a worthless hairpin. "He was a 'man.' *The* man of my dreams. The father of my beautiful children."

"Hope you plan to marry first."

Lorette enlisted her well-connected friend to find out what she could about Mr. Culhane in her English Literature class. In one day's time, Gay Iris reported, "His name is Hepburn Culhane from Colt, Texas, a town founded by his father. He grew up on over one thousand acres of Texas prime on a horse and cattle ranch until he went to Northwestern University and then World War II—"

"I knew it!"

"...where he was stationed in North Africa and Italy. Wounded in the shoulder, came home, has sisters, no brothers and the car he's driving was given to him by Ma and Pa Culhane. He lives off campus and so does his girlfriend."

"What?"

"Yep. She works at the phone company," Gay Iris intoned knowingly.

"Oh." Lorette knew the girls who worked in and around Nashville, who were not in college but wanted college guys for boyfriends then husbands, were reputed to "put out" when their men "needed release." "That's good," Lorette said unconvincingly. "'Cause I'm saving myself for marriage. So it all works out."

"Really. Well, you have to get his attention first. Sounds like he has everything taken care of. And I do mean *everything*."

"Why are you so mean?"

"What is he going to do with five foot two you when he's playing house with another woman?"

"I want that man."

"Stand in line."

"E tu', Gay Iris?"

"Heck no. But I'm probably the only one who doesn't and that includes teachers too. I mean, Rette, the man has traveled and been to Europe. He's probably had Italian women." She extended her hands beyond her chest fondling imaginary breasts. "He's dating these girls for fun."

"I just have to let him know I'm the marrying kind."

"Nowhere in my report did I say he was looking for a wife."

"Why else would he be here?"

"He's a man who wants an education. Wants to be a congressman or mayor or… something which means law school. Which means years and years—"

"Men don't know what they want until a woman tells them," Lorette dismissed.

Lorette dressed carefully for Monday's class, sporting a modest pompadour, a drop-dead-Fred outfit, tasteful but showcasing her petite frame. She sat expectantly on his side of the room. He didn't show. She looked at the rain and wondered if his off-campus girlfriend went to work today or were they sleeping in.

On Wednesday, she arrived purposely late in another coordinated frock and, with all the seats taken around him, strolled across class to the seat by the window. He never looked up.

When class began Mrs. Davenport grinned all over herself and asked, "Mr. Culhane, your voice lends itself so readily to the recitation of literature. I wonder if you might read for us."

"Certainly," he boomed.

Maybe I should just leave the two of you alone, Lorette thought. *Between mooning teachers, sorority types and off campus chippies, li'l ol' me doesn't have a chance.*

She watched him rise as his long legs carried him out the door before she realized class was over. By the time her legs transported her to the hall, he'd vanished.

What is he, a magician? Lorette asked herself, as she snaked her way through the hall, down the steps, throwing open the door. She ran smack-dab into his back.

He turned.

"Oh, excuse me," Lorette apologized feebly, aware she was giving him the opposite first impression she'd intended.

"Hey, hey, hey!" his buddy beside him piped up. "Looka here. Looka here. Now this is what I've been fighting for. Put a little spice in my life, brown sugar... do you party?"

"Down, Ozzie," Hep directed. "Excuse him, Miss. He doesn't get out much."

Lorette watched Hep pull his friend—still in mid-drool—away until they disappeared around the side of the building. Lorette stood there feeling anything but sophisticated thinking she'd sure made a lasting impression on him. Hopefully not. As she began to walk the two guys drove right by her in Hep's car. Neither man glanced her way.

Angry and embarrassed, it was she who cut class on Friday and again on Monday. On Wednesday she came early and left late so Hep wouldn't notice her. She watched him in the company of Jannelle Hunter and later Callie Simpson. *Umph,* she thought, even his off campus cutie's days were numbered.

~*~

Lorette stood on the corner at Jefferson Street waiting for Annie to come and pick her up. The Nashville air had turned decidedly cold and she vowed to drive tomorrow instead of waiting on their horrifically late maid. She'd moved back home as she always did when depressed; home, the only place where she could be both nurtured and left alone. She shoved her hands into her pockets and the more she tried not to think of Hep Culhane, the more she did. Not only had she never met or fallen for a man who didn't know she was alive, her mind was consumed with the coup she'd garner if she married him. No ordinary doctor or lawyer, dentist or professor that'd been done to death in her family, but the son of a rich Texas rancher who founded the town he'd grown up in. She could hear the tongues wagging with that news. "And he wants to be mayor of a major city." Lorette would be a perfect First Lady of... wherever. She was special, her paternal grandmother had told her so. The bus came, stopped and opened its door, only then did Lorette realize she was standing at a bus s top. She shook her head and stepped back. What would Grand'Mere say about her now?" she wondered absently. *Was she still alive?* Lorette wondered.

She couldn't have been more than six or seven when she first met her Grand'Mere Gabrielle. Prelude to the trip was the first time Lorette ever remembered her mother and father having a "loud discussion" about returning to New Orleans. Years later her sister told her that Mama wanted their father to accept the invitation for a visit because his mother was sick and supposedly dying. Their father wanted no parts of it. "She's just curious is all." Seems their mother, Fern, had sent the "Old Bat" as their father called his mother, birth announcements for all five girls—Gabrielle Giselle had sent them all back except Lorette's. After all those years Gabrielle sent for her son and his daughter, "the one with the French name." Alexander thought it offensive and divisive that she'd single out just one of his daughters. Fern looked at it as an opportunity and opening and time to heal old wounds. "You give her too much credit!"

Alexander certainly moved on and made a life for himself and his family in Evelyn, Tennessee where he'd been banished for "staying too long at the fair." His mother's invitation rankled up all long buried feelings, the first being fetched from Paris, France after he'd finished up his studies at the Sorbonne. Like his brothers before him, he'd done the "Grand Tour" of Europe before returning home to work the family businesses. Unlike his brothers, he'd stayed two years longer and as punishment, he was sent to a backwater town in Tennessee called Evelyn. Alexandre', as the family called him, showed them all what he could do and turned the mill into a successfully operating enterprise. Summoned back to New Orleans, he'd declined as he'd fallen in love with a pretty brown-skinned beauty to which the family objected loudly. They acquiesced suggesting that he keep her in the city's cottage section where all mistresses lived. Intending to marry her, he refused and the Javier family cut him off personally and financially, giving him only the mill he'd revived. Her father had shown the New Orleans elite-bigots, whose sole mission remained to banish any Negro-tainted blood from their lineage, that he had a mind and heart of his own. Alexandre' had become Alexander and never thought about cooperating or perpetuating inner-race bigotry.

On the long trip, the young Lorette relished having her father all to herself and going on a train for the first time in her life. She recalled the huge gold letter "*J*" on the gate fastened in place by a high brick wall and opened into a courtyard with an ornate fountain and open gallery steps. It was a wonderful hotel that smelled of fresh flowers and lemons with fine furnishings where she could see herself in their reflection, and rugs and a bevy of maids in black and white uniforms. "This is not a hotel, Cher," her father'd said. "It's the house where I grew up."

Lorette remembered how a white lady summoned her closer. The lady smelled so good and had on fancy

152

clothes, and jewelry, and a cane that she tapped on the floor for maids to bring them tea, sandwiches and little sweet cakes. She only recalled staying a night or so and she was led to a canopy bed like she had in her room now. To the displeasure of her father, she'd begged for that bed once home. "You see!" he'd said to her mother... but Lorette didn't see.

"How'd you like visiting your grand'mere," her mother had asked.

"It was alright," Lorette said.

"Do you want to go back?"

"I don't think so. There was nothing to do. No children to play with. It was boring."

Her mother had chuckled.

"She told me something to always remember," Lorette said.

"What was that?"

"She said I was *special*. The most special little girl in all the world. That I should never settle for anything less than what I want. That I should live like a princess and that my Prince Charming will come."

"Really?"

"Is that possible, Mama?"

"Yes. I have my Prince Charming. He's your daddy."

Eerily, Lorette now thought, *well, I've found my Prince Charming too, but he doesn't know it yet.*

Like an omen from the "Old Bat" herself, Hepburn Culhane's car slid to a stop by the light. Lorette couldn't catch her breath. She stared at him, hoping he wouldn't look to his right. He reached over to his glove compartment and glanced at her. She yanked up an insincere, jittery smile.

"Oh. Hey. Hi," he spoke, not knowing her name.

"Hello." She looked up and down the street, cursing Annie anew.

"You look like an orange freeze standing there. Can I give you a lift somewhere?"

The car behind him honked that the light had changed. Hep ignored it waiting for her answer.

"Yes. Thank you," she heard herself accept nervously.

He reached over to open the door and she leaned in, "I live out in Evelyn."

"Then we better get going."

They filled the car with light banter about weather, classes and occasional directions to her home. "Here I am. The house ahead on the hill."

Hep pulled up and let her out at the bank of steps leading to the Victorian porch. "Nice."

Her house had been called a lot of things but "nice" had never been one of them. Of course, he had a Texas ranch. "Won't you come in?"

"No. Thanks. I have an appointment."

"Oh. Alright well, thanks again."

"You're welcome," he dismissed.

Her hand opened the door.

"See you in class," he added.

"Right. Thanks."

154

Hep glanced at his watch and steered back towards town to pick up Barbara Babcock from work. He wanted to take her out, but she preferred cooking for him, staying in and letting nature take its course… usually they were dessert for one another. Sometimes he stayed over, other times he headed back to his apartment. It depended on how he felt and what he had for class the next day. Anticipating the after-dinner activities required him to flick his just lit cigarette out the window as he was losing the taste for them now, though they'd served him well overseas. Now, he had other things to fill his mouth and occupy his time. He and Barbara had settled into a companionable rhythm. He'd met lots of women in his time but never one who enjoyed the carnal pleasures as much as she did. She'd do nicely until he graduated college and head out to the west coast. For now, a mature, undemanding adult woman augmented his dreams perfectly. Now that Lorette he'd just dropped off would be another story altogether. Like most college girls these days she was looking for a husband. *Poor sap wherever he might be,* Hep thought. He knew her type: cute, pampered, an indulged child of the black bourgeoisie, exposed to all the trappings—clothes, house, maids, all controlled with the flutter of her long eyelashes.

Marriage to anyone fell to the bottom of his list of priorities. After graduating Fisk he had three years of law school. *"From the son of a slave to mayor of a city,"* he thought. *Great campaign slogan. Wouldn't Miss Felicity Rudd be proud?*

*R*eaching for a piece of gum, a thought popped into his mind. Perhaps he'd meet the future Mrs. Culhane in law school. A woman with the same commitment, values and goals who'd roll up her sleeves and pitch in for the good of their family and the black constituents he served. A woman who could hold her own with any group of people in any situation where clothes and money would take a back seat to domestic harmony and career success. Someone like his sister, Selena; capable and confident. Hep smiled as he U-turned to pick up 'Fast Barbara Babcock' as Ozzie'd called her after she'd spent the night at the apartment on the second date. *They were going to take it nice and slow tonight,* Hep thought. *Yeah, I'm staying over.* With his solid 3.8 average securing his academic success and Babs taking care of his manly urges, his life just percolated according to plan.

~*~

"No, thank you. This was just great, Mrs. Javier. Thank you both for your hospitality."

"We are just glad you could finally join us," Fern Javier said.

"It only took three Sundays," Mr. Javier remarked. "A fine strapping man like you must get tired of cafeteria food."

"Ah. Yes, sir," Hep offered, wondering just how this happened that he sat across from Lorette Javier in the formal dining room of this fabulous house.

156

She'd asked if he would tutor her in math. He'd picked Sunday afternoon so as not to interfere with his Saturday night and early Sunday morning loving with Barbara. He thought he could help the co-ed out, but there he sat while Annie cooked, served and cleared for them.

Hep opened his mouth to say he'd better get back and tend to his own studying when Mr. Javier said, "You like cars, Hep?"

"Yes, I do, sir."

"Then come with me. I have a '37 SJ Duesenberg I'd like you to take a look at."

"Oh, Daddy."

"You've had him for a few hours. Let me talk cars man-to-man. It's cherry red."

As her father and Hep disappeared out the side door of the kitchen to the garage, Lorette couldn't suppress her smile.

"Let's not count your chickens before they hatch," Fern warned.

"Oh, Mama. You are far too late for that. Look at them. The two most important men in my life," she gushed.

Annie rolled her eyes as Fern eyed her love-struck daughter.

"Mary, Jesus and Joseph. Help us all."

Ain't Misbehavin'

"Selena!!" They all called out startling her with unabashed gratitude. The South Side USO Canteen always jumped with gorgeous girls, fantastic nibbles and *the* best "Dew Drop Inn" stars that Negro America had to offer. A mecca for free black entertainment, it drew plenty of the devoted. Even from overseas Hoyt'd continued to hear about the South Side Canteen and he'd told Selena how proud of her he was. As a senior hostess, she continued volunteering with a vengeance to feel close to her husband while he was away, pinch-hitting wherever she was needed from mending uniforms, writing letters home, filling empty pretzel dishes, helping register soldiers for War Bonds, spinning records and sitting in for stars when they were late appearing. She began playing the piano mostly and one GI made one request: "I'll Be Seeing You," she sang with such poignancy that all eyes were wet at the song's end. Feeling guilty for the somber mood, Selena shouted "This is supposed to be a party!" and launched into a rousing rendition of "Boogie Woogie Bugle Boy" that got everyone's feet happy and she kept it up so long that when the main stars appeared, the soldiers were disappointed in the break from lively, good music. A feeling they got over quickly once "Miss Horne" took center stage. "She is gorgeous," Selena had to admit to Mazeda.

It was still no easy feat to get Mazeda to come and replace her fixation with missing Mil, the riveter job and growing bank account. "At least I didn't replace him with another person as he seems to have done with me. He got another woman, that's why I haven't heard from him."

"You don't know that," Selena said, knowing that Mazeda vacillated between another woman and 'he's dead.'

"A woman knows."

"Would you like to dance?" a GI asked and Selena pushed her friend toward the respectful man and the dance floor as she went to finish coordinating a meal delivery from Itch's.

Selena'd remained preoccupied with FDR's announcement about having soldiers serve for two and a half years instead of the original one. *Did that mean Hoyt too? He was press not a soldier.*

A soldier asked to dance. "No thank you. Come get me when a fast one comes on." She proudly wriggled her third finger left hand. With a smile, the soldier acquiesced without pressure.

Being there at the Canteen continued to save her life, filling her days and leaving her exhausted enough to sleep through the night although she woke up earlier than she wanted. Missing her better half made her so piercingly lonely. She relished remembering the mundane to the miraculous. The way he liked extra pepper on his grits so they were gray in color when he finished stirring them. The way they never passed each other without touching; acknowledging their importance to one another or the promise of more later that night. Thanksgiving was his favorite holiday; he had "so much" to be thankful for, mainly her coming into his life. How they'd stay in their pajamas all day on Sunday, not answering the door or phone, eating reheated Chinese food for dinner in bed, making love, showering and changing into fresh PJs before nightfall. Her buddy, her best friend, her confidant, her heart. Her husband Hoyt. Often after only a few hours of sleep, she'd awake without reason and lay there listening to the other tenants go to their jobs and try to fall back to sleep; sometimes successful, other times not. Before rising she always prayed for Hoyt's safety overseas and gave thanks for bringing her baby brother home with just a bum shoulder. She prayed for Range's soul and all the other women who'd lost their husbands, brothers, and fathers. With her work at the Canteen she only continued with a few music lessons for serious stalwart students, which she gave for free. She didn't go to church but she religiously called her parents on Sunday which always ended with an invite home for a visit.

Through her Canteen gig, Selena grew more comfortable with performing for live audiences and crowds, judging their musical needs and desires and she savored the control she had over their moods. She used her music like an elixir to heal homesickness and boost morale and egos and the soldiers hated to see her leave. She received offers to perform in homes for anniversaries, birthday parties, social clubs and once, a debutante cotillion, all paid handsomely and augmented her budget. The money Hoyt sent went straight to the bank. She wondered if she could make a living singing; she knew Hoyt would be for it as he always pushed her to stretch herself. They could get that four-story brownstone in D.C.'s LeDroit Park sooner. He could set up his photography studio on U Street, get into moving pictures like his idol Micheaux and she could get a teaching position at Howard University and a permanent nighttime gig at Crystal Caverns on 11th and U, and their lives would be perfect.

"Just come home to me, Hoyt. Home. Home. Home. Dear Lord." She squeezed her eyes shut. "Amen."

Mid-week, Selena stood in front of the oversized microphone, knees knocking, stomach in knots and the orchestra cued up again. She hadn't slept all night with the excitement of recording another V-DISC and it was showing. This time, Hoyt was not just out of eyeshot. She had "amateur" written all over her face and her voice. She closed her eyes and imagined Hoyt there. Standing just behind her, a big, proud smile on his face and she sang into the song, took hold of it and led the orchestra where she wanted to go. She savored the feel of controlling the session and the orchestra responded like they were dealing with a professional who knew how to work with them. She did six V-DISC records. Hoyt'd heard them all and wrote her gushing letters about her talent and sexy letters about his plans for her... for them when he came home. "Let him come home. Home. Home. Whole... Dear Lord. With all his parts in place and working."

Smile

Naked winter trees noted the coming and going of Hep and Lorette as they scurried across the campus, stiff with cold. Unbeknownst to him, they had become an item; the handsome GI giant and the pretty Campus Queen. Lorette so proud of being beside the tall Texan likened it to being with a celebrity or her father as people gravitated toward Hep wherever he went. Hep peeled off to his class and Lorette kept going. He hadn't gone home last weekend and hadn't accepted the Javier invite, and Lorette still tried to figure out what he'd done. Hep offered no explanation. She didn't care. She'd received a B as a midterm grade in her math glass, done more for him than for herself, as she realized that Hep Culhane would not want a dummy for a wife.

Hep listened intently at the Economics professor and once the class was over regretted that he'd accepted the invitation to the Javier's for this Sunday's dinner. He knew the Sunday dinners would soon cease as Lorette's mastering math would bring them to an end. Barbara Babcock could cook in the kitchen and the bedroom, and he looked forward to returning to the simplicity of his life where his needs would still be met, but he'd miss his conversations with Mr. J, as he'd been instructed to call him over the last few months. Not since his father had

Hep found a more successful and worthy black man. Under the hood of a classic car, Hep learned pearls of wisdom to live by. Colt Culhane and Alexander Javier, two men, worlds apart, built dynasties, advanced their families and communities which led to their prominence and success. Eliciting and maintaining respect, while enduring and prevailing over adversity. Colt Culhane arrived at the zenith of success by sheer ambition, determination, perseverance, guts and vision of combining cattle, horses and land. Mr. Javier's route via education and diversification from lumber and gist mills to brick masonry and now concrete. He'd learned how a rumor had started that they thought him a Negro. "It was too late for the true businessmen in and around Tennessee. I'd already established a reputation for fair prices, superior wood, professional and dependable service, shrewd negotiations. Excellence and Javier Mill became synonymous. The 'well-heeled' knew I sent my men up north to be trained in the latest techniques to remain competitive and the moneyed gentry would settle for none less. Finally, the Chamber of Commerce president over four counties decreed that Javier 'must be a white man who married a Negro woman. That's his business. I ain't gonna let his taste in women ruin mine.'"

Hep chuckled and Mr. J concluded, "Can't let folks define you. You do your own defining. Got to walk the dog, can't let the dog walk you."

Hep smiled. It sounded like one of his daddy's quotes.

164

"Don't be afraid to change with the times," Mr. J intoned. "If you don't, you'll get left behind. When this war is over, I'll parlay my lumber and brick masonry into construction for all those GI's coming home that'll need houses for their families. The concrete aggregate for all the roads this nation will be building. Gotta have vision beyond what's in front of you and the gumption to take a chance."

"I like that boy, Duchess," Papa J proclaimed after dinner once their guest left.

"I wonder why?" Fern quipped knowing that they shared qualities. "He's the only one who listens to you when you talk all that business stuff." She opened the kitchen door, stuck her head in and said, "Night, Annie. Thank you."

Papa J waited for his wife by the newel post of the stairs. "You know I took him to the mill then the plant and he asked some very intelligent, interesting questions."

"The son you never had," Fern teased, as she climbed steps before him.

"Certainly not the sons-in-laws we have."

"Be nice. They provide very well for our daughters. Give us cute grands."

"That boy Culhane is gonna be somebody, Duchess."

"I'm sure his parents think he is already."

"Yeah. You see when I offered him a job this summer he said he'd have to go home and check on his parents first and attend their Founder's Day Parade."

The Duchess smiled, recalling how she'd liked that answer.

"Family is important to that boy."

"Yes, it is. I'll be out in a minute," she said to husband as she glimpsed her daughter and closed the bathroom door.

"Night, Mama," Lorette sang out, as she cut off the lights and pirouetted gleefully into her bedroom.

As Fern washed up for bed, she thought of her dewy-eyed daughter. She was both relieved and happy to discover that Lorette had the capacity to love someone other than herself but remained reserved, allowing her husband and daughter to make over Hepburn Culhane; the son Alexander never had and the man Lorette wanted so desperately to love her back. The Duchess and Hep were probably the two coolest individuals in all of Evelyn, Tennessee. She'd watched people fawn over him all the time—his stature, looks, intellect, but none of it seemed to mean as much to him as his opinion of himself. She liked that he was worldly, secure, sophisticated and confident without ego yet honest, and unpretentious—but she didn't want her baby girl hurt. What could Lorette offer him but blind adoration which he'd already proved he didn't need?

Same thing makes you laugh makes you cry, Fern thought.

They Can't Take That Away from Me

Mazeda bolted upright in bed. Her heart beating fast like it pumped outside of her chest. She surveyed her room and nothing appeared out of place. She caught her breath and paced her breathing. Not knowing what awoke her, she fluffed her pillow and lay back down.

Then a wail-scream pierced her quiet efficiency.

"Selena?" Mazeda drew on a robe and went to the door, peered out to see two uniformed white men coming from her apartment. Men she didn't know.

"What's going on?" she asked approaching them.

"You know, Mrs. Colson?"

"My best friend."

"She needs you. Her husband died in France," one said without ceremony.

"What!?" Mazeda pushed past them into the apartment and found Selena crumbled on the floor where she had apparently slid down the wall and collapsed.

"No.No.No." Selena held herself and looked at Mazeda without seeing. She let out another plaintiff wail. "He promised."

Mazeda went and closed the door on the small crowd that gathered in the hall, returning to the slumped Selena and guiding her into a standing position. "C'mon. Let's sit over here."

Selena stood then jerked her arm from Mazeda.

Selena only wanted to be touched by one person... Hoyt. If what the white men told her was true, that would never happen again. She dissolved into tears, slid down again past the couch to crumple on the floor. She didn't have the strength to sit or stand upright.

Stoic days turned into frightful nights and back to days for such a long period, Selena lost track of time. The only constant was pain. Her friend Mazeda became her sole protector as she turned away the curious and well-meaning friends. Selena didn't know how to live a life without Hoyt in it. Didn't know how or what to think or how to be in a world where he was no longer. All of her hopes and dreams died with him on some distance shore. Selena had never known how to wallow, Culhanes didn't wallow or bathe themselves in self-pity and "why me?" But it seemed really easy and she was learning fast. Finally, sick of herself and her behavior, Selena rallied quietly. She smelled bad, looked worse and decided to take a shower and eat something before Mazeda came home from work. Not wanting to venture out or answer the door, Selena had finally succeeded in having her friend leave her for work. Selena busied herself with tidying the apartment, a whirlwind of activity, and before she knew it, she'd organized Hoyt's prints and separated clothing. Hers from his. Her mind had ordered her life where her heart couldn't deal. Selena looked at the piles and, unbeknownst to Mazeda, began making arrangements. She carefully packed up his prints, camera equipment, boxed his negatives, his clothes and the piano he'd gifted her one Christmas to be sent to the attic at Cherokee Ranch to keep Hep's WWII memorabilia company. Her parents threatened to come to Chicago and Selena forestalled them only by promising to come to them. Slowly, she allowed friends and tenants of her building to come in and take what they liked, releasing property only if she knew it'd have a good home. After a few more weeks, the task was done and the time had come for her to follow Hoyt's things home. Tired physically and emotionally Selena steeled herself for rest, relaxation and rejuvenation. As he'd suggested, she only wish she had Hoyt's porkpie hat that she told him to keep for good luck.

"Humph," Selena harrumphed aloud. "For all the good it did."

She offered Mazeda her apartment until the lease was up, but Mazeda wouldn't budge from her efficiency across the hall where she still waited for Mil's return. One day, someday... soon, she still held out hope. For the very first time, Selena truly understood.

One day while Mazeda was at work, Selena slipped a letter under the door of her friend, thanking her for all her support and help and included her address for her and her only to have and use whenever she wanted. Selena quietly closed the door to #3G, her happy home, descended the well-worn steps for the last time, hailed a cab to the station and boarded a south-bound, one-way train ticket to Texas. Going back home, back south, back to a nurturing place where she was herself and all who know her would accept her without curiosity. Only thing, as the train rocked her back in time, she was not the same Selena who'd left with the handsome husband years ago, with all the excitement of facing the unknown together. She wondered if she'd ever truly be herself again. All she was and who she wanted to become died on a French battlefield... taking pictures. Still mad at him for leaving her, she hoped he didn't suffer. Selena could not bear the thought of that.

Once home in Colt, Texas, the widow Colson slept for several days in her childhood bed and allowed herself to be comforted by her mother and father. Then her brother unceremoniously left school to check on her, the conversations between the two from Tennessee to Chicago were one thing, but his sister's return home signaled a deeper trauma that even she failed to recognize. Prompted by Hoyt's death and his sister's need, then their father's "touch of pneumonia," Hep followed his sister home.

"What you here for, son?" Colt asked when Hep appeared at the door. "School out?"

"Selena said you had a 'touch of pneumonia.'"

"Say what? I know you didn't come all this way for me," Papa Colt called them both out. "Your mama will have me tip-top again in two weeks with her magic garlic tonic."

"Hello son," Keely greeted him. "Welcome home."

"You know there's nothing wrong with you coming to check on your sister," Papa Colt said.

"Where is she?"

"Upstairs."

Hep took the stairs by two and knocked on her bedroom door. With no answer he eased it open only to see a lump of humanity in the middle of her bed. He stood over her bed and said, "Some people will do anything for attention."

At the sound of her brother's voice, she looked up and jumped into his arms. Clinging to him around his neck and sobbing. "He's dead, Hep. Gone forever."

"I know," Hep soothed. "Whew! You sure your breath didn't kill him?"

Selena laughed for the first time since the news of Hoyt arrived. She laughed and laughed... too hard, too loudly, but it felt good. Colt and Keely glanced upstairs at the unfamiliar sound, one they thought their daughter would never make again.

"Family," Colt declared, "ain't nothing like it."

"Cures what ails you," Keely agreed.

After Selena showered and ate, Hep suggested a walk to the swimming hole to take advantage of the unseasonably warm weather.

"So, how you doing, sis?"

"Bad."

"He was a good man."

"Who you telling?" She pulled a length of last year's honeysuckle from a tree and strung it along.

171

"I don't think I can do this."

"You can and will. Hoyt will see to that."

"You feel him too?"

"I do. Not like you, but I do. A man like that touches you. Changes your life." His eyes filled with tears he didn't allow to fall. Weary of death and dying he continued, "I couldn't believe it when I heard."

"He was supposed to be safe. The lying bastard."

"Mad at him?"

"Oh, hell yeah. And when I see him he's going to get an earful."

"No time soon, I hope."

"I'm not going to hurt myself. Hoyt would hate that."

When they reached the water, Selena crumpled to the ground, held her head but wouldn't let her brother see her all "tore-up."

"I hope you never lose anybody you love, Hep." Not realizing what she'd said, she pulled out the stem of the fragrant honeysuckle flower and ran the one drop of sweetness over her tongue.

The gesture reminded Hep of when they were kids. His big sister seemed very child-like and there was nothing he could do for her.

"I gotta do this myself. Right now I'm sick of me. Tired of feeling bad and shiftless. No direction."

"What do you want to do?"

"Go back to the way it was." She peeked at him beneath the vine in her hand before tossing it away. "And never let him go. I wish I had his hat."

Blues in the Night

"He's cutting ties, Mama!" Lorette declared. "First he disappears, then sends a letter to you and Dad apologizing for missing dinner. And wishing you a Happy Thanksgiving."

"I thought that was very nice—"

"Not to me, Mama. Sends it to you! 'Tell Lorette hi,'" her voice filled with pain. "He should have sent the letter to me."

The time Fern dreaded was upon them and she had to figure it out while Alexander was in Ohio on business. "Perhaps he didn't feel it necessary." She sighed searching for the right word, not wanting to hurt her daughter's feelings. "Maybe you two don't share the same feelings—"

"What are you saying?" Horror scrambled across her face.

"Perhaps he doesn't know how you feel. When he comes back you two can discuss it. You can tell him how you feel and he'll—"

"You're right. Oh, Mama you are brilliant!" Lorette hugged Fern, quickly leaving the mother confused that she'd accepted her explanation. "I have to tell him. He's not a mind reader." Lorette turned and bolted up the steps to her room. Opening her wardrobe, she eyed her clothes while backing into her walk-in closet and retrieving her suitcase from the top shelf.

Annie and Fern looked at the ceiling above, listening to the footsteps and trying to figure out what the young Javier was doing up there. Annie shook her head and returned to the kitchen while Fern climbed the stairs to investigate. She opened her daughter's bedroom door to find clothes strewn about the room; on the bed, in the chair, on the chaise by the window, over the sink. "Lori what are you doing?"

"I'm going to tell him how I feel."

"What do you mean?"

"I'm going to Colt, Texas and profess my love."

"No. No you cannot."

"Why not?"

"When he comes back, Lorette. If his mother or father is sick and his sister is going through her loss—"

"Ozzie said her husband died in the war."

"OK. Then this is not the time for an outsider to intrude on family business."

"But if his answer is that he loves me then I will be family too. Don't you see?"

"No, Lorette I do not. No decent, well-raised, young lady even considers traveling across country by herself to go after a man who may or may not be interested. It's ridiculous, Lorette."

"Oh Mama. Don't you remember how it feels to be in love?"

"As a matter of fact I do. Now and then."

"Then you should understand."

"Stop," Fern stated firmly. "Sit." She patted the mattress beside her. She began slowly, "Hepburn Culhane is under no obligation to clear any of his plans with you, honey. Were you engaged or even going steady?"

Lorette began to cry anew.

Never in her entire life had Lorette Monique Javier felt she meant so little to a person. Never had Lorette Monique Javier ever loved someone so deeply, so completely. She felt Hep Culhane slipping away from her.

"You cannot go tearing off to Texas, uninvited and expect him to love you just because you love him. Just because you show up."

"I do love him, Mama," her resolve returned.

"What about his parents? What are they to think of a girl chasing their son home? It's unseemly, Lorette."

"If he loves me, they will love me."

"Why not wait until your father comes home. He can take you—"

"Oh, Mama. How would that look? I'm trying to show him how grown up and womanly I am. I can't do that with my father escorting me—"

"Suppose there is someone else in Colt, Texas?" Fern blurted out in sheer frustration.

"I've thought of that a thousand times over the past few months. I don't know. I only know I can't sit here and wait and wonder. I have to know, one way or the other. I can't be in love-limbo anymore. If he doesn't want me… I'll live. I'll survive, but I don't want to find out twenty years from now at a reunion that it was me he loved. That he wanted to be noble and spare me the struggle while he becomes… whatever."

"Oh, Lori," her mother used her childhood name again.

"I'm scared, Mama. Scared of being rejected but not half as scared of facing a life without him. One way or the other, Mama, I'll be OK."

Fern watched her determined daughter tuck her favorite combs in the side pouch of her valise. Her maternal terror was not directed toward the parents' reaction, but Hep's. Despite Lorette's professing, that man had been given the power to mortally wound her sheltered baby girl.

~*~

Their daily trips to the swimming hole ended only when the ravages of hunger drove the brother and sister back home after dark. A Texas gulley washer sprung up and dissipated just as quickly, the Culhanes barely making note of it as they ate in the dining room. A timid knock settled on their front door. They almost didn't notice until a pounding came. "That's the way you rouse the Culhanes," a male voice came from the other side. Hep opened the door onto the face of Lorette Javier.

"Lorette?" Hep couldn't believe his eyes. "What are you doing here?" An astonished Hep asked as the rest of the family drifted out and gathered behind him.

"So you do know her?" Silas asked. "OK then," the driver set her suitcase and valise down and left.

"Who is this?" Keely asked, as Selena folded her arms.

"Lorette Javier. These are my parents and my sister. I tutor her at Fisk."

"Long way to come for a lesson," Selena quipped.

"Welcome, come in li'l bit," Papa Colt invited the scared young girl.

Regret seized Lorette immediately. This was not the reception from Hep she expected. Only now did she wish she'd listened to her mother.

"You not as big as me. How tall are you?" Papa Colt continued.

"Colt," Keely said tersely. "Why are you here?" she asked the girl.

Lorette's mouth opened as all stood around her waiting for the answer.

"My mother asked me not to come, but I wanted to see Hep. Make sure he was alright."

"Really?" Keely asked. "My son can take care of himself. Been to the war and back. You, on the other hand—"

"Keely, why don't we let li'l bit here get something to eat and get a good night's sleep. We can discuss it all in the morning," he offered sensibly.

"I don't know this girl. She may rob us in the night—"

"Keely," he soothed, surprised by his wife's uncharitable nature.

Keely fought to hold her tongue against this woman who'd come for her son, uninvited.

"Thank you," Lorette said quietly.

A still-perplexed Hep stood in disbelief before his sister nudged him in the back. "Ah, yes. Are you hungry?"

"No," she shook her head and beamed at him in a way Selena hadn't seen since she'd looked at Hoyt.

"May I call my parents?" Lorette asked. "They'll be worried."

"Humph! The gall," Keely huffed. Her son had already been hurt by one woman, Feather. She wasn't going to let him be duped by another, just because she followed him from college.

"Sure," Papa Colt piped up. "Hep, show her the phone."

"Well, well, well my little brother has a following from Fisk," Selena laughed.

"This is not funny, Selena," Keely snapped. "What kind of woman follows a man home? Unannounced and uninvited. It's unseemly. No home training."

"Maybe a woman in love, Mama."

"Excuse me, Mrs. Culhane, my mother would like to talk to you," Lorette interrupted.

The little hussy's mama wants to talk to me now, Keely thought.

Keely fumed all night through to the next day only momentarily relieved after speaking to Mr. and Mrs. Javier who'd apologized for their daughter's intrusion and asked that they send her home which they would gladly reimburse. Keely tossed and turned until the dawn broke and she began breakfast. She didn't like that her husband did not share her sentiments. Her husband thought it "funny" that this pretty gal had come here after their son.

"She is a cute little thing," Colt said with a gleam in his eyes. "They'd make some pretty babies."

Going through all of her chores, Keely said nothing to her family as she resisted this girl's compliments to her cooking and offers to help. In short order Orelia had come to meet Lorette bringing her daughters and, later, nosey other folks dropped by to see this "forward" girl in the flesh.

"Ma, I'm taking Lorette to show her the town. Want me to pick up anything?"

"No. But you can drop off that—"

"Ma—"

Hep'd never thought of Lorette in a romantic vein but he watched her effect on his friends and neighbors as he squired her around. She seemed to dazzle them all with her smile and easy manner. Respectful, gracious, articulate and polite.

"You are going to invite her to Thanksgiving dinner?" Selena asked of her mother.

"The girl has a family and I'm sure she'll want to spend it with them."

"She's not just any girl, Ma. She could be—"

"Don't say it," Keely held up her hand as if it alone could prevent the unthinkable. "How am I to respect such a selfish, disrespectful girl who comes unchaperoned from Tennessee to check on a boy—"

"Man."

Keely continued peeling potatoes with a vengeance.

"Say what you want, Ma. Why can't you just think the woman has gumption?"

"Oh, is that what you all call it now?" She threw the skins into a scraps pile for the garden. "You weren't raised like that!"

"I don't think she was either Ma. Did you notice her clothing? The fine material, the almost invisible stitching, the way her clothes fit her perfectly? The details in her dresses, the pleats alone expertly ironed and she didn't do it. I don't think her mother did either. Her hair, nails and skin? She's quality, Ma. Not like some of the women who coulda followed him home." Selena thought of some of her brother's Chicago conquests. "I know quality, Ma. Those who really have it, those who've recently acquired it and those who fake it. This girl has had it for a while, I mean for generations."

"That suppose to excuse her bad manners and impress me?"

"You see the way she looks at Hep? With awe and wonder. Like she can't believe her good fortune to meet him."

"Fortune. You said it."

"You think she's after his money? He's got none," Selena laughed.

"She's spoilt-rotten to the core."

"Don't think so. She's a different kind of women who's never been told 'no.'"

"So when he tells her 'no,' she'll fall apart and kill herself... if she doesn't get him?"

"Oh, no. Not this girl. She'll try her best and if that's not good enough, she'll move on. Behind that sugar-sweet drawl and that smirky half-smile is a tenacious will that'll win out. She's an iron butterfly. Flighty and lacey and delicate appearing, but really strong and wiry. Don't let the outer girl fool you. She's got a whim of iron. Like a dog with a bone, once she's had enough of the bone not giving her what she wants, she'll move on."

"OK. Is Hep the dog or the bone?"

"Besides how bad can she be, he met her at college?"

"Yeah, he was *tutoring* her, so she's a dumb-cluck to boot. Looks aren't everything."

"OK, Ma."

"He is not in love with that girl!"

"Not yet," Selena sassed, grabbing an apple before disappearing up the back steps.

Thanksgiving came with Lorette Javier as the Culhane guest.

182

"Li'l bit, come sit here," Papa Colt directed Lorette.

When the rounds of "what are you thankful for" circled the table, Lorette said, "Being my first Thanksgiving away from home, I thank all the Culhanes for their welcoming graciousness."

The unimpressed Keely rolled her eyes. *Ain't we the lucky ones,* she thought.

The dinner discussion ranged from the war to politics to travel, each regaling the other with family history. All familiar with their own, Selena seized the opportunity to ask their guest about hers.

"So what does your family do in… Tennessee, is it?"

"Yes, Evelyn, Tennessee. Almost like Mr. Culhane, my father founded Evelyn too."

"Do tell," Keely feigned interest.

"He was sent from New Orleans there to run the family grist mill. He then built a lumber mill and lately an aggregate quarry with all the construction using concrete. Buildings and roads," Lorette drawled to a close.

"So your family's been there awhile," Selena helped her out.

"Oh yes. All of my sisters and I were born there. There are five of us."

"What does your mother do?"

"A homemaker like yourself, Mrs. Culhane."

"I doubt that seriously. Please pass the rolls," Keely said, evenly.

"Her father graduated from the Sorbonne," Hep offered proudly, knowing his father would like that.

"In Paris, France?" Papa Colt interjected.

Lorette beamed, excited that her only ally had chimed in. "Yes he, my grandfathers and all my uncles. It's a tradition and a graduation present that they do the 'Grand Tour of Europe' before returning home. My father stayed a little too long so they sent for him and punished him with reviving the Javier Mill. Or so they thought. He resurrected that family mill, parlayed a few others and the townspeople loved him for it. He gives his employees medical care and even sends their children to college. They call my parents the Duke and Duchess of Evelyn, Tennessee."

Lorette watched the unimpressed Keely pour giblet gravy onto her mashed potatoes, making sure the brown liquid didn't touch her sweet potatoes. Lorette's heart sank realizing Hep's mother was no fan.

"Is that where your parents met? In France?"

"Oh, no. My mother worked at the mill, -- a bookkeeper. She was a school teacher."

"Oh, so was I," Selena smiled.

"The Javiers were upset with my father choosing her so they cut him off. Financially. Besides being brilliant, I think that's one of the reasons he did so well. To prove them wrong and that he could do it all himself."

"So tenacity runs in the family," Hep offered with a quick smile.

"Yes," Lorette grinned at him.

"Why did the Javiers of New Orleans not like your mother?" Keely asked.

184

"Because she is dark," Lorette answered innocently, regretting it the minute it slipped out.

"Oh. Like us?" Keely said. "Excuse me." She threw her napkin beside her plate and got up to serve dessert.

The silence was deafening.

Lorette thought about apologizing but knew any further explanation probably wasn't a good idea. Still she couldn't help herself. "That was the Javiers in New Orleans. Not us. We don't feel that way at all. Color—" Lorette looked over at Selena who had one slender dark finger over her dark lips, telling Lorette to "shut up." "Dinner is delicious," Lorette offered weakly.

"Yes, Keely can cook. Bet you thought about your Mama's meals a lot overseas," Papa Colt deflected to his son.

"I sure did. Worth the wait."

"I think you put on a couple of pounds since you been back," Selena said.

The discussion remained light and airy for the remainder of the meal. Keely began clearing the dessert dishes and this time Lorette helped Selena and Mrs. Culhane without asking. Lorette offered to wash or dry the dishes. "No, thank you," Keely declined.

"Let's take a walk around the ranch," Hep rescued his ersatz house guest.

"All right," Lorette jumped at the chance and they donned their coats and gloves.

Once outside, Lorette broached, "That was a disaster."

"No, it wasn't. If you've ever fought in a war... you'd know it wasn't anywhere near 'a disaster.'" He lit a Lucky Strike.

"You know I didn't mean anything about color. You've seen my family. You know we are all colors—"

"Most black families are. The Russian roulette of black genes."

Was he trying to make her feel better or was he dismissing her? Had coming here been a mistake? She now not only felt nervous but stupid for taking too much for granted. Hep had never tried to hold her hand or kiss her. She prattled on about his family, the town in which he grew up, his friends, the swimming hole. But she needed answers so she could save face.

"How about you, Hep?"

"How about me what?"

"I know how everyone in your family feels about me. But I don't know how you feel about me. I need to know if I've made a fool of myself as my parents think."

Hep looked out over the corral fence.

"I need to know if I should just go home and forget all about you. Move on because you could never like me the way I like you."

"How old are you?"

"What? What's that got to do with anything?"

"A lot. You are so young."

"I'm twenty next year."

Hep remained silent.

"I know what you are thinking. I've …I've never… My life has been easy…but not …" Lorette tried to harness her thoughts. "I know you are a man of the world. I know you've had …experiences that I have not. That's OK. That means you'll know what to do. How to…please…"

"OK, "Hep rescued Lorette. "What did you expect to happen?"

"I thought my coming here would make you see me as a viable choice for you. Maybe we could just date and see. I might not really like you once I get to know you."

A rumble started in his chest and turned into a laugh once it hit the air. Hep laughed… and laughed… and laughed.

"Is that so unfathomable? That a woman would not find you irresistible?" Lorette posed. As if really hearing what she'd just asked, she began to laugh with him. It was sweet relief for them both.

Selena helped her mother place the washed dishes back in the breakfront and the laughter from the corral startled them.

"Yeah, Ma. I think you better get used to this one."

I Got A Crush On You, Sweetie Pie

The ivy-wrapped building of Fisk University welcomed students back from their Thanksgiving break and against the chilly weather, immediately, they launched themselves into studying for finals and research papers, anticipating the upcoming Christmas holidays. Football games played themselves out in the stadium in their usual rivalry with Tennessee State, co-eds hid curvy bodies beneath corduroy and cloth coats as their legs grew brittle against the elements they thought, *if only girls could wear pants like the guys.*

The campus was alive with activity, both academic and social, as Hep Culhane and Lorette Javier not only resumed Tuesday/Thursday tutoring sessions but added movies, dances, parties and lunches on campus as a couple.

Lorette continued to enjoy most of Hep's visit to her house for Sunday dinner when she had him all to herself. When, after dinner despite the briskness of winter, her favorite sight remained seeing her father and her man disappear into the garage and tinker with her father's car. Two weeks after their return from Colt, Texas, Hep finally kissed her. She kissed him back and Gay Iris had to hear about it all ad infinitum.

"I hope when you two 'do the do,' I won't have to hear those details," Gay Iris lamented.

"We'll be married then and I can't tell you what goes on between husband and wife," Lorette chided.

That Monday, the couple dined at the off-campus hangout, Louie's, on Jefferson. As Hep reached for the sugar to sweeten his black coffee, he saw Barbara Babcock enter the door.

Seeing him, she smiled and walked directly to him, ignoring Lorette she said, "Oh, so you're back. Your Dad's OK, I hope."

"He's fine. Thanks for asking."

"Had a nice Thanksgiving, I hope."

"I did. Hope you did as well."

"Call me. I'll make those smothered pork chops you like," Barbara said, eyeing Lorette like she was an underdeveloped twelve year old.

Hep smiled stiffly.

Lorette placed her straw in the vanilla milkshake. "You know I've never seen your apartment," she said none too coyly.

"It's a small two bedroom at 12th and Hyman. Really nothing to see."

"Has she seen it?"

"She has but mostly we go to her place. She has an apartment about five blocks away."

Lorette bristled at his honesty. "Does she go to Fisk? I don't remember seeing her."

"Do you know everyone who goes to Fisk?"

"Why are you being so mean?"

"I'm simply answering your questions. If you don't want to know. Do not ask. I'm not that type of guy, Lorette. I will not lie. I have not seen her since I got back."

"Are you going to?"

"Yes, I have to let her know that we are over and I am dating you now."

Lorette beamed at his mandate. "Can I go?"

"No."

~*~

"So good to see you, Hep," Barbara answered the door with her assets on full display. No one had to ask her age, her body screamed full-grown, red-blooded woman at him.

"Thanks for seeing me," Hep said.

"Why so formal?" She closed the door behind him. "I'm far from a stranger."

"Smells good in here."

"I made many of your favorites: smothered pork chops, fried chicken, macaroni and cheese—"

She sauntered up to him and pressed her body against his. "Things that'll still taste good in the midnight hour or tomorrow morning." She smiled as she felt his body respond to her despite his best efforts.

"Can we talk?" Her scent, intoxicating and he had to say his piece and leave. It'd been too long since he'd enjoyed a sexual release, especially from a woman who required no coaching or gentle approach and already knew what to do to get his peak performance... a few times a night.

"Sure. I have a bit of news myself." Her cleavage led them to the couch. She sat provocatively, crossing her long, lean, bare legs, exposed to mid-thigh. He knew what lay above.

She has gorgeous gams, Hep thought. Perhaps he should have brought Lorette. He tore his eyes away from her frame long enough to notice the table set for two, romantic candlelight flickered as he inhaled her perfume, aptly named Tabu.

"It's been a few weeks and I've met someone."

Barbara recoiled and raised an eyebrow.

"We've started dating and I thought it best to let you know. So you can move on as well."

Barbara shot up from the sofa like a pin stuck her derriere.

She looked down at him. She wanted to slap him.

He stood, "I didn't want you to hear it from anyone else or see us. That'd be insensitive."

Barbara couldn't remove her eyes from him. Hep Culhane was to be her future, her way out of Nashville to the Big Time. Where else would she meet a more likeable candidate? Sexually matched, Hep could give her everything she ever wanted. Her chances at the phone company and otherwise were slim to none now and, would be bleaker still when the war ended.

"You're a wonderful woman and you'll meet someone who deserves—"

"I deserve," she spat indignantly. "You gonna tell me what I deserve? I deserve…a…father for this baby."

"What?"

"You heard me. 'We' are pregnant."

It was Hep's turn to look stupefied and bewildered. "How can that be?" He sank back on the couch.

"I think you know how. We are fierce together in bed, Hep. Or wherever we've dared to make love. Sex was never our problem."

"I always used a condom."

"Only 'no sex' is 100% foolproof." *Discard me like an old, used-up shoe,* she thought. *I think not.*

Hep held his head and rubbed his fingertips across his eyebrows. He and Barbara enjoyed each other sexually but never had he envisioned a life with her. Never considered marriage and children with this woman. With the things she did to him, he'd never want her to kiss their children.

"It's not that young little chippie I saw you with at Louie's is it?" she challenged. "She can't possibly give you lovin' like I do. She can't know how. Does she know how to give a good—"

"Is the baby mine?" Hep interrupted.

He caught her fist mid-slap.

"How dare you! Get out!" she shouted.

Hep rose and walked calmly to the door. "I will provide for the child, but I will not marry his or her mother."

"You bastard!" she yelled and slammed the door behind him.

Had it not been for finals and the upcoming Christmas vacation, Hep would have been consumed with his impending fatherhood. Not convinced Barbara was pregnant, he knew time would tell, but the issue of paternity loomed large. If the child were his, he could perhaps send him/her to Colt, Texas to be raised, but he suspected Barbara would never give it up. Wouldn't his parents and Feather love that? He refused to marry a woman he did not love, but he would care for the innocent child. As the child grew, Hep would be more involved in his or her life if the mother permitted.

On Christmas Day, Hep joined the Javiers.

"Oh thank you, Hep," Papa Javier said, unwrapping his imported leather driving gloves. "I bet these were hard to get with a war on."

Hep helped clean the floor of colorful Christmas wrapping paper and went with Papa J to turn the smoked turkey one last time. "Ever have smoked turkey?"

"No, sir."

"Call your folks?"

"Yes, sir. This morning."

Lorette looked at her father and future husband out the window and smiled. This Christmas everyone was home, even Dr. Coke and her husband. Of all her brothers-in-law there, Hep and her father shared the closest bond. Of all the men there, none were going to be the mayor of a major city. Lorette Javier had hit the jackpot with Hepburn Culhane. No one could top her; the First Lady of a major American city.

Hep still could not get all the Javiers and their children's names straight and there was a houseful of kids of all ages. They devoured the well-planned meal, mostly prepared in advance so Annie could spend the holiday with her own family. At the meal's end, the tradition of telling the story of the Duke and Duchess of Evelyn began. All riveted to the telling like it was the first time. When everyone sat in the front parlor with the ornate Christmas tree in the background, Lorette whispered to Hep, "I love my lavalier."

"I'm glad." In the presence of family and the absence of an engagement ring, she kissed his cheek. "Daddy used to tell us this story as a fairytale when we were growing up. All five Javier girls would stretch out in their big bed."

"Once upon a time," Papa Javier began, "there was a Prince of New Orleans, Alexandre' Javier whose family reigned supreme in The Crescent City. The most prominent, richest family in all the land. All their sons studied in Paris, France and when the young prince stayed too long, the King sent for him to come home.

"The penalty for his dalliance of staying 'too long,' they dispatched him to Tennessee to revive and run the mill there, knowing he would fail as it was in much

194

disrepair. At first, the Prince thought the backwoods borough beneath him. He lived in a little cottage and figured the sooner he whipped the mill into shape the sooner he'd be back in New Orleans in the castle with the gold J etched upon its gates, the better. The Prince worked hard and drove his workers to do the same and they hated the Prince. Into his life one day he heard a lilting laugh. A laugh that made him happy. The kind of laugh that makes you laugh too. It was the first time he'd laughed since coming to Tennessee. Do you know whose laugh that was?"

"Grandma's," the children would chant and laugh.

"Ah! I have such smart grandchildren!" Papa J exclaimed.

Just as it was when the five Javier girls were small, the youngest of those present lost their battle with the sandman and were carried upstairs after a very full and exciting Christmas Day.

"That's quite a story," Hep concluded.

"Not as exciting as your dad's."

That's All

With the war still on, the brand-new year slipped in unannounced and without much fan-fare. Too many losses for everyone to be jubilant about another year of fighting. After the Culhane Christmas party, New Year's proved just another day as Selena pulled her old coat around her shoulders and eyed the bleak Texas terrain for answers on what she should do next. No Hoyt Colson. No Club Alabam celebration this year. Hep Culhane and Lorette Javier returned to Fisk's campus beginning the spring semester. Despite his calls and even stopping by her apartment, Hep could not get in touch with Barbara Babcock whose waist should be thick with child by now. He'd decided not to tell Lorette until the entire fiasco proved to be an "affaire complet" achieved between the would-be parents. When Hep told Lorette, he intended to tell her the full story in one fell swoop, not bits and pieces. Then Lorette, with all the information needed, could decide whether to stay with him or pursue another life. With this life-changing challenge, he'd made another education and career decision about his future. Below the Mason-Dixon Line seemed to be Hep-inhospitable. After the freedom of living in Chicago, attending college up north, and fighting in Europe, he'd had enough of the south's *de facto* Jim Crow laws and oppressive environment and sought freer horizons. After he completed that year and possibly summer school, he finally decided to transfer himself and his credits to the west coast... UCLA. He hoped Lorette would join him after she graduated.

"Happy New Year," Hep told his sister over the telephone as he checked phone messages from his roommate."

"Thanks."

"You weren't around before we left. How you living?"

"One breath at a time," Selena sighed. "Feather had her baby. A girl—"

"That's nice—" Hep cut her off.

Selena got the message.

Hep came across a note from Barbara Babcock. "Listen, I got to go. Catch you later."

Hep pushed open the glass door leading to Louie's where they'd arranged to meet. Always prompt, she was already there holding down a booth. Offering a quick anxious smile, he slid across the vinyl seat.

"You're hard to get ahold of," Hep said.

"Nice to see you too."

"Coffee," Hep answered the waitress. "I thought we should touch base and see how we're going to proceed with... this situation."

"Paying me to get rid of it?"

"Not an option. I don't believe in that. This baby is innocent and deserves a chance."

Seeing him, reinforced for Barbara what a decent guy Hep Culhane was. Too decent for what she had planned. Too decent to trap him into a financial relationship since he'd made it clear he'd take care of the baby but not her. Already exhausted at the thought of fighting with him for the next eighteen years, she blurted out, "I lost the baby, Hep."

His gaze pieced hers.

"Guess God intervened after all," she said.

He almost asked if there had ever been a baby. He almost asked if she was just letting him off the hook. He almost asked when? Where? How? But he heard Range tell him, "Let it go, man…"

"So I guess that's it for us," she said brusquely. "No harm no foul, huh?" She opened her hands. She got up and took her coat from the rack. Hep's eyes fastened at her waist which looked as slim as ever. She ran her hand over her stomach. "Nothing there."

"Sorry for your loss," he said.

"No. You're not." She slung on her wrap and buttoned the first three. "Have a nice life."

Once she cleared the threshold of the diner, Hep breathed a sigh of pure relief. He washed his face with his big hand and smiled, not realizing he'd been so tense. He'd tell Lorette, but there was no rush.

~*~

Without realizing it, Hep's mood and attitude adjusted one thousand percent. He hadn't noticed but Lorette had. Not sure whether it was her chasing him to

198

Colt, Texas forcing him to realize he loved her or the fact that he'd made the Dean's List or that she got a "B" in the math for which he was tutoring her or that Hep fit seamlessly into the Javier family, she was happy. Hep'd even charmed their no-nonsense housekeeper, Annie, who was charmed by no one. Hep and Lorette were invited to all the social events, accepting some and declining others, which in the past would have irked Lorette, but now staying home or going to the movies with Hep beat any of the invites they declined. Perhaps she was maturing. Spring sprang and painted Evelyn, Tennessee with colorful variegated crocus, flame tulips, chartreuse forsythias, purple lilacs and other heady and delightful scents of hyacinths that May; the end of the semester was upon them. Hep spoke freely of his newest plans, failing to see panic consumed Lorette's dark flashing eyes.

"You would transfer to California?" her voice screeched, getting his attention.

He took both of her hands in his. "I was thinking that after you graduate you could join me there."

"That's two years from now!"

"I know, but it's not that long."

I could have at least one child by then, she thought but said, "I know it's just one year for you."

"And I could get things set up for you to come out. We'd marry here first—"

"Ah!" Lorette gasped, and covered her mouth. "We've never talked about marriage."

"I know. But surely you've thought about it."

"Every waking hour of the day."

"Hyperbole."

"Whatever. But if you think I'm letting you go out to the west coast without me you got another thought coming."

"But Lorette, you have to finish college."

"I can finish out there just like you can."

"Your parents are not going to let—"

"Let? I am a grown woman now and I can decide for myself when and where I go and I am going to the west coast with my husband."

He looked at her, blinked and swallowed. This was too fast. "Well—"

"OK," she continued. "When shall we get married? August? That will give us enough time to plan a wedding fit for us."

"Wait!"

"What?" she looked at him, her bright eyes shining with expectation, excitement and innocence. "You do want to marry me, don't you Hep?"

"Well, yes. But. It's just that this is so soon."

"Time's awastin'. We're not getting any younger. Wouldn't it be better to have me with you from the very start? Make your home, iron your clothes, cook your meals—"

"Do you even know how to do any of that?" He chuckled.

"I will learn. I promise." She giggled.

She was so pretty, anxious and willing to help make his dreams come true.

"I guess we better get you a diamond engagement ring."

Lorette squealed and hugged him tightly around his neck. "OhMyGod.OhMyGod! OhMyGod!" she chanted and fanned herself, hoping some of the excitement would evaporate. Like fortune found, she'd garnered The Grand Prize—Hepburn Culhane. She'd tell their children how hard it was to snag their father... "I love you, Hepburn Culhane. With all my heart and soul."

"I love you too, Lorette," he replied, half revelation, half admission. Unlike other women he'd dated, he never thought of a future with any of them. His needs met and satisfied his only goal. Unlike his buddy Range, Hep'd always considered himself a serial monogamist. He hadn't given in to Lorette as much as allowed her to work her wiles on him all the time knowing her intent. They were alike in that way. She had a naïve audacity that all things were possible, attainable, doable if you wanted it badly enough and worked toward it. As a grown man and a soldier who fought overseas, he had a more realistic outlook on life. He'd seen some things, done some things and had some things he wanted to forget. But he needed someone like Lorette in his corner. Everyone did. When he said "I love you" to her just then for the first time, he meant it. It felt good, honest and right. The fact that she'd said it before... that she loved him first? All gravy.

The next evening, Selena called her brother. "So what's this I hear about a wedding between you and some girl who followed you from Fisk?"

"You been talking to Ma."

"I should have heard it from you," Selena teased and asked, "Is she in trouble?"

"What kind—" Realizing his sister's implication he emphatically responded, "No. I have too much respect for myself and my future. Besides we haven't even... you know, done..." he stumbled.

"Made love," Selena filled in the blanks. "Do you love this girl?"

"Yeah. She has good qualities. We can go far."

"Damn, Hep. You ain't buying no horse."

"Dad used this technique and it worked out for him and Ma."

"This ain't the turn-of-the-century. We have inside toilets, electric lights and refrigeration now."

"I'm saying that she is a good match for me. We share the same values and ideas about things."

"Ummm. How romantic."

"She believes in where I want to go and intends to help me get there. She is the only one who didn't laugh at my wanting to be the first black mayor of a major city."

This caught Selena's attention. Believing in someone. "That's a power thing, Hep."

"Don't I know it?"

"It may be more important than love. To have someone on your side helping you and not fighting you,

202

or doubting you every step of the way." She smiled into the phone. "You know I love you and just want the best for you. Don't want you to hurry into anything that might hurt you in the long run."

"No guarantee for any of us."

"Too true."

"I remembered what Range asked me one time. 'How'd you feel if she got away and you never took that chance?'" He stopped before continuing, "I don't want to take that chance with Lorette, lose her and find out later she'd been the one."

"The one that got away. Well, there's gonna be a wedding. What can I do to help?"

An August wedding date was set. Evelyn, Tennessee and Colt, Texas abuzz with all the preparations which began with the beautifully engraved, pearled ivory invitation that arrived in only a few Texas post office boxes, which Keely proudly took to choir practice. As per tradition, Selena was asked to be a bridesmaid. She declined but accepted the request to sing "Always" as the newlyweds' first dance. *That sappy song,* Selena thought, *surely Lorette's choice. It's no* "Stardust.*"

All too soon, the Culhanes converged on the Javier House in Evelyn. Their mouths agape as they lit from the chauffeur-driven car and approached the palatial house perched on the hill surrounded by lush flowers and foliage. Each feature captured a Culhane; Colt, the craftsmanship in the scalloped shingles and the sturdy-hung shutters; Keely, the beveled and stained-glass windows "in a house!" Orelia, impressed with the triple balconies attached on three floors. Selena eyed the total splendor of the gorgeous fairytale-like home and scoffed, "well, this explains a lot."

Once inside, Annie, who'd been with the family since the second Javier daughter was born, served them refreshing lemonade and ice tea while the chauffeur and other maids hired for the event, took the Culhane luggage to their respective rooms, unpacked and hung the clothes in the wardrobes. Prepared not to like Ma and Pa Javier, Selena was forced to change her mind by the gracious and hospitable couple known as the Duke and Duchess. They sat in the front parlor exchanging pleasantries and introduced their other daughters and their husbands. One remarked that Coke couldn't come as she had an emergency at the hospital at which her baby sister was momentarily miffed. Selena not only liked them but grew suitably impressed by their accomplishments in having all four daughters educated with their professional rosters including; lawyer, dentist, teacher and Corrine "Coke," a medical doctor who met and married her husband in med school. Selena tried hard to find a way to be critical, but nothing materialized.

The rehearsal dinner, reserved and arranged by the Javiers at a local restaurant and hosted by the Culhanes, showed an affable commingling of two middle-class, black families from drastically different vantage points. The next day Selena noticed how her father, Alexander Javier and Hep disappeared under the hood of a car as her

204

mother and Fern Javier settled in on the back porch chatting away, a pitcher of ice tea and canapes between them.

~*~

The wedding party seated and perched on the edge of their seats as Hep's best man stood claiming all the attention.

"Hey man," Hep warned Range, "keep it clean."

"I got class, man. I know how to act," Range casually brushed the side of his suit. "You look good, man," he said, as he strolled to the podium and looked at the assemblage before him.

"You too." Hep grinned widely.

"Hep-cat and Hipster," Range said into the mic and, only he, Hep and Selena chuckled.

"I didn't think this day would ever come for my buddy," he told the bridal party and the guests seated around tables of ten listened to the best man's toast. "But here we are. Only one girl could get him here this fast. Lorette Monique Javier. No question she loves you. Girl had her mind on the mission." Range stopped and looked at Hep. "You love her, man?"

"I guess so," Hep answered.

"Yeah, you do. You settled for fogging up car windows and sought no other sexual release from her or anybody else? You must love her."

Hep bolted upright. He shook his head and chuckled into the dark, quiet room before punching his pillow and lying back down. "You should be here, man," Hep uttered in his mind's ear.

"I am," Range answered in kind.

Hep grinned and stared at the ceiling, a muted glow danced upon its surface from an outside lamplight. He smiled again at the thought of Range coming to reassure him on the night before his nuptials. *Thanks man,* Hep thought, turned on his side and fell back to sleep.

When I Fall In Love

Selena sat in the upstairs window seat in front of one of the house's strained-glass windows.

"Hey sis," Hep greeted.

"Well, the groom," Selena responded. "I have to admit it. These are nice people."

"I agree."

"How you feeling. Nervous?"

"Surprisingly, no. A little sad."

"Why so? Death of freedom?"

"Missing my best man." The name Range hung between them.

"Yeah, Sam Rudd is a come down."

"Our brother-in-law is OK. He's just not Range."

"He's here." She touched his heart. "You know he wouldn't miss it for the world."

Hep smiled in agreement. "Had a dream about him and he said as much."

"Dreams from the heart tell you what the mind will not. You're never gonna be rid of him," Selena teased.

"Hope not."

"Hep," Lorette drawled from downstairs.

"Gotta go."

"Get used to it," Selena teased. Her baby brother was marrying and marrying well. Marrying "up," not in terms of finances but in class. She wondered what this meant for him; wondered if Lorette could keep him interested.

On that unseasonably mild August day in 1943, seemed all of Evelyn, Tennessee turned out for the wedding of the youngest and last Javier girl to witness her marry a man whose father found a Texas town, owned and ran a horse and cattle ranch of over one thousand acres. As Selena watched a bevy of young, giggly bridesmaids saunter down the aisle and assume their places at the altar, she was reminded of her good decision not to be the oldest one in the bunch. Hep stood young, tall, erect and handsome in a black tuxedo awaiting then watching the demure Lorette Javier glide down the aisle on the arm of her father; poised, confident, her happiness escaping from beneath her veil. Already duly impressed by the cache' of calla lilies and white orchids which comprised her bouquet and the bows with white roses and baby's breath that punctuated each pew, Selena had to admit that the voluminous wedding gown studded with glistening seed pearls was stunning. Lorette Monique Javier looked fairytale-princess… gorgeous.

As her father stepped back, the couple joined hands and the preacher began. Selena was reminded of her own wedding to Hoyt Colson. She twirled her wedding band on her third finger left hand and the memories damned up behind her eyes and spilled down her cheeks. The way it was for them would never be again. She only hoped that her brother and his new wife would be half as happy as she and Hoyt were. Selena finally rejoined the wedding just in time to hear Lorette's vows.

"From the very first moment I heard your voice and saw you, my life changed. I knew you were my destiny. I knew we belonged together. Forever. I knew God sent you for me. I knew this day would come and here we are. I can't wait to begin our lives together. To make a home for you and our children to come. I love you, Hep Culhane with every beat of my heart." She smiled up at him.

"Hep," the preacher prompted.

"Lorette." He took a deep breath, "I take you as my lawfully-wedded wife and I promise to love, protect, provide and care for you and our children. To be faithful and true and honest with you always. I want to uphold our tradition and have our marriage be as successful and loving as our parents' before us. I intend to do my part to make it happen. I love you and our children to be."

The reception proper held in the church's hall was only a prelude to those privileged enough to return to the Javier home. Both destinations, overflowing with copious amounts of scrumptious home cooked and catered food and drink, easily satisfied all who came to wish the newlyweds well. They were to honeymoon in Niagara Falls, surely Lorette's idea and New York City before migrating to Los Angeles in time to find a one bedroom apartment before Hep started at UCLA the day after Labor Day. Lorette opted to wait a semester before she enrolled; as a new wife she wanted her home perfect for her perfect husband.

Selena had picked out several places in the Watts neighborhood for them to look while they stayed at Shanghai and Sugar Dee's. Her old friend and her new sister-in-law were chalk and cheese and Selena chuckled at the thought of the two of them together in the rooming house. Selena, sure that Lorette's sensibilities would be adversely affected by lodging in a type of place she never knew existed. Selena predicted the new Culhanes would find a home in a week.

In seven days' time, Hep carried his bride over the threshold of their new, first floor, one bedroom apartment on Flora Street. Lorette, ecstatic about their home, as she could not stand living in one room and sharing a bathroom with strangers. As Hep made it to his classes, Lorette busied herself turning their apartment into a replica of the hotel they'd stayed in at Niagara Falls, full of seaside accents which fit the L.A. motif very well.

"My happy home." *How many more will we live in before occupying the mayor's mansion,* she wondered.

~*~

Colt, Keely and Selena returned to Colt, Texas in the midst of hell-hot heat. Selena resumed the posture she'd claimed before her brother's wedding. She slept late, bounced around the big house and the little town and, after seeing everyone she wanted to see, grew restless again; anxiousness bordering on depression.

"Hello!" Selena answered the ringing phone.

210

"Hey Kiddo. How you doin'?"

Selena smiled at the unmistakably smooth voice. "Miles Syphax."

"On the line. Listen, the news of Hoyt's death just caught up with me. I am so sorry, Selena. He was a special man."

"I must agree."

"Stand-up, solid guy who loved his work. Took the only pictures of me where I didn't look like a black ribbon on the bandstand."

Selena chuckled.

"He loved you too. You all were some kinda couple. Let me know if you need anything."

"I'm fine."

"Hard to find is more like it. I had to practically bribe Mazeda to give me this number."

"She's a friend."

"Hope you consider me one too. I'm still traveling too much, but you can always catch up with me if you need to."

"Thanks, Miles."

"Right-O. Take your time healing. Let me know where you land, Mrs. Colson."

"Will do."

Selena sauntered through the front door and sat on the porch swing beside her father.

"Who was that?"

"A friend of Hoyt's and mine. Expressing his condolences."

"That's nice." They rocked a while in silence before Papa Colt asked, "What else is ailing you?"

"Funny question for someone who's just lost her husband," she snapped, immediately sorry but couldn't say it.

"Well, you are welcome to stay here as long as you like. This is your home. Always has been. Always will be." He puffed his pipe and the smoke perfumed the fresh air. "What are your plans?"

"Dunno, Dad."

"You need a new dream 'cause this one is done."

"Gee thanks, Dad." Truth was this was all "new" for Selena. She'd never felt this lost before. Abandoned really. Never felt like she didn't belong and life didn't fit her, leaving her chaffed, itchy and anxious.

"Well, you can jus' pretend you're sixteen as long as you like. Sleep in your childhood room..."

"Tsk!" Selena remarked, stomped from the porch and went into the yard.

"What'd you say to her?" Keely asked, coming to the porch with liquid refreshment.

"What she needed to hear."

"Colt, it's only been a few months." Keely watched her daughter walk up to the cemetery.

"Life goes on, Keely. Just want her to know what's what. She needs direction. Can't move forward looking in the rear view mirror."

Selena looked at the graves of her father's boys and then at Range's. A sight she thought she'd never see...

another generation of dead friends. With Hoyt buried overseas among other GIs who died in France, Selena didn't have a home side grave. She second-guessed her decision to let him lay there with those he'd served. She'd have to go to France to visit him; make that trek one of these days. France... a zillion miles away on foreign soil.

With her brother off starting a new life, her beloved Colt, Texas grew cloying and suffocating. What about her? What lay in store... a life without Hoyt? Selena held herself. Hoyt wasn't over there; he was here with her. At night as she still laid in bed, waiting for his touch. To feel his body encompass hers. To smell his naturally clean scent of bleach and lime soap. To feel his velvet skin. His hair. At times, awakened by his light snore. But when she sat up in bed... she was alone. The sheets cold, her loins on fire. Her mind ablaze. Tired of Colt, Texas, Hep and her daddy were right but where would she go? What did she want to do?

"You know you can't run from him, Selena," her mother said at the River Bend Station. "That'd be like throwing raindrops back up into the clouds."

"I know, Mama. I'm taking him with me." She smiled. "I like to think I'm running toward something. Don't know what but at least I'm hopeful, not hopeless."

"All aboard," the conductor yelled.

"I spend too much time saying goodbye at this station," Keely remarked.

"You fixed for money?"

"Yes, Daddy. And I gave you Zen's address where I'll be staying."

"Is it nice? Safe?"

"Yes, Daddy. I'll be staying with her and her family. It's a new apartment complex. Only a few years old. I'll be fine."

Keely's concern was palpable. She wouldn't speak it, but they knew that last time Selena left, she left married, with a husband who would take care of her. This time she left a single woman... like Star, who they hadn't heard from since.

Reading her mother's mind, she reassured, "Mama. I'm not Star. I'm older, wiser and I've been out there before. I'll be fine." She smiled and added, "I'm taking a page from Lorette Javier."

"Umph," Keely sniped.

"Life is too short and too precious to just fiddle with it. If you want something you've got to go after it."

Keely wouldn't trust herself to speak. It'd all been said.

Selena boarded the train and sat near a window so she could wave at her parents as it pulled out. She blew kisses and felt the seat next to her where Hoyt had been the first time and should be now. She felt his presence and his blessing all around her. She was going to be a 'citizen of the world' as he'd predicted. Being on this adventure felt better than staying put in Colt, Texas. Zen lived uptown in the Magnolia Projects near the iconic Dew Drop Inn over on LaSalle where she and Hoyt had visited while in New Orleans. The owner remembered her and told her to "drop in" when she got to town, and that was Selena's first stop. If that didn't work out, there were a million clubs in and around the French Quarter where she could audition. Worst case scenario, she'd end up with Zen at the Blue Plate Mayonnaise Plant.

Selena chuckled aloud, "That'll never happen."

She smiled out of the window and watched the countryside whizz by as she catapulted towards the unknown.

Don't Get Around Much Anymore

While completing her engagement at the Dew Drop Inn, The Onyx downtown off Bourbon came calling and Selena couldn't resist answering. In the smaller, less notorious club, she could perform as suited her. With slightly higher pay, she could get a room nearby and not have to travel in the wee hours up to Magnolia. Besides, she loved Zen, but living with her family and sharing a room with another grown woman proved to be taxing. Selena relished a place all to herself where her clothes, makeup and jewelry wouldn't be "borrowed" without asking and the piece of chicken she'd thought about through her sets would still be in the refrigerator when she got home... no matter the hour.

Selena sat at the piano, accompanying herself on "Don't Get Around Much Anymore."

"A for-sure piano player," a man gruffed as he watched her dark fingers tickle the ivories while her five octave range voice accompanied in perfect pitch.

"You worth your weight in gold, girl," the vaguely familiar man continued.

At her set's end he asked, "Come sit with me. I got some talk for you."

"No thanks. But you're welcome to stay for the next set," she lied, hoping he'd move on to another bar.

"Don't flatter yourself. You too skinny and young for me. I got some pointers for you—only if you wanna go somewhere in this business."

"Oh, you gonna 'make me a star' is that it?" she sassed and went into the back room.

He came every night for two weeks after that, yelling out directions, "Too loud! Don't let the music drown out your voice."

"Slow down, this ain't no race," he directed another time.

"Got damn you can play that thing. Don't know whether your voice or piano-playing is the best."

The banter remained the same... a few words before Selena disappeared on him until her next set. Annoying was how she characterized him, mostly rolling her eyes when he shouted out suggestions, but doing them all the same. Then the third week he didn't come. She did her three sets in silence except for the admiring applause of the growing crowd. *Yeah,* she thought, *he should be here to see how I please this audience without his guidance.*

"You're doing great, Selena," Manny complimented as he paid her.

"Yeah, because that heckler is gone." She counted her money and smiled.

"Who?"

"Old dude who came in a few weeks back."

"Zack?"

"I dunno his name."

"Zack Fluellen?"

"That's who that was?" Selena recalled his name as one of Star's favorites but she and Hoyt had seen him a couple of times at Itch's on Chicago's south side.

"You should consider yourself lucky. Know how many folks would love to be coached by him?" Manny locked his money back in the safe.

Selena stood there.

"He's probably out on the road or in New York at a recording session or maybe just at his own club around the corner...Devil's Cauldron on Basin. If he likes you, he'll be back. If not... you blew it."

For the next few weeks, Selena sang and played her heart out, to the adulation of the crowd, some of whom she recognized set after set. She was developing a following. "Old dude" Fluellen, never came back. One night between her sets she meandered around the corner to Devil's Cauldron and peeked in. Packed to the hilt, SRO which usually meant the owner was in residence, doing his thing. She slid in and stood in the back and watched him. *He must have at least ten years on me,* Selena thought, *but he was light years away from anyone I've ever heard on that sax.* Immediately, she realized that her husband and sister knew a real genius when they heard one.

"He better than Pax Peques any day," the man in front was saying as Selena decided to return to The Onyx.

"Selena Colson," Zack recognized from the stage. "Have you all heard this girl?" he asked his audience.

"She's around at The Onyx, but maybe we can get her to sing one for us before she leaves."

At the sound of her name, Selena froze, but the spotlight swung around and heated her up. She thawed and smiled, making her way to the stage.

She cut her eyes at Zack who grinned in answer.

"What should I do?"

"Anything you want. Woody, get up. She plays her own keys."

Selena sat on the bench and her fingers began picking at the black and whites.

"We ain't got all night," Zack gruffed, his audience laughed.

With that, "My mama done told me," Selena launched into "Blues in the Night" with a fierce, crowd-grabbing, church-going piano intro that got everybody clapping and finger-popping in sync and then showcased her voice … the crowd went wild.

"We went to church this evening," Zack said when she finished. "Thanks. Selena Colson around at the Onyx. Go check her out."

An elated Selena ran around the corner all the while thinking, that's the kind of club she wanted to be a part of. With that as an appetizer, Selena showed-out there for the next few weeks. In her element, she played wild and free while controlling her voice and the crowd.

Zack came into the Onyx from time to time. Selena never knew when but found herself excited when he showed up in the crowd and sat near her but didn't heckle as much.

"Missed your mouth the last couple of nights," she said.

"I got a business of my own." He took the offered drink. "'Sides you don't need my coaching anymore. You doin' all right."

"Folks can always improve."

"Zat right?" He threw back his drink. "Even me?"

"Even you."

"We'll see 'bout that."

One night at the Devil's Cauldron, Selena completed her song to thunderous applause and, bowing gracefully, she noticed a well-dressed woman coming towards her. Fast, furious with diamonds flashing and a fur stole wrapped around her upper body despite the hot and humid temperature.

"Selena Colson," she assaulted as Woody disappeared.

"Yes."

"Allow me to introduce myself. I am Lucille Fluellen."

"Ah. Nice to meet you."

"Zack Fluellen's *wife*."

"Oh?"

"Zack hasn't invited you to dinner yet so I thought I'd come and see his latest trick."

"I'm afraid there has been some misunderstanding. Zack is coaching me. That's all—"

"Oh, little girl, that's how it starts. You don't think you are the first one and you won't be the last. Of that I am sure."

Summoned from his office by Woody, Zack approached, "Lucille. You not supposed to be in here, unless you want the payments to stop."

"Don't you threaten me, Zack Fluellen," she continued, "I will never give you a divorce!"

"Ain't nobody asking for one." He nodded towards Woody and the bouncer who approached Lucille.

"That's right, get your coons to do your dirty work. Get your hands offa me." She jerked from their grip and proceeded out the door.

Selena stood frozen in her tracks, amazed. "Well," she finally said.

"Sorry 'bout that."

"A wife. Your wife. Interesting."

"And four kids so she says. I have doubts about the last two. You know, Momma's baby. Daddy's maybe."

"You take marriage vows lightly, Mr. Fluellen?" Selena asked.

"Guess it depends who's on the other end."

Selena stared at him.

"Lookit, until just now I haven't seen her in four, five years. She heard about you and is just marking her territory. Seems there are a lot of perks that go along with being my wife and she doesn't want them to stop. She's trying to scare you off. Did she?"

"Like I told her, and you already know—you are simply coaching me with my music and career. Nothing more."

"Zat right?" Zack's gaze held Selena's.

She was the first to blink.

~*~

They walked with their backs to the Calliope as directed. Two blocks west into an alley. The stifling heat concocted a strange brew, a stench of urine, garbage and discarded humanity stinging their senses as they trudged through the darkness in silence. The sound of their shoes echoed in the vacuous emptiness as they looked for the building. It had all been said and now, only the deed was left.

Zen stepped on a piece of broken glass. "Shit!"

"Here it is," Selena said.

They both looked at the unpainted door that had once been green, slightly off its hinge. A dog barked in the distance as they pushed the wood aside. They proceeded alongside the vacant shotgun house, sure that they were being observed. By whom they had no idea. The shed sat off-side in the back and Zen knocked quietly. The door creaked open as a black cat careened across their feet.

Selena and Zen eyed one another silently noting the bad omen.

"You know it's not too—"

"I'm doing this," Zen snapped in a whisper. Once inside a broken down discarded, blotchy, red couch sat on three legs. A couple of cockeyed, folding chairs and a few stained mattresses announced this was either a dope house or where teens stole sex-filled moments, hurriedly climaxing before straightening out their clothes and going on with their meaningless lives.

A woman appeared from a door they hadn't noticed. "I told you don't bring nobody."

"I needed—" Zen began.

"Who are you?" the bony woman assaulted Selena with harsh accusatory eyes.

"Nobody," Selena replied.

"A wise-ass, huh?" She pointed to the room behind her, a cigarette dangling from the side of her bulbous lips, painted a garish red like she was going dancing afterwards. "You stay here," she ordered Selena as Zen proceeded slowly towards a rickety green, Formica table holding a set of crude instruments. "Take off your drawers," the woman directed as she closed the door to hide the crime.

"Shit. Shit. Shit!!" Selena cursed and paced.

She'd argued it out with Zen for three days. They could take care of the baby. Zen's mother could add her baby in with her other grandchildren she kept. Zen countered with not wanting to bring a baby into this world without a father; to have it live in the projects and die in the streets. Finally, Zen told Selena she was doing it with or without her. It brought them to this day. This place. This hour. This horror. Her friend could die on that discarded Formica table or after she got home. Why can't Negro women get "taken care of" in a hospital like white girls? Have a "D and C." Or like Negro stars. She knew that the lifestyle of the musician scene produced many unexpected pregnancies, and very few babies. No stars she could think of had babies, but they had plenty of sex. They knew people. What about the common woman? The unconnected woman? Was she just supposed to have babies she wasn't prepared for? Make her bed and lie in it for the rest of her life. Mess up two human beings: mother and child.

The irony wasn't lost on Selena. She and Hoyt's much wanted baby ended in a mass of rejected cells in her toilet bowl and what was of Zen's unwanted, unplanned baby was being scraped from her uterus by filthy instruments which could render mother and embryo dead. *God got this one wrong.*

One of Papa Colt's sayings popped into her mind, "you can't live your life with 'what if's' and 'might could be's.'" "What if" their baby had lived then Hoyt wouldn't have gone overseas? "Might could be" the Colson family of three would be living in LeDroit Park right now and Selena would be spared this horrendous experience of helping a friend end the life of a child.

"All you got for sure is now," Papa Colt'd decreed. "Don't squander it."

Suddenly, Selena felt nauseous. Dizzy. Her head spun, she felt hot, her heartbeat raced faster and faster, and finally she barged through the prohibitive door.

"Stop!"

"What the hell? Get outta here!" the woman yelled.

224

"No. You get outta here," Selena shouted back and stepped forward toward her friend.

"What are you doing?" Zen yelled, sitting up, she burst into frustrated tears.

"I don't need this," the woman gathered up her utensils. "No refunds!"

"I can't have this baby, Selena. I can't." Anger turned to hysterical desperation.

"C'mon. It'll be alright. Let's go before we have company."

"I can't. I can't. I just can't…." Zen sobbed all the way back to Selena's room.

Once Zen slept, Selena slipped out and found Zack at his club. "He's upstairs," Woody told her.

Selena approached his apartment door and knocked quietly.

"Welcome said the spider to the fly," Zack grinned, and stepped back so she could walk in.

"Don't get happy."

"You come here uninvited? Not very lady-like, college girl." He watched her switch past him, admiring her form. "But since you're here. What can I fix you to drink?"

A pleasantly surprised Selena eyed his tasteful furnishings. A small, neat everything-in-its-place apartment.

"Cool your jets, old man. This is not a social call."

"And I thought you'd come to your senses."

Selena did an about face to look directly at him so he'd know she was not playing with him.

"If a girl were to get in an uncompromising situation and wanted to get out of it. Who would she see?"

"Talk English, college girl."

"You know what I'm asking."

He shook his head in utter disappointment. "I thought you were smarter than that."

"It's not for me, fool. I haven't slept with anyone since my husband," she said quietly. "For a friend."

"How far gone is this 'friend?'"

"Two, no more than three months tops."

"Where is she now?"

"My place."

Zack disappeared into the other room but Selena could hear him on the telephone as she feigned looking at his album collection. He returned. "It's all set. Take her to this address. The garage behind this house."

Selena glanced at the number written on the paper. "Pretty toney address."

"He's a real doctor. Abortions are illegal so you and your friend cannot—"

"We won't. We want this all behind us."

"Woody's waiting for you downstairs. He'll drive you."

Selena stopped by the door and turned, "Thank you."

"Glad I could help."

As Selena went downstairs, through the club and into the waiting car she thought, *of all the lessons she was learning, it's all about "who you know."*

That Old Black Magic

"Look at you," Zack approached her seated at the bar after she finished her last set. "You got all of Nawlins packing The Onyx just to see you."

"Not Devil's Cauldron," Selena teased of his club.

"They all eating outta your hand. 'Do no wrong' Selena." The bartender slid Zack his usual drink.

"This all you want? To be Big Time in Nawlins?"

"Not bad. Better than most," a pleased-with-herself Selena said.

"Who knows how far you could go if you stop Star-chasing."

"I'm not chasing stars."

"No, Star your sister. Stop trying to live her life. Do what she did." He took a swig of his drink. "You do what you want to do. Make your mark on music. You already have here but there's more out there."

"Suppose this is all I want?"

"Then you're done. Buy a club, open it up, get a house...New Orleans will be your home." He drained his drink and tapped the bar lightly for a refill. "You'd be content?" He eyed her and could almost see the wheels of her brain turning. "This is all very seductive. But is it enough?"

"Since you're so smart, old man, what do you suggest?"

He chuckled at the old man reference he hadn't heard in a while and continued, "You need to pay your dues. Go on the road. Get an appreciation for artistry. Cut your eye-teeth on the hardships; see what you are made of. Go to school... another type of education, college girl."

"I know how to do all that."

"No you don't. You playing with it. You got to declare it. Take it seriously. Claim it." He finished his second drink and hit up for another. "Besides you got to leave your fans now. Give 'em a chance to miss you. Can't miss you if you're always here." He swigged his drink and asked, "What do you do?"

"I am a singer... a damn good singer and a piano player."

"What do you want out of life? What's your wildest dream?"

Selena thought. Tucked her teeth over her bottom lip and said, "I want to own my own club."

"Named?"

"Selena's"

"Where?"

Selena paused only for a moment and said, "Paris. Paris, France."

As Selena sat in the middle of the bus amid all the men of the Lionel Hampton Band, she couldn't believe she'd done it. Were the seeds planted with her sister Star but she never said anything because that had been Star's dream? Was it solidified for her once she stepped foot into Maybelle's in East St. Louis with her cousin Butch? Where she first met the love of her life, Hoyt Colson? Had her dreams always run just beneath the surface of her life and not come full-throttle until Zack Fluellen asked her questions and she gave voice to them? She'd picked Paris, France because of Josephine Baker and Bricktop and all the other Negro stars that had sung the praises of Europe, but most importantly because she could visit Hoyt Colson's grave.

The route south stank as much as the pig intestines it was named after; The Chitlin' Circuit. Selena hated it. Being on the bus with a bunch of handsy men and only one other woman, the manager's wife who kept a watchful eye on their singer, but was not on duty most of the time, leaving Selena to fend for herself. Selena's reputation boarded the bus with her and she had no problem with the guys but the lack of available daily hygiene for herself and her companions annoyed her. Although she grew up in Texas, she was not familiar with whites serving food from the back of an establishment, if at all. Sometimes they seemed proud to say they "don't serve niggers," as if it were a badge of pure white superiority. Water, gas, food and accommodations had to be pre-planned to avoid such humiliation. She had her own room, but on two occasions only a chair propped against the doorknob served as her security. She longed for the places she and Hoyt stayed as they travelled the country, including Shanghai and Sugar Dee's in L.A.

230

Sometimes the food was so greasy it sat on top of her stomach and gave her diarrhea more times then she cared to admit. But the people. Her people, black people, were pure gold. When she sang before them, she quenched her thirst, fed her soul and made her heart sing. She often went over her time because only when on stage did she feel the trip was worth its while.

As Zack predicted, this "college girl's" education exploded. She'd picked up smoking if only to fit in, often lighting then just dangling the thin reed between two fingers to puff out every now and then. Her drink of choice, more coke than rum. She cursed with "damns and hells," working her way up to "shit's" but could not abide the other words. During their considerable down time, she learned to play cards, and, by the tour's end, took all the guys' money, mainly because she remained sober. Only one thing she couldn't understand... the sleeping around, single or married, bedding various women for sport. As if a religion, the sin was to go home alone on Friday and Saturday nights. So after the Friday night set, Selena found herself making her own way back to the hotel. She walked solo along the dimly lit street a few blocks. A car eased up beside her.

"Hey, pretty lady," it slowed to a stop. "Need a ride?"

Selena glanced over to decline and looked at a handsome, almost familiar face in a convertible. His hand flung across the seat he was offering.

"No, thank you."

"Oh, you'd rather take a chance with the Klan."

Selena stopped. Although poorly lit where she stood, she looked ahead at the long stretch of dark woods before lights could be seen again in the distance.

"What they could do with a pretty Negro lady like you."

"I'm going to the Hotel Zanzibar."

He reached over and popped open the door, "Get in."

Selena got in and closed the car door, wondering if she should ask the man to put his top up.

"Pax Peques," he offered by way of introduction.

Ah, yes, Selena thought. *Pax "the sax" Peques, the man that Mazeda, Sugar Dee and countless other females drooled over at Itch's Club in Chicago.* Selena hadn't recalled him being this good-looking before, but she was in the company of her super-handsome husband Hoyt at the time and only had eyes for him.

"Selena—"

"I know you. You don't think I just pick up any brown-skinned beauty do you?"

The term made her think of Star.

"You can wail, girl!"

"Thank you."

"Caught you a few times in Nawlins."

"At The Onyx?"

"Naw. Zack's place."

Selena smiled as those "in-the-know" always referred to the Devil's Cauldron as Zack's Place.

"I got to make a quick stop."

232

"I got to watch you and the Klan too?"

"Got to get the baby's milk home. You gonna meet my Mama. Not many women can say that."

"Lucky, me."

The car pulled down a secluded road. Selena didn't relax until a two–story, white frame house came into view. She followed Pax and the porch light through the front screen door. Selena stood in the hallway of a modest, neat and clean entry which reminded her of Colt, Texas in miniature.

Pax handed an older woman the milk and both disappeared into the kitchen. In the dining room by the table a little voice blew bubbles, letting the stranger know she was not alone.

When Selena made eye contact, the baby threw up her arms.

"Hi, pretty baby," Selena whispered, bending to lift the little girl from the play pen. The baby looked at Selena, blew spit-bubbles and smiled. "Look at those chubby-cheeks."

"Hello," the woman said entering the room. "I'm Mrs. Peques. Paxton's mother. The reverend's wife."

"Pleased to meet you," Selena replied.

"You have a name?"

"Yes, ma'am. Selena Colson."

Mrs. Peques all but ignored Selena as she went for the baby in her arms. "And this is my precious KiKi. I have your bottle."

"She's a beautiful baby," Selena said.

"Yes. She is. Yes, she is," she repeated as the little girl settled into her arms. "I can say that. She's my grandbaby."

As Pax returned to the room, the little girl broke suction with her bottle and identified, "Da Da."

"Hey, baby girl. Jury's still out on that one. Ma is my white shirt pressed?"

"Upstairs." She watched her son disappear up the steps. "I love that boy with all my might, but he is spoiled rotten. I can say that but I better not hear nobody else degrade him. Wasn't me or his Dad's fault. Women. Won't leave him alone and he is all too anxious to oblige as many as he can." She looked back at the baby and kissed her forehead. The baby smiled.

"He'd have a real go with this baby's mother, but he's too blind and young to see. Be a good husband once he finishes running. Truth is I don't know if the woman's been born who can settle him down."

"Where is she now?" Selena asked. "The mother?"

"She works Monday through Fridays at the shirt factory next county over. Can't keep a baby over there and don't make enough money for day care. Mother comes home Friday nights and leaves either Sunday night or Monday morning to go back to her one room. I dread the day she can afford a small apartment and day care and takes my baby away from me."

Selena thought of Zen. No matter how much you love your child and want the best for her... life can just beat you down. Selena'd pointed out the pros and cons,

234

but, once made, never questioned her friend's decision. Clearly, Zen didn't have the support this baby did. She'd never mentioned who the father of her baby was. This grandmother loved this little girl unlike Zen's mother who'd have just added her baby to her four other grandchildren she already took care of.

Zen could've gotten her own room, but who would have cared for the baby while she was at work? Selena wondered and said, "That's very nice of you."

"She's my grandbaby. Aren't you, sweetie?"

"My bleeding heart mother." Pax came down the steps. "Not your baby, Ma."

"Should be. We can give her a good stable life. I'll work on that. Right Kiki? Huh? That's my sweet baby."

"She had all boys," Pax interjected, disappearing through the dining room into the kitchen again.

"You seem to be a decent girl," Mrs. Peques offered. "He's a good man, will settle down and make a great husband and father …someday. Can't say when that'll be. So you just bide your time—"

"Oh no," Selena interrupted. "We just met. He was just giving me a ride to my hotel."

"Um Humm. That's how it starts, sweetie."

"Ready?" Pax returned, chomping down on a chicken leg.

"Pax," his mother admonished his bad manners.

"Yes." Selena stood. "Bye chubby-cheeks," she said. "It was very nice meeting you, Mrs. Peques."

"Nice meeting you as well," she managed before looking back into her granddaughter's loving eyes. "Remember what I said. You seem like a nice girl."

Pax looked from his mother to Selena and back again. "What's that all about?"

"Women-folk talk," his mother dismissed.

This time Pax opened the car door and asked, "Where to now?"

"The Hotel Zanzibar. I'm beat."

~*~

Selena's tour ended in New York City. Too dark-complexioned to be a Specialty Singer at the Cotton Club, she accepted the gig at The Savoy Ballroom where she and Ella Fitzgerald sang with Chick Webb's band and did a stint with Earl Hines band at the Apollo; Billy Eckstine sharing the vocals with Dizzy Gillespie on far left and Charlie Parker on far right. Selena Colson on piano. While staying at the Hotel Theresa, Zack called to welcome her back and offered his apartment on Edgecombe Avenue on Sugar Hill, in Harlem until she could find her own.

"Oooh, high-cotton," Selena teased over the phone. "You all must have some at-home jam sessions with Duke Ellington, Count Basie, Coleman Hawkins, Johnnie Hodges—"

"Lena Horne and Joe Louis," he interrupted. "But that's up at 555 Edgecombe. I have a more toney address at 409. I live in the 'mythic center of the Harlem Renaissance.' Although Stephanie St. Clair, the numbers

Queen of Harlem, lived there back in the twenties we now have judges, Thurgood Marshall and W.E.B Dubois to name a few. We're the quieter, more sophisticated sister. "

"Oh, forgive my faux pas," Selena relented.

"You making a real name for yourself. Playing with the right people, making good contacts. That's how you work it."

"And friendships."

"Uh huh. But the offer of my crib is just to you, Selena. I don't want no other folk up in there."

"Will you be there?" Selena tested. 'Cause I don't want no junk and jive."

"Don't flatter yourself. I'll be in L.A. A friend of mine is opening a club on Central Avenue and while there I'll be recording with Miles Syphax at Capitol."

"He didn't tell me that."

"You talked to him?"

"He's an old friend and called with condolences when Hoyt passed."

"Well, he was tired of the traveling and he could help out the teetering company."

"If anyone can, he can."

" I'll get the super to let you into my apartment and give you a key."

"Thanks. It shouldn't take me long to find a spot."

"What's with this language, college girl? 'Don't want no junk and jive,' 'spot'. What else you learn on the road?"

"That was the reason I went, right?"

"Umph," he grunted in his familiar style.

"How many 'spots' do you have anyway?"

"Enough. Home is here in Nawlins, 409 Edgecombe and one in Chicago. I need a secure place for my instruments, music and what-have-yous so I don't have to worry about stuff being stolen since I'm away for months at a time."

"Nice problem to have." She waved at a customer. "Where are you staying in L.A.?"

"Either The Dunbar Hotel on Central with everybody else or at Shanghai and Sugar Dee's."

"They're old friends too—"

"Of course they are."

Selena laughed. She'd talked to Sugar Dee before she left on tour.

"Seems that's the place to be and The Satin Doll is the new club to be and be seen. Gonna be upscale and tight. Give Club Alabam a run for its money."

"Uh huh."

"I ain't kidding about having company over my place, Selena. Nobody needs to know where I live and no visitors."

"Your secret's safe with me," she said and added. "Thanks."

"One more thing… I wouldn't just show up at my pad 'cause you're there. When I come, you'll want me there. Later." He hung up leaving Selena holding the receiver.

Cocky old man, she thought with a grin.

Selena only stayed at Zack's for two weeks before she found her own place on St. Nichols, also in Sugar Hill. A three-story, one-bedroom brownstone walk-up, nicely furnished, a little pricey, but she was making good, steady money at The Savoy and pop-up gigs at the Apollo and needed a safe place to stay. She missed the mood music of the USO Canteens because folks at The Savoy Ballroom were into jump and jive; lindy hopping gave way to the jitterbug, showing off their dancing prowess that did not include laying up against a slow moving brother grinding all night. Energetic, fun and lively with the occasional fight out front for those who couldn't get in. Too professional to try out for Amateur Night at the Apollo, she counted some of the former winners like Sarah Vaughn, Ella Jane Fitzgerald, Billie Holiday, Dinah Washington and Pearl Bailey, as friends.

At a post-show jam session, she and some girlfriends sought a little peace and quiet at an after-hours club. While sitting quietly Pax Peques entered; tall, lean, suave and debonair.

"Park his shoes under my bed any time... day or night," one woman said, eyeing him like a fine cut of meat hanging in a butcher shop window.

"He has," the other woman reminded.

"I couldn't keep him interested."

"Some men are meant to roam. He's a fine, gypsy, mothafu—"

He sidled up to the table and greeted the women, "Ladies" and then focused on Selena. "Good to see you again."

"And you," Selena replied coyly, sipping her drink.

The other girls eyed her in awe.

"So, how do you two know each other?" a curious third woman asked.

"Selena and I go way back. She's met my mama," Pax teased. "May I have this dance?" He held out his hand.

As Selena's taffeta dress rustled past the ladies, one remarked, "Ain't that a blip?"

"You look smashing in that midnight blue," he intoned into her ear as he held her tightly.

"So I'm told."

The less interested she seemed, the more he came around. She supposed men like him were used to having women fall all over them. She presented a challenge. Still, she was willing to play with him knowing she wouldn't keep his interest any more than other women had. Selena's popularity soared; as a free agent, she did gigs along the 52nd Street corridor: 3 Deuces, Club Downbeat and Minton's Playhouse up on 118th. Often Pax Peques escorted her to various chic parties and one night when he dropped her off he asked, "Mind if I come in?"

In one swoop her eyes fell over his frame; she looked at him and surprised herself by saying, "Why not? I thought you'd never ask."

"I was being a gentleman."

"Don't go changing on me now, Pax the sax.'"

Fortified with standing ovations earlier that night and three drinks of rum and coke, Selena felt as if she were playing a part in a Micheaux movie. She didn't know who she was supposed to be, but she knew she hadn't been loved in almost two years and she was ready. No disrespect to Hoyt intended. She smiled in thinking he was saying to her, "Damn, Lena. It's about time." Like her, Hoyt knew it was all physical. Pax or any man could have her body, but Hoyt always held her heart and soul.

On this night Selena wore a gold yellow silk dress that hit all her curves and shone brightly against her dark skin.

"I think I like you in this color best of all," Pax said as she sauntered to the Hi Fi and let a record drop.

"Zat right," she said a la' Zack Fluellen.

"I'm partial to the dark-skinned beauties."

"Really?" She turned toward him and held out her hand for a dance. "Why is that?"

"You know everybody got preferences." He gathered her into his embrace. "I like to see the color difference between them and me."

Selena reared back. "You not considering yourself high-yella, are you?"

"Low-tan, maybe. Most folks think I'm Puerto Rican on my daddy's side."

"How'd they get that idea?"

"I mighta told them."

"Why would you want to be anything but what you are?" she asked.

"How long have you lived in America?" He kissed her lips quickly and slid his hot hands up and down her torso. "You breakin' the mood."

"Do tell." Selena murmured as her body fell into a rhythmic sync with his.

"Got that right," he managed just as he slid his wet-sticky tongue into her waiting, hungry mouth.

Selena suckled it like she'd thirsted for years. His lips tasted vaguely of gin and fruit juice. He smelled of faded cologne and ...man. Of want and need and convenience. His hands traveled up and down her spine eliciting the unquenchable feel of long-buried desire. Everywhere he touched, longing blossomed under his magical fingertips. Intense, familiar yet intangible. Why have it appear full-force if there were no chance of resurrecting the authentic feeling of long ago? When you loved and were loved as she was by Hoyt Colson, there was no hope of recapture.

Pax's hand expertly separated her bra from her skin and he buried his head between her breasts and masterfully devoured her nipples, so he demanded center stage in place of her past remembrances. He returned to her lips as he carried her to the bed and deftly applied a latex sheath then he began to trace her body from her lips, to navel to hairy triangle and she writhed in reaction to, not the neglect, of all the attention she received. He caressed, played with and toyed with her like the

242

showman he was, bringing her to the brink, yet postponing their consummation. Then he presented her with his love muscle posturing it for her admiration before seeking and melting into her throbbing orifice. They twisted and turned while he murmured all the correct and admiring words with increased thrusting intensity. He came with her only seconds behind. Her never-involved heart watched, but once her mind returned to her body she noticed how the two lay in a puddle of their own heat, she noticed his attention to foreplay, as if her pleasurable gratification was part of his performance. She admired his attention to detail, pleasantly surprised at his well-endowed maleness. He was a man who enjoyed and knew how to please a woman. He liked sharing himself and receiving praise for his expert loving. Satisfaction satiated, she realized that she'd never find a man to love her as Hoyt had, and that she in turn would never love as she had because that level of loving required exclusive trust. But she lay there as the pulsating subsided and the razzle dazzle passed. Her singular thought was "he'll do."

Tea for Two

Lorette and Hepburn Culhane relished their newly wedded bliss as only a married couple starting out their new life could. Hep carried Lorette over the threshold of their new one-bedroom apartment in the quiet section of Watts. They'd spent just a weekend in Niagara Falls as a honeymoon, saving New York City for later, and Hep began his studies at UCLA. He engaged in his courses while Lorette busied herself with making their new abode comfortable and homey, staying within the budget necessary for them to achieve their goals. Hep, disappointed that Lorette preferred to join him next semester, couldn't complain as she doted on him hand and foot when at home. She cleaned and went to the grocery and had meals waiting for him when he came home from school and before he left for his evening security job.

On the weekends, they shopped for furniture and frills to make their home just as she pictured it. Besides the wedding gifts shipped from Evelyn, mostly linens and kitchen utensils, they purchased a Mediterranean bedroom suite with two lamps for the night stands. Slowly they added a couch, a coffee and end tables as well as a kitchen table which doubled as his desk when he didn't go to the library. Hep relieved and ecstatic when he'd made the Dean's List as he didn't' know how the curriculums at Northwestern and Fisk had prepared him for UCLA. He'd never imagined and was pleasantly surprised at his wife's interest in lovemaking which seemed to be her central focus and recreation when he was around. When he'd tried studying at home, she always tempted and distracted which finally sent him to the library as his only hope. He had no idea the innocent, reserved Lorette Javier Culhane would be an adventurous, insatiable and avid partner in all respects. He smiled, remembering the previous night when she placed three strategic bows on her person and declared she was the dessert for the night. He'd bought her a television with a stand for the living room but it did not hold her attention as she seemed far more interested in them entertaining one another in color over the black and white box. Her sexual appetite brimmed with curiosity and enthusiasm and he had no complaints. He smiled remembering his buddy Range, "If you want to be happy for the rest of your life marry a virgin. She don't know whether you're good, bad or otherwise." He wondered what Range would have thought of Lorette.

Hep lit a cigarette, more habit than need, and walked across the beautiful campus marveling at how breathtakingly beautiful California was, reminding him of the Italy he saw and surely the Tuscany he never did but Tavio had so aptly described. He knew back home in Texas, Mother Nature painted the leaves in autumnal colors before dropping them to the ground, providing a crunchy carpet beneath your feet accompanied by air with a snap to it. Hep noticed the number of males in attendance but he didn't know their circumstances any more than they knew his. As the war raged on, Hep kept up with the Allies' effort, aware of the postponement of The Italian Campaign that he and Tavio Orsini helped plot, the latter paying for it with his life. He stopped and looked on the bulletin board for a more fulfilling part-time job than the one he currently held. Anxious to finish himself and have Lorette join him and complete her education still reigned as the supreme goal for him. He'd promised his father-in-law that she'd get her degree like the four other Javier girls. Hep smiled at the thought of his wife. He supposed this feeling was what his father meant when he said, "marry with the mind and your heart will come along." "If you choose someone logically, the folly will follow." Range always used the wrong head in his selection process, but his buddy had no intention of marrying before he was thirty when he'd pick a twenty-year-old wife. Hep chuckled. Funny how Hep never thought of Lorette as a lover as his father probably never thought of his mother, but it all worked out. "If it don't, at least you haven't loss nuthin but time. Your heart can stay intact," Papa Colt'd told him.

Hep jotted down the announcement from the Los Angeles Police Department and wondered if they hired blacks. Good salary, paid holidays, health plan, everything a young couple would need, but Lorette wouldn't go for the life-on-the-line danger. He thumbtacked it back to the cork board; they had their plans on track and it didn't include any detours. He glanced at his watch; it was their three-month anniversary and he had just enough time to stop by the florist to get three, long-stemmed red roses. He'd get thorn-less, as he wondered where she'd stick them.

Using Halloween decorations, Lorette put the finishing touches on the table setting to celebrate their month-anniversary in paradise. The Velvet Crumb Cake made from a Bisquick box recipe perfumed the apartment. The couple's mutual reprieve for independence occurred when he studied and she attempted to expand her cooking expertise. She'd never learned since Annie performed all the domestic duties growing up, freeing her mother to dote on her five girls; going on every field trip, volunteering at school, at church, and going shopping with her daughters, always in need of something. The Duchess held fundraising teas in the front parlor seemingly every other Saturday. Lorette never thought it would be her mother she'd emulate. Of course, she supposed she'd have to wait until her second child to get "help" at home, wondering when they'd be able to afford it, certainly not while Hep was a student. They'd need someplace for the help to sleep. No place in a one-bedroom apartment. No place for her parents, sisters, their families or Effie and Gay Iris to visit them either. Shanghai and Sugar Dee's was out of the question!

As her best friends continued their college pursuits, Lorette reveled in her marital status, trying not to gloat that she'd indeed grabbed the brass ring in the carousel of life. Being Hep's wife fulfilled her in indescribable ways, even better than she thought it would be. Not only his phenomenal love making which she thoroughly enjoyed, but his patience with her cooking experiences, enduring all the mistakes and often offering to pick up something on his way home from school. Cooking was not the disaster that ironing was for her, scorching most of his white dress shirts with an iron tattoo. Washing at the laundromat proved easy enough but she didn't like using public machines available to anyone with a quarter. The phone rang. "Hello?"

"What you doing, girl?" Gay Iris asked.

"Being happy. What about you?" Lorette asked as she arranged the brown and serve rolls on the baking sheet.

"Only been three months. Give it time," Gay Iris teased. "Oh, Effie is going to Europe on a study abroad program. Brussels, Belgium and Vienna, Austria."

"Who knew you could piano-play your way to Europe?"

"All expenses paid, college credit and exposure."

The friends chatted affably until Hep stuck his key in the door.

"Oh, my handsome husband is home," she told Gay Iris, accepting a peck on the lips from Hep. "Ah! For me? He brought me flowers and a bottle of wine." Hep went

248

to change his clothes and wash his hands. "Gay Iris says 'Hi'."

Hep waved, disappearing into the bathroom.

"Gotta go," Lorette said abruptly.

"Don't do anything I wouldn't do!"

"You have no idea. Bye."

"Something smells good," Hep said, returning to their dinette table. "Looks good too."

"All for you. Since you didn't want a pumpkin pie." She sidled up in front of him. "How was your day?"

"Better now." He leaned in for a long languid kiss, his nature predictably rising seeking expression.

Surrounding the vase of red roses, they dined on lemon chicken, mashed potatoes and peas and carrots. She, giddy with happiness, and he, satisfied that their shared goals were of the utmost importance. After dessert, they talked quietly. "Do you miss not being in class like your girlfriends?"

"Not at all. I have what they are all looking for."

"I have something for you."

"Really," Lorette's eyes glazed over and she clapped her hands like a child receiving a Christmas gift.

Hep presented her with a paper folded in thirds. He smiled and said, "An application for the second semester."

Her smile even brighter, she countered with, "we're going to have a baby!"

Let Them Talk

The sun stepped through the window and jarred Selena awake with its blaze. She staggered to the window to let down the shade and turned around. There lay Pax Peques sprawled across her bed. *Looking fine even in his sleep,* she thought, admiring his form.

"Hey," he rolled over and drew back the covers exposing his soldier, swollen and standing at attention. "Get in here. Let's continue."

"Bathroom," Selena said, pointing and left.

She relieved herself, washed her hands and looked at her image in the mirror. She looked a fright. *I can't date a man who looks better than me,* she thought, as she tried running a comb through her short, rough hair and, after a few tries, smoothed it out enough to be presentable. *Where's Sugar Dee when you need her.* No matter how long she stayed in this bathroom she knew her hair was not going to change into a grade better than Pax Peques. They'd sweated it out with last night's loving. She decided to brush her teeth while there. She wasn't greedy but it'd been so long since her bell had been rung, she reasoned, why not. No harm, no foul and with Pax Peques, always latex protection. Neither of them were going to fall in love. Both incapable for different reasons, but both had needs.

Selena had a brand new boyfriend. Pax Peques dated the star of the hour. Great publicity for both. After about three weeks, Selena learned of Pax's birthday and, on her day off, decided to cook for him and have an intimate party-for-two at home. She called his mother for his food favorites and dressed in all white which accented her skin perfectly. She'd bought naughty undies intending herself for dessert with a can of whip cream by the nightstand. With the lights dim and the music low, she sat by the beautifully set table, not lighting the candles until he came.

He never did. At three a.m., she chucked it all and went to bed. At about 8, he slithered in the door and slid into bed beside her like he belonged there.

"Where were you?" she sprang up like a Jack-in-the-Box who couldn't stand his lying beside her.

"What? It was my birthday."

"I know. I cooked for you. Had a small surprise birthday party planned for you."

"I guess the 'surprise' was on you." He chuckled.

"You think this is funny?"

"Oh, c'mon, Selena. I didn't know. Everybody wanted to buy me drinks. We hung out—"

"Did it ever occur to you to call me so I could join you? I am your girl."

"My girl," he repeated. "What are we? In high school?"

"Are you drunk?"

"Little bit." He held up his fingers separated by an inch.

Selena flew into the bathroom and came out dressed.

"Where you going?" he asked.

"Out."

Adored and treated as a queen by two men: her father then her husband, Selena had no experience in dealing with a selfish, spoiled, good-looking man who held little regard for anyone not named Pax Peques. And if her husband had lived, she would still be spared this ordeal. She wasn't used to being the last consideration with men or women. She recalled returning to Colt, Texas after Hoyt's death and how far apart she, Francie Bivins and Delilah, her old friends and bridesmaids, had grown. Both married with children and very happy with their lives, Selena had little in common with her old pals who'd taken different paths. Selena'd offered them an all-expenses paid weekend to see her in New York but their husbands nixed it. They were Colt, Texas guys, happy with their wives at home and providing for their families. Like her father was. Selena could not fault them. Her daddy wouldn't want her mother to go off to spend a weekend in New York with an old friend. Strangely, Selena'd suffocate in a town like Colt, Texas. The home that had nurtured her, taught her, seemed small-time and cloying. Francie said it best when she admitted "it's like you've become Star. You went away and became this singer on the radio and in records and came back here to see us." That'd not been Selena's intention, but it happened. Cosmic forces beyond her control. Her husband'd set it in motion. He saw in her and Hep more. He showed them more. Hoyt gave them a curiosity for the world beyond their birthplace. She had Hoyt to thank for so much. But still, Selena missed her girlfriends. No one could take their place.

She'd call Sugar Dee, but with the time difference it'd be impolite. Besides, if Zack were still out there working in the new club, she didn't need him getting wind of this affair with Pax. She'd talked to Mazeda a few times a month trying to convince her to come for a visit but Mazeda had no taste for New York or New Orleans and had become comfortable waiting for Mil Yarborough's return; the dissolution of her friendship with Zen had been her biggest hurt. She'd stood by Selena since the moment she went to Nawlins and then when Selena had the opportunity to be a real friend to her... Zen closed up and off. Selena'd called a number of times but Zen's mother always said, "She's out," or "can't come to the phone right now."

With Pax left in her bed, that night, Selena went straight to The Savoy and changed into one of the gowns kept there. She opened the door to her dressing room and couldn't get in for all the flowers strewn about the room. Fragrant, abundant and gorgeous all with the same card, "I'm sorry Selena, baby. Love, Pax." Everyone was terribly impressed.

Selena was not.

Later, they'd made up in grand style. Breathlessness their only conversation for the moments to follow.

I'm going to have to buy one of those stove-top pressing combs if I'm going to continue this relationship with Pax, she thought, as she rolled from his nimble, fine body in satisfied ecstasy. Her hair and entire body, one big sweat-wad.

"You are a wild woman!" Pax proclaimed as he made his way to the bathroom, smacking her firm, bare butt.

Selena lit up a cigarette as she covered her breasts.

He came back, plopped on the bed, laying on her stomach. His hair wet as he often ducked his head under the spigot to rinse out the perspiration from his face and head. Naturally straight without conk or pressing comb, he still had nothing on the "good-haired Criquis of Colt, Texas." She longed to tell everybody so impressed with his locks about the family back home with hair straighter, shinier and prettier than any white folk they'd seen. Selena still puzzled as to why folks out here remained so preoccupied with hair texture and skin color.

I guess there are just some things I'll never figure out, she thought, like the deaths of Hoyt and Range.

"We going to Dinah's party?" Pax asked.

"Want to?"

"Hell, yeah. I'm going." He looked up at her. "Pick you up after your last set?"

"Yep."

Selena not only appeared at the party but was coaxed into a jam session, paired vocally with her buddy, Ella; a scat-off which Ella easily won. "I give!" Selena teased, throwing up her hands and mock-bowing to her friend.

Beat, Selena begged off, leaving Pax partying with the best of them. At about 4 a.m., he came into the apartment followed by a bunch of folks. "What's going on?" Selena asked, pulling on her robe, as one guest flipped on the Hi Fi, another went into the refrigerator, another took a "whiz" in the bathroom and the last one flopped on the couch.

"Had to bring the party here," Pax said, as he took off the dining room table centerpiece to set up poker chips.

"I'm tired, Pax."

"We won't bother you none," he dismissed.

"Why not go to your house," Selena asked him quietly.

"Oh, that's cold. Baby, don't be like that. We'll be quiet."

"Get the *hell* outta my house!" she yelled, stopping everyone in their tracks. She looked at them individually. "You want to try me?" she challenged, nostrils flaring.

They all scrambled, like a vaudeville comedy routine, and piled out the door.

Pax looked at her.

"You too," she advised. Her eyes bore into him until he complied.

She double-bolted the front door, closed the bedroom door behind her, jumped between the sheets while grabbing her sleep mask.

Later that day, after finishing her conversation with Sugar Dee, she'd passed Zack the phone without asking Selena.

"Hey," he'd said.

"Hey," she answered straightening up to talk to him, not knowing why. "You're staying in the best place in L.A."

"I agree. You need to come on out here," he gruffed.

"I was thinking about that. I need to visit my brother and his wife."

"Cool."

"I'm going to stop through Chicago and see Mazeda. It's been awhile."

"Bring her," Zack advised.

"It'll be a miracle if I can pry her away. The change would be good."

"See you when you get here."

Selena hung up the telephone just as Pax walked in.

"Who dat?"

"Not for you," Selena said and looked at him. "Pax, what do you want out of life?"

"I got the life I want."

Selena showed her impatience.

"What? Where'd that come from?" he asked.

"Where do you want to be in five, ten years?"

"Alive."

Selena looked at him. "Do you want to travel? Own your own club? Buy a house?"

"I ain't got nothin' to prove to nobody. Just making a living and having fun. That's what life is all about."

I think your parents disagree, she thought.

Selena'd finished her full-time stint at The Savoy and was attracted to California, the land of opportunity. Hep loved it.

In two days, finally making up her mind, she took her suitcase from storage and checked her wardrobe; what she needed to get cleaned. What she needed to buy. Dropping her earring, she got on all fours and stuck her hand under the bed. She withdrew an earring. Not hers. She didn't have pierced ears. She, like her mama, felt God gave her all the holes needed.

When Pax came home whistling, the affable mood changed immediately when she held up the cheap, silver earbob. For effect, Selena dangled it between two fingers.

Pax first expression was "Oh," like "you found it." Quickly changed to "Oooh..." like "Oh shit!"

"You've been in this bed with another woman," Selena stated clearly.

"Naw. Baby. I think that belongs to the cleaning woman."

"She doesn't have pierced ears either." She rose. He backed away. "No more sugar in this shaker for you. Get your shit and go."

"Now Selena. We need to talk this out. She felt sick and I said my place—"

"*Your* place? This has never been *your* place. Gimme my key." Selena held out her hand, palm side up. "Put it in this brown-skinned hand and get out."

"So this is the way it ends?"

"Exactly how it ends. I have no further use for a sorry excuse of a bitch-raised man like you."

"Don't talk about my mama."

"She'd be so proud of her baby boy."

"You'll be sorry." Bravado claimed him as he dropped the key into her palm.

"I already am."

He left, flippant, arrogant and sauntered down the steps. "There's more of you waiting in line. You ain't that special."

With that Selena opened up the closet and took his expensive suits to the window. Opened the glass barrier and tossed his suits high up into the air so they fluttered down just as he hit the front door.

"Here! You forgot something!"

His clothes rained down and landed on the iron fence, the cement stoop, the patch of grass and into the dog doo on the sidewalk. Selena went and got more stuff: his toiletries, his after shave, his pomade, and cufflinks which fell with a cheap, hollow rattle on the hood of a parked car as his cologne smashed on a trash can and stunk up the entire neighborhood. A crowd formed and began laughing which vexed Pax "the sax"

Peques. A roving reporter from "The Amsterdam News" captured it all and for three days, big, bold headlines later read: **"No Reason to Come Back!" "Who's Playing the Blues Now?" "Pax the Sax Sent Packing."**

The Best Is Yet To Come

The shrill bell summoned Sugar Dee to her front door, the California sun rendering the image before her in an unrecognizable silhouette on the other side of her sheers. When she saw her friend through the side plate-glass transom she couldn't open the door fast enough.

"Girl!" She tackled Selena in a bear hug and held on for dear life. "You are a sight for sore eyes. I didn't think you were coming."

When Selena managed to take a breath she said, "I had to detour and picked you up something special."

Selena stepped aside.

Mazeda popped into view. "Surprise!"

"Oh my God!" Sugar Dee repeated the same gesture. "How'd you get her way from Chicago?"

"Wasn't easy. Now, you have to convince her stay,"

Selena laughed as Sugar Dee took her back into the embrace. Holding each of her friends on either side she couldn't believe how much she'd missed them both. "Am I crying? Shit! I'm so damn happy." She let go and looked at them again and then said, "Well c'mon in. Shanghai! Shanghai!!" she yelled.

"Went on a liquor run," a familiar voice shouted back.

"Oh yeah. Forgot that fast. Mazeda Yarborough. I'm so glad to see you, girl. You hungry? Tired? Need to lay down?"

Selena watched the old friends catch up without uttering a word and sauntered into the kitchen. As she poured herself a glass of tea she eyed the high palm trees, the clear blue sky and the way the sun slanted on the Spanish-tiled roof of the garage. Her brother'd settled there for a reason. Los Angeles was seductive. She moseyed out onto the back porch.

"Hello stranger," greeted from below.

On the patio, seated at a table in the shade surrounded by peanuts and their shells sat Zack Fluellen.

"I thought I heard a voice I knew," Selena said as she began her slow descent down the stairs. "This is a publicity moment. The Great Zack Fluellen eating goobers at Shanghai and Sugar Dee's. An Afro-American Daily Newspaper moment"

"I'm just regular folk." He pushed the peanuts towards her. "Of course, it's nothing like that piece on you and Pax in *The Amsterdam News*," he teased.

"Hummm," was all an embarrassed Selena could say. "That got all the way out here?"

"Are you kidding? Not only on billboards but folks sent clippings of it." Zack laughed. Selena offered a tight smile. "A woman finally gave Pax his walking papers? Men and woman cheered you on. You got quite a reputation. A following. Becoming a legend. Free publicity."

Selena sat and sipped her refreshing ice tea.

"Ninety days of my life I'll never get back," she muttered.

"You gave him eighty-nine more than I thought."

Selena cut her eyes at him.

"I'm just jivin' you, college girl."

"I really messed up."

"Somebody die?"

"It was a mistake. My mistake for taking up with the likes of him."

"There are no mistakes. Only lessons."

"Yeah, so I've heard," she recognized her daddy's saying and countered, "Don't make him a priority when you are just his option."

"Now you know the type of cat to avoid."

"Sax players?" Selena joked.

"One apple don't spoil the whole bunch." He shelled another peanut. "The only 'mistake' is if you haven't learned your lesson and keep picking the same kinda man over and over again."

"On no. I'm a quick study. I'm done with smooth, good-looking, ladies-men who don't think the sun shines until they get up." She took a peanut and cracked it with her fingers. Selena recalled the wonderful two men at the beginning of her life and wasn't settling for scraps now. "I learned it takes a mighty good man to beat having no man at all."

"Can do bad all by yourself, huh?"

"His mama tried to tell me."

"His mama? He took you home to meet his mama in ninety days? You must got some good—"

"I ran into him when we gigged at the Red Bird Café in Frenchtown Tallahassee, Florida. He gave me a ride is all. At the time." Selena crossed her legs. "Had a baby there I think was his; although neither of them said directly. Cutest little girl." Selena smiled. "I was in a tough place. The baby made me think of Zen's baby and then of Zen. How much I missed my friend. Talking to her. Bouncing things off of her."

"You all been out of touch?"

"Yeah," Selena sighed.

"How long?"

"Too long and I don't understand it. After you helped out with that …situation, I thought that'd make us tighter than ever. That we shared that bad time will make it on to the good. Can't get a hold of her to even have it out. She avoids my calls."

"Well, Selena, everything isn't always about you."

Selena looked over at him.

"Sometimes it's about the other person. What she's going through. Must've been hard to find out you're pregnant and alone; to battle with the decision to have the baby or not. Abortion. Have it. Or give it up for adoption. It's all a bad scene."

Selena shook her head and looked away.

"And maybe after all you went through to give her what she wanted and it was over…she's still wrestling with it. Was it the right thing to do? I'd think a woman would think on it all the time. And you're just a reminder of that bad time she's trying to forget. You didn't have the experience. Didn't have to make the decision for yourself. You get to go on with your life. Your career."

Selena absorbed and weighed each word. "Never thought about it like that."

"Might could be she'll either come around or not. Nothing you can do about it, but be there if and when she does."

Selena looked at the skyline over the garage's red-tiled mosaic roof.

"Everybody who *comes* with you, Selena, can't *go* with you." He hunched his shoulders. "That's life."

She looked at him then down at her fingertips.

"Folks come into your life for a reason, a season or a lifetime. Maybe Zen came and taught you what you needed to know and moved on."

~*~

From the kitchen window above, Mazeda eyed Selena and Zack and asked Sugar Dee, "What's happening down there?"

"Dunno exactly. But something is," Sugar Dee said, smiling at the couple below. "Don't want to spook them by drawing attetion to them. Let's leave them be. You got more *pressing* problems."

"I do?" Mazeda became distracted.

"What's going on with them edges, girl? Let me work my magic."

~*~

"You know you'd make a good girlfriend," Selena said, draining the last of her ice tea.

"What?" Zack feigned mock-indignation. "Not the role I was going for."

"Got a cigarette?" She asked more as a diversion.

Zack obliged.

"So what have you been up to?"

"Same ol', same-ol'. Nat and I finished the album; should be another hit. Met his new wife."

"Really?"

"Maxine was ten years his senior."

"I know you're not talking about age, old man."

"It's different when the old one is the female."

"Negro, please."

"He wants children."

"Do I know her?"

"Anita Chatman used to sing with various bands."

"You like her?"

"I don't have to. Nat's crazy about her. A bit hincty for my taste."

"He's a good guy. Just so he's happy."

"Everybody's looking for that special someone."

"Not me."

"And yet, here I am." He winked and smiled.

~*~

The Satin Doll on Central Avenue hit its mark, aiming to be the premier Negro club for Los Angeles, it did so with flying colors. Zack and his partner set out to supersede the Club Alabam which was housed on the first floor of The Dunbar Hotel. Distinguished as the first club built by and for Negroes from the ground up through three floors of rooms, built by Dr. John Somerville, the first black graduate of USC, School of Dentistry; that is until The Satin Doll opened its doors a few blocks down on the corner. Folks still patronized Club Alabam but The Satin Doll reigned supreme as the upscale, classier club for Negroes, and ordinary folks saved up to celebrate special occasions at the club which became the hang out for those "in the know," especially celebrities. The plush décor, drinks and dinner reservations, valet parking and a raised, semi- revolving stage on which Selena and Zack Fluellen insured a packed house for three weeks.

Sugar Dee visited Selena back stage between the sets.

"You think Mazeda's gonna stay?" Selena asked.

"She went for a job interview today."

"That's a good sign," Selena said, letting Sugar Dee curl her hair again.

"You got the gal-darnedest hair. It looks rough and nappy but it's fragile and soft to the touch. Problem is yahoos don't know how to treat this grade of hair. They want to press the hell out of it and fry it too hard. Your hair can't take that."

"Work your magic, girl. Truth is," she returned to the subject of Mazeda, "she's been working hither and yon and likes it, but I think she's ready for a change."

"I've been watching her with Dewey too."

"Who, the manager? I haven't seen that. And I share a room with her."

"That's 'cause you got your own thing going."

"What?"

"You know, you're occupied on stage singing and what not." Sugar Dee didn't let on about Selena's getting closer to Zack.

One evening as The Satin Doll closed up for the night, the staff ran the vacuum cleaner, bartenders checked inventory, the chef decided his menu for the week and the cashiers closed out the registers. Selena sat alone at her favorite table, the one she reserved for Hep and a pregnant Lorette.

"We did good tonight, Selena," Dewey offered, joining her. "I can't thank you enough for being our guest vocalist."

"Glad to help," Selena said, not knowing what she'd be doing otherwise. Clueless to her next career move beyond giving the east coast a break. "I'm enjoying myself."

"It sure shows," Dewey grinned as Mazeda came up and sat next to Selena.

"Mazeda Yarborough," Selena greeted. "I'm sure glad you came."

"Me too. Chicago's about to get colder than a old maid's bed." She looked at Dewey and immediately said, "Oh, sorry."

"No need to apologize. Mighty refreshing that you feel the need." He paused and then repeated, "Mazeda Yarborough."

"In the flesh."

"Mazeda Yarborough," he repeated again.

Selena and Mazeda exchanged quizzical looks, chalking it up to liquor and a great take at the gate.

"That's a mighty unusual name. Mazeda."

"Tell me something I don't know."

Dewey hedged then asked, "Do you happen to know a cat named Mil Yarborough?"

The world stood still. The air sucked out of the club, rendering both women speechless. They looked at one another for confirmation that this man had just spoken the name of "Mil Yarborough." A name neither had heard in years. A name that Mazeda continued to hope but thought she'd ever hear again. Not wanting to spook the man or miss one word of what he was about to say, Selena asked, "How do you know Mil Yarborough? When was the last time you've seen him?"

Mazeda, not sure if she was breathing, waited for the answer to the questions she could not ask and was not sure she wanted the answers. Like if he were happily married and living down the street with his wife and five children.

"I met him awhile back in Florida," Dewey began slowly, wondering how much he should reveal.

Mazeda clutched her heart, then held her mouth.

268

"Why don't you just tell us about him," Selena urged while patting Mazeda's free hand.

Dewey looked from woman to woman, gauging if his disclosure would be the end of his career. He'd put all that behind him; had worked hard to make something of himself. But if this was Mil's Mazeda, she had a right to know.

"Maybe I should just talk to Mazeda—"

"That won't be happening," Selena said. "Just tell us what you know."

"I've been waiting a long time," Mazeda found her voice, and held his gaze without blinking.

"I met him in a turpentine camp in Florida, Sarasota County. Arrested as a vagrant which wasn't true for me or him. I was visiting my family just like Mil was visiting his sick Mama."

Mazeda burst into tears.

Selena held her around her shoulders. "Go on," Selena prompted the hesitant man who looked at the pain his words caused Mazeda. "She needs to know."

Dewey took a deep breath and then smiled. "I remember the first time I saw Mil coming through the misty woods in the striped prison uniform we all wore. It was dark. Always looked dark 'cause the sun didn't shine through them trees. It was something about the way he wore them stripes that just said, 'I don't belong here. You can't keep me here. I got somewhere else to be.' There were some roughnecks there, no doubt. But, then there were those of us who got there just 'cause we were black and they figured no one would miss us."

Mazeda's tears fell on Selena's shoulder.

"What you call that?" Dewey searched his mind for the word he'd heard used about them over and over again.

"Expendable."

"Yeah! We was at the camp that only had leased convict labor. Weren't no way for us to get word out to our loved ones. Mantee County. They expected us to just work and die. Anyhow, long story short. Mil tried to escape three times. Each time they took a little piece of him; not so much as to keep him from working but enough to keep him in line. That third time, we all went with him. We made it to the swamp edge and Boss-man cut him down. One shot to the back. Man behind him strangled that beefy, white boy with his own chains; wrapped them twice around his fat, red neck until his eyes bulged, his tongue stuck out and he fell face first into the mud." The pleasure and relief that all the prisoners felt showed on Dewey's face. "We all ran for our lives."

Mazeda's face streaked with tears as Dewey handed her his handkerchief.

Dewey continued, "He loved you, Mazeda. Talked about you all the time. Had a little crumpled up picture of you he kept near his sleep-blanket. All he talked about was getting back to you in Chicago. He said, knowing you, you thought he'd run off with some woman."

270

Mazeda smiled through shimmering tears.

"With his dying breath, he made me promise that if I ever got out, I'd call on you in Chicago. Made me promise not to tell anyone else his real name was Millicent. That was 'the tell,' the code to let you know I wasn't lying."

With that revelation, Mazeda threw up her hands and hugged Dewey. She laughed. "He never told nobody that. You did truly know him."

"Yes, I did. Because of him. I'm here. I made it out." Dewey began to well up. "He was a good man. He just knew he was getting out and going home to you."

Selena looked at the strange embrace of the two who only knew each other in passing and now, one word, one revelation, one shared experience made them bond forever in a way no one else could. Turpentine camps. She'd never heard of them. Prison camps where blacks were railroaded on trumped up charges by law enforcement who'd sell/lease them wherever needed never to be heard from again. Did they treat women that way? Could something like this have happened to Star? Confiscated slavery. Involuntary slavery. De facto slavery… it is still happening.

At about four in the morning after the last set, Selena sought the refuge of the quiet backyard patio before she turned in. Stars twinkled high in the sky on a canvas of black velvet. It'd been a heck of a week with Mazeda reconciling that Mil's gone for good. The purgatory of unknowing over. Happy that she finally knew for sure.

Sad that he wasn't ever coming back to her. The release cleansing but hurtful.

"Got something for you," Dewey had said before he left that night, and laid Mil's harmonica, Myrtle, in the palm of Mazeda's hand. She'd looked at it still, cold steel and remembered how much Mil loved that "lip harp" and how much he loved her. She closed her warm flesh around it and carried it to bed with her. Selena sure she'd curled up with it and her memories. The house was quiet and Selena sat in her chair noting how the night held a certain serenity and comfort.

"Want some company?" Zack asked from the top of the outside stairs just in case the answer was no.

"Why not?" Selena took her feet out of the other chair so he could join her.

"Helluva week."

"Yep."

They sat in companionable silence for a while.

"So what's next for you?"

"Don't rightly know, Mr. Fluellen."

"You hit another one of those plateaus. Gotta kick your career in the butt if you still want it."

"I do. Kind of in a quandary."

"There you go using five-dollar words when a two-dollar word will do."

Selena chuckled.

"You need a manager."

"No, I don't."

"How you know?"

"I don't." Selena pulled her sweater around her shoulders against L.A.'s inviting crisp air.

"You don't want to have to consult nobody or be told where to go or what to do. Or what's best for you… and you don't want to pay for it."

"You got me," Selena acquiesced.

"Suppose I offered to be your manager just until you find one you like. Otherwise, your career can stall and plummet as fast as it rose."

"Who's using five-dollar words now?"

"I'm more than just a pretty face."

"Why would you do that?"

"I don't just offer this expertise to any old body. I got to believe you have talent. Have a shot at the real Big Time. Not going to attach my name to a loser.

"What's in it for you?"

Zack lit a cigarette offering Selena one and when she declined he put his lighter back and took a deep drag. "I'm at the point where I've done it all. Well, almost. What I haven't done I don't want to do. I'm flush. Comfortable, musically and financially, thanks to royalties coming in whether I perform or not. I've achieved all my goals and then some. I played everywhere I wanted and with everyone, on and off vinyl. I travelled this country and the world. Dominated charts and articles in music magazines and create a crowd wherever I go with whatever I say. I have a street named after me in Paris like Armstrong and Bechet. I've met the queen. I have flourishing clubs and a place to hang my hat in three major cities. I've had my turn. Still having it, but I'd like to lend help to another aspiring artist. I'd like a protégé to make it."

"There are plenty of musicians who sing your praises and give you credit for innovations."

"Yeah, but those beboppers are on my heels now. Dizzy, Charlie, Thelonious… and they're good. So good and complicated that nobody can steal their stuff."

They chuckled. "So you want to make your name on my back?" Selena teased.

"Keep my name in the mix," he countered. "You know how it is when Christmas comes every year. You're happy. You celebrate. But nothing brings the *feel* of Christmas back until you see it all brand new in the eyes of a child."

Selena thought of Orelia's children's Yuletide excitement. "So now I'm a child?"

"You're an infant. Maybe a toddler. Just want to see you at least reach adolescence… musically speaking." He took a drag. "You're more my project. What you got to lose? Success. Popularity. Making history?"

The house inside awoke when Sugar Dee and Shanghai came in and laughing, went to their room.

"How much?"

"You haven't been listening, college girl. I don't need your money. But I sure do appreciate a woman who wants and can make her own money 'cause you ain't getting none of mine." He took another drag and continued, "I'll teach you that too. I'm not like other

274

Negroes who spend their dough on clothes, cars, jewelry, furs and other foolishness that don't last. You need to invest in a house or two. Some land. Watch your money *grow* and not *go.*"

"Sounds good," Selena thought of the other black stars who had white men manage their careers. Men, some they'd married, who opened doors and catapulted careers for their black women. Zack was a black man who could do the same with no strings attached.

"So what, do we sign something?"

"Nope. Gentleman's agreement. We can shake on it." He stubbed his cigarette butt in the ashtray. "Two things."

"Oh, no. Here it comes."

"Your sister, Star."

"You knew her!" Selena accused.

Zack sighed. "I was aware she was around in Nawlins, a skinny kid with a good voice but I didn't *know* her. We never had a conversation. I was busy traveling, recording, running my own club and then the war. Unless you already had a foothold in the business, the war caused others to flounder and fail. Heard she went to New York. That's it. I know as much as you."

"You'll tell me if you ever hear anything about her from here on?"

"I will."

Selena slumped in her chair. "What's the other thing?" she asked quietly.

"Your name."

"What's wrong with my name?"

"Wrong is the word. No disrespect to your late husband but Colson ain't got no pizzazz. Not like Fluellen."

"What are you saying?"

"I'm willing to give you my last name or at least lend it to you."

"You can do that?"

"It's mine to give. Folks change their names all the time. Ain't no thing. Selena Fluellen is snazzy. Jazzy... 'And here she is Selena Colson!' Leaves you cold."

"How about Selena Culhane?"

"Selena Fluellen. I will gift you my last name."

"So you're gonna adopt me, old man?"

"Have you noticed when they introduce us at The Satin Doll they say 'Selena and Zack Fluellen' like you're one of those one-name stars, and me. Or we could just let it slide like it has."

"If I can sing, what difference does my last name make? All my records have Colson. "

"I'm sure Eleanora Fagin could sell records too but not as many as Billie Holiday. Or Ruthie Lee Jones but Dinah Washington has a certain ring to it."

Selena's face scrunched up, hating that he was right.

"It's not really so much 'show business' as it is 'the business of show.' Or," he hesitated. "You could just marry me."

"You already have a wife."

"Details."

276

"For you." Selena rolled her eyes. "I wasn't raised to be second fiddle."

"How about once I take care of that?"

"I've met Lucille Fluellen and she ain't goin' nowhere." Selena stood. "And neither is this conversation. Good night." She walked up the steps. "Lock up when you come in."

Over the next month Selena watched Zack wheel and deal on her behalf. He set two-night minimum dates for her in and around L.A. and Las Vegas. He refused some recording deals and accepted others only with artists that could boost her profile like with her old friend Miles Syphax. Zack handled publicity, promotion and required a private dressing room for her, a non-refundable deposit at booking and full payment at the gig's end. Zack demanded that she be respected by management and audiences alike and she was guaranteed payment whether or not they complied. Selena began to understand what it meant to have a savvy manager who took excellent care of her, her voice and steered her career in the right direction. She felt less like she'd made a deal with the devil and more like she'd acquired a guardian angel.

A Boy For You and A Girl For Me

In the game of life, baby trumped college application. Baby trumped college attendance and a degree. Hep was happy but not ecstatic but wouldn't rain on his wife's parade, though he foresaw clouds in the future unless he met the challenges head on. He wouldn't insult Lorette by asking how or why she became pregnant. He knew his part in this derailment of their goals; they'd been horny and careless but satisfied. As his wife's belly grew and her wardrobe changed she was lucky not to have any morning sickness, only sheer pleasure at being healthy and pregnant. Not knowing whether the baby was a girl or boy, one thing Hep knew, this birth necessitated careful planning. UCLA hadn't accepted all of his Fisk credits but he'd finish out this semester, find a full-time job and attend school part-time for the remainder of his last year.

Due in May, Hep and Lorette were blessed with a healthy little boy that April. Too preoccupied with their child-wonder, the new mother and father hardly acknowledged D-Day, June 6, 1944 when the war ended, with the exception that now life would be great for everyone and there'd be no war for their son to fight. Three months later, Tavio Range Culhane sat in his high chair and helped his parents celebrate their first

278

anniversary. Tavio Range Culhane, a cafe au lait, little baby with curly black hair and affable personality, exactly what Lorette ordered and had worked hard to conceive as she had no desire to return to school. She relished her role as wife and mother, her dreams came true with every waking day. If only her cooking would improve. Being a homemaker suited her but her joy was playing with her son and waiting for her husband to come home from school to discuss the happenings of the day. When Tavio began walking, the demands on keeping up with the energetic little boy challenged her. The clothes he outgrew, the food he consumed, the timely visits to the pediatrician all taken in stride for the young wife and new mother. Hep completed his academic year on the honor roll and then reality of the increased expenses came calling. He shared his educational and career plans with his wife.

"The police department?" Lorette questioned at dinner as she fed Tavio peas and carrots which he spat out reaching for the drumstick his father held.

"Yeah. The hours are good. I'd work in the neighborhood. Be a beat cop. Could come home, eat dinner with you two before night school."

Tavio kicked his chubby legs in delight as he chomped down on the chicken bone.

"Is that safe?"

"Safe as anything else. The pay's great. Uniforms, no clothes to buy." Hep came up behind her and hugged her waist. "You worry too much, Lorette." He kissed her cheek. "We need a room for Tavio."

The rambunctious boy had the habit of waking up early and peering at them from the crib, stifling their early morning lovemaking. "He'll be climbing out to join us soon."

"Oh, Hep." She blushed playfully then said aloud, "Two bedrooms?"

"At least. I'd like three. Just in case we have to double them up after his little sister or brother is born."

Lorette planned a girl as her next child so it'd be nice to have three bedrooms.

"What does this do to our schedule, Hep?"

"Throw it off by about six months to a year. After I graduate, I'll apply to law school but there are other ways of becoming mayor. Get on the city council first. Do some community organizing. Make a name for myself and run for a seat. Being a beat cop will help with the votes for that." Hep grabbed another piece of chicken and tore off meat for Tavio. "I can't lose with my perfect family. We three right now and later more."

Only one more, Lorette thought. A girl. If it were a boy she'd double them up in bunk beds and use the third bedroom as a guest room or a room for the help to stay. But at least Hep still spoke of becoming mayor and appeared invested in the shortest way to get there.

"The way this boy eats, and outgrows clothes, more money is the key. What do you think?"

"Sounds like you have it all figured out." She went and sat on his lap facing their son. "But you always do. You know I'm behind you one thousand percent."

"That's my girl." He kissed her lips. "Ummm is that Peach Melba I taste?"

"Your favorite," Lorette smiled.

Bewitched, Bothered and Bewildered

Huddled in the recording studio listening to the final playback, Selena paced slowly and Zack stared at the floor, not the linoleum's pattern but critiquing the quality of her voice, looking for flawless and finding it.   As Selena held the last note of the last song , the musicians, arrangers, and Selena herself erupted into a ferocious satisfied "Whoop!!"

Heady from her first self-titled album; SELENA! her happiness could not be contained.   Zack threw a celebratory party for her at The Satin Doll right after the taping.

"How you feeling?" Zack asked on the way to the club.

"Like Christmas!" Selena enthused.

"We should get those sales too."

She turned to him and said, "Thank you."

"My pleasure. With your talent? It's easy."

"You lie like a rug, but thanks."

They pulled up outside.   A banner across the front door stated, "Closed. Private Party!"

Selena hesitated. "I wish my folks were here."

"They may be inside."

"Really?"

"No. But you'll see them at Christmas."

282

"Yes."

"Some of your other folks are in there and they're waiting on you."

Selena threw back her head as the doorman opened the plate glass.

"Sell it, Selena," Zack teased.

The party-people clapped and whistled as she entered. All of her friends in town came out for her celebratory debut. They danced, drank and took turns showcasing their own talents in homage to their friend's first album.

In the wee hours of the morning, Selena and Zack walked to their rooms at Shanghai and Sugar Dee's. Past the House of the Rising Sun still jumping in full swing.

"Night cap?" Zack asked as they filed through the front door, heading for their favorite place—the patio, strung with fading stars and the sliver of a setting moon.

He stopped in the kitchen brought down two glasses, one with ice and a pitcher of water.

"Champagne on ice?" Selena asked.

"No. I got scotch for me." He found his flask in his right jacket pocket.

"Straight. No chaser."

"Ice water for you."

He poured and asked. "So what you gon' name your next album? Can't do SELENA II. That don't flow."

"We have to decide that now? Can't we wait to see if this first one is a hit?"

"Oh, you know it is. No one sounds as good as you."

Selena blushed and swallowed the ice water. "Ummm. Best drink in the whole wide world."

"I'm telling you 'Selena Fluellen' is the way to go."

"You sure know how to mess up a perfectly good night."

"Just the opposite. I am giving you the chance of a lifetime." He took a swig and poured himself another short one. "Neither one of us is this morning's milk. You must be pushing up on thirty."

"You silver-tongued devil. Pointing out a lady's age. Classy move."

"I been watching you over the years. How you finally filling out."

Selena chuckled.

"You were too skinny before. I like a woman I can hold on to. A woman who fills my loving-hands to overflowing. Not no skinny woman I can break in two."

"I'm sure there has been no shortage of either."

"That's how I know. Did a scientific study on it." He drained his glass. "I love you, Selena."

Shock registered on her face.

"I have for a long time. Square business. You had to mature and I had to make sure you were the one."

Selena blinked once but continued to look at him like he was speaking Chinese in tongues.

"I'm no angel. Never said I was. I know what you're thinking. We've never-done-the-do. Never even kissed. Sex is sex; necessary. A bodily function like eating, sleeping and crappin'. But love...you can love somebody without ever making love to them. You can love everything about them. How happy they can make you just by being around. How they just make you feel good. Missing them when they're gone." He stopped. "You are everything I want and nothing I don't."

"Wow." Silence held her tongue.

"Might could be we each other's answer." He looked squarely at her. "Each other's chance at lasting happiness. After all the sunshine, lollipops and blooms of first love, we get down the road to you and me. The way it was meant to be. The long haul."

Selena stared at him for a long time as the silence screamed loudly about them. She broke her gaze, scooted the chair back and walked towards him. Bending down, she took his face in the palms of her hands and kissed him. Kissed him hard and long, his lips parting, his eyes closing, her tongue darting into his mouth. Exploring, romping, enjoying the taste of him. She broke the connection and took his hand, led him upstairs, passed the room she and Hoyt occupied all those languid nights and went straight to Zack's room on the back near the bathroom. He shut the door gently behind him and watched her slowly disrobe, moving to music only they heard. She liked that he wasn't over eager. Cool. Like this was supposed to happen. He liked the same of her. Unbuttoning her last button near the zipper, the sound of the metal descent filled the room and Zack approached her. Her heart beat faster.

"I like to open my own gifts," he whispered, taking the top and letting it fall away. He slipped the strap of her bra from her shoulder and watched it fall and reveal the substantial, high breasts he'd imagined being there all this time. Bite size yet voluptuous, the dark nipples arched and aching for attention. He turned her around, as he peeled her panties from her hips, she leaned into him naturally as if they'd done this a thousand times. His expert saxophone hands traveled up and down her body teasingly as he did on the keys of his brass instrument. How often had she watched his hands caress the sax and now they did the same to her skin. She liked that he teased and taunted her pulsating womanly triangle, evoking the sweet manifestation of her desire. Slippery, wet and tantalizing she wanted him now and couldn't believe how painstakingly technical he was, savoring his visual and tactile exploration of her body, like he had all the time in the world. Not urgent, not inexperienced, not too anxious, Zack was a lover with a slow-hand and Selena relaxed and reveled in it. He massaged, played with her and she moaned in the most unladylike way. She turned into him and he kissed her hungry lips. She felt his maleness, supple and firm, against her throbbing center, not sure if she was a good candidate for slow loving.

Looking up at him she began undressing him.

"Slow down, college girl. What's the rush?"

She couldn't answer him. She didn't want games. She wanted him.

286

He smiled down at her as she shucked his shirt and tie and undid his belt so his pants loosened and dropped.

"My turn," he said huskily as he backed her up and laid her ever-so-gently on the comforter of the bed. Lowering her down like a pro, smoothly, in one motion, like a needle finds its groove, he slid into her without hesitation.

The feel of his swift sword entering her moist scabbard sent an explosion of sensation through her body, closing her eyes and curling her toes. The rhythmic undulating movement against her womanly center forced her eyes open. His gaze held hers.

As he towered over her, looking into her eyes with every joyful thrust, Selena recognized it. In her bare feet and bottom on white cotton sheets in a California rooming house she saw it. The way Zack Fluellen held on to her transcended his words spoken earlier. His eyes confirmed and verified how he felt about her without uttering a word. Selena knew the way a woman does. She heard, loud and clear, "I love you." She'd found what she was looking for and thought she never would again. Zack Fluellen felt like home.

They mutually climaxed to an end and he let out an uncontrollable growl.

Selena smiled. She wanted to jump for joy.

"What are you grinning about?" he asked as he rolled from her to her side.

"I will never call you old man again."

"Zat right?"

They captured their breaths and lay in absolute and complete ecstasy, basking in a feeling she thought would elude her for the rest of her life. Nestled beneath his chin, she snuggled as he held her tenderly. With the sound of quiet shrouding them she clearly asked, "Will you catch me if I fall in love with you?"

"No doubt."

God Bless the Child

On August 6, 1945, the U.S. and its Allies dropped an atomic bomb on Hiroshima and on August 9th repeated the gesture on Nagasaki. On the 14th, Japan surrendered and World War II in the Pacific was over. After the initial jubilation, everyone grew preoccupied with how America would revert to absolute peace. As a policeman, Hep realized more servicemen would be returning home in various stages of health and he thought of the influx of men herded into designated areas where, despite their income and ability to afford better, housing covenants prevented blacks from moving elsewhere. A toxic stew brewed among men who'd seen independence, garnered respect, self-reliance, carried guns and defended their country… to be relegated, and expected to quietly resume the oppressive positions of a pre-war society an unrealistic goal.

Selena, gleeful for everyone who'd be embracing their loved ones, knew she would not. But her jubilance reigned supreme as the returning vets with disposable incomes and sophisticated tastes, sent her albums soaring on the charts along with her requests for guest spots at clubs and on the relatively new format, televised TV shows. Lorette's elated outlook had little to do with the war's end, but was familial in nature. The Culhanes moved into a brand-new, three story apartment building on Alvaro Street, Apartment #3G. Selena declared it a good omen full of promise, love and happiness as the apartment she and Hoyt shared in Chicago also had 3G under its door knocker. *The Culhane home,* Lorette thought. *The last before the mayor's mansion,* she hoped.

As the adage goes, "new house-new baby;" Lorette did not disappoint. Months after occupying their new home, she told her hard-working husband the good news while their active son ran track through the spacious apartment. "We're going to have another baby." Lorette not only loved the scale of the three bedroom, one bath and being the first family to inhabit it, but it was built on a short street which dead-ended at defunct railroad tracks, perfect as there was no traffic except from the folks who lived there. She wished that they'd had one of the two detached homes at the corner, but in time they'd move into a proper home with an upstairs and a front and back yard with space to spare.

From the front door of apartment #3G to the left, an open kitchen with an eating counter and a long wide living room; the only other door on that side, was to the master bedroom. To the right of the front door a hallway, first door to a huge bathroom with both tub and shower large enough to accommodate Hep's big frame comfortably, plenty of storage, and a window. Straight down at the end of the long hall was TC's room, far enough away from his parents' amorous late night and early morning trysts. To the left of TC's door would be her baby girl's room which she'd tackle when she finished decorating her son's room in blue. Using all the furniture from their first apartment they added TC's furniture; twin beds, bureau, night stand and drapes for all the rooms from master, living room and both other bedrooms. Lorette felt little pressure to complete her daughter's room as she'd sleep with them for the first year anyway; bassinette, then crib as crib-death remained a prevalent concern and their daughter would not be moved until that threat was over.

"Brittany?" Hep asked. "That's a big name for a little girl."

"You said I could name the next child and I like it."

"And if it's another boy?"

"It won't be."

In seemingly just moments, Hep paced the maternity waiting room as his wife gave birth to their second child. A little girl just as Lorette had predicted. Brittany Melba Culhane who Hep called "Mel" almost immediately. The nickname took just as Tavio, when not called Champ by his father, had become TC last year. All manner of cutesy clothes came in boxes from Evelyn, Tennessee, Colt, Texas and even St. Louis from Aunt Summer. Selena and Zack brought their new niece a frilly, crocheted, pink layette.

"How do you like your little sister, TC?"

"I want to hold her!"

They positioned the rough two-year-old way back on the couch, fashioned his arms to accept the precious baby which he held until he grew bored.

"Isn't she just the cutest tiny perfect little baby?"

"Yes, she is Lorette. You and Hep make pretty babies," Selena said.

"Look at all that hair!" Zack gruffed.

"It'll change a thousand times before it settles in."

"Cute little button nose and those big, round, pretty eyes. Who has eyes like that? Her face is practically all eyes."

A natural, gender demarcation emerged and divided the family Culhane with Hep and TC, and Lorette and Mel. When home from work and school, Hep naturally took TC with him which Lorette didn't mind at all. Happy for the break, she napped when Mel napped. For the young mother, having two children under the ages of two and one half, proved more than a notion. On Sunday afternoon, the parents put Mel into her pram, canopy down, and took TC on his tricycle and paraded around the block amid all the well-wishers on Alvaro Street before getting ice cream cones, going home for naps and rising for Sunday dinner. It was especially nice when Selena and Zack came over to babysit. Holding, feeding, changing Mel's diaper and playing board games with TC. Anything to tire them out before Hep and Lorette came home from the movie. Lorette wanted to see Barbara Stanwyck in *Stella Dallas* but Hep vetoed it for John Huston's *San Pietro* that had finally been released after years of controversy. The War Department thought it too graphic to show civilians San Pietro falling to the Allies in December 1944 after a ten-day siege and the loss of 1,100 Allied soldiers. Hep wanted to see the thirty-two-minute film as it contained the intelligence he and Tavio worked hard to create. Hep kept abreast with all the maneuvering of the Italian Campaign and this film showed the second phase before the Allies moved onto Cassino. As usual, Lorette acquiesced to Hep, knowing the dark, quiet and comfortable theater, invited a nap on her part.

Hep's abrupt rise and leaving his seat jarred her awake. She followed him as he headed for the bathroom. *Was it something he ate?* She wondered, as she waited for him in the lobby.

Emerging five minutes later, his face wiped clean with cold water. "Sorry," he said.

"You alright? Is your stomach upset?"

"No. I'm O.K." He headed for the front door.

"Don't you want to see the rest?"

"It's over. We'd better get back home." He swung the door open for her. "Get some ice cream for the kids and the babysitters."

The couple opened the door to apartment #3G.

"You all back so soon?" Selena asked as Mel, seeing Lorette, reached for her mother.

"We had dinner and a movie," Hep offered before disappearing into the kitchen.

"Daddy!"

"Hey, Champ, bought you some ice cream."

"Chocolate?"

"And chocolate ripple for your Aunt Selena."

Lorette lugged Mel over to the couch and sat down. "Whew. You are growing."

"Wait until she starts walking," Selena said, to which Lorette did not respond.

"Don't look like no time soon," Zack said. "Miss Anne likes being carted around."

With the kids bedded down, Zack and Selena stayed for adult conversation as Lorette nodded off.

"Makes you wonder how our mother did this day in and out," Selena whispered, pointing at her sister-in-law.

"Did what she had to do and loved it. She was older, more experienced than Lorette," Hep defended.

"Don't make them like Keely Culhane anymore."

"Was the show any good?" Selena asked her brother.

"Nothing I'd recommend to a civilian," Hep said.

"No, Oscar Micheaux?" Selena countered.

"No."

Once Selena and Zack left and Lorette had gone to bed, the house eerily quiet, Hep could not sleep. He'd seen Frank Capra's 1944 tribute to *The Negro Soldier,* a documentary by the U.S. Army, War Department which affected him quite differently. But *San Pietro* devoid of any black soldiers, hit him harder. Vexed by the realness of this movie, he hadn't known what to expect, but it grabbed him in places he hadn't thought about in a long while. Besides the black and whiteness of the film, the pictures of the terrain, scruffy and dull, and the entire pallor a flannel gray, lackluster, it was the soldiers being piled into white body bags that gave him pause. Not a black body among them which made him angry, but the white soldiers reminded him of Tavio, and how priceless and precious life is and can be. Tavio's death spun off into Range's dying, all equaling resurgence of memories and no sleep that night. Hep's mind ablaze, questioning why his life was spared. Psychiatrist called it Survivor's Syndrome. Hep poured a glass of buttermilk and drank its thickness slowly like welcoming an old friend. Mel stirred and Hep went and got her, taking her from their room to the living room couch, Lorette dead to the world. He smiled at his big-eyed, cooing daughter, "You can't sleep either, huh?" He put her bottle in the electric bottle warmer. Maybe his legacy hasn't anything to do with him beyond bringing exceptional children into the world to make it a better place.

That Christmas, Selena and Zack forwent a Colt Christmas and stayed in town to be with the Culhanes of Alvaro Street on their first Yuletide in apartment #3G. Festive and full of fun, they'd put the Christmas tree in front of the big window in the living room. Folks stopped by to spread cheer. Selena sang, Zack played his sax and Nash Byrd, bassist for Duke Ellington's band, home from the road, came down with his wife, Eunice, to join in the fun. Apartment #3G filled to the brim, rocked and no one complained.

New Year's Eve found Selena headlining at The Satin Doll with the usual suspects at her favorite table and those celebrity friends of hers in town, sharing the stage. After the collective singing of "Auld Lang Syne" and the partying resumed, Dewey took Mazeda aside, dropped to one knee and asked her to "start the year off by being her wife."

"What you gonna do?" Selena asked her old friend.

"Marry him!"

~*~

"What?" Lorette blinked uncontrollably.

"Congratulations. You and your husband are going to have another baby."

"How is that possible?"

"You have two children. I'm sure you know how."

"We've been careful. I can't have any more children. I'm not supposed to have any more children."

"The Lord says otherwise. You two are very fortunate."

A stunned Lorette walked home not realizing she'd done so until she turned the doorknob of #3G.

"Where have you been?" The babysitter, Mae Tilgman, from across the street asked. "I was beginning to worry. You said you'd be home a hour ago."

"Sorry."

"You alright?"

"No."

296

"You look dazed. Sit down." Miss Mae went and got her a glass of water just as Mel reached for her mother.

"Where's TC?"

"In his room playing trucks and railroad."

"Hey," Hep said, entering the apartment and, hearing his voice, TC bounded down the hall, jumping straight into his Daddy's arms.

"Hey, Champ!"

"Daddy can we go to the playground?"

"Sure. Let me change my clothes and you put on your sneakers." He then tweaked Mel's chubby cheeks and looked at Lorette. "Hey, Lorette." He looked around and noted that the kitchen showed no sign of starting dinner. "Want me to pick up something while I'm out?"

Lorette turned to him.

"What's the matter?" he looked from his wife to Miss Mae.

"She walked from the doctor's office."

"Why'd you do that?"

"I needed to walk and think."

"About what? You had a good checkup, right?"

"Dr. Russell said we were lucky."

"Ready, Daddy?"

Over the next few days, with his own change in work schedule, added duties and "more money," Hep hadn't noticed Lorette's preoccupation.

"When are you going to finish school?" Lorette asked her husband one morning before work.

"What?" the question caught him off guard.

"I mean, when are we going to get a proper house and more room?"

"With all the added responsibilities, you know I had to skip this semester and probably the next until things settle down."

"But you love it, Hep. You love your life. You are fulfilled."

"Yes, I am. I make the best of whatever, knowing that somewhere down the line it'll all—"

"I don't have your faith," Lorette blurted out, and left the room.

"What the heck?" He gathered his keys, kissed his daughter and rubbed his son's head and said, "We'll talk about this when I get back. Gotta go to *work* now. Have a good day." He put his hat on his head. "TC, take care of Mommy."

"OK, Daddy."

Must be her time of the month, Hep thought, as he took the stairs by twos.

Hep came home with a hand-packed quart of butter brickle ice cream, Lorette's favorite, and found her in a much improved mood. "Feeling better?" he asked.

She hunched her shoulders.

"I know things aren't working out as we planned but it'll come. Know that I am always working on it."

"When Hep. What about school?"

"In fact, I have good news. The request for the shift change finally came through. That'll leave my afternoons free to finish up my courses before I go to work evenings."

"When will you sleep? Or study?"

"You know I've never needed much sleep and as for studying—"

Lorette burst into tears.

"Lorette?" He went to her. "What is it?"

"I'm pregnant!"

Hep laughed with relief. "You mean *we* are pregnant." He held her. "That's good news."

"For whom?"

"Us."

"No, it is not working out, Hep. You'll never get your degree at this point. More children, more responsibility. This was not our plan."

"Apparently, it's God's plan." He rocked her. "It'll all work out. Just a little delay."

"I'm tired of delays. Tired of making due. Tired of our plans not working out."

"Honey—"

"We should be finished with your degree and then it's my turn when our two children are in school. Two children, Hep but now… another baby?"

"Lorette—"

"So I was thinking. There is a way we can get back on track." She fiddled with the top button of his shirt without looking at him.

"I'm all ears." He smiled down at her, overjoyed with the news of welcoming another Culhane.

"Since we already have two, healthy, wonderful children; a boy and a girl, one of each. Nothing would be gained by having another child. I can ask the doctor if he could... I mean, I could even have my doctor-sister...but then I wouldn't want my family knowing *our* business..." Lorette glanced up at her husband, ill-prepared for the terror registered in his eyes.

"What are you suggesting!?" he roared and strong-armed her away from him.

He held both of her arms by her side. Mistaking his silence for agreement, she had never seen him so enraged. Mad-dog angry. He looked as if he could hit her.

Afraid he may strike her if he let her go, Hep continued in a lethally low voice so as not to disturb TC and Mel. "If any of my children, those here now and those to come, 'inconvenience' you or 'wreck' the plans you have for yourself, you let me know. Me and my children will let you go to pursue whatever you think is more important than being a loving mother to any of them."

"You mean you'd pick your children over me?"

"In a heartbeat. If that is your choice, then you are not the woman I thought you were, and *we* have no future." Fire and ice fought to control his stance. He released her from his grip and walked out of the apartment.

Hep could not contain his anger at the mere suggestion of aborting one of his children. He thought of

300

his partner, Truck Macmillan, over the moon because his wife, after multiple miscarriages, was expecting. To have Lorette not understand the blessing that each child brings, vexed him beyond words. Beyond forgiveness. On something so basic, how could he have been so wrong about the woman he chose to be his wife? His life partner. The mother of his children.

He found himself at the all-night diner where he and Truck usually ate lunch. He sat in their usual booth and the waitress came over.

"Hey, Officer Culhane."

Hep looked up and into the eyes of their regular waitress. "Oh, hey, Amy. You're working late tonight."

"So are you." She smiled at the fact he was alone for a change and out of uniform. "One of the girls couldn't come in so I took her shift. I can always use the money."

"Humm."

"You OK?" She noticed his uncharacteristic preoccupation.

"Sure. Coffee, please. Black."

"I know that," she smiled again. "How about a nice slice of lemon meringue pie too?"

"Just the coffee. Thanks."

Hep nursed the coffee for more than an hour and she refreshed it often. When he looked up Amy stood behind the counter with a ready smile. Once when she came over she offered, "I get off in a hour so if you want to talk… I'm a good listener."

Hep looked at her quizzically. "Thanks but I'm fine."

301

Only then did he think perhaps Truck was right. His partner always teased Hep about his female following. Hep always laughed it off with a "not my thing." Truck countered with a "it must be nice to know you're wanted on any terms." Hep would tease, "All my life man. Have you seen my wife and children? What would be the point?" That always closed the discussion. This was when Hep thought he knew his wife.

He looked at the pretty tan-skinned waitress and his only thought was why would he choose to complicate his life with another woman? He constantly wondered why men jeopardized their homes and family with a side-woman. Even when your wife lets you down in unimaginable ways, the commitment to the institution of marriage should keep you faithful to your vows until a resolution can be reached. Any energy expended should be toward working on the marriage not going outside of it. It was a given that marriage wasn't all sunshine and bubbles but if the love cannot be restored then man-up, get a divorce and date until your eyeballs fall out.

Hep sipped his coffee and looked out of the window to the dark, empty street. His reflection bounced back. He wanted to always be able to look at himself in the mirror and see a man his son would be proud of. Be a living example of the type of man his daughter would marry. Abortion-talk between healthy, able married folk was absurd to him and between him and his wife...unfathomable.

It was the way he was raised. He recalled his father always saying "Religion aside, you go to bed thankful and wake up grateful. Grateful that your bed wasn't your cooling board. Grateful that you had the next 24 hours to live your life to the fullest and know you could handle whatever life threw your way." Hep supposed that's how you lived when your life depended largely on Mother Nature. Lorette's family of origin and mindset wasn't the same. He and his wife's differences were showing. He'd said it plain. It was up to her now.

~*~

Hep stayed out all night and returned home in time to shower and change for work. In his absence, Lorette had run through all of her options which included leaving her children and returning to Evelyn, Tennessee to do what? Finish college? Be the brunt of town gossip… a mother who left her husband and children to live in her childhood room? After she fumed and ranted it came down to one thing… she loved Hep more than herself. Right now, she hated herself for loving him so much. If she left, she knew he'd be alright but she knew she'd die without him. She heard his key in the door. Right this minute, she was relieved to have him come home.

"I'm sorry," she said when he finished his shower and dressed in his uniform in silence.

He walked to the front door. His hand on the knob, he turned without looking into his wife's eyes. "Unless you are ready to leave me and my children, we will never speak of this again. You cannot possibly realize how deeply you hurt me." His eyes flashed down into hers, "And if you *ever* harm one of my children. I will not be responsible for my actions."

Part III
1947

That Old Devil Moon

An interminable amount of time passed before Hep could even be civil to Lorette. A tribute to his current children, especially TC who kept rubbing his mother's belly and asking his father to do the same. It was the only touch Lorette had felt from Hep in weeks. The sight of the growing belly comforted the father-to-be who forgave his wife for her momentary insanity, chalking it up to hormones, but he'd never forget it, or bring it up again.

"Thanks for doing this," Lorette complimented Miss Mae Tilgman, the older neighbor from across the street. "I didn't know what to do with her hair."

"Of course not. You got different hair. Not much to work with but she only a year old. Her hair can still grow some."

"Too bad she didn't get TC's hair."

"Now that's the truth but that's how it works sometime. Boy, who don't need the good hair gets it and his sister gets the bad."

"Ummm," Lorette said, rubbing her stomach.

"He giving you the blues?"

"Or she. I didn't have any morning sickness with TC or Mel, but with this one I'm sick all the time."

"It'll go away soon. Oh!" Miss Mae glanced at her watch. "Time for my stories." She jumped up and scurried out the front door.

"Are you sure I can't give you—"

"Phish! No chile. See you tomorrow." She flew down the front stairs and Lorette watched her move spryly for an old lady. *The World Turns* waits for no one.

Tomorrow, Lorette thought. Lorette hadn't cottoned to any of the other residents in the building. Truth be told if it weren't for Miss Mae's working magic on Mel's hair they wouldn't be "friends" either. Miss Mae, up from North Carolina living with two grown sons and an assortment of other folks, had little in common with Lorette. Lorette tried to befriend Eunice Byrd, who lived in one of the two houses at the end of the block. She had two daughters about the ages of the Culhane children and her husband played bass with Duke Ellington's Orchestra and was gone a lot. But Eunice only seemed interested in Lorette when Zack and Selena came to apartment #3G. Once at the grocery store she'd struck up a strained conversation which Eunice quickly excused herself from as she had to go pick up one of her daughters from dance class. When asked where the other daughter was, Eunice reveled in saying "home with the housekeeper."

Absently, Lorette stood at the top of the stairs recently vacated by Miss Mae and looked at them. Tall, steep, yet narrow. Concrete overlaid with linoleum tiles. About fifteen steps to the first landing where the low-oblong window allowed you to see out. Over the last few days, Lorette had thought about a fall. It happened all the time in movies. She could fall and lose the baby and not be able to have any more. Hep wouldn't be the wiser. But God would punish her by paralyzing her, or killing her off. Sometimes, when she stood there, at the very edge, Lorette could feel herself teeter.

Just then Mel ran out of the front door and grabbed her mother around the legs. "Mama. Up!" She held her hands and Lorette picked her up.

"How's my little princess, huh? Are you hungry? Let's go see if TC is hungry. TC's always hungry." She closed the door behind her.

The routine began. Right after Hep left for work, Lorette knew the next knock would be Miss Mae. She wished there were some way to whittle Miss Mae's visits down to three times a week. Mel's hair held on that long. Or she wished Selena came by more often. The chanteuse seemed to have the gift but she came around when her brother was there, not to just visit her and the children. Although, Lorette recalled how Selena was exceptionally helpful when the kids were first born. After Lorette's mother spent her week up here, Selena came over for a few hours in the afternoon if she were in town. *Where would her mother stay this time?* Lorette thought, answering the door. With Mel? Then she'd end up taking care of the wrong baby as the newborn would still be in a bassinette in their room.

"I brought donuts," Miss Mae held up the paper sack.
"Thanks."

308

Mel ran to Miss Mae and her bag of goodies. "You got coffee?"

Lorette wouldn't dare antagonize Miss Mae, especially when Hep was about to change his shift... again. He'd be home during the morning hours and gone in the afternoon and night getting off at 11 p. m. and home by 11:30 p. m. At four years old next year, TC would start school just in time for the baby to be born. Mel would be her never-changing one constant. "Mama, up!" She demanded and Lorette obliged.

"You know it's none of my business and tell me if I'm out of line, but I been watching you hoist that girl up, lifting groceries. Pulling TC in the wagon."

"Just being a good mother," Lorette said, as she tried folding clothes with one hand.

"Eyeing the steps out front—" Miss Mae hedged.

"What are you saying, Miss Mae?"

"You having a baby and should be more careful. Folks could think negative on you."

Lorette's eyes locked with the older woman's.

"Maybe you just a young, modern mother. In my day, we'd milk our 'family way' for all it's worth. 'Cause if that is your intention, there are easier ways to miscarry—"

"Miss Mae." Lorette jumped up and looked around making sure no one could hear. "I'm afraid I'm going to have to ask you to leave for suggesting such—"

"Settle down. I said if I was wrong to tell me. Apparently, I was wrong. Sorry."

Lorette began to fix TC a snack of Ovaltine milk and Graham crackers.

"It's a boy," Miss Mae announced. "Rambunctious. Too active to be a girl child."

"A little football player," Lorette tried civility. 'Well, I got a ways to go yet."

The visit would not end, Lorette dying to know what Miss Mae knew but knowing better than to ask. *I bet she knew plenty about potions and concoctions taken during a full devil moon coming from the woods of North Carolina,* Lorette thought. Miss Mae stayed longer than usual and Lorette looked at the clock, "Well, time to start dinner. Hep'll be home soon." Miss Mae groaned as she rose and kissed Mel on the cheek.

Lorette took out pork chops and laid them on the counter before joining Miss Mae at the door. "Quinine water and red pepper. At least three times a day. More if you can stand it."

Lorette said nothing. "Thank you for doing Mel's hair, Miss Mae."

Miss Mae winked which Lorette in no way acknowledged. Once the door closed, Lorette ran to the kitchen cabinet, took down a glass, filled its bottom with red pepper and drank it down. It burned her throat and tongue. She coughed and choked, rinsed then drank another glass of water and began cooking dinner for her family.

~*~

Besides being obnoxious, Miss Mae was also wrong. The baby came two weeks before the due date and was a girl who made her mark early. First born TC put his mother through four hours of labor. Mel only two. After enduring labor for twenty-four hours, this baby came into the world through C section. Lorette's first, leaving an incision on her mother's stomach for all of her days. TC and Mel weighed in at six pounds eight and nine ounces respectively. This baby weighed eight pounds three ounces. TC and Mel breastfed beautifully. This baby couldn't get enough mother's milk and had to be bottle fed. This baby's name... Jasmine Bianca Culhane.

Once home Jasmine moved directly into a crib in her parents' room as a bassinette proved too fragile. Once Lorette's mother returned to Tennessee, Selena to Las Vegas and Hep to taking TC to school, the task of mixing Karo syrup and evaporated milk into sterilized bottles fell upon the new mother. Jasmine's lungs superb and, like her father, she required little sleep. Lorette flirted with wit's end.

Jasmine boasted a reddish-color skin tone, and a head full of hair which she promptly lost by the third month. When Aunt Selena gave her butterfly kisses, Jasmine's delightful squeal made TC laugh. Mel, a little rough with her baby sister, lost interest in the newborn preferring her mother's attention. Jasmine walked in eight months, ran in nine and already had the kind of personality that wouldn't allow her to be ignored in a room. She'd captivated her father, Aunt Selena and brother immediately.

"Can't you send Annie up here for a few months?" Lorette asked her mother on their usual long distance calls.

"Oh, honey Annie is too old for that. You want us to hire someone—"

"Oh no," Lorette interrupted. "Hep would hate that, besides there is no place for 'help' to stay." She knew better than to even intimate that this child required anything extra than what she'd provided for her first two. "The diaper service is quite enough."

The family spent the following Sunday at the beach. Selena, in Bermuda shorts and a striped top, walked with her brother to the car, while Zack, TC and Jasmine frolicked across the sand chasing a beach ball. Beneath the umbrella spiked into the sand, Lorette and Mel spread out the lunch waiting for Hep to bring the cooler. Hep hadn't received the response desired from his wife about his career coup and rising in the ranks so he shared them with his sister. "I was eligible for promotion because they applied my military service to three years of college which allowed me to jump over a lot of whites. Needless to say, many are none too happy. Only the second time a Negro would be over a white squad. A little dicey that first time."

"I bet. Well, if anyone can you can, brother dear. You got that cool, calm temperament."

"Yeah."

"You should be proud."

"I am." He gave her the bag from the trunk and grabbed the cooler. Returning toward the beach he watched his children play.

"How's Lorette doing?" Selena asked.

"She's worried about Jasmine's hair."

"She's got none."

"She's afraid our little girl will be bald."

"Then she won't have to pay someone else to take care of it like Mel's."

They saw Jasmine run straight for the waves with no fear, before TC intercepted his baby sister. "See her eyelashes? Got more than you and me put together. You best be believin' when her hair comes in it's gonna be aplenty. Tell Lorette to rest up."

On her sturdy legs in the shifting sand, Jasmine toddled toward her father and aunt, and presented them with a sea shell. "See?" She offered and hobbled off again, bypassing her mother and sister for TC who remained at the water's edge.

"No one has mistaken her for a boy yet," Hep teased, thinking of how irate Lorette used to get when Mel was.

"Are you kiddin'? Nothin' on Jasmine says 'boy.' The lashes, intelligent eyes and that bow mouth. Folks who do my make-up try to put those full lips on grown women."

"She is inquisitive. Unlike her siblings were."

"Where'd she get those light eyes?" Selena asked.

"They'll change. Mel's did."

"You done good, brother. Pretty, healthy children."

"I'm happy."

"Ever think of the linkage of living events in our lives?"

"What do you mean?"

"Started with Micah Rudd entering Dad's life bringing Felicity Rudd who brought Hoyt Colson, the love of my life, who influenced you and Range... dubbed you 'citizens of the world.'"

"Hep-cat and Hipster," Hep said with a chuckle. "I have him to thank for broadening our horizons."

"You could be married to Feather with a bunch of kids living on your spread in Colt, Texas. Safe, simple, happy life."

"Instead of being out here at a L.A. beach with my family? Kicking butt in the LAPD?"

"It's scary to think of what we would have missed," Selena recognized.

"I'll take this life any day I breathe," Hep said.

"Me too."

"To Hoyt Colson who got us here," Hep toasted his Nehi orange soda. "And Zack Fluellen who's taken you the rest of the way."

"I've taken my own damn self," Selena countered, playfully. "He has helped," she admitted.

"That's mighty white of you."

"Truth be told... I don't know what I'd do without him."

"You had the talent and he had the Golden Key to open doors for you. Sounds like a marriage made in heaven."

"Star had the talent but not the access."

"It does take both. Any news?"

"None. Like she just vanished," Selena concluded.

They both fell silent.

Shortly after her two and a half year's birthday, Jasmine's bald head sprouted hair which grew and grew and didn't stop until it almost reached her waist. "Well, Lorette wanted her daughter's hair to grow. She got her wish," Selena remarked.

Miss Mae said, "Land sakes alive, I never seen such hair on a little girl before." That red-colored complexion and that blondish, reddish coppery hair…you think it was the red pepper?"

Lorette shot Miss Mae a look of pure venom but she needed her now more than ever to tackle Jasmine's long, thick, peculiar hair, probably from her father's Javier side of the family.

"I guess that old devil moon makes me say such. Sure can't take her with you to The Cardozo Sisters," Miss Mae commented. "Folks that do Mel's hair will burn up Jasmine's. What you gon' do? Send her to Sugar Dee's?"

Miss Mae knew how Lorette felt about the rooming house. Trying to wean her way free of Miss Mae, Lorette refused to ask her for help with yet another daughter. On one of her visits, Miss Mae caught Lorette, pressing comb in hand, poised to run it through Jasmine's hair.

"Stop! You will ruin that girl's hair. Not fine like yours but it's good if you treat it right." Miss Mae took a glass of cold water and a wide tooth comb and sat on the living room couch. "C'mere Jasmine." The little girl sat on the floor between Miss Mae's legs while she worked magic on the almost three-year-old girl's hair.

Parted in the middle with two long braids, Lorette accepted the compliments as if she'd done her daughter's hair herself. Hep, Selena, Zack even Eunice Byrd commented on how nice it looked at the grocery store. By day's end, after roughhousing with her brother and father, wild hair sprung up framing Jasmine's features, her face pocked with sweat. "Oh, Jasmine," Lorette lamented, as she washed up her daughter for dinner. In the mornings she brushed the once neat plaits with a "lick and a promise" to do better and make it last until Miss Mae returned. Since Hep had arrested one of Miss Mae's sons, her visits became more infrequent.

Red Top

Selena returned to Colt, Texas for the annual Culhane Christmas Party. Disappointed her brother couldn't join them because of a work schedule conflict, Selena managed to have a ball reconnecting with her old neighbors and friends especially Francie, Delilah and their families and her twin nieces, Orelia's girls. Far more relaxed this visit than previous ones. Far more confident and less uncertain about who she was and where she was going in life. Even when Francie said, "Just think. You are married to one of Star's idols." This time Selena knew who she was, where she was going and with whom. A man who loved her, claimed her, protected her, supported her, inspired her and had her best interests at heart. A man who satisfied and titillated her like a man... not an old man either.

"I said it before. Like you living Star's life," Delilah said.

"No. It's my life," Selena claimed it. "And I love it... a lot."

Selena and her father put on a show worthy of a paying public. They traded barbs and piano and vocal renditions and, after the kids fell asleep, Colt even sang a few of his repertoire from the old days, delighting all who listened. Even persnickety Orelia seemed to have a good time.

By New Year's Eve, the chanteuse was back at The Satin Doll. Her brother and his wife at her favorite table along with Mazeda and Dewey, and Anita and Miles Syphax. Her presence and performance electrified the crowd and at midnight, for the first year, thousands of black and gold balloons fell from the ceiling, confetti flew and horn blowers rang in the New Year. 1950. As Selena led "Auld Lang Syne," Zack appeared beside her and sang along hand in hand. Selena, so happy she could cry.

"Red Top! Spinning round and round," blasted from apartment #3G. Selena, Zack, parents, brother and sister clapped as Jasmine spun around and around the Christmas tree to Earl Garner's advanced release before falling and exploding into infectious laughter, the kind only a three year old could incite. TC migrated back to the upright piano his Aunt Selena and Uncle Zack had given him for Christmas. Over the past six months, they noted how the gifted seven-year-old boy could hear a tune and play it by ear instantly. "You got to cultivate that," Aunt Selena had said. Having already sung two carols, Melba, the songbird of the family, wanted to sing again. While Mel and Lorette decided on what should be next, Jasmine piped up and said, "Red Top, again!"

"I got sumpthin' for ya," Zack told her and fired up the Hi Fi, putting on Bill Doggett's "Honky Tonk" and the lively little girl started dancing again. At the song's

318

end Uncle Zack declared, "Jasmine, you got some moves!"

"Jaz is jazzy!" Aunt Selena said, "Jazzzzzz," she repeated and threw up her open-palm hands and shook them. "Hot cha!"

Picking up on the gesture, the three-year-old sang, "Jaz, Jaz, Jaz... that's my name."

"Yes, it is...Jazzzz," Selena declared, and the little girl giggled and giggled.

They broke for the ice cream Aunt Selena and Uncle Zack always brought with them to accompany the Christmas sugar cookies the Culhane children had made, sprinkles and all. Hep and Selena sat on the couch while Zack sat at the piano with TC.

"Look at us," Selena said to her brother. "I know it sounds sappy but I am continually astounded. Did you ever think we'd be this happy again?"

"We hardly noticed when the war was over. We'd both suffered such losses."

"You ever think about Range?"

"All the time. He's just below the surface. Someone will say something that sounds like something he'd say. Every time I have a baby I wonder how many he would have had. What would he have named them? Where or who he'd be with today. On certain days I think I can call him and say, 'hey, I got a promotion, man.' "Ah! Congrats 'Bay rum and buttermilk.'" "Thanks 'perfume and peppermint.'"

"I recall Hep-cat and Hipster."

"Yeah," Hep laughed, good to discuss an old friend with someone who remembers him too. "It's a thousand things and then it's nothing." He realized he'd gone on the way only siblings allow and understand. "Homage to Hoyt again. And you?"

"I'd be the Old Lady Culhane still living at home in my childhood room 'cause there sure was no Colt, Texas boy I wanted to marry."

"And if he'd lived?"

"Wow. We'd have a three story row house in LeDroit Park. He'd have his photo studio on U Street. I'd be teaching music at Howard University days, playing at Bohemian Caverns at night. Maybe have kid or two to fill up those five bedrooms. Did you know he wanted to do films?"

"No. I know he loved Oscar Micheaux."

"One of the reasons he went overseas…to get priceless experience on the army's dime. Turned out to be expensive; he paid with his life. His dying impacted my life too."

"Hoyt changed our lives," Hep mused.

"I still think of him and smile. They always use his picture "Separate but Not Equal" and Gordon Parks' "American Gothic" for civil rights ads. The white magazines ask permission. I can be flipping pages and Boom! There it is. There he is. His work is still all over the place. It seems like a lifetime ago and like yesterday all at the same time."

"He and Zack would have gotten along."

"Same taste in women." Selena took another bite of cookie. "They didn't *know* each other but they respected one another. Each their own uncharted paths. Each going after their passions. Ever think of Feather?"

"Not really. When I do, I think of her as a mother who lives in Colt, Texas. We were literally kids. Had no idea the promises we made couldn't be kept. Youth gives you that optimism. When I came back I was riding on vapors. I didn't know it until I found out Range had died. That was the last straw; it all caved in on me. His sister married the right man."

"And you married the right woman?"

"Pretty much."

"Ummm."

"Alright, that is my wife and mother of my children."

"I didn't say a word."

"You never did."

"You didn't ask."

"Don't let yesterday take up too much of today. We were so innocent. Naïve. We're adults now. With adult hopes, dreams, responsibilities."

"I think it's called maturity."

"You seem happy with Zack."

"I am." She smiled.

"Life works out best for those who make the best out of the way life works out."

"Amen," Selena signified. "Those are folks from our past that now and always, live only in our hearts."

"So what's next for you?"

"We're thinking Paris, France."

"High cotton! You'll like Europe."

"I'm just tired and real pissed at the way we're treated here. Can perform but have to use the service elevator. Can't swim in the pool or even stay where you play. Getting only partial money for a better show than the white girls and guys. It's getting old. I'm getting old. I hear about playing in Europe where the only color they're interested in is green. Where they treat you like royalty."

"How many have to go overseas to make it big and then come back to U.S.?"

"How many never come back?"

"Can't blame them. Go where you are celebrated not tolerated. You'd come back."

"To visit," Selena teased. "It's in the talking stages. But one day ofays'll piss me off and I'm gone. I'd send for you all. If you can get off work."

"... And when he's not working, he's coaching his team at the Boys Club," Lorette interjected on her way to the kitchen.

"Mostly weekends," Hep picked up. "TC's in a baseball and football league at the Police Boys Club and it gives us quality time. When things are quiet on the streets, they let me do my shift there. A lot of the boys don't have dads who can take off. Good community relations."

"You're a good man, Hepburn Culhane."

"Yes, I am."

322

"So you staying with the law enforcement gig."

"Yeah. It's been good to and for me."

"The first black cop."

"Hardly. Besides my partner, Truck MacMillan being black, the initial honor goes to Roscoe "Rocky" Washington and Earl C. Broady about five years ago out of the Newton Street Division. LAPD was segregated, and no white cops were going to take orders from blacks so they created an all-black watch for Washington and Broady to supervise. Story goes somewhere in the middle of his probationary period, Broady was demoted to patrolman and when unsuccessful at getting his positon back, he resigned in '45. At 42 years of age he went to law school, but just last year in '49, Washington became the first black Watch Commander to oversee white officers. So far, so good."

"That what you want to do?"

"I'm going to take a stab at the detective exam when the time is right. I like what they do. I'd be good at it."

"How does wifey feel about that?"

"She'll adjust."

"You think so, huh?"

"When are you leaving for Paris?" he joked.

~*~

The hot sunshine burned brightly over Los Angeles. The palm trees rose high to try but failing miserably to touch the sky and the street below percolated with an aliveness, a mixture of hopes, dreams, successes and failures.   Hepburn Culhane's career progressed in unprecedented and circuitous ways unlike many black police officers of the LAPD. Unfortunately his reputation had attracted the ire of both Negro and white cops, but in his indomitable way, Hepburn Culhane remained a man of integrity and vision and, above all, a man who could be counted on regardless of the complexion of his partner; his only color was blue. He didn't gossip or join in reindeer games, known as a "decent," "fair" guy, the resentment began to subside, replaced with quiet respect for the man who respected all who wore the badge. Slightly opposite from his partner Truck McMillan who could be hot-headed when provoked.

Apartment #3G settled into a rhythm. With two Culhane children in school only one remained home with her mother. The luxury of having a housewife for a mother meant a child could sleep late and Jaz usually arose at ten after her mother had cleaned up the kitchen of breakfast dishes and lay on the couch to watch soap operas and game shows. Her mother put a bowl, a box of cereal and a spoon on the kitchen table for Jaz who got her own milk. If she wanted a hot breakfast, she had to get up early with everyone else. Jaz preferred to sleep. After her breakfast, the little girl'd put her dish in the sink, go and clean up and dress for the day with the clothes laid out at the foot of her bed. If the Spic 'n Span sat on the counter with the pail and mop, Jaz knew she had to decide where to be for the couple of hours it took her mother to mop the linoleum floor and let it dry. Her

324

choice was either up front in the living room with the television and her mother or alone in her bedroom where she had access to TC's room too. The long wet hall up to the bathroom remained the challenge; could she hold it for two hours?.

"Shuussh!" was her mother's response when she tried to ask a question or discuss what they'd do today; Lorette wasn't to be interrupted from watching her shows or her chance to rest before starting dinner. Jaz's only outings occurred if they went to the laundromat or store or to pick up Mel from school. Otherwise, Jaz stayed inside waiting for her brother to come home.

Often, there were fewer than ten words spoken to the little girl; "Jasmine clean up your dish." "Jasmine pick up your shoes." "Jasmine put away your crayons it's almost time for your brother and sister to come home." All directives. No conversation. Jaz didn't mind as she thought all houses ran this way. But when company came over, the astute little girl noted how engaging her mother became. "Yes, she is a sweetheart," her mother would say to a visitor. "Jasmine show her your paper." But company apparently tired her mother out because right after they left, her mother went back to her couch and lay down. Her mother seemed the same when her father and siblings were at home. Death to anyone who bothered her mother before the end of Art Linkletter when she seemed enthralled by strange children who seemed "to say the darnedest things." Lorette seemed to have a flesh and blood kid she didn't care to say anything to. This show served as her mother's cue to get ready for the return home of her first two children; it was Jaz's cue that her brother was on his way.

Jasmine's life-line to the outside world was her big brother, TC. As Art Linkletter entertained Lorette in the front room, Jaz would go to her bedroom window and wait for TC to come up the walkway. She'd run to the front door and open it for him just as he climbed the steps. With a "Hey, Jaz," her day began.

First her mother had to shower him with kisses and questions about what happened at school while Jaz'd follow him down the hall to his room. She'd jump up on his spare bed as he shucked his school clothes and changed into his play clothes. While her mother wasn't interested in the least, TC would ask Jaz what she did today. What did she play? Did she go out?

TC never said anything about his mother's lack of interest in his baby sister but started to quiz Jaz on colors, shapes, her numbers and while he ate his grilled cheese snack at the same table where she'd had her cold cereal, they'd recite the alphabet. When Lorette displayed TC's "A" papers on the refrigerator with a magnet, Jaz took an interest in them. As TC finished his homework, he gave Jaz work to do as well. TC started leaving Jaz work to do during the day and grading it while he ate his after-school snack. The first time Jaz got her arithmetic right he rushed to show his mother, "Look what Jaz did. They're all right!" "Nice," Lorette said. "Aren't you goin' to put it on the refrigerator with mine and Mel's coloring?"

"I will when she's in school, dear. Now clean up before your father gets home."

The seven-year-old TC noted the disappointed sadness in his sister's eyes. The next day TC was late coming home but when he reviewed Jaz's spelling and she got them all right he said, "Good, Jaz. You get a gold star!" He'd clapped and Jaz'd beamed. He'd stopped by the Five and Dime on his way home and bought a box of gold stars and five squirrel nuts. "Wanna go outside?"

"Yes!" Jaz'd say and jump around. Often when TC took her outside it was the first time she'd left apartment #3G all day. He'd toss her the ball or watch her jump rope and try to impress him with cartwheels or show off her progress on what he'd taught her about tying her shoe.

Jaz's worse days were when TC and her father had practice three days a week at the Boys Club. On those days Jaz had to go with her mother and sister to various activities designed for Mel. Whether hair appointments or dance class, the waiting seemed an eternity. Jaz would have rather stayed home by herself and watch TV or do the homework TC'd left, but her parents said she had to go. At almost five years old her sister, Mel, had become a singer and sought out by many choirs to appear in plays and talent shows around town. Dubbed "The Little Girl with the Big Voice," this meant in addition to hair appointments, there were auditions, rehearsals, and shopping for dresses, fittings and alterations. Her mother seemed to enjoy these more than Mel who always wanted to sleep. While Jaz and TC played outside, Mel preferred taking a nap after school.

Her father's and brother's activities were much "more funner" than her mother's and sister's. Besides growing resentment, Jaz grew tired of her mother's act of fawning over her when she had an audience and ignoring her when it was just the two of them. Jaz longed for the day when she'd be in school and learning and her recreation could be with her father and brother.

~*~

The familiar pop pierced the quiet Watts neighborhood, alerting residents that bullets threatened their safety. Hep identified the sound as gunshots while he and Truck approached the small crowd gathered across the street from a modest bungalow. The smoke emanating from the front window marked the source of the problem.

Ever since the end of the war, there had been an increase in these minor offenses. Veterans who fought for freedom in the war denied it when they returned. Tired of Jim Crow tactics and wanting a better life for themselves and their families, blacks swelled the population in Promised Land of California, only to be crammed into certain sections of the city. When Japanese were sent to internment camps, Little Tokyo became Bronzeville to reflect the skin color of the new residents. Watts, Willowbrook and Linwood's hues changed, all enforced and upheld by the restrictive housing covenants which prohibited blacks living elsewhere even if they could afford it. Tensions, frustrations, scarcity and lack of good-paying jobs exploded and spilled over with an occasional veteran who'd brought a gun back with his newfound pride. Letting off steam was predictable and Hep's job was to make sure the release vent exorcized oppression without harming any innocent neighbors.

"Who is he?" Hep asked a bystander.

"Bennie."

"Bennie," Hep called out. "I'm Sgt. Culhane. Can I talk to you?"

"'Bout what?" '

Hep recognized the type; half drunk, part crazed with suffered indignities of being a black veteran in America and all mad. "Anyone in there with him?"

"Naw. Wife at work. Children at school," the bystander informed.

"Tired of talk. Out of talk," Bennie spat and took another swig from the bottle. "You the man in black face?"

"My job is to serve and protect you and this community."

"Serve and protect this—" Bennie let off a wild shot that whizzed by Hep's ear, causing Truck to duck.

"I'm calling for back-up," Truck announced, hunching his way to the squad car.

"Look. I'm putting down my gun. Can I come and just speak to you?"

"What?" Bennie couldn't believe his eyes. "You simple mothafuc—I could take your head off with one shot."

Hep figured if Bennie had wanted, he could have killed them all by now. That wasn't his intention. "Where'd you learn to shoot? In the Army?"

"Yeah. I served in the Army. They treated us like shit then and they still treat us like shit. Double V, my ass. 'Victory overseas and Victory at home.' What a crock."

"Where'd you serve, Bennie? I was in Italy."

No response.

Hep took his opening and advanced slowly into the middle of the street. "Did you see Italy?"

"Naw. France."

"Yeah? I had a buddy in France. My best buddy as a matter of fact." Hep stopped at the curb, not invading Bennie's space. "He said there were good times and rough times. Sometimes he'd deliver supplies or bombs and they wouldn't even let them eat a hot meal in the mess tent. They had to eat K-rations and sleep in the trucks."

No response from the house.

The large crowd hushed, watching the drama unfold. Bennie's front door squeaked opened just a crack. Hep stood tall as the crowd ducked.

"He was with the Red Ball Express," Hep continued.

The door opened wide, Bennie visible. He eyed Hep with a dazed expression. A gaze of disbelief and walked slowly toward him.

"Put the gun down!" Truck yelled and advanced, gun drawn, aimed at Bennie's head.

330

Hep held up his hand to his partner. "They want you to put your gun down, Bennie."

"I was in the Red Ball Express," Bennie whispered directly to Hep. "Nobody knows about us."

"My buddy told me all about your company. Listen. Could you drop the gun, Bennie?"

"What was his name?" simultaneously, Bennie asked and dropped the gun. It clunked to the ground. Truck swooped in and grabbed it as Hep said, "Range Criqui."

"Ah damn! I know him! That was my boy! Did he talk about me?" Bennie asked as Truck reached for Bennie's hand to cuff him.

Hep shook his head no to Truck.

Truck's eyes asked Hep, "Are you crazy?"

"There's no danger right now. Why don't we talk until your ride comes?"

"Yeah. No danger," Bennie spat at Truck and rolled his eyes back to Hep. "They called me Red 'cause I'm so black."

"Red..." Hep stumbled remembering, "SkeeKee Benton?"

"Yeah! Hot damn! Yeah. That's me!" Tears sprang to Bennie's eyes.

The crowd laughed with relief and humor. Hep and Red sat on the porch of his house like old friends as two squad cars poured into the neighborhood. The two veterans spoke of Range and some of their exploits, Red not believing Range had died. "Once we exchanged seats mid-air. We were flying. He was as crazy as I was." He stopped. "Sorry he didn't make it."

"Me too," Hep offered. "I wish he had a wife, a house like this and kids in school."

"Yeah."

"It's not perfect, but you got a lot to be thankful for, Red."

"Yeah. I do, but it gets so frustrating."

"Yep. Being a black man in America hasn't ever been easy, but we need to do what we can to make it good for ourselves and our families."

Hep dismissed one police car as the other one waited.

Skee Kee shook his head mournfully.

"All of us have broken lives in one way or another. But there's always redemption. We need to make better choices."

"You right."

"Listen, I'm going to have to cite you for Disturbing the Peace, Red. And Discharging a Weapon in city limits."

"I know. You do what you got to do, brother. It was worth it. I'm gonna straighten myself out."

"Good luck. I'll be checking on you."

Hep watched Red be handcuffed and led to the squad car. His head palmed and protected as he ducked and slid in the back seat. A man who only wanted to be recognized, remembered and reminded of all he was and what he could do… given the chance. With the sun glinting off his handcuffs, Red waved goodbye.

"You are the slickest MF I've ever known. Lock the man up and he's throwing goodbye kisses," Truck teased.

"All in a day's work," Hep countered as he opened his car door, thinking at least no one was shot.

"The Red Ball Express," Truck inquired. "Was that for real?"

"Yep. Triple Nickels too. The 555th. Buy me a burger and I'll tell you all about it."

Amazing Grace

Driving along the tree-lined streets of Evelyn, Tennessee the Culhanes of Los Angeles, California had come to bury the woman who helped raised the "Five Javier Girls." Annie had passed peacefully in her sleep and the service proved as dignified as her life had been. The Javiers paid for the funeral and hosted the repass at the Javier home. "She was family," the eulogy stated.

The three Culhane children proved to be hits of their own. Everyone was interested in Lorette Javier Culhane and the exotic life she lived thousands of miles away in glamorous California. Lorette missed her dear old friends; Effie, a concert pianist, met and married an opera singer and lived in Belgium, but sent a fabulous display of spring flowers and a letter recalling Annie's generosity to her as a young girl. Gay Iris married with children lived in Ohio, also sent her regrets and remembrances of how Annie would feed them anytime day or night along with her mother-wit and advice. Lorette missed her dear old friends who now only kept in touch via Christmas and birthday cards since they all had distant and busy lives of their own. They weren't present, but other old friends and neighbors marveled at the Culhane children; all different but all equally beautiful. Many singled out TC with his olive, Indian-brown complexion and astounding mass of curly ebony hair. Mel for her unbelievable voice and soulful rendition of "Amazing Grace" at Annie's funeral, but Jaz… stunning.

"How can a little girl be 'stunning?'" Lorette fumed to her husband quietly.

"Why does that bother you? All of our children are healthy, smart, talented and cute," Hep teased.

"It's not funny, Hep," Lorette snapped.

The California Culhane children climbed all over the mansion of a house. Explored all the rooms and every nook and cranny and porch, playing hide and seek. When Papa Javier could pull himself away from his grands, who he'd only seen once, he lured his son-in-law to the old Duesenberg stored in the garage. "Lorette sent us the newspaper clippings of your heroics in the streets of Los Angeles," Alexander said to Hep. "Impressive."

"Just doing my job, sir."

"Off-duty patrolman running into a burning house and rescuing an old lady and her cats. Single-handedly saving that white cop surrounded by a black gang until reinforcements came." He looked over at Hep. "Didn't have to do that."

"Yes, I did." Hep anticipated Mr. J'd need a wrench and passed it to him.

"How about talking the man down from the ledge and saving him and his wife and children."

"That's why they pay me."

"Seems to me you're building a good reputation as a man who can handle explosive situations and diffuse them. A man to be counted on and respected."

"Learned that compliments of Uncle Sam."

"That's why you've advanced to lieutenant." He handed Hep the wrench back and took the screwdriver. "Your wife is mighty proud. You don't tell her all of it."

"Not by a long-shot."

Papa Javier grinned his consent.

Lorette paused at the window, smiling as she glimpsed her father and husband working on the Duesenberg.

"Like old times," the Duchess remarked, putting silverware back in the drawer.

"Seems like just yesterday."

"You still love him?"

"More than I ever thought I could." She beamed at her mother before returning her gaze to her handsome husband. "His touch still makes me tremble."

TC went over to his dad who pointed out some gizmos under the hood. "The three most important men in my life, Mama," Lorette said with a wide grin and a blush.

"Anyone with eyes can see that."

That night, miles away, Selena Fluellen wowed the audience at The Sands in Las Vegas. The packed house hung on her every note, felt every nuanced lyric, their eyes drank in her dark form draped in a loose-fitting, elegant sequined gown, witnessing the change of colors from the spotlight, shimmering as she treated them to the five octaves of her unique voice. The all-white audience snapped their fingers as she sang "They Can't Take That Away from Me," rocked in their seats as "Old Devil Moon" fell from her rubied lips, became reverent and church-quiet as she sang, "Cry Me a River, " and dabbed their eyes when she closed with her signature song, "Stardust." A standing ovation and shouts of "encore" brought her back twice before she finally left the stage for good.

Signaling the end of her engagement, Selena remained full of energy and awaken early, leaving Zack in bed deciding to take a dip before they returned to L.A. In a white one piece with a flowing, lacy cover up, she decided to have breakfast at the pool bar where many patrons who'd seen the show last night greeted her. Donning her sunglasses, she claimed a lounge chair near the pool and accepted a towel from a nervous cabana boy. "What's the matter, son? I won't bite," she teased and closed her eyes waiting for her food to digest.

The heat of the dry, hot sun awoke her. She rose, shed her cover-up and sauntered to the steps of the pool descending and becoming soothed and invigorated by the welcoming coolness of the blue water. "Ummm," she cooed, immersing her body, letting the water close around her neck, not allowing her hair to get wet.

"Excuse me, Miss Fluellen," an officious white man in a suit and tie approached. "I'm going to have to ask you to vacate the premises."

"What?" Selena shielded her eyes and looked up into the man's beady gaze.

"You cannot swim in this pool. It is reserved for 'whites only.'"

Selena thought, *This man certainly doesn't know who I am. The revenue from her performance last night probably paid his salary.* She looked around and saw that all the white people had left the pool and stood around the edges waiting for her to leave. Embarrassment. Angry indignation swirled in her mind. These very people who loved her last night, couldn't get enough of her, now couldn't stand the thought of sharing the same cool water on a hot day. Thought she was dirty. Had cooties. Anything but the right to be in the same water with them.

Sick. Hypocritical white folks, she thought. Too stunned and hurt to curse them out, she could have easily burned down this hotel and all of Las Vegas.

"Selena," the familiar voice pierced her stubborn anger. "We have to get going. Ready?" Zack asked in a soothing, dignified tone.

Seeing him holding all her belongings from the lounge chair, extending his hand gallantly toward her almost made her cry. Regally, she climbed the pool stairs and took the proffered hand, "My knight in shining armor," she whispered to him.

"My queen," he countered with a smile that stilled her heart.

"You got everything?" she asked non-plussed, looking back at the lounge chair she'd vacated.

"I believe so. Which route do you want to take back to L.A.?" he asked amiably like they were vacating a garden party and had all the time in the world.

Selena couldn't open her mouth again. Not as adept as her husband, she remained silent until they reached their room. Once the door closed, Selena crumbled. Furious tears stung her eyes. She wanted to cuss every ofay out. Never had she been so humiliated. Hurt by the very people who loved her less than twenty-four hours ago. She dissolved into Zack's arms. Mortified by her reaction. Disappointed in herself that these no-named, irrelevant, clear-white folks had gotten to her.

"What do you expect of people who come to an occupied country and 'discover' it?" Zack held her. "You give them too much credit. I have very low-expectations when it comes to white folk. And they seldom disappoint. I don't ask them to give me nuthin'."

"Just open the door and you'll get it for yourself."

"Precisely. One monkey don't stop no show."

"I'd heard the stories about how The Flamingo Hotel treated Lena Horne," Selena sighed. "Set her up in a cabana and burned her sheets every morning. And the way they treated Miles Syphax when he bought his house in Hancock Park back in the late 40s, paid $75,000 for it. White folks didn't pay that much for those houses in that neighborhood. First, the Neighborhood Association tried to block the deal then tried to buy it back. When Miles didn't back down, they poisoned his dog and burned 'nigger' into his lawn. He stayed. He's a class act."

Selena recalled her last visit to Miles' home where they discussed their co-optic audience.

"This business is not for the thin-skinned. I know what they call me. Blackie, Darkie, if he closes his eyes he disappears in the dark. Sooty Syphax, Shine Syphax. My favorite is Sambo Syphax. I like the alliteration." He chuckled.

"But they also call you the best crooner of all time. The Velvet Voice. Mr. Cool. Mr. Smooth. Give you credit for saving Capitol Records," Selena offered.

"I learned a lot about folks growing up in Eutaw, Alabama. If you believe folk, any folk, when they tell you 'you're great,' then you are obliged to believe them when they 'call you out your name.' That's why I answer to me and only me. I know when I'm doing good and when I'm not. No comments from the peanut gallery needed." He'd thrown a beach ball back to his son in the pool. "It's not what they call you, kiddo. It's what you answer to."

"I know what they call you at the bank," Zack had interjected. "Mr. Syphax." They'd all laughed.

"It's a gorgeous house," Zack said, bringing her back to the present.

"Yes, it is," Selena agreed as she slid into the passenger's side of the car. "I'm never coming back here."

"Never say never."

They drove back towards L.A. in silence, stopping for gas and an ice cold Coke Cola. *The U.S. is like an*

340

abusive parent, Selena thought. *Black folk keep trying to give them a chance to redeem themselves and they never do. It's time to cut bait.*

Once back in the car Selena spoke, "I'm ready."

"For what?" Zack asked, not removing his eyes from the monotonous road.

"To go to Paris, France."

Zack smiled. "Yeah?"

"Yeah."

"You'll love it. And they will love you."

"Where do we stay? At Bricktops?"

"You can stay wherever you want."

"The Ritz?"

"That's fine." He glanced at her. "We can stay there for a few weeks until we find a flat."

Selena laughed. "Yeah. Right. Until they tell us we've got to leave."

"Selena. Europe is interested in one color... green. Fans are interested in whether you have the chops or not. It's a whole other world over there. They never colonized this country. They don't have ofays' hang-ups. They're not still fighting the Civil War hoping for a different outcome. I been there several times. I know. Any musician who's been there knows. You'll see. We'll go. If your schedule allows, we'll stay a month. Scout out whether it's a place where you can live or not. If so, we'll get a house so when we go there, we don't have to stay at The Ritz."

Selena looked over at him. "You jivin'?"

"Square business."

It Had To Be You

"Can we go and see your grandparents now?" Jaz asked, standing behind her father in his ear as he drove his family back to L.A. from Evelyn, Tennessee.

"My grandparents are long gone. You mean *your* grandparents," Hep clarified to the four year old.

"GrandPa Colt and Grandma Keely in Texas," TC piped up.

"Yeah," Jaz agreed, "The ones we talk to on the phone. I've never seen them."

"Sit back," Lorette said.

Jaz ignored her and continued, "Have TC and Mel seen them?"

"No," TC said from the window seat behind his mother. Mel, sitting in the middle, kept writing in her notepad.

"We've seen Lorette's mom and dad and I want to see yours."

"Jaz, don't call your mother, Lorette," Hep admonished for the umpteenth time since their trip began. He glanced at his wife questioning where she'd picked up this habit, to which Lorette just hunched her shoulders.

"That's what people have called me for the last week," Lorette told her husband sotto voce.

"No excuse," he said.

"Don't make a big deal out of it," Lorette advised quietly, patting her husband's leg.

"That'd be good, Dad. To put faces with voices over the phone," TC continued from the back seat.

"I agree, son. We'll work on that. You all start school in a few weeks and I have to work out my schedule."

"Yippee. School," Jaz enthused. "Finally. I've been waiting *all* my life."

~*~

The third week of school, Hep and Lorette were summoned by the teacher to school.

"It seems we have an issue with Jasmine answering to her name."

"I beg your pardon?" Hep asked.

"She does not answer to 'Jasmine.' She declares her name is 'Jaz.'"

Hep chuckled out loud.

Lorette and Mrs. Lloyd did not.

"It's very disruptive. I call her name and I, along with the rest of the class, wait for her to answer."

"I'm very sorry—" Lorette began.

"Wait. Is she doing her work?"

"Why yes. She's very bright which is why I've been so lenient. Bright children are often rambunctious. Tavio is equally as bright but he's more reserved and—"

"Mrs. Lloyd. With all due respect, we are not here to discuss Tavio or Mel. We don't compare our children with one another and we'd appreciate that you see them as individuals as well. You called us here to discuss, Jaz, whose only offense seems to be not answering to the name Jasmine. May I suggest that you call her Jaz? What harm is there in that? In my line of work I run across many children with far more serious offenses than four letters on the end of their name. She is not wrong. We do call her Jaz. Perhaps she is putting you and the rest of the class in the family-friend category. I'd think of that as a positive. Now," Hep stood, adjusted his gun and billy club, "If ever there is a serious behavioral problem or a school challenge, please feel free to call me from work to discuss it. A professional such as yourself, I am sure you'll find a way to compromise with a four year old and find a solution to this classroom 'dilemma.' I trust your judgement. Have a great day." Hep strode to the door in only four steps and opened it for his wife.

Offering pleasantries along the way out through the corridor and to the car, once seated Lorette said, "You totally stood up on Jaz's side."

"I did. It's her name. She can be called as she sees fit. Whatever she wants in life, she'll have to fight or bargain for it. Never too early for children to learn how to do that."

I'm in trouble with this third child, she thought.

Right before Christmas vacation, the Culhanes were called to Park View Elementary again. This time to the principal's office on a disciplinary action. Jaz had punched Johnny Green in the nose and made it bleed.

Outraged by the red on their son's white shirt, the Greens, who called for the meeting, were also in attendance.

"Let's call the children in," Hep suggested.

Once done, the principal, Mrs. Seuter, asked the reason for the playground melee.

"She hit me for no reason just because we wouldn't let her play 'Witches and Fairies.'"

"You lie like a rug, Johnny Green!" Jaz shot back.

"Jaz," her father tempered.

"What is your version?" Mrs. Seuter asked her.

"He said my sister had a gorilla nose and started making monkey noises and they all laughed at her. I told them to stop and they kept on going. So I punched him in his   nose."

"Johnny, is that true?" Mrs. Green asked of her son.

"Yes, ma'am."

"That is not the way you were raised, young man. Apologize."

"Sorry."

"Didn't call me gorilla nose. You got to apologize to Mel."

The adults chuckled which confused Jaz.

"I will see to it, alright?" Mrs. Green asked.

"And Jaz," Hep began. "You cannot go hitting people you disagree with. That is no way to settle any differences. You either talk it out or walk away. You apologize to Johnny Green."

"But Dad—"

346

"Jaz."

"Sorry."

On the way home Hep suggested that they pick up Mel and TC and go out to eat. As Jaz ran up the steps to get her siblings, Lorette said, "Hep, you are rewarding her for bad behavior."

"I am rewarding her for standing up for her sister. Not sure if Mel would have done the same for Jaz."

At bedtime that night, Jaz confided to her father that he'd probably be called to school again because someone said Mel was 'adopted.' "Because she didn't look like me and TC. It was a girl. I didn't punch her!" Jaz said proudly. "They tattle-tell on me all the time. So you can expect another call."

"Thanks, punkin," he told his daughter. "I'll wait for it."

It never came.

Thus by the time Jaz was five, school had settled down and everyone had survived. Allowed outside to mingle with other girls of the block, Jaz learned bat and ball, jacks and pick-up sticks but her favorite activity was jumping—Double Dutch—a challenge she soon mastered by sticking the ribbon of her ponytail into her mouth so it wouldn't interfere with the rope. Many girls populated Alvaro Street but Jaz's main friends were Dedra, Alice, Valerie and Echo Blake, even if she was double-handed and couldn't slap the rope on the concrete like the rest of them.

TC came home, laid his bike against the tree and ran upstairs. The shiny blue metallic, two wheeler called to Jaz and she went over and hopped on. She tried to steer it and promptly fell, scraping her knee but, thank God, not TC's bike. She repositioned it and waited in line for her turn with the ropes.

"Jaz, your knee is bleeding," Dedra informed.

Jaz ran upstairs to tend to it.

Bursting through the door her mother noted her blood.

"Jaz—"

"I can fix it," she dismissed, heading for the bathroom. She wiped off her scratch with toilet paper and stood on the top of the commode seat to reach the mercurochrome in the medicine cabinet.

"What are you doing?" Hep poked his head in the bathroom door.

"Fixing a scrape."

"Let me help," he reached for the red medicine and she sat back down on the toilet. "You've got to clean this off."

"I did."

"Let's see if we can't get rid of this gritty dirt."

Jaz watched her father put her leg on his lap and drizzle water over the scrape before rinsing it then patting it dry. He patiently applied the mercurochrome and plucked a Band-Aid from the cabinet under the sink. "You got this jumping rope?"

Jaz shook her head, no. Eyeing the hallway for her brother, she then whispered, "I tried to ride TC's bike."

"Jaz. You'll get your bike this Christmas."

"I know. I won't try it again. It's too high and has that bar."

"Yes it does. Go change your socks," he said, looking at the spattered blood.

"Thanks, Dad." Jaz could hear Mel singing from the hallway. Jaz opened the door to see Mel standing on her bed with a brush in her hand and a crinoline on her head.

"Don't you know how to knock?" Mel shouted at the intrusion.

"It's my room too. What are you doing with a half slip on your head?" Jaz asked as she rummaged through her sock drawer to find the perfect pair that matched the pink pedal pushers. "When are you going to clean your side of the room?" Jaz asked kicking a pair of her underwear towards its owner.

"I told you I don't have to. I'm going to have maids when I grow up."

"Well, you don't have them yet." Jaz, tired of her sister's show asked, "Jumping Double Dutch, you wanna come?"

"Heavens, no," Mel answered, predictably.

"Enjoy 'Mel Land,'" Jaz said sarcastically.

By the time Jaz got back up front, her father was gone and TC's bike was propped against the wall near the closet. Her brother was fishing for something off the closet's top shelf and an article fell and hit the floor.

"What is that?" Both Jaz and her brother reached for the object at the same time. "A hat?" Jaz said and plopped it on her head. They both laughed.

"It's Dad's hat from the olden days. And it's too big for you."

Jaz looked up at her brother from under its wide brim. "I'll grow to it."

"It's a man's hat," TC said.

"Don't I look cool?"

"No, you look a fool," Lorette said, coming up from behind, chuckling at her own little rhyming joke.

Mother and her son laughed.

Jaz did not.

"Give it to your brother," Lorette mandated.

"But I found and wore it first," Jaz protested.

"Jaz, it's not for a young lady to wear. I'll get you one with flowers—"

"I don't want one with flowers. Here!" Jaz tore the brown felt fedora from her head and shoved it into TC's chest. She rushed from the apartment down the steps to rejoin her friends.

"Your father's waiting for you in the car," Lorette said to her son. "Have a good practice."

Hep waited for his son in the car at the curb. When TC came through the outside door, wearing her hat, Jaz left the car and went to get in line for her turn at Double Dutch. She couldn't look at TC.

He walked over to her, took the hat from his head and put it on hers. "Looks better on you."

350

Beneath the large brim, Jaz smiled up at him with such unabashed gratitude. "Thank you!"

"Mess it up and I'm taking it back!" he warned, climbing into the front seat beside his father.

Jaz loved the 1940s fudge brown fedora, which became her comfort when she wasn't with her father who'd owned it or her brother who gave it to her. The fact that it irked and embarrassed her mother so, just a bonus.

~*~

"Paris, France?" Lorette asked at dinner after TC's Little League game.

"Yep," Selena said proudly.

"When?" Hep asked.

"Now that I've finished my contractual obligations, the first of the year."

"After New Year's at The Satin Doll?" Mel asked.

"Yes."

Mel nodded agreement. She'd come to count on her picture with her famous aunt which appeared in JET Magazine's "Picture of the Week" two Christmases in a row. Better than the EBONY article on Selena Fluellen which only mentioned Brittany Melba Culhane once.

"How long?" Jaz asked from under her hat.

"Just a month or so. Got to find out if I like it."

"And if you do?"

"Then we might move there for a little bit."

"What? That's a long way to get my hair done," Jaz remarked with a sigh.

"Well, I thought about that," Selena said. "I already have a headband for Mel, and two ponytail barrettes for you. You gather up your hair and clamp them on in place. You're old enough to start taking care of your own hair."

"Okay," Jaz said skeptically, "but I'm not washing it."

The next week, they all sat in the audience as the "Little Girl with the Big Voice" belted out "Somewhere Over the Rainbow" and won the talent contest. She posed for pictures wearing a pretty dotted Swiss, yellow dress and the headband Aunt Selena had given her.

"I'm going to have to move out of my room with all of her awards," Jaz teased. Once back home, TC played the upright piano accepting requests from all of them. He started with Jaz's favorite, "Canadian Sunset." At the end of the night, he became uncharacteristically sentimental and said, "I have something for you, Aunt Selena." From behind his back he presented her with a thin roll of paper.

"What is this, handsome?" She opened the sheet music and read the top, "Beauty Black." Composer, Tavio Range Culhane. "Oh, my Lord!!" Selena bear-hugged her nephew and almost bumped him from the piano bench. "Play it for me..." and he did. At the song's end, Selena had dissolved in tears. "I have the most talented family in the world. TC, this is lyrically complicated and... priceless."

"Wait until I do the words," he beamed.

As the family settled in to play a quick game of Chinese checkers, brother and sister sat at the kitchen counter.

"I can just see Zack loves being with the kids," Hep said, handing Selena another piece of cake.

"I told him once I couldn't have children. He told me he had his own, plus they are 'overrated.'"

Selena and Hep chuckled. "You met them?"

"Only Renee'. She's in college now."

"By the way. They're not 'overrated.' They are gifts from God, especially these three."

"A little biased?"

"Just look at them. Different but the same. Know who TC reminds me of?" Hep asked.

"Who?"

"Range."

"Really? The same coloring, skin, hair...he could be a Criqui."

"Or a Javier," Hep offered.

"Psh! There's no denying Mel. She, me and Star got that Saida-hair. Grows if and when it wants. Although Mel has a coffee-and-cream complexion; Star and I have her on that. We are Beauty-Blacks."

"According to Dad, sounds like Mel has Saida's eyes. The ones Lone Wolf couldn't get enough of."

"But that last one. Jaz. Seems like all of our ancestors piled up in her. That coppery-bronze complexion got to be African-Indian. Her hair more

Indian than ours... it grows, shot through with that gold and those light eyes—"

"Javier."

"You keep bringing them up," Selena smirked at her brother playfully. "When I saw Jaz with her Grandpapa Javier...they shared similar coloring. I'd never thought of that before. But hers is deeper, richer."

"I'm sure the Javiers appreciate your giving them some of the credit."

"Her features are unbelievably mature on such a little girl. Too early for the nose but those kiss-me lips."

"Selena! I'm not thinking about my daughters kissing anybody any time soon."

"Mel's are nice and full, but Jaz's have that little pouty, saucy, Frenchy thing going on."

"Cheeze. You're not even there yet." He took a swig of beer. "You're staying aren't you?"

"I dunno. I know I'm sick and tired of these garden variety ofay-clear-white-folks over here. I'm going to give France time to piss me off."

"It's not like that over there."

"You sound like Zack. But you two have been over there." She ate the last of her cake. "You saw what they did to Paul?"

"Robeson? Yeah, he presented a paper to the U.N earlier this year, 'We Charge Genocide,' and that McCarthy committee has been on him like white folk on rice. And The NAACP's distanced itself calling him a 'dangerous gadfly.'"

"Well, I still call him friend. Hate leaving him over here but his passport's been pulled."

The doorbell rang and Hep went to get it. "Hey, Truck."

"I don't want to interrupt the celebration," Hep's partner said.

"Just family. C'mon in," Hep instructed.

Introductions were made all around before Truck accepted the offered beer and settled in with Hep and Selena. "It's a pleasure to meet you, Selena Fluellen. Who believed this cat really knew you?" Truck MacMillan teased.

"You're just a tall drink of water. I bet white folks get you two mixed up all the time," Selena sassed.

"Hep's got a few inches on me. Oh, here are the keys before I forget. Taking the family on a much-needed vacation," Truck explained. "I leave my house in Hep's capable hands."

"You're the one who suggested him for the Watts Division awhile back."

"Guilty. I'd seen how he handled himself in the streets with blacks, whites and Mexicans alike. Never rattles."

"That's my brother."

"I'd already witnessed his perfect score at the range. So I dug into his history. Northwestern University, sniper in WWII, which explained his shooting ability. So when Brass asked who I'd want to take with me to man the new post, his name topped my list."

The two men clicked bottles in a toast. "When preparation meets opportunity."

"With all LAPD's corruption, I needed someone I could trust. To have my back. Be able to follow through." Though he didn't mention it now, Truck had noted how all sorts of women came onto Hep but he never broke his professional stride; not a stare, a leer or a comment. After he'd seen his pretty wife, Lorette and their children at various promotions ceremonies, he understood why.

"Don't leave out integrity," Selena prompted.

"Plus we both knew Morse code, compliments of WWII and learned sign language…made up our way of communicating and the rest was history. Drove white folks crazy with our 'jungle talk.' He's certainly gone on and up the department ladder."

Selena smiled proudly at her brother.

"Of course, the department pulls him just as often for the Boys Club. Seems the youth in the area go for organized sports but stay for Coach Culhane. Whenever anything happens with the gangs, they call Culhane to calm the waring boys. He seems to have their respect," Truck elaborated. "And much-needed patience."

"Don't you have to get going?" Hep joked.

Truck glanced at his watch. "Matter of fact I do." He stood and addressed the room, "A pleasure meeting you. Goodnight to all!"

"Safe travels. Here's your Green Book." Hep plucked it from the top of the refrigerator and handed it to him.

356

"It was helpful?" Truck asked of the book for Negro motorists published by a postal worker that detailed all the places Negroes were welcomed to eat and stay in the country.

"You bet. Maybe one day we won't have the need for it."

"Did I mention optimistic?" Truck said and saluted a final farewell.

The next day, Hep left the team going through their paces on The Boys Club field to run home and get Truck's keys to check on his buddy's house. From nowhere, Jaz called out and ran to him, "Hi Daddy!"

Hep watched his daughter come from across the street as one of Mae Tilgman's boys fell back and returned to his apartment building. His daughter jumped into his arms.

"Jaz, where are you coming from?"

"Getting my hair done."

"In her house?"

"Yeah."

He looked at his daughter for signs of trauma.

"I go over there and she washes and plaits it for me. She says 'the key is to get it while it's wet. Your hair takes water.'" She laughed at her own impression of Miss Mae. Her father didn't chuckle at all. "Where are you going? Can I go?"

Hep opened the door and Lorette stood in the middle of the living room. She looked at her daughter's neatly braided hair and her husband's icy glare. *What is he doing home now?* She thought then said, "It looks nice, Jaz. How's Miss Mae?"

"Fine."

"Jaz, why don't you go to your room and change your clothes."

"I'm already in my play clothes," she responded quizzically. "Can I go outside and skate?"

"Yes," her father said without removing his eyes from his wife. "Don't leave the block."

"I know." She got her metal skates from the closet and put the key around her neck. "Bye."

Once his daughter cleared the threshold and closed the door Hep fought to contain his anger. "You let our daughter go over to the apartment of known felons to get her hair done?"

"Now, Hep—"

"No Lorette. There is no excuse. I work hard to keep my family safe and you send her over there in the midst of them because of hair?"

"You make it sound so simple—"

"Let me ask you this… would you send Mel?"

Lorette looked at her husband, mouth open, nothing coming out. "They're different children—"

"What does that even mean? That Jaz can handle herself and Mel can't?" Hep wiped his hand over his head in frustration. "I don't care what you have to do, but you find another option for our daughter that does not have her in the presence of the Tilgman brothers. You take a class if need be. Or I will gladly do my daughter's hair

358

before I go to work. Fathers who don't have wives do it all the time. Is that what I'm going to be, Lorette? A single father? You just let me know when it's all too much for you."

From where she stood, Lorette silently watched her husband go into the bedroom and get Truck's house key from their dresser. He grabbed his baseball cap and said, "I'll be at the Boys Club field with TC."

~*~

The New Year's Eve celebration was stellar that year at The Satin Doll. That year it seemed the banner was bigger, the cache of balloons larger, the confetti guns poised at the ready as all the beautiful people glided in; women in their fur stoles and gowns and men in their tuxes. Even Mel was impressed with the mood and attire after she was told she could not lead "Auld Lang Syne." The Culhane girls wore sumptuous red velvet dresses trimmed with white French lace and TC had been fitted in a tux. Word ran rampant that Selena and Zack were the next French defectors and it seemed all who attended were intent on giving them a send-off to remember. Decorations dripped from every nook and cranny and, at the tables, centerpieces of horn blower fountains festooned with other noisemakers awaited the magical hour. Every available singer wanted to perform one of their songs that night which made the air sizzle as they tried to outdo one another. A photographer from EBONY Magazine circulated among the patronage snapping pictures of all who fought to pose in front of its lens.

"Jaz, she looks like Ma." TC pointed to a star he'd seen before. "Isn't she beautiful?"

Jaz looked at the woman and refused to admit any resemblance, and hunched her shoulders nonchalantly.

"She is pretty," Mel admitted.

"Hey sweetie," Aunt Selena sat beside them momentarily. "You having a good time?"

Jaz watched her mother pose for a picture with the star.

"I love this dress, Aunt Selena," Mel gushed. "It's divine."

"I'll be sending you all school clothes from Paris. What do you want, my man?"

"A beret," TC said, and they laughed.

"Your hair looks exquisite," a stunning woman in an off-the-shoulder, organza, cream-colored gown walking by said of Jaz's French braid.

"Thank you," Jaz replied and looked up at the lady. "Now *she* is gorgeous."

"That's Dorothy Dandridge," Selena identified. *Too bad Lorette doesn't look like her*, Jaz thought then said, "I'm going to miss you, Aunt Selena."

"I'll be back, Jazzy."

"Promise?"

"Promise. How else can I give you butterfly kisses?" Aunt Selena grabbed her niece and kissed her cheek just as the photographer came upon them. "Smile pretty." A picture snapped before he moved on.

Someone To Watch Over Me

The Fluellens boarded the *LLe de France* at New York City harbor, ascended the gangplank and followed their purser to the deluxe stateroom like Black Hollywood personified. Selena wanted to take the sister ship, *Liberte'*, she thought more apropos, but Zack insisted on this one with its reputation for the rich and famous as a more appropriate vehicle for entry into their new phase of life. "We'll take the Queen Mary back," Zack decreed as the whistle sounded and they took places at the balcony rail watching the ocean liner sail out from New York City past the Statue of Liberty into open sea. Selena inhaled the fresh, briny air. "We're on our way," Selena enthused, excited about her new adventure.

As the Fluellens joined their fellow, first-class passengers in the gorgeous exteriors and sumptuous furnishings, the words "Art Deco," bounced from the lips of many of their knowledgeable diners. Of the 1786 passengers, 535 joined Selena and Zack, 603 in cabin-class and 646 in third. They enjoyed hob-nobbing with the cabin and third class passengers who more than likely knew of and appreciated their celebrity, while first-class tried to figure out who they were. The comely black couple breezed about the decks, dined and danced when they felt like it and wrapped up in blankets in the lounge chairs as the ship cut through the salty sea. Arriving early in the morning at LeHarve, at the mouth of the Seine River, France's second largest port after Marseille, a limo awaited them and drove them west, down the coast, Selena oblivious to their destination. Too excited to care as this was her first trip out of the country.

"The signs to Paris say we're going the wrong way," Selena observed.

"Nothing gets by you, college girl," Zack stated. "We going right."

After another few miles the limo slowed and pulled into The American Cemetery and Memorial, perched twenty-eight acres above Omaha Beach.

Selena's heart caught and she squeezed Zack's hand. Her gaze pleaded, *what have you done?* Tears filled her eyes as Zack gave the driver instructions. She'd thought about visiting Hoyt's grave but said nothing of it to Zack. And yet, there they were.

The car stopped on the road by neatly arranged white crosses, U.S. flags billowed and beat against a crystal clear blue sky, waving in the wind. A soldier opened her door. She looked at Zack who said, "He's waiting on you."

Following the soldier, Selena passed many graves. Tears streaked her face and fell off of her chin for the loss of lives and how their deaths rippled through other lives back home. She knew this was one of fourteen permanent American World War II military cemetery memorials. She knew that one in Saint James Normandy

362

France held four thousand four hundred and ten World War II American soldiers who'd lost their lives in the Normandy Brittan campaign.

The soldier stopped, saluted a marker and Selena looked down. *Hoyt Colson* chiseled on the front of the white cross looked back. She clutched her wildly beating heart then held her mouth so a single plaintiff wail would not escape and fill the cemetery, competing with the sound of wind that whipped her hair about her head. She stood on the edge of memory and fell into its soft center. She looked up into the azure blue sky, where she knew him to be. She closed her eyes and sank to the soil that held the remains of her husband. She felt his name form beneath her fingertips, infusing and receiving all the love they'd shared. She'd been mentally numb and emotionally drained when the army asked if she wanted his remains repatriated to the United States or permanently interred on foreign soil. She'd thought, *What would I do with his "remains?"* The Colsons'd never considered their deaths. Since Hoyt had no family, the only other place she knew was Colt, Texas and Hoyt would die all over again in the Mt. Moriah Gethsemane Cemetery with folks he didn't know. He'd be bored witless. Here, among the men with whom he'd spent his last days, was where he belonged. Selena sat back on her heels and eyed all the men who kept him company. She could hear them swap stories and escapades. She could hear him ask, "Ain't my woman fine?" Selena smiled and wiped tears mixed in with the pancake foundation from her cheeks. "God, I loved you." She touched the top of the cross. "And you loved me."

He's not here now, Selena thought and stood. Dying long before the Normandy invasion she didn't know how his grave got here and only imagined the feat Zack had in locating it. Who knows what the service does in wartime. This physical grave was good enough for her. She looked at the expanse of the sea below. This was just the kind of day he'd love. She kissed her lips and touched the cold white marble. "Goodbye, Hoyt Colson. You were the love of my life." She straightened and said, "See you on the other side." Absently, humming "Stardust," she tore herself away and began walking down the winding path and came upon an impressive chapel in a Romanesque design. Carved in its granite base:

I Have Fought the Good Fight
I Have Finished My Course
I Have Kept The Faith.
(2Timothy 4:7)

"Youth Triumphing over Evil" etched on the exterior.

On the chapel door in a sculptured group—an eagle, shield, stars, laurel and arrows representing the Great Seal of the U.S. was flanked by two angels. Below, "In Memory of the Valor and Sacrifices which Consecrate this soil."

Selena stood at the entrance but couldn't go in. There was no point. *Every storm runs out of rain*, she thought.

The limo pulled up, Zack opened the door and she got in. He followed and once situated, she leaned on his chest.

"Thank you," she whispered.

"You're welcome." He rubbed her hand.

"I didn't even know if—"

"I did." His chin grazed across the top of her hair. "You gotta respect a man who knew his woman's worth. He took good care of your heart so I could come in."

"He did," she agreed and smiled up at Zack.

"He may have been your first, but I'm going to be your last."

"I love you, Zack Fluellen."

"How could you not?" he teased.

"It's both terrifying and comforting that you know me so well."

"Because of him—I can. He knew how to treat a good woman who could later recognize another good man." He kissed her forehead. "He got the girl; I have the woman."

In three hours the Fluellens checked into The Ritz, disappeared into their suite and stayed for two days. On the third day, they strolled the streets of Paris as tourists: The Eiffel Tower, Notre Dame, spent two days in the Louvre, Musee Jeu de Paume and de l'Orangerie, the Tuileries Gardens and Musee Rodin before calling on the vivacious Bricktop and then a real estate agent to help them escape the perpetual liveliness of the city and find a chateau just outside of Paris proper. They stayed out nights through early mornings and slept until noon. Ate, sauntered and sampled all Paris had to offer; small intimate cafés on German des Pres, picnicked by the Seine, shopped only a little but mainly engaged in the number one Parisian pastime... people watching. Zack proudly showed her the confluence of streets where Rue Bechet, Armstrong and Fluellen intersected.

"That should be your next album cover," Selena suggested.

The winding, skinny streets seductive, urging one to traverse and discover what lay at the end. The smells of freshly baked bread and constantly-brewing coffee intoxicatingly perfumed the air. Paris, a cacophony of sights, smells and sounds that never gave your senses a rest. Individual willpower never a match for the City of Lights that had been at this for centuries.

On their way to Monet's Giverny, Zack took a wrong turn and they ended up lost in the labyrinth of winding Parisian countryside, quiet, beautiful landscape, worthy of any painter, conspired against them. They drove leisurely practicing their French, knowing they'd eventually find their way back to a main road. Selena felt such freedom there, miles away from home. She couldn't feel as free while being lost in the United States; couldn't explore in a southern state where danger lurked behind every insincere smile of a white man giving directions. Or a white woman in a store indignant at the audacity of her shopping where she shopped... or being eyed, marked and followed around suspected of stealing. Paris already provided more freedom than her own country had. Freedom in not knowing, or caring what people were saying to or about you... secure in knowing it would not lead to losing your life. Freedom from worry of misinterpreting intent. Freedom from wondering if Star were here, in France. Selena and Zack did whatever they wanted where they wanted without fear of maltreatment or retribution. Selena felt twenty years younger here and fully understood the allure of this place for black musicians, artists and writers, how it not only appealed to, but inspired their freedom of expression.

"Oh, Zack, backup!" Selena said, passing a long tunnel of mature cypress trees which led right up to an exquisite three story, limestone chateau, where lush green ivy climbed over the façade up to windows on the second floor. "It's a fairytale house."

The black couple would have never thought to explore if they were in upstate New York or Charleston, South Carolina but here, Zack boldly drove down the mile-long private drive into a huge circle formed around a fountain. The car tires crunched on stone as they pulled to a stop. "Looks vacant."

"But well-kept. Maybe the owners are visiting America or Italy."

"Might could be." They got out and looked at the house. "Not too big. Not too small."

"Just right, huh, Goldilocks."

"Let's get the address and have a realtor check it out," Zack suggested as a man approached from the gatehouse.

"Bonjour. May I help you?"

"Oui. Is this house for sale?" Selena asked.

A lively exchange ensued and the couple left with the history of the chateau and its amenities as Marius apologized for not being able to take them inside.

"I want that house," Selena told Zack, as she flicked the realtor's card across her fingers.

In two days' time, on a blindingly bright day, they returned with the realtor and toured the inside and the surrounding acreage. The first floor flowed, arranged for entertaining with two half baths on either side of the house. The sunken, stone kitchen small, but ample for a staff of two or three. Four bedrooms with sitting areas upstairs, one in each corner of the house, boasted seventeenth century touches, stone archways, outer walls and floor-to-ceiling windows bathed each spacious room in natural light. The third floor was reserved for house staff except for Marius and his family, who occupied the three-bedroom gatehouse.

"Slave cabin," Selena whispered to Zack.

"OK. Not over here, Selena. Slate-tiled roofs, fireplace, separate bedrooms... no slaves lived like that in America."

In the back, a pergola wrapped from one side of the house to the other. "Listen," Selena directed Zack. "Absolute quiet."

"Crickets. Birds," he teased as the realtor walked them to the pond. "Like Monet."

Walking back, Selena noticed the gazebo in the distance and asked of another stone building with a few windows, "What's that?"

"The old kitchen," the realtor said. "Back then no cooking was done in the chateau for fear of fires burning it down. Plus it was too hot to cook in the summers; it would heat up the chateau."

"We can make the kitchen into a guest house for—"

"Say what now?" taking his eyes off the property, Zack glanced over at her. "That's what hotels and whatnot are for. I don't mind you doing all this 'entertaining' but then it's time for them to go. Don't have to go home but they got to get the hell outta my house. No overnighters."

"Zack?"

"What? I don't know why we need four huge bedrooms for the two of us."

"For Hep and his family. Orelia's twin girls. Your daughter. My parents."

"They ain't coming over here. We can't get them to L.A." They thanked the realtor and got back into the car. Zack made a left turn onto a secondary road that led to the highway. "OK, so you're saying just family?"

"You know Shanghai and Sugar Dee will be the first over here. Then Mazeda and Dewey. That's 'bout it."

"Umph. Can't stay forever. They got jobs."

Selena laughed, recognizing her Daddy in her husband. He felt the same about Colt, Texas when they were laying down the rules. "No hotels. Can't stay in Colt, Texas... got to leave when the sun goes down."

~*~

The February 1952 Issue of JET came to the Apartment #3G; a comely black woman on a hot pink cover which included an article entitled; *Negro Hair: A Million Dollar Business.* Jaz flipped through the pages stopping at the one of her mother and the movie star with the caption "Actress, singer and former GI Pin Up girl, beauty Lena Horne poses with Lorette Culhane, a Los Angles housewife, mother of three. Separated at Birth?" *Umph,* Jaz kept going and there, *Picture of the Week,* was her and Aunt Selena smiling for the photographer. Jaz giggled as she read; "Chanteuse extraordinaire sassy Selena Fluellen and her adorable niece, Jaz Culhane, celebrate New Year's Eve at L.A.'s posh Satin Doll. Two dolls indeed."

Jaz went into the kitchen junk drawer, got two thumb tacks and ran back to her room. She knelt on her bed and, over the headboard, sunk tacks into the photo, attaching it to the wall; one top and one bottom. She laughed, giggled and smiled. She looked over to Mel's side with all her pictures, trophies and ribbons, all could not compare to the one picture of Jaz and her aunt.

"Jaz, let's go!" Lorette yelled from the front door.

"Bye," Jaz kissed the picture and ran to catch up with her mother and sister.

Once in the car, Jaz asked again, "When will I be able to go with Dad and TC to The Boys Club?"

370

"When you become a boy," Mel said from her front seat perch.

"That's not nice, Mel," Lorette said, as she negotiated a left turn, still delighting in the Cadillac Selena and Zack had left them, not wanting to take the car to Paris. "You'll grow to love dance class as much as Mel and the other girls soon. Give it a chance, Jaz. It's only your second time."

Jaz sighed and looked longingly out of the window in the direction of The Boys Club. Once past, she sat back in the car's seat wanting to get the class over with. She'd finally been dragged into her mother and sister's realm just because she was a girl. At Mrs. Therell's Dance Studio, Jaz shed her PF Flyers to don black ballet shoes which matched her black leotard and tights like all the other girls. Luckily, the Culhane sisters were in different groups, Jaz a beginner and second-year Mel accelerated beyond her age group. After Jaz's class had done movement and the five positions they sat against the wall as the advanced girls showed their stuff. Mel pranced and glided across the slippery floor. "She loves this stuff," Jaz said out loud.

"She's really good," the girl next to her remarked.

"She farts in her sleep," Jaz said.

The little girl laughed and laughed, covering her mouth trying, but failing miserably, to stop the mirth.

"Tracy Sommerville!" Mrs. Therell thundered.

"Yes, ma'am." Tracy popped up and went to her teacher's side. Sitting where her teacher silently pointed before proceeding with the class. She now faced Jaz.

After class Jaz watched Mrs. Therell talk to Mrs. Sommerville, expecting to be called to account at any minute for her part in disrupting the class. Jaz changed out of her ballet slippers into her tennis and saw the pretty little girl with the upturned nose and the black hair listen to the adults. As Jaz proceeded out with her mother and sister, passing the three in deep conversation, Tracy smiled at Jaz who returned the gesture.

Tracy Sommerville, the only child of a housewife and mail carrier, went to private Catholic school and lived in a house about four blocks away; her eyes followed the other girl until she cleared the doorway. Priests, nuns, conformity, uniformity, obedience and respect had never met the likes of a Jaz Culhane.

Jaz, impressed that Tracy did not snitch on her as the cause and reason for her laughing spell, respected her. Each of the girls looked forward to seeing the other in class every Saturday morning at ten o'clock, until they were both summarily thrown out due to 'lack of aptitude and interest.'

~*~

When Jaz saw a strange car parked at the curb, she instinctively knew it belonged to Aunt Selena and Uncle Zack. Jaz broke away from Dedra and raced up the stairs by two's. The front door banged open and Jaz, the last of her family to arrive, jumped into her aunt's arms. "Whoa!

You are getting too big for this!" Selena said, falling back on the couch, clutching her niece without letting go. Jaz buried her head in her aunt's neck and cried.

Without saying a word, she unhitched her hold and went to Uncle Zack and hugged him before returning to her aunt.

"Lookit, Jaz. See what Aunt Selena brought us?" TC said to break the solemnity of the mood.

"We all got berets," Mel said, donning hers over her short hair.

"The real thing," Hep said.

"And I got a porkpie hat," TC said and cocked his head with a jaunty gesture.

Jaz laughed.

"Now we all have hats."

Jaz joined Mel at the box of girls' clothes, Selena pleased that the girls liked what she had picked out for each of them.

"Didn't think you all were coming back," Hep said to Zack.

"I think she's found her place in the world," Zack said.

"We bought a chateau outside of Paris," Selena beamed, zipping up the dress Mel'd tried on.

"How exquisite," Mel enthused.

"You all will have to come. There's plenty of room," Selena invited.

"We're going to see Grandpapa Colt and Gran'ma Keely," Jaz informed, stepping into a black patent leather T-strap shoe. "In the summer."

"After that, of course," Selena said to Jaz and continued with her parents, "That is wonderful! They will love Colt, Texas."

"We're going to ride horses and swim in the swimming hole and do everything," Jaz said, fastening the slender buckle.

"Can I come?" Selena asked.

"Sure. They have plenty of room too. Do you have horses in France?"

"No."

"How long you staying?" Hep asked, passing Zack a cold beer.

"She only came to be on Ed Sullivan's Cavalcade of Stars."

"And to see my children," Selena interjected. "Don't be modest. Bird asked Zack to play a few cuts with him on his new album, "Live at Birdland." We're gonna have dinner with Paul and Eslanda Robeson. The government still has his passport and they can't travel."

"Boy, I'd love to have him and Papa Colt have a conversation," Zack interjected.

"While in New York, Steve Allen's gonna do an entire broadcast from Birdland."

"Black people on TV."

"Get out the Jolly Time popcorn and Royal Crown ice cream floats."

374

"Aww. When are you leaving?" Jaz asked.

"In a few weeks."

"Can I come?"

"You are still in school. The house will be there. And I'll be back and forth."

"Going on a ship again?"

"No, flying."

"In a airplane?" Jaz said excitedly. "Way, way up in the sky?"

Selena shook her head yes. "Boat's too slow for me and Uncle Zack."

"I'd be scared."

"Gotta conquer your fears. You'd get used to it."

"Are you?"

"I'm getting there," Selena confessed.

"Going to buy a club next," Zack shared with Hep.

"Really? Expatriating?"

"Maybe dual citizenship. Too soon to tell. She may end up hating it."

"What about you?" Hep asked.

"Makes me no never-mind. Anyplace I hang my hat is home."

The Very Thought Of You

Back in New York, Selena sang two songs on The Sullivan Show; "That Old Devil Moon" and "They Can't Take That Away from Me," piggybacked a duo of "Young At Heart," with Sinatra on his Frank Sinatra Timex Show. Ratings for both shows went through the roof. Zack brought her the latest editions of *Down Beat*, *Metronome* and *Billboard* with Selena Fluellen stories sprawled all over them. "You'd think I'd just been discovered." She laughed.

"Ofays are slow." He popped open *Variety*. "Black folks known you for years."

Zack quoted: "'I hesitate to categorize Selena Fluellen as "just a jazz singer" because she defies categories; she's part swing, part torch, part saloon-singer, even some opera when she treats you to all five octaves of her voice. Vocal acrobatics. It's because of the partnership between her voice and her piano that she can sing with such authority and passion. A pure voice like Ella's but a clarity, phrasing and style all her own. Inimitable. She has the technical perfection to feel a song beyond the lyric. She can make you feel sexy and she can make you cry. Pure entertainer. She deserves every award she's received.'"

"*Ebony* wants to do a spread," Zack said as he flipped to another paper. "I like this one," he continued to read, 'Selena Fluellen is sassy, classy and a little bad-assy.'"

They howled with laughter.

"We can use that to promote you in Paris."

"Let's wait until after we open the club and our country house is ready before *Ebony*," Selena suggested. "I can't wait to get home."

"Why not do it then and now."

"You don't know nuthin' about timing."

"C'mere," he grabbed her hand and pulled her down on him. "I'll show you timin'."

~*~

"Right there. Perfect!" Selena exclaimed as the mover carefully set the highly polished, Baby Grand piano in place by the Palladian window to one side with the French doors to the garden behind her. "Zack! Zack!"

"That's it," he agreed, entering the room.

"Finished. Our country home is finally just the way we wanted."

"Finished? You? Ha." He sat on the sofa in front of the 17th century marble fireplace. "All I need is you in it."

"You got that."

"Play me something."

Selena started with "The Very Thought of You," "You made Me Love You" and "It Had to Be You" their own love trilogy of songs and two hours later ended with "Gimme a Pig Foot and a Bottle of Beer."

"And that's why Perry Como and Ed Sullivan want you back."

"Just so I'm not sharing a bill with that Italian mouse."

"Topo Gigio? Naw. You got Harry Belafonte."

"Two black people on the same show? Well, la de dah."

"One Black Queen and one Calypso King."

"Miles is talking about a TV show so you know I'll have to go back for that."

"Yep."

"I am famished," Selena said, slapping her knees and standing.

"You sound like 'big-word' Mel." Zack rose from the sofa, took her hand and they danced into the kitchen. They ate cold chicken, the last of the salad Nicoise, took out brie to reach room temperature as Zack opened a bottle of cabernet.

"Lisette did all this," Selena offered.

"She did good."

"She stocked the house. Cooked. She's gonna work out fine."

"Just so she don't live here full time."

"We'll need her here full time. You and I aren't going to have time to shop and cook and clean."

"She can come a couple of days a week and leave."

"Oh, Zack. This is too far for her to do that. We gonna buy her a car?"

"Hell no. Get somebody who got a car or a boyfriend to bring her out here."

"Oh, so you want strange men in and out of your chateau?" She rolled her eyes. "You talking nonsense." Selena accepted the proffered glass of red wine. She knew when to change the subject. "So we going back for a final walk through of the two club contenders?"

"Tomorrow at three. I like them both."

"Me too. But I wonder if Montmartre has been overdone. I love to party up there and it's historically black, but I'm talking future. Plus, I don't like that if SELENA'S is packed, they have other options so close. When they come to us, they'll have to make a special trip and have to wait for the next show 'cause Montmartre'll be too far."

"Look who's becoming a savvy businesswoman. They gonna hear you blowin' from inside and not want to go nowhere anyway." His teeth cracked the gristle from the chicken bone. "This is good. Lisette cook this?"

"She did."

"Taste like my mama's."

The next day Zack and Selena Fluellen decided on the skinny little street off Rue TreMarc, near the Rue Saint Honore' just off Rue Rivoli. They commissioned the neon vertical letters, SELENA, in hot pink on the side of the building projecting outward so folks could see it in either direction from afar. They set about configuring the inside. A horseshoe stage up front echoing the horseshoe shaped bar in the back.

"That's gonna take up a lot of space," Zack noted.

"I don't want more than twenty tables of four."

"Eighty people? You need at least six butts per table."

"I want a cozy, intimate club. I like my people close to me. Like I'm entertaining in my living room. Besides Bricktop only had fourteen tables and she was a rousing success."

"Maybe Cole Porter'll write you a song too."

""Miss Otis Regrets?" ...Miss Fluellen has none."

"Well, it's your club," Zack conceded.

"You'll hire the staff? You know how to outfit it."

"I do. I'm hoping we can convince Dewey and Mazeda to come over. Lure him away from The Satin Doll."

"That would be perfect. They should be ready for a change of venue."

"They can't live with us, Selena."

"I know."

In three weeks' time a line formed on the sidewalk under the hot pink sign, SELENA. Inside the tastefully glitzy foyer with the floor-to-ceiling picture of her, Selena watched every patron as they entered the well-lit vestibule with hat check to the right of the front door past steps with a prohibitive velvet rope which led to the upstairs dressing room. From there, behind a two-way mirror, Selena witnessed folks file in with all the jubilance of Christmas time. "This night has finally come," Selena said, and felt Zack come up behind her in a tight caress.

"You worked hard and you deserve it all."

"Couldn't have done it without you."

"Yeah, you could. But not this fast."

They laughed.

From the foyer below, invited guests surrendered their ornate, engraved invitations for opening night and entered into a dark, cozy room with only the horseshoe stage spotlighting the mic, her piano and the band's vacant seats. Selena had wanted stalactites dripping from above like the Bohemian Caverns in D.C. but the ceilings were too low. The tables filled quickly and the doorman halted and manned the front door while folks continued to line up outside for the next set. The anticipation of being there on this vanguard night, the night Selena's opened in Paris, France, already garnered bragging rights; her guest list a virtual who's who among the elite, the royal, the bon vivant, press, and most fervent music lovers Europe had to offer. The centerpiece candles shimmered in the darkness atop their linen cloths as scantily dressed waitresses shuffled back and forth filling drink orders before the show started.

An hour later, the lights on the bar dimmed and the spotlight on the stage brightened to signal the coming of the main attraction. The bassist, the sax and coronet players and drummer assumed the stage and the audience clapped, pointing and identifying notables on stage and off.

Zack walked from the open door and claimed the stage amid applause and whooping.

"Bonsoir Madames and Monsieurs," he spoke in French, as he gestured for them to calm down. "This is not my night. This night belongs to you and Selena." The mention of her name caused a swell in admiration. "This is the club she wanted for a few of her personal friends and that is what you all are on this night. So relax and enjoy her inaugural appearance at her club. I give you SELENA!"

Thunderous applause erupted as everyone looked at the main door but she came from another entrance off the hallway to the kitchen and restrooms, surprising and titillating them all as she passed by the bar, shaking hands, sharing kisses, commanding the room by her sheer presence.

She glided up the three steps to her platform, while her flowing, richly-woven caftan shocked with gold threads glinted off the lights. The audience stood, applauded and she hadn't sung a word. They wouldn't allow her to begin and Selena thought of Star, of Maybelle, of all the women who'd gotten her to where she was. Of Hoyt and Zack, her brother, her daddy and mama, even Saida. She raised her hand in cease fire to stop them before they reduced her to a bundle of tears.

"Welcome to Selena's!" she finally interrupted and cued her band. She began with the bouncy, finger-popping "The Best is yet to Come," and the crowd settled down only enough to join in and bounce and snap fingers; men kept time with wing-tipped shoes and silky-satin covered butts of skinny women wriggled in the chairs to the beat.

Selena grabbed each patron and took them on individual journeys of three "Opening Nights;" the press in France and at home chronicled her sweeping success, "a true artist, innovator who learns the rules so she can break them in the most delightful way, a richness of tone, but she has the chops to stand next to an instrumentalist and not only hold her own, but challenge them to keep up with her. Playful yet harmonically sophisticated with flawless chord changes accompanied by her range from soprano to baritone. Melodical experimentalist. Her instrument is her voice. Sassy, classy Selena!"

After two solid hours, Selena, drenched with perspiration and glowing, told the audience, "I'm sorry I have to go. They said I have another set soon."

The crowd jumped to their feet.

"Will you all come back?" She cajoled the audience and said, "I'll be here. Promise."

"Merci!" She motioned to the band and bowed deeply before she left the stage, this time through the main door and up the velvet-roped steps to her dressing room.

"You did it, baby!!" Zack grabbed her as she came in.

"I did, didn't I?"

In the three weeks before they were to leave for Colt, Texas, Selena sang and courted the crowd like it was their first and last time together. The packed club rocked and the patrons outside anxiously awaited their turn for the second show. Selena looked down on the crowd and asked, "What's that little girl doing in here?"

Zack joined her at the two-way mirrored wall, "Where?"

"She just darted in there. My material isn't for the under eighteen."

"Who you tellin'?"

When she walked down the stairs towards the stage the little girl appeared and presented Selena with an earring she'd dropped. "Thank you." Selena bent over and asked. "Where's your Mom or Daddy?"

The little girl scampered away just as Selena heard her name announced by Zack. In yet another ornate caftan that was becoming her signature garb, Selena flounced to the stage in her sensual gait, kibitzing with folks on the way. She sauntered up the steps, snatched the mic from the stand and greeted, "Bonsoir!" The crowd cheered, applauded and whistled a welcome. She stared shimmying to the music her band played as they waited for the thunder to die down.

"Alright. You all feel good tonight?"

They answered, "Oui!"

"I'm gonna make you feel even better," she sassed. "As Bricktop used to say, 'Every time I shimmy, a skinny gal loses her man.'"

384

Anything Selena sang… fast, slow, mid-tempo, they were there with her word for word. She gauged her repertoire by the crowd with her, letting them set the tone and pace and they were never disappointed. It had become Selena's habit, between songs, to recognize notables in her audience and engage in light banter.

"Whew!" she mopped her brow with a colorful hanky after a rousing rendition of "Blues in the Night." *"Mercy.* It's hot up in here. I saw a little girl in here earlier. Is she still here?" Selena shielded her eyes against the spotlights. She reminds me of my niece back home. She's always giving me lost earrings. I don't have pierced ears. God gave me all the holes I need."

Laughter erupted from the crowd. "Sassy, classy and a little bad-assy!' a table yelled back to her.

Selena laughed. "I'm gonna slow it down now. Mama needs a rest." She cued her band who began with strings. "This is for my man, Zack." She began, "You made me love you… I didn't want to do it—"

At the end of the second show, Selena let them know she was going home.

"This is your home!" a man yelled out and the crowd applauded in agreement.

"Why thank you. But I'm going to Texas for a bit of the summer." Then she asked the band, "Who in their right mind goes to Texas for the summer?" She laughed at herself. "But I'll be back in a few weeks," she returned to the audience. "And we can pick up where we left off."

A collective sigh rose from the darkness. "I'll meet you back here. Is it a date?"

"Oui!!"

~*~

Selena's manicured finger strummed the announcement. "You told me never to say never, didn't you, handsome?"

"I did. But you got a mind of your own," Zack gruffed.

"I also know I'm not letting you loose in Las Vegas with your old buddy, Joe Louis either."

"Hey, he's the greeter at the Moulin Rouge. I can swing by the club, see some old friends, and stay a few nights and meet you in Colt, Texas."

"Humm," Selena hedged.

"Three sold-out shows per night since it opened in May. First interracial hotel in Vegas," Zack continued. "All the black stars from Miles Syphax to Belafonte and some white ones like Cary Grant, Humphrey Bogart are in the audience. I hear Sinatra comes over from The Sands after his gig and the Dorsey Brothers from New Frontier. Even though Miles is getting $4,500 a week from the Thunderbird, he still can't stay there but he's being well-compensated."

"Humph," Selena grunted at the racist policy.

"The club is drawing all the big talent away from the regular clubs 'cause after finishing their gigs, they all converge on The Rouge and jam until the cows come home. Tourists know that and bypass the individual clubs knowing they'll all end up at The Rouge. Sounds like a blast." He eyed Selena. "I'll meet you in Colt in a few weeks," he repeated.

"Sounds like a transplanted SELENA's."

"It does."

"You haven't named any women."

"I'm sure they'll all be there too."

"And so will I. I'm coming."

"Oh really?" Zack teased. He knew his woman and how to get her back there.

Home on the Range

The gray on gray Dodge loaded down with the five Culhanes, luggage and anticipation, set out down Alvaro Street heading for Colt, Texas. Hep'd taken an uncharacteristic two weeks' vacation for the first time and although he spoke to his parents frequently by telephone, couldn't recall the last time he'd visited his hometown. Lorette, apprehensive about being in Keely's presence again, looked forward to seeing Papa Colt with whom she'd always felt a special connection, being the smallest in the family. She closed the Green Book Truck had brought over in exchange for the keys to their apartment. She knew her husband had this sojourn from L.A. to Texas all planned out. Hep glanced at his children in the back seat; TC at the window behind his mother, Mel in the middle flipping through a magazine and Jaz, standing right behind his ear.

"On my side, I see a yellow poppy field, and two cars," Jaz relayed.

"On my side, I see cows, a silo, a red barn and chickens," TC countered, as he scanned the comic books, Scoey, his best friend, had given him for the trip.

Anxious for his parents to see their grandchildren, like everything else in his life, Hep wasn't sure what had taken him so long. Life, his career, their schooling, Mel's myriad of performances...but now, it was time and the excitement, palpable. Three hours out from L.A., they'd stopped at an open pasture and consumed the picnic lunch Lorette had prepared.

"Are we almost there, Daddy?" Jaz asked, piling back into the car.

"Not quite," Hep answered.

They assumed their seats, Jaz pulled her fedora down over her eyes and fell asleep. Mel, right beside her sister, remained wide awake, while TC continued being totally engrossed with the comic books, knowing at this rate, he'd have nothing left to read when he reached Colt, Texas.

Jaz awoke, stood and laid her head on her father's shoulder.

"Sit back, Jaz," her mother said.

Jaz switched sides to his other shoulder where she couldn't hear or see her mother because of the wind rushing through the window. "She's OK," she heard her father say.

After what seemed an eternity, Jaz'd fallen to sleep again and when awakened popped up like she knew they'd arrived. A big white house, with a wide porch, a swing hanging from the ceiling and fence with a gate greeted her. "This is it?"

"Yes, punkin."

"Oh my! Here they are!" Keely shouted from the screen door, pushing it open, running down the steps and banging open the gate. She hugged Hep first, "My son. My son," half praise, half prayer.

"Hi, Mama."

Keely stepped back, kissed Lorette's cheek and said, "Well, who are all of you? My grandchildren?"

"Yes, ma'am," the young male said.

"You must be TC, the handsome, smart one."

"Yes'um."

"Come give your grandma a kiss." He obliged and Keely turned to the next girl. "You must be Mel. The Star!"

"That'd be me," she said, stepping up to kiss Keely without prompting, her grandmother's reward for recognizing her as the star of the family.

"And you must be Jazzzz," Keely said with a pizzazz the little girl hadn't expected.

She giggled. "With a missing tooth? Did you eat too much candy?" Keely teased.

"No, ma'am."

"C'mon in."

Hep and TC gathered the luggage. Mel picked up the mirrored travel case Aunt Selena'd given her for her birthday.

"Your father must not have heard me," Keely said and continued, "You and Lorette can take the guest room with the double bed. I thought TC could have Orelia's old room and the girls could take Selena's room with the twin beds."

Ugh! Jaz thought. "I still have to share a room with Mel?"

"Jaz—"

"But she's so messy. I can't stand it."

The L.A. Culhanes filed into the house and Jaz felt immediately dwarfed by the size. It wasn't like her grandparents, the Javiers' house with all the furniture and doo-dads...it was mammoth. As she walked past the grandfather's clock, by the open rooms toward the steps, she looked at the guns, rifles and a single feather mounted on a huge floor-to-ceiling fireplace she could get lost in. They turned to climb the hidden staircase and Jaz spotted him. Out by the corral. Papa Colt. *It had to be him.* She'd heard about him. Talked to him all these years. Now face-to-face she was going to meet him. Her legendary grandfather who tamed the west, fought Indians and founded this town.

She announced her entry into his world with a slam of the kitchen screen door. He looked over at the noise but didn't say anything.

Jaz sauntered up to him. "Hi. I'm your granddaughter Jaz. All the way from California." She grinned up at him from beneath her hat.

"Well, pleased to meet you, Sporty."

"No. I'm Jaz."

"I heard you, but that's a mighty sporty hat you're wearing." He tapped the brim lightly and smiled.

Jaz's eyebrows furrowed, not knowing whether it was the long ride, or the fact that she still had to share a room with Mel but this meeting with her grandfather was disappointing. She turned on her heel and marched away.

"Hey, Sporty! Where you going?" Papa Colt called after his impish granddaughter.

A few minutes later, Hep found his father still watering the horses. "Hey, Pop." They engaged in a bear hug and a couple of back-slaps.

"You don't look the worse for wear. I guess she's feeding you alright," Papa Colt teased. "Where is li'l bit?"

"Upstairs settling everybody in. You look good, Dad."

"You sound surprised." Colt punched his son's arm playfully. "Got a little hitch in my gitty-up from time to time. But there's no stress here in Colt, Texas. Good food. Good sleep. Good air and water."

"I hear you."

"Met your youngest."

"Jaz?"

"She's a little high-strung, ain't she?"

"Dad, you have no idea what high-strung is."

"Got another one worse than that?"

Hep shook his head.

"Females young and old. A puzzle."

Despite the gruff old man known as her grandfather trying to get her attention with eye winks and funny faces, Jaz steered clear of him as she helped set the table; to her he was just the man who couldn't get her name right. That night on her way to bed she passed a dark, vacant room and asked, "What's in there?"

"Used to be my room," her father answered.

"Really? Why can't I sleep in there?"

As her grandmother Keely walked by with more fresh towels Jaz asked, "Grandma, can I sleep in there?"

"Sure. I thought you'd want to be with your sister."

"No, ma'am. She's a slob."

Jaz flipped on the light and helped her father make up his old bed with fresh linen. "You have a extra bed in your room?"

"Yep," was all Hep said, thinking the death of his older brother not proper nighttime discussion before his daughter went to sleep. Jaz slipped between the crisp sheets that smelled outdoor fresh. He listened to his daughter say her prayers and then kissed her on her forehead. "Night, Punkin."

"Night, Daddy."

Little by little folks dropped by to see Hep and meet his young family. Every time Jaz came down from washing up in the morning, a new cast of characters stood ready. Her Aunt Orelia and Uncle Samuel with her cousins among the first, followed by friends of her father and Aunt Selena. Church people, town folk, people of Colt, Texas who all said the same thing, "Next year you'll have to come in time for Founder's Day in June."

After a hearty breakfast Jaz joined her father, Papa Colt and siblings by the corral where Hep saddled a pony and hoisted her up onto its back. She rode in wide rings around the stable like Mel and TC. Mid-week, TC and his friends Tulsa Rudd, Tate Truax and Canaan Redbird, left the confines of the fence heading for the open range.

"I want to go with them," Jaz said, pointing to the boys.

"I'll take you out," Hep offered and grabbed her reigns before going in the opposite direction. "I want to show you something. Mel, you want to go?"

"No. I'm going back inside," Mel said, inching off the animal, relieved when her feet hit terra firma.

"Can I come?" Papa Colt asked the pair.

"Sure," Hep piped up before Jaz could object.

The three galloped and the motion made Jaz laugh, like bubbles in a glass. When they reached the swimming hole, Jaz slid from her pony and ran towards the rim of the bank. "Look at the waterfall!" Jaz pointed out excitedly. "Can I get in?"

"Sure. Take off your shoes and be careful," her father said.

"I been meaning to change this rope," Papa Colt said, walking toward the hanging tire.

"Oh, this feels so good!" Jaz flipped on her back before diving down into the clear, clean wet.

"I remember this tire," Hep smiled. "I can climb up—"

"Those days have passed when you could climb up; you'll break off the limb," Papa Colt teased and began untying the rope.

"I touched the bottom!" Jaz exclaimed, before gasping a mouthful of oxygen and disappearing again.

"Spunky little thing," Papa Colt said as he began climbing the tree, scooting out toward the edge where his son threw the rope up to him.

Jaz broke the water's surface again and saw her grandfather in the tree. The sight mesmerizing. She swam to the shore just as the hemp doubled over the rubber tire and dropped again. "That ought to do it. What you think, Sporty?"

Jaz screwed up her lips in protest and asked her father, "What's that for?"

"The tire? You swing on it, out over the water then let go."

"Show me."

"I don't have on my trunks. You test it out for us."

"OK." Jaz made her way over and into the ring of rubber and began swinging farther and higher until both her father and grandfather shouted, "Let go!"

She did and splashed into the waiting water. She surfaced laughing with delight. "That was so fun!"

Twenty-five splashes later and one two-mile ride back home, the three put up their horses and dragged in through the kitchen door.

"You all look a sight!" Keely said.

"We only here 'cause we got hungry. What's for lunch?" Colt asked.

"Jaz," Lorette crumpled with disappointment. "How'd you get so dirty? And you are all wet. Your hair... Hep—" She pled.

"We had fun," he said, silencing his wife with a kiss on her lips.

That night, after the dinner dishes had been washed and put away, the adults sat on the porch while the children played hide-and-seek before catching lightening bugs in glass jars. One by one parents gathered their children and went home leaving only the Culhane kids to stagger up the stairs delightfully tired. Faces washed, teeth brushed, prayers said, and jars of glowing bugs on their nightstands, they drifted off into blissful sleep. In the dark morning before the sun rose, Jaz turned over in her bed to discover a blanketed lump in the other bed. Too tired to object to Mel's presence, she fell back to sleep.

Later that morning, Jaz rose, observed the rumpled bed, signaling that Mel had slept there, as she went to wash up and ventured downstairs. She loved it there. *Why did her father ever leave? S*he wondered. Descending the steps she heard a familiar voice. "Aunt Selena!" she ran toward her and flattened her hard body against the softness of her aunt.

"Ooof!" Selena exclaimed like the air had just been knocked out of her. "Surprise!"

"Now *this* is just the best vacation ever!!" She hugged her again before asking, "What are you doing here?"

Selena knew Jaz had little interest in her being a guest on The Ed Sullivan Show or Uncle Zack's guesting on John Coltrane's latest album; she simply said, "I had to come and see you!"

"That's a good reason," Jaz concluded. "It is so much fun."

Aunt Selena removed her niece's hat. "Oh, Jaz!"

"I've been swimming every day," Jaz explained with a hunch of her shoulders.

"You know what we'll be doing tonight," Selena warned.

The next two weeks was a volley of swimming, riding horses, eating and being free to be and do whatever they wanted whenever. No Vacation Bible School necessary for the Culhane kids although they relished Sunday morning services at Mt. Moriah Gethsemane Baptist Church. Mel and her brother were more than just spectators like Jaz, as TC played the organ for his grandmother Keely under her deceased son's Henley's tribute steeple and Mel took center stage each Sunday, wowing the congregation with her vocal rendering of spirituals, picking a different hymn for each Sunday she was present. The excitement when the brother and sister assumed their respective places, exhilarating. Hep spoke of having to return home and all three children held their collective breaths while arrangements were made for them to stay another week.

Sunday meals reigned among the Culhane favorite activities with greens left simmering on the back burner and rolls rising into delicious gooeyness under a cloth while the residents were at church. If there was no planned church activity, all scurried home and changed from their church clothes. Women-folk set about helping with the finishing touches on the Sunday meal while the men tossed horseshoes, and manned a built-in BBQ grill. Children took to back porches with rock salt and a churner to press out the most delectable ice cream this side of the Sierra Nevadas; fresh cherries, peaches and berries were among the most favorite summertime flavors.

"Hey, what is today?" Jaz asked mid churn.

"July 15th—" TC surmised, not missing comic books at all.

"We missed the Fourth of July," Jaz reminded.

"We only celebrate Founder's Day here, not the Fourth of July," Papa Colt answered.

"Why?" Jaz asked.

"That is the most significant day for Colt, Texas."

"Do you have fireworks on Founder's Day?"

"Yep. And a parade and games and races—"

"Wow. We do have to come back next year for that!"

The children of Colt, Texas splashed in the swimming hole while Lorette and Selena picked a nice shady spot under a poplar tree on a blanket, drinking ice tea they'd transported along with towels. Mel laid hers far enough away from any threat that water would reach her carved out sanctuary.   With white, cat-eye sunglasses and magazines as company, she dared anyone to interrupt her.

"Look at Miss Anne," Selena teased to Lorette. "She's already quite the star."

"Hep thinks it's me who is pushing her, but Mel loves to sing and she loves the attention it brings especially since winning Ted Mack's Amateur Hour. This is her calling."

"Two-thousand dollars is no joke, Lorette. She's luckier than most. Look how long it took me to find my passion in singing." Selena lit a cigarette. "Plus she's good. No denying that."

"The true test will be when she reaches high school. If she still loves it or not. I don't want her to be dependent on a man for her livelihood or happiness."

"Amen. Happiness is an inside job anyway. No other person can make you happy. Your other two kids are no slouches either. That TC is a musical genius."

"My saving grace. He is literally no problem. I hope it stays that way."

"And then there's Jaz."

They both chuckled; a subject too big to tackle on such a pleasant afternoon.

"And how are you doing Lorette Javier Culhane?"

"I'm happy," she relented. "I mean... life isn't where I thought it'd be, but I love my husband and children."

"Where'd you think it would be?"

Lorette sighed. "I thought I'd have a house by now. Maybe in Compton. Hep and I both grew up in houses, I never thought we'd be renters this long. Thought that my children would be in private schools or at least Windsor Hills in View Park. That Hep would be mayor."

"Dreams are good. Reality can be a motha…" She took another drag and noted that Lorette named all-white areas. "Would you do it all over again?"

"What? Marry your brother?"

Selena shook her head.

"In a heartbeat. I mean look at him. Isn't he handsome?"

Selena eyed Hep. "He's OK. Not my type."

They laughed. "It's more than just looks or the way he makes me feel every time he touches me—"

"Whoa!"

Lorette grinned. "He's such a good, honorable man. Takes such good care of us. Everyone I know loves and respects him. He's so smart. Has zoomed up the career ladder at LAPD—"

"But you rather he didn't?"

"Every time he gets a promotion, becoming mayor sinks farther and farther away. He's happy. He loves his job and coaching TC's teams. It's enough for him. He became lieutenant reluctantly because he wanted to take the Detective test, which he passed with flying colors. He loves it."

"Life works out best for those who make the best out of the way life works out," Selena quoted her brother on a stream of smoke.

"Yeah. Maybe that's the key to a good life."

"Sometimes, you got to let go of the life you planned so you can live the life that's waiting for you."

"Yes, exactly," Lorette said, in awe of her sister-in-law's wisdom.

"It could always be worse. Like if you'd never met Hepburn Culhane. Or if I'd never met Hoyt Colson. What dreary lives they would have been."

"That's frightening. I couldn't stay in Evelyn, Tennessee any more than you could have stayed here."

"Or return for good." Selena took the last drag of her cigarette and stabbed the butt in the ground. "We're pretty lucky. Some women never get a man worthy of them. I got two."

"We didn't have to kiss any toads either."

"Speak for yourself. I had one toady. Just one. Lesson learned." She picked a piece of tobacco from her tongue. "Learned to never put the key to my happiness in somebody else's pocket."

"Pax Peques?"

"That'd be the one. How'd you know about him?" Selena side-glanced her sister-in-law.

Lorette answered her with her knowing eyes.

"Humph. Not everybody can handle my personality," Selena continued. "Not my fault or problem. Can't change to accommodate every Tom, Dick or Harry."

"So true."

"Talk about a lapse in my judgement. Trying to make that Negro into something he'd never be. At least not with me. I supposed I used him because he was established and he used me right back. No harm no foul." She leaned back on her arms. "He's probably still out there doing' the same-ol' same-ol', unless he's been shot by some woman's man. He believed it wasn't cheating unless he got caught. A Preacher's Kid who didn't know Amen from what-when."

"I've only known one man all my life. Thank goodness he was the right man for me. He makes me feel important and good about myself."

"Good. That's what he saw growing up. That's what he gives. Pax Peques always acted like a back row sinner at a tent revival. Shifty-eyed and jittery. And most days he made me feel like I wanted my middle finger to answer every question. Your man ought to at least make you feel good about yourself in and out of bed."

Selena lay on her belly facing the kids in the water. "Even though he wasn't, he acted like a 'bitch-raised man.'"

"What?" Lorette answered with a chuckle; she loved bonding with her worldly sister-in-law.

"You know how a woman who didn't have a husband in the home will say she's been 'both mother and father' to her son? That's a woman who also didn't grow up with a father. If she did, she'd know that no woman, no matter how loving and well-intentioned, can teach a boy how to be a man. Only a man can do that. Only another man can teach a boy how to love and treat a woman…show him how to treat his mother—by telling and by example. Don't nobody want a 'bitch-raised man.' I've seen enough of them in my lifetime but never had to tangle with one, thank goodness. You want "mama's boy" who's been taught by his daddy how to respect, revere, love, honor and not be threatened by a smart, independent woman. My daddy and your husband are mama's boys… I hope TC becomes one and Mel and Jaz marry one. What boys know and see is what they become. Papa Colt always told us a man's one job on this earth is to make sure he provides and cares for his family while he's here on earth *and* after he leaves. 'Raise 'em up' so when he dies the family doesn't fall back into poverty or despair. That's a man's work. Attain, sustain and maintain. Your husband and mine will see to it. No bitch-raised men here."

Lorette laughed at her savvy, no nonsense, colorful sister-in-law.

"Excuse my French," she added and they both laughed.

"I've shed my tears. For Hoyt 'cause I didn't know how to live in a world without him. So broken hearted I jangled when I walked. With Pax the sax, I cried 'cause I was so colossally stupid. But with Zack… he put me back together. With him I cry tears of sheer joy."

"Thank God for Hepburn Culhane and Zack Fluellen," Lorette toasted with her ice tea.

"Amen!"

~*~

"Hey, Grandpa," Mel greeted as she walked into the dining room.

"Hey, Bright Eyes. I heard you singing the other day. You got a mighty pretty voice. Like an angel."

"Thank you, but I don't like my eyes."

"What? Why?"

"They don't look like TC's or Jaz's."

He reared back and looked at her. "So?" He slapped his knee. "C'mon here." She sat on his bony knee. "They got their eyes and you got yours."

"Yeah, but it's not the same."

"Not supposed to be. They can't sing like you either, can they?"

She thought awhile then shook her head no.

"Cause we all got our own attributes. Know why I called you 'Bright Eyes?'"

She shook her head again.

"Because you have eyes like my mama."

"I do?" She looked into his.

"She had big, pretty, round eyes like you. My daddy loved them and I loved them too. Nobody in this family got her eyes... but you. 'Cause you are special. I loved my Mama," he said wistfully. Like he'd just lost her this week. "Your color is more like Aunt Pearl. 'Elephant grass,' my mama used to say. Aunt Pearl is no blood kin but she loved and took care of me and my mama for a time."

404

"Everyone clean-up for dinner," Keely called out. "Oh, good. Mel, wash your hands and put the ice in the glasses for me."

"Will you remember that?" Papa Colt asked. "Like your voice, remember how special your eyes are. You are the only one in the family with that gift."

"OK," Mel grinned.

"You look good when you smile," Papa Colt told her. "You ought to try it more often."

As everyone scattered to the one big bathroom upstairs and the one Selena had put in downstairs off the kitchen, Hep went into his old room to open the window and walked across that one squeaky floor board. He smiled and pried it open and there, just like yesterday, was the old cigar box with all his hidden treasures. A couple of bottle caps, a whistle, tickets from a Founder's Day cake that Feather'd baked, a baseball card and birthday cards for him from Star with a flyer from New Orleans. Selena entered just as he unfolded it. "I have to look at these to remember I had a sister named Star. Was she really real?"

"You weren't but nine going on ten."

"About TC's age."

"I thought we'd've heard something by now. Anything."

"We know if she'd done well she would have high-tailed it back here to rub Daddy's face in it."

"So are we to presume the opposite?"

"Not ready to concede that yet. I still look into every discarded female's eyes to try to find a glimmer of recognition... but nothing," Hep shared. "I press five dollars into strange women's hands. They are not my kin but they are somebody's. I hope someone has been as kind to her. Lorette hates when I do that."

"She has no idea how a loss like that can affect you."

"We wouldn't know Star if she came right up and served us coffee," Hep said.

"Don't I know it? She has to come to us," Selena said.

"That ain't gonna happen." Hep tucked the cigar box back under the floor board and followed his sister out and down the stairs. "Heading back to Paris Monday?"

"Yep."

"Can't believe you left your new club after only six weeks."

"Give the wolf a taste then leave him hungry," she quoted Zack. "Always leave them wanting more."

"Saw you on Frank Sinatra's show. You tore it up, sis."

"You have your popcorn and RC cola ice cream floats?"

"Keep up these guest shots, we'll be big as a house."

After dinner Jaz asked, "Grandpa Colt, what are those things on your fireplace?"

"Guns," TC answered.

"A little more than just guns. That's history. My history and yours."

Mel was the first to sit on the couch in the reception hall in front of the mammoth stone.

"Didn't your Daddy tell you about our people?" Papa Colt asked his grands.

"No," Jaz said.

"Not yet," TC added.

"Well, sit right down and let's have a lesson."

"Pst!" Selena went into the dining room and motioned to the adults, Hep, Lorette, Zack and Keely. "You all should see this."

Papa Colt, surrounded by his three grandchildren, sat on the sofa while the adults filled in on the floor and the various chairs. "We started in Africa. My Mama, Saida, was born there. The daughter of a king. She was at her sister's wedding when all of a sudden white folk came and took them. Stole them away. She had big round 'Bright Eyes.'" He winked at Mel. "Nobody got those eyes but you and my Mama."

Mel beamed at the comparison.

"When she and her mother came over on the ship, her mother gave her a cowrie shell…that one there…" He pointed on the fireplace façade. "She put it under her tongue and kept it so no one could take it. And when her mother jumped into the water—"

"For a swim?" Jaz asked.

"No. She didn't want to be a slave…so she drowned herself to be with her husband and children."

The Culhane-three mouths fell agape. "So my mama Saida was cared for by Aunt Pearl on the plantation.

Although she was no blood relative, she took care of Saida until she left with my daddy, Lone Wolf, a Cherokee warrior."

TC's body swelled with pride.

"They went off and had me and then brought me back to visit Aunt Pearl, but they killed my daddy and captured my mama. Aunt Pearl took care of me and her, until my mama died birthing my baby sister."

Papa Colt paused, gauging if this was too much for the very quiet grandchildren. "It was hard and terrible."

"Why didn't you leave?" Jaz asked.

"Couldn't. It was slavery," Papa Colt answered.

Jaz looked totally confused but remained silent.

"Finally the Emancipation Proclamation came and Aunt Pearl and I set out for Washington, DC. After Aunt Pearl died I came west."

"How old were you?" TC asked.

"Twelve. I was twelve."

"Who'd you stay with?" Mel asked.

"Well, I got a job and stayed where I worked. Met some guys and we all hung around together. Then I bought this land, built this house with their help. Asked your grandma Keely to marry me. Then we had children."

"Aunt Selena and Daddy," Jaz piped up, happy she could finally relate to this harrowing story.

"Yep. Then they had you and here we all are!" Papa Colt eneded on a high note.

"Yaaay!!" Jaz said. "Grandma Keely can I have another piece of cake?"

"Jaz, no," Lorette said.

"Sure you can." Both Keely and Jaz ignored Lorette. "Anybody else want anything?"

The orders came in and they took dessert number two out on the porch.

Hep sat on the steps near the corral. He eyed the purple-colored sky infused with hot pink as the sun finally set sending up a gush of stars. "Daddy," Jaz said approaching, "What are the stars called again?"

"Constellations." He helped her sit by him. Their legs swung loose from the porch over the yard as he continued, "See that one there? That's the Big Dipper."

The adults listened as the father answered his curious daughter's inquiries. "Don't forget you have to finish teaching me how to whistle like you and TC."

A while later, Jaz helped her Aunt Selena take her father's, grandfather's and brother's plates to her grandma Keely in the kitchen. Lorette and Mel disappeared upstairs to get ready for church tomorrow.

With Jaz in tow, Selena passed the front door and saw three generations of Culhane men on the porch. The sight gave her pause. *This is the type of picture Hoyt would have snapped for posterity,* she thought. Grandfather, father and son exchanging information, having a manly talk, basking in shared heritage. She guided her niece upstairs.

"So what's the real history, Grandpa Colt?" TC asked.

"Nothing gets by you." Papa Colt's body pushed the porch swing in motion and TC joined him on the hard surface. "What's TC stand for again?"

"Tavio Culhane."

"From the way you ride those horses and how perceptive and smart you are, I thought it stood for Top Cat."

The three men chuckled.

"It could," TC said with a smile.

"Tell you what, Top Cat. I'll give you all the family history you can stand when you come back next year. Deal?"

"I'd like that. Deal, Dad?" he spoke to Hep.

"Deal."

Upstairs, Selena fashioned Jaz's hair into long Shirley Temple curls which she proudly showed off to everyone who'd look, especially Lorette. She went on to the front porch and asked Papa Colt, "What time do we go to church?"

"You all go about ten."

"You're not going again?"

"Got to watch the house and make sure it don't burn down with the supper simmering on the stove."

"When's the last time you've been to church?" Jaz pressed on as the adults eyed one another.

"That's a good question. I guess when my baby, Selena, got married."

"Baby?" Jaz giggled.

"I go to church right here on this porch every Sunday," Papa Colt concluded.

"But don't you want to *see* Mel sing? I hate to admit she's pretty good even if she is a slob."

"Nobody's perfect."

"If you're afraid, I'll sit right beside you."

"You will now?"

"Yes."

"Might could be."

Jaz eyed him quizzically.

"Anything's possible," he clarified to her confused light eyes. "We'll see," he finally translated.

On Sunday, everyone gathered in the front grand hall to make their way to church. From upstairs a familiar shuffle-step, shuffle-step was heard overhead. Keely grinned like a school girl, knowing her husband used his cane only for long distance walking.

"Where's Jaz?" Hep asked.

Rounding the corner of the concealed steps, all eyes on that spot, appeared Papa Colt dressed in a spiffy shirt and tie. Jaz held his hand.

They passed the group in the center hall, passed the mammoth fireplace with the heritage relics.

"C'mon. We're going to be late," Jaz prompted.

Papa Colt winked at his wife.

"That girl is pure magic," Keely remarked, tears brimming her eyes. "C'mon, you heard the girl. We're going to be late."

Papa Colt sat between his wife and granddaughter, Jaz. He refused to let folks make a fuss about his appearance but Reverend Gassaway recognized him from the pulpit. With his grandson on the organ and his granddaughter, Mel, center stage with her soul-stirring rendition of "The Old Rugged Cross," Papa Colt beamed with pride so powerful he thought he could ascend up through Henley's steeple, never to be seen again.

"Told you," Jaz whispered to him of her sister.

Selena caressed his shoulder from behind and Papa Colt patted it twice.

My grands, he thought, *expert at "being who they are."*

After the service, Papa Colt appeared to be the celebrity, not Selena and Zack. Finally walking away from the church, Selena said, "TC, when I get back to L.A. we have to go to the bank."

"Why?"

"I want you to use your money to open your own account. You're never too young to learn about money. I've got your royalties for *"Beauty Black."* Over five hundred dollars."

"What?" a wide-eyed TC exclaimed.

"The next few months' rent is on you, son," Hep teased.

"Wow."

"The pay for 'genius' is good."

~*~

412

Colt's body set the porch swing into motion. The August heat settled down sending up a tranquil night flooded with twinkling stars and happy memories. He missed his children and grandchildren like he never thought he would. This house at Cherokee Ranch was too quiet and still with no promise of high energy until they returned, summer of 1954. He wondered what the years ahead held for not only his family but all black families… across this nation -- men, women and children. He wished he had a crystal ball and could just see five or ten years down the road. Ten years ago in 1943, pockets of race riots broke out in Mobile, Alabama, Beaumont, Texas, Detroit, New York City's West Harlem and even in L.A. He wondered what ten years ahead, 1963, will bring. He hoped he'd still be around to witness it. He planned to be. If black folks would get together and rise up at once, these *United States* would have to deal with all the inequality that runs rampant across the country.

Papa Colt took another swig of his liquid refreshment and smiled at the thought that his grands are surely home by now readying for a return to school with plenty of fodder for their "What I Did for My Summer Vacation" essays.

In his aging and prophetic bones, Papa Colt, a rancher in Texas and his son, Hep Culhane, a Los Angeles detective, shared a singular thought. Both sensed something in the air. A change was coming. Not knowing what, how or when but a change, good or bad, was hurling its way for all people of color.

"Heaven help us all," Papa Colt prayed.

DISCUSSION QUESTIONS

1 What is your interpretation of the title, **MIGHT COULD BE**?

2 Who are your favorite characters and why?

3 What scenes spoke to you most?

4 On their wedding day, there is no question that Lorette loved Hep.

    a) How did he feel about Lorette?

    b) When plans went askew, how did the coping patterns of the couple differ?

5 Family and friendship dynamics are plentiful in the novel. Which relationship(s) resonates most with you?

6 Characterize the personalities of the three Culhane Children: TC, Mel, and Jaz

7 The good, bad and ugly are passed down from generation, knowingly and unknowingly. Selena and Hep learned of the possibility of life, of what might could be, and the expectation that a Culhane can handle anything that comes their way. What other characters had coping traits passed down to them?

8   Which characters lived their lives opposite to their families of origin, not repeating traditions but blazing their own paths?

9   Discuss Selena's three concepts:

   a) When a single mother states that she's been both mother and father to her son, Selena believes that no matter how loving or well-intentioned a mother is, she cannot teach her son how to be a man.

   b) Bitch-raised man

   c) Mama's boy

10 Compare and contrast the marriages depicted therein: Colt and Keely; Hep and Lorette; Alexander and Fern; Selena and Zack.

11 Zack believes in the separation of sex and love. Admitting that he loved Selena without the consummation of it. Discuss.

12 Instead of numbered chapters, the author uses song titles of the 40s and 50s with one exception where she skips ahead to the 60s. Do you know which one?

13 While the author's main objective is enjoyment, what treasured tidbits tucked into the narrative were new info to you? Entertainment and education are not mutually exclusive. Was your knowledge-base expanded in any way?